The Sum of All Parts

A Teapot Cottage Novel (#8)

by
Annie Cook

www.Anniecookwriter.com

About The Author

Annie Cook is a writer of women's contemporary fiction, and literary fiction. This is her eighth novel in the Teapot Cottage Series. She has also written a number of 'filler' novels as stand-alone works that link by adding different dimensions to some of the characters in the TC series. Annie is also a podcaster and guide to women who want to tell their own stories. She is originally from New Zealand but divides her time between the UK and her home in Southern Italy.

www.Anniecookwriter.com

Other Novels by Annie Cook:

THE TEAPOT COTTAGE SERIES
No Small Change (#1)
The Power of Notes and Spells (#2)
When It's Meant to Happen (#3)
Ruin Reins and Redemption (#4)
The Stuff You Fail to Notice (#5)
The Choice Between Safe and Brave (#6)
From Raw To Very Well Done (#7)

~ * ~

A Moral Swerve
Thicker Than Water

~ * ~

This book is for every woman 'of a certain age' who has had
to rebuild her life, rediscover herself, and find a way to
release her own power in making her dreams come true.

*"Be strong, be fearless, be beautiful. And believe that
anything is possible when you have the right people
there to support you."*

– Misty Copeland

Chapter One

Adie Raven looked up as her husband Mark came wandering into the living room. His hair was wet from his shower, and he was already in his sleep-shorts, dressing gown and slippers. Occasionally, if he was feeling more tired than usual, he didn't bother getting dressed again. It was nearly half-past six, and their lamb and veg casserole dinner was gently bubbling away in the Aga. The potatoes were almost at the mashable stage, and ready to have the finely chopped spring onion added, along with a decent knob of butter, a good shake of black pepper, and a grated cup of the seriously strong cheddar cheese that Mark was so fond of. A nice bottle of red wine was quietly breathing on the table.

'Hi, darling. How are you feeling? Dinner won't be long. If you'd like to drain and mash the spuds, I'll just get the last of my invites addressed and stamped, and they can all go off tomorrow.'

Mark nodded. 'Aye, I'm a'reet. Just a bit weary, lass. I don't think I'll be long out o' bed tonight.' He gestured to her small pile of envelopes. 'There don't seem so many o' them, love. Is it worth 'avin' a party if that's all that'll turn up, even if they do all say they will?'

Adie grinned at him. 'The usual suspects, as you call them, will all turn up for the Christmas party like they do every year, remember? These invites are just for the people who have never been to a party here before. I think it's nice to have a hand-written invitation to something, rather than just a text or an email or something, like most people send these days. It makes an event feel a bit more special. These are mostly for some of the tenants we've made friends with since I started renting out Teapot Cottage. I can't believe it's been eight years!'

Mark chuckled. 'Yep. We've been married fer eight, yer've rented out cottage fer eight, an' it's yer sixtieth birthday. An' it's Christmas, an' all! That's a lot to celebrate. They've been a grand eight years though, 'aven't they, Adie? Yer still 'appy, lass?'

'You know I am! I've never been happier in my *life* than I've been since I met you, and you know it. If you're fishing for compliments, you're out of luck. You know I adore the very bones of you, and I wouldn't change you, or a single thing about our lives together, and that's all you're going to get.'

He winked at her. 'Well, if them's as good a net o' fish as yer've got, I'll take 'em. An' I do think it's nice, 'ow some o't tenants 'ave become good friends over't years. Even though yer only keep in touch by email, mostly, it's still summat special, in't it?'

Adie nodded. 'Yes, it is. It will be great, if even *some* of them can come. Most people are really busy with their own family and friends at Christmas, and they probably won't want to come all this way, but I guess that's what I get for being born on Christmas Eve! But my sixtieth celebration may as well be on Christmas night, when we always have a big bash here anyway. No point in trying to have two parties!'

She gestured to her small pile of envelopes. 'If any of this lot can make it, I'll be truly astounded! But I do have to try. It's why the invitations are going out so early. It gives people enough of a chance to consider what they might want to do at Christmastime and maybe see this as a nice option. Not everyone wants to spend time with family over the festive season, and even the ones who do can't always make it work.'

She shook her head, almost absently now, as she turned her attention back to finishing the job of getting her invitations ready to send.

Her thoughts drifted back to her first-ever Christmas here at Ravensdown Farm in Torley town. She'd been alone, housesitting at Teapot Cottage on the edge of the farm's estate, after separating from her first husband. Her marriage was in tatters, most of her family weren't even speaking to her, and she'd been suffering mightily from being cannoned headfirst into the menopause without any real warning. Her symptoms were severe, random, and wretched. She hadn't felt like she'd been in control of anything!

Life had seemed pretty bleak back then, and Adie had never forgotten how important a refuge might be, to someone who couldn't or didn't want to be with loved ones at Christmas. Sometimes, the people they felt obliged to spend time with *weren't* 'loved ones' at all! A Christmas like that could be nothing more than an endurance test for them, with people they generally avoided for the other 364 days of the year. Adie had experienced similar in the past, spending the day with her much older brother Raymond and his astonishingly horrible wife. That had been no picnic, and she'd vowed never to repeat it. Perhaps a party at Ravensdown House would be a nice alternative for some others who might feel that way about family.

'We can put a few o't gang up 'ere,' Mark mused. 'Then they can all get rat-arsed and not 'ave to think about getting' to where they're stayin'.'

'Yes, I've mentioned that, in the invitations. Stuart and Fiona have offered their lodge, Ford's Haven, if everyone says yes and we end up without enough beds between here and Teapot Cottage. Not everyone gets drunk, do they? Some guests don't drink much alcohol, if any at all, and they could drive to other lodgings after the event. Wait – I know! Maybe we could hire a minibus and driver to move people around, if we end up with a 'yes,' to every invitation?'

Mark pulled a face. 'Well, yer'll pay well over't odds for a driver on Christmas night, even if yer could bloody get one, which I doubt. But rentin' summat like a seven-seater SUV or van would work if we could get some bugger to agree to drive it.'

Adie nodded, trying not to smirk at his astonishingly broad Lancashire accent that still always made her want to burst out laughing at times, especially when he swore. It wasn't far short of hilarious, the way he rattled on. It was so endearing too, that he had no idea himself, what he sounded like.

'Good point. I'll work on that. Maybe Stu Thompson would drive it? He's more or less teetotal. One way or the other, everyone who needs a bed will have one.'

Adie secretly hoped that everyone she was inviting to her sixtieth birthday party *would* be able to make it. The event was more or less piggy backing onto the annual Christmas night 'do' they always put on at Ravensdown House, but it didn't make sense to have two parties in a row, and she really didn't want to wait until later in the year. Turning sixty was a big deal, and she wanted to celebrate it when it happened, not at some obscure time further down the track, when the impact of it would have been lost. Having it the night after her actual birthday made sense, every which way she looked at it.

Expecting any of the extended 'Teapot Cottage gang' to turn up was a serious long-shot. For some of the guests she was inviting it was a long way to come. Minty Cartwright was way down in the south of France, for goodness' sake! Adie doubted very much if she and Marcel would come but there was always a faint glimmer of hope. It would be so lovely to see Minty again, meet her man, and catch up on a lot of the gossip that never made it into their emails.

She was a lot more hopeful that Wendy Whitelaw-Briggs, and her husband Billy would come. They were only half an hour away and could easily attend, if they were free, and bring their baby daughter Robin with them. Chefs tended to be flat-out if they worked over Christmas, but it would all depend on whether Wendy had decided to have an event of her own on Christmas night, at her adults-only restaurant; 'AyO.' Adie had already assured her and Billy that there would be a quiet room set aside for the 'little' guests who came to the party. She was determined that the challenge of getting a decent babysitter on Christmas night wouldn't have to stop anyone with kids from coming along.

She was confident that their good friends Stuart Thompson and Fiona Winterson would be here too, although she wasn't sure what Stuart's daughter Meghan might be doing on Christmas night. She was nineteen now and although she still lived at home, she had a busy university and social life, and a very nice long-term boyfriend. Parker Truman was a local Torley guy, also at university. She'd met him when she and Stuart had been staying at Teapot Cottage one summer, a good few years ago now, and she'd gone to the local Friday night youth club in the town. They'd eventually got together and they'd been an item for a few years now. Adie hoped they would be around, to come to the party, but she wouldn't be surprised if Meghan's plans involved being as far away from her 'fuddy-duddy' dad as she could get. She and Parker were popular, by all accounts. They probably had invitations to a *hundred* Christmas parties!

Adie's daughter Teresa and her fiancé Chris (and their baby son Lewis) were definites. They would be staying down at Teapot Cottage, along with Adie's son Matty, his wife Marie and their two daughters Milly and Sophie. Adie's stepdaughter Feen always called them 'Silly and Mophie,' but nobody was offended. Everyone was well used to her tendency towards Spoonerism, where she swapped the starting letters on a pair of words, especially the names of close-friend couples or family. She'd done it all her life, and she couldn't seem to help it, so there wasn't much point in taking her to task for it.

Carla and Dave (Darla and Cave) Holloway were definites too, as were Carla's parents 'Han and Stazel,' as they were known to everyone now. Darren and Debby Davies came every year, with their kids, Ruby and Tom. Darren's parents, Barbara, and Pat (Bat and Parb) usually came up from Exeter for Christmas, and it was always nice to see them too. They usually tagged along to the Christmas party anyway, but Adie was sending them their own invitation this year.

Her stepdaughter Feen and her husband Gavin would be at Ravensdown House all over Christmas and New Year with their twins, Alder and Willow. Adie's first-born daughter Ruth, her wife Gina, and their daughter Chiara would also be in the house for Christmas, and so would her oldest and dearest friend Miranda and her husband Max. The older grandkids and the children of friends would all be having a gigantic sleepover upstairs, in a big bedroom at the back of the house, which Adie was sure they would all be excited about. It would have its own Christmas tree and strings of fairy lights, to make it feel a bit magical for them all, and puptents would be erected so they could all quietly snuggle down for the night at different times, depending on when they felt tired enough to sleep. The babies would be sleeping in Mark and Adie's room, until it was time for their parents to take them home.

It was hard to believe that she and Mark had six grandchildren between them now! Thankfully, the relentless demands of the farm kept them both fit. Between that and Adie's regular yoga sessions, she managed to keep up pretty well with the young ones.

The usual Christmas night crowd of locals would be here too, as always. If it was going to be anything like the previous Christmas parties, it would be a really good night.

A smile played across her lips, as she remembered the first party she'd attended here, as a guest. Mark had invited her after she'd inadvertently met him down in the town, and he'd realised that she was the house sitter at Teapot Cottage, at the edge of his land. He'd asked her into Peggy Wilde's café, Ye Olde Torley Tea Shoppe, for a quick cuppa so she wouldn't feel so much like a stranger in town. That had quietly turned into lunch, and he'd generously invited her to the party.

Walking into a room full of strangers for the first time, with wildly fluctuating hormones, a shattered heart, and an uncertain future, had been incredibly daunting. Thankfully, her 'new' friend at the time, Peg Wilde (now Tripper) had picked her up from Teapot Cottage so she wouldn't have to go to the party alone. Peg was now one of her closest and most treasured friends, and so were some of the other people she'd met that night. It seemed like a very long time ago now, when she'd been here without the faintest clue that by the time the next party rolled around, she would be hosting it and married to Mark Raven!

He'd been the most eligible bachelor in the county at the time, but he hadn't been looking for romance. Far from it. He was widowed with very firm plans to stay that way. He'd made no bones about that, right from the start, but unexpectedly falling in love with Adie Bostock had swiftly put paid to his best intentions and the rest, as they say, was history.

Along the way, Adie had managed to 'inherit' a whole new family. Mark's delightful sister, Sheila Shalloe, was the same age as Adie. She was a 'keeper;' honest, pragmatic, and generous to a fault. She and her husband Bob were close friends now too.

After Feen had got married to Gavin and had their twins, Alder and Willow, Gavin's beloved grandparents Stan and Hazel had also become part of Adie and Mark's lives. So had his mother Carla, who had then got married to local high-end car importer and hobby-farmer Dave Holloway. The family had swelled dramatically on both sides, and the 'party-mix' of people was always entertaining.

Carla Walton-Holloway was razor sharp, and witheringly sarcastic, but incredibly funny with it. Her husband Dave was sweet and indulgent but, whenever Carla threatened to stray beyond the boundaries of what most people regarded as acceptable speech or behaviour, he still somehow managed to keep her in line without having his head snapped off in the process. That was no small thing, but he was no faint-hearted man, and he had helped to mellow Carla dramatically.

Adie and Carla had history, going back to when Adie had first arrived in Torley to house-sit, and Carla had sensed a romantic threat. She'd had her sights set firmly on Mark at the time, and she became tactically ruthless in trying to prevent him from getting together with Adie. It had all been stressful, and horrible. The situation had got even more tricky when Feen met, fell in love with, and married Carla's estranged son Gavin. But then Feen was involved in a serious car crash out on the road to Torley town. She'd been airlifted to hospital where, under sedation, she had been given a Caesarean section to deliver her and Gavin's twins at just twenty-eight weeks.

The accident had been horrifying and terrifying, and the fact that Feen and her desperately premature babies came so close to losing their lives had been a defining turning point for the entire family. Everyone finally understood the need to put their differences aside and pull together. Adie and Carla would never be bosom buddies, but they were friends now. Carla had worked on her demons and was a much nicer person these days. Seeing the softer side of her had been a revelation for everyone who knew her – even herself. She and Gavin had had been estranged for a long time, but they had finally mended their fences, and the family was in as good a place as it ever could be, all things considered.

Mark was right. It *had* been an amazing eight years! So many wonderful people had come into Adie's world and so many life-affirming things had happened. Her life was now so far removed from her previous one that she didn't even feel like the same person she'd been, all that time ago.

And she wasn't the only one to have found true love! Her best friend Miranda, who was also invited to this year's party, had met and married a wonderful man, after many years 'playing about with toyboys' and ending up abandoned after the passions had fizzled. For a long time, it very much looked as if 'Mand' was destined to end up alone. She was a very successful stage actress who had trodden the West End boards for decades and always lived life on her own terms, but she'd been getting to the point where her age and circumstances were starting to get in the way of her living that carefree, commitment-free life. She and Adie had both known that something needed to change, and then it did – without much warning at all. Maxwell Kennedy ('the Third,' no less!) had wandered into Miranda's life and turned it upside down, and she was now as loved-up as anyone could be, secure and happily head-over-heels in love with a man her own age who absolutely adored her right back. Adie hoped, with all her heart, that they'd be able to make it to her sixtieth birthday celebration.

She was already looking forward to spending a few days with them, early in the New Year. They'd just bought a beautiful house in Surrey, and had invited her to go and see it, and stay for a few days. She'd decided to travel by train, had already booked her tickets, and was thinking about buying a few nice new things for the trip. She figured her good friend Trudie Sangster, who owned GladRagz boutique in the town, would help her pick out a few pretty outfits. Trudie had styled her when she'd first arrived in Torley eight years ago, with her world in a million pieces, hormonally hysterical, with no idea what her post-menopausal body shape was going to end up being. She'd already given up trying to be *stylish,* without even realising how far she'd stumbled down the track of looking completely washed out and shapeless.

Trudie had quickly come to the rescue, like Superwoman, swooping and in and saving the day. Adie's waist had more or less disappeared, so her beloved skirts had stopped being a comfortable option after they'd started drifting upwards to sit like matronly tents that splayed out from below her boobs. Trudie had courageously raided her new friend's wardrobe and throw out bags full of shapeless tracksuit pants, faded t-shirts and oversized, unflattering baggy tops. She'd replaced them with slim-fitting dark jeans and other stylish pants, quality jumpers that didn't just fit where they touched, and tailored shirts and jackets that made the most of Adie's figure which had – mercifully – stayed quite slim. She'd started wearing dresses too, in styles that flattered and gave the *illusion* of a waist.

She'd also put herself in the capable hands of Madeleine Murphy at Torley Tresses. When she'd first arrived in town her hair had been almost long enough to sit on, but it had started going straggly and limp, thanks to her plummeting oestrogen levels. She'd always loved her long hair, but she'd ended up being at her wits end with it. Maddie's senior stylist had given her a short, sassy, wavy bob that had flattered her

face and taken the eye away from her softening jawline –
another unhappy testament to the menopause!

The combined efforts of Maddie's stylist and the utterly
brilliant Trudie had taken years off Adie's appearance, and
Sheila Shalloe had persuaded her to tag along with her to the
yoga classes at the Torley Community Centre. Within a few
months of first arriving in town, Adie Bostock was almost
unrecognisable. Nowadays, she was a million miles from the
frumpy, lumpy, washed-out woman who had arrived here with
her life in ruins and no clue how to pull it back together.

She sent a quick text to Trudie now, while she was thinking
about it, to ask her to keep an eye out for a few nice things she
could take with her to Miranda and Max's. That was another new
development since menopause had messed with her head – she
forgot things a lot more easily! Acting on a thought as soon as
she had it was sometimes the only way she achieved things
anymore. These days, the fridge and the wall of her dressing
room upstairs were littered with post-it notes to remind her of
what she had to do or where she had to go, and when.

She was grateful for Trudie's friendship. The two women had
instantly 'clicked' when they'd first met, and they were good
friends now. Trudie always had an eye for what would look good
on Adie, and whenever she went on a buying trip and had
anything coming into her shop that would suit her to a tee, it
never took her long to say so. Adie was confident that Trudie
would find her some lovely clothes and a few nice accessories
for her trip to see Miranda and Max.

Their new home, in a very exclusive pocket of Stoke
d'Abernon, in Surrey, looked amazing and Adie was excited to
see it. The photos Miranda had sent her showed a spectacular and
substantial Victorian villa, set in five acres of gorgeous gardens,
and bursting with character and original features. The house
boasted six bedrooms, seven bathrooms, and a swimming pool
and separate 'pool house,' complete with sauna, steam room,
jacuzzi, and ensuite accommodation. Happily, the property also
offered a tennis court. Adie hadn't played for a long time and
although she wasn't great at the sport, she did enjoy it. Miranda

didn't play, but apparently Max did. Maybe there would be a chance for a few matches!

They'd only moved in a few months ago after selling Max's house in Hampstead and Miranda's flat in Soho, where she'd lived for many years, because it was literally on the doorstep of the West End where she nearly always worked. After making the decision to pull back and do a lot less acting, she and Max had decided to move out of the city. Their new location meant an easy route back in, whenever they wanted to go to dinner or to a show (or whenever Miranda was doing one), but they had the chance to relax more in the countryside. They'd got a couple of German Shepherd puppies and were in the process of housetraining them.

Adie couldn't wait to see the house. The photos and video footage they'd taken were stunning, and Miranda had been so thrilled about inviting her to go and stay for a week or so, it simply hadn't been possible to refuse! The chance to get together and 'chew the fat' like they used to before Adie moved to Cumbria was far too tempting to resist, and seeing her son, daughter-in-law and granddaughters would be the icing on the cake. Matty and Marie lived in Epsom, less than ten miles from Stoke D'Abernon, and spending a couple of days with them would be something to look forward to after the anticlimax that always followed Christmas.

Feen and Gavin were the only ones who stayed around for a while after a Christmas visit. Whenever her own kids came, they were always on flying visits and needing to be somewhere else immediately after. There was never any real 'quality time' to be had when they came and went so quickly.

At least they come! Some parents can't get their grown-up children to come home for Christmas, for love nor money. Being my birthday does help, and I'm sure none of them could live with themselves if they didn't come for my sixtieth! I know it puts them on the wire to fulfil their other Christmas commitments, but this year I just want it to be about me.

Mark seemed unusually tired after dinner tonight, so she suggested heading to bed early. Sitting up in bed of an evening with a cup of chamomile tea, properly catching up with him and having a snuggle, was her favourite time of the day. They usually just chattered about largely meaningless things, and it was always comforting and sweet, but tonight she could see his eyelids drooping and she knew he needed to go to sleep even if she didn't. She quietly admitted defeat and let him nod off. She had a quick look at her Teapot Cottage social media pages, then plugged her phone in to charge and turned out the light. She snuggled down next to Mark and smiled to herself as he snorted softly in his sleep. She wasn't sleepy herself, so she decided to think about the Christmas and birthday party, and how much fun everyone was going to have.

*   *   *   *   *

Chapter Two

Minty Cartwright held her arms out to Adie, as she came through the kitchen door.

'Merry Christmas, Adie! And Happy Birthday for yesterday! The front door was off the latch, so I just barged straight in!'

Adie laughed at her, with pure delight. 'My God! You're actually here!'

'Well, I did say I was coming! You did get that email, right?' Minty stepped forward and hugged Adie tightly.

'Yes, of course, but I wasn't quite ready to believe it until you were actually walking through the door! God, it's *so* good to see you, Minty! How has your trip been so far? It's quite a journey to drive here all the way from the south of France in the middle of winter!'

Minty shrugged. 'The drive was as good as anything ever can be, I suppose. Marcel's car is fast and comfortable, which helps. The ferry from Calais was jammed over the weekend, with everyone trying to get here in time for Christmas, and the various motorway dramas on both sides of the ditch have kept me concentrating whenever it's been my turn to drive.'

She yawned and made a couple of circles with her nose, to stretch her neck. 'It was a long haul, but we stayed a night en route with a friend of Marcel's in a town called Saint-Pavace, just north of Le Mans. We saw a car on fire just north of there not long after we left the following morning. It was well ablaze. Not the nicest thing to see in Christmas week, some poor sod escaping a burning car with their lives and the clothes they stood up in!' She grimaced.

'Then, at Calais, a car in front of us lost control on the way onto the ferry and somehow ended up going over the ramp and landing on its roof! Nobody really knows how that can even happen, but it did. It held up our departure for almost an hour and on the way here this afternoon a car had broken down near the Lancaster turnoff and closed two bloody lanes! But despite all the fun and games we haven't have many delays overall.'

'That all sounds like more than enough. I hope your journey home will be a bit less eventful. It's a long way to come, by car,' Adie observed.

'Yeah, it is, but it made more sense than anything else, to be honest. I want to get around and see a few people while I'm over here. I have three weeks off now until the clinic reopens midway into the New Year, so I want to make the most of it. It was going to be really expensive to fly and hire a car for the time because it's Christmas and the prices get hiked on everything. Marcel was prepared to pay to do all that but the cost of everything really was ridiculous, and it's a question of conscience. I can't afford it, and even though he can, I didn't want him to. It seemed a bit unfair. He was happy enough to do it this way. It is a lot easier anyway, to have our own car. Sharing the driving helps.'

'Where *is* the man in question? I can't wait to meet him!'

'He's still in the car, on the phone to one of his sons. He'll be in, in a minute. Thank you for organising a room for us at The Feathers pub, Adie. We do appreciate that. On their website it said they were full.'

Adie nodded. 'Well, it's a full house *here*, so I literally couldn't make it work to fit you in as well! We don't even have any floor space! But the publicans at The Feathers are good friends. I threw myself on their mercy and they let me muscle in and bag you a room for tonight.'

'We've already checked in and picked up the key. It's lovely there and the weather looks reasonable, with no rain forecast, so it'll be an easy-enough stagger down there later if we've had too much to drink.'

Minty had already suggested to Marcel that they leave their car at Ravensdown House and walk back into the town, after the party. That way, they could have a few drinks and not have to worry about driving or parking later, when Torley town might be busy with Christmas night revellers.

'Don't worry. We've hired a mini-van, and the habitually sober Stu Thompson will drive people to where they need to go later tonight. Is everything all organised for your son's wedding next week?'

Minty's son Ethan had arranged his wedding to his boyfriend Cal to coincide with her trip over from France for Christmas. She'd been excited about it for weeks. She'd mentioned it to Adie the last time they spoke, when she'd confirmed that she and Marcel would be at the party.

'Yes! Everything seems to be in hand. He and Cal have organised the entire thing themselves. Most of Cal's family have already flown in from Toronto to spend Christmas here and then attend the wedding before flying home. Then the boys are off on honeymoon – to Hawaii, of all places! Belle and Tim are putting me and Marcel up at theirs for some of the time we're here then we can use the boys' house while they're away. I'll get to see as much of the kids and as many other friends as time will allow.'

'Gosh, it will be so great to do that *and* to see some friends and ex-colleagues too! This is the first time you've been back since you emigrated, isn't it?'

Minty nodded, bemused at how excited Adie seemed to be, for her. It was very sweet.

'It is. The kids have been out to see me, of course, and so have a handful of friends. But I'm still waiting for *you* to make the trip! You and Mark are welcome anytime – you know that don't you?'

'Yes, and we absolutely *will* take you up on it, probably around the end of spring after we've got a handle on stuff that will need doing on the farm. Spring's our busiest time around here but later, before the summer heat kicks in, we can surely manage a few days. I want to spend some time in Paris too so we might do it all by train and take our time a bit coming home.'

'Good. It will be lovely to show you around down there. It's a really nice part of the country.'

Minty recalled now that Adie had asked her in a previous phone call if she was still in much contact with Fiona Winterson. Minty knew that it wasn't because her friend had wanted to 'dig' or seem nosy. She was simply asking, in her own way, if Minty might find it uncomfortable to be in the same room with Fiona. It was Adie's way of approaching what might have been a delicate subject.

Fiona's affair with Minty's husband Leo had been devastating and had led to a very acrimonious divorce. It had also destroyed a friendship that had spanned forty years. The loss had been profound for their daughter Belle too because Fiona had been her godmother. The two had been close before the affair had come to light. Fiona and Ethan had always enjoyed a light, bantering friendship too.

But, thanks to Fiona's decision to help herself to Minty's husband, all of those previously cherished relationships ended up in tatters. Such deep, devastating betrayals had cut the entire family to the quick and it simply wasn't possible to repair damage done on that scale. Ethan no longer had any time for Fiona, Belle couldn't find any forgiveness at all for her godmother *or* her father, and Minty had ultimately concluded that hers could only go so far.

Admitting that had been hard. Moving on had been even harder, but Minty was in a good place now, with all the drama behind her. She had a new home in the south of France and a lovely new man who she was gently getting to know.

It was why she'd come to Teapot Cottage in the first place; to take some time out and try and get her head around the events that had rocked her family's world. She'd needed a quiet space where she could think about what her life was going to look and feel like in the wake of it all. She'd never expected to end up divorced, with her oldest friendship smashed to pieces and her daughter's heart completely broken too. She'd suddenly found herself facing an entirely different future from the one she'd always taken for granted. She'd gone back to her maiden name of Cartwright, after ditching her cheating scumbag of a husband's name; McLeod.

Minty swallowed down her nervousness now, at the prospect of seeing Fiona tonight. But they were grown women – surely, they were capable of maintaining dignity at a mutual friend's party? She was pretty confident that Fiona wouldn't want to cause a scene, any more than she wanted to herself.

She'd hastened to assure Adie that there wouldn't be anything to worry about. She'd had a couple of conversations with Fiona in recent times, and they'd been fairly light. One was Minty's call, to see how Fiona was doing after her double mastectomy for Inflammatory Breast Cancer, and how it was being managed. A few months later Fiona had called *her* to offer an update. Both conversations had been painfully superficial compared to the ones they used to have but they'd been fine.

Minty knew that Fiona and her new husband Stuart Thompson were good friends of the Ravens now, and she was determined that Adie wouldn't have to be nervous about having both women in the same room. The last thing anyone wanted was to have an awkward atmosphere. There shouldn't be any animosity. She'd see to that herself, even if it killed her.

Mark had said something similar, apparently, and he'd told Adie that if people couldn't at least be civil, he'd be having a strong word, and if they still wouldn't play nice after that he'd be throwing offenders out. Minty had laughed when Adie told her what he'd said. Knowing Mark Raven as she did, she had no doubt that he'd make good on his word, if push came to shove. He was a lovely big bear of a man, with a heart of solid gold, but he wasn't one to stand for any nonsense – especially if it might affect his family.

It was still a vaguely niggling worry, however, that there might be some kind of eruption. The annual Ravensdown

Christmas party was legendary for its generous amounts of food and alcohol, and people typically made the most of it. Bearing that in mind, nobody could predict what might come up in an unwise 'tipsy' conversation. Thankfully, Stuart and Marcel were both more or less teetotal and eminently sensible, and they would ensure that nothing got out of hand.

By all accounts, Mark didn't drink as much as he used to so he would keep a good eye on things too. But Minty didn't want him – or anyone else for that matter – to be in a state of hypervigilance all night. That would be no fun at all, especially for poor Adie. But Feen Raven would also be a good barometer tonight. She picked up on nuances most other people didn't even know existed. She would soon draw attention to any bubbling tensions and hopefully nip them in the bud. All in all, Minty concluded, the party was probably in excellent hands. She still did a mental 'finger-cross' though, before finally shrugging off her worry.

She dug around in her shoulder bag for a small, square box, and handed it to Adie.

'Here. Happy Birthday! I got a friend in France to make this especially for you, so I hope you like it.'

She watched as Adie quickly wiped her hands on her apron and undid the wrapping on the package. Her eyes shone, as she took the lid off a small silver jewellery box, to reveal a double belcher chain with a delicate pendant on it, of a rough-edged and only semi-polished blue-lace agate crystal with a small, shiny silver heart set within it. The pendant was stunning, and Minty felt compelled to explain the origins behind the stone she'd picked out.

'Blue lace agate is the crystal for your voice. Expressing yourself, with conviction and clarity. We've talked a few times, haven't we, about how important it is, to make sure our voices don't get 'lost in the noise of life' as we get older? This should help to ensure yours never does.'

She was astonished, to see that Adie had tears in her eyes.

'Oh, my God, Minty! This is gorgeous! I do know about blue lace agate. Feen taught me quite a lot about crystals a while ago and explained their power to me. But I don't know if I've ever had a gift so thoughtful, and so *meaningful*, as this. Thank you, so much!'

'My friend Lisanne de Truell has a tiny shop in my town, where she produces the most exquisite jewellery. She takes a few commissions, so I chose the crystal, and we decided together on setting the heart within it. I figured a milestone birthday like a sixtieth deserved an appropriate stone. I'm glad you like it.'

'I do! It's beautiful.'

'Are Feen and Gavin here tonight? Adie? Um… hello?'

Minty snapped her fingers in front of Adie's face, because she appeared to have 'tranced out' a bit. Adie instantly refocussed and rolled her eyes.

'Sorry, Minty! I drifted away into my own head for a minute! One minute, I was appreciating this gorgeous gift, the next I was back at my first-ever Christmas party here eight years ago, when Feen gave me a beautiful pair of earrings that she'd made for me herself. I think I've just experienced some weird kind of déjà vu thing.'

She grinned, apologetically. 'I seem to be drifting off more and more often these days, since the menopause. I now have what Mark and the rest of my family call 'post-menopausal sponge-brain!'

Minty laughed. 'Don't worry. I'm menopausal too now, and I'm having the exact same problem. I sometimes get in the car and forget where I'm supposed to be going. And I've lost count of the number of times I've had to leave a patient in the clinic and rush off into a quiet corner somewhere and will myself *not* to spontaneously combust with the absolute worst hot flushes! It's awful, all this horrible hormonal stuff. I never know what I'm going to say, do or forget next! I feel like I'm in a constant state of semi-panic, with it all. I'm considering taking HRT now, to see if it helps.'

Adie grimaced. 'Some say it does, others can't get along with it. I went through without it, but Feen helped me a lot, with her natural remedies. I also made some dietary concessions, worked to achieve a better sleep schedule, a good exercise regime, and a few other adjustments. I do a lot of yoga, and the work around the farm offers a good workout. It all made a big difference, and I'm through the worst of it now. I just get the occasional hot 'rush,' and I have dryness in certain areas that we don't discuss at the dinner table, but I did okay with it, overall. There *is* a sense of finally climbing out of a pit, though, after bouncing around and pinging off the sides of it for forever and a day.'

'Hmmm…' Minty was thoughtful. 'You know, it might not hurt for you to see a dietician again, and get some new tests done to see what deficiencies you may have that a bit of adjustment might sort out. We have to do more to support our ageing bodies once the oestrogen has taken a strong one-way dive, with all the juicy support it gave us on so many levels! Good quality supplements help a lot. But I was just asking if Feen is going to be here tonight, with her family?'

Adie nodded. 'Yeah. She and Gavin are already here with the twins. They arrived a week ago. I think they're all still upstairs. My best friend Miranda and her husband Max are up there too, getting ready, and so are my daughter Ruth and her wife Gina, and their daughter Chiara. They'll all be making their way down soon, I suppose.'

'I'm sorry we're so early. It seemed a bit silly to just hang around down in the town, with everything shut, once we'd got ready to come. We should have stayed in the pub I suppose, for a drink or two. I was surprised they were even open, to be fair, since it's Christmas Day and everything.'

'They're closed through Christmas Day, but they always open the pub for the evening. The town's other pub, the Bull and Royal, won't open at all today. And, God, no – it's totally *fine* that you're here early! Maybe you can give me a hand in the kitchen?'

Minty grinned. 'I seem to remember being hoodwinked into doing that once before, when you were trying to get me to stop wallowing at Teapot Cottage on my own and help you with a certain 'pot-luck' dinner! I don't imagine you need much help at all Adie, just like you didn't back then, but I'm happy to keep you company and do whatever's needed. You know, I introduced that 'pot-luck' concept to friends in Landes, and they love it! It's a regular thing there now.'

Adie smirked at her. 'Everyone bringing a contribution makes sense these days. My sister-in-law Sheila and my friend Peg Tripper do most of the catering for this party every year, and I do a fair bit as well, of course. But without the contributions from guests, it would all be a lot less interesting *or* adequate than what it needs to be, to feed the masses.'

'Peg runs Ye Old Torley Tea Shoppe, doesn't she? I remember her. She's lovely. Gosh, it'll be so nice to meet everyone again! Is Trudie coming? She made me over when I was here. I'm into totally different dress styles nowadays and I have her to thank for it.'

'Yep, she'll be here with her husband Kevin.' Adie pulled her bottom lip with her finger and thumb for a second. She seemed to be debating whether to say something further, and then she lowered her voice.

'Trudie and Kevin are going through a bit of a rough patch, Minty. Just so you know. None of us knows exactly why. Trudie won't say much about it, other than to say that she has no idea what she and Kevin have in common anymore. We're all hoping it's a temporary hiccup and they'll get themselves back on track. Just tread carefully with her if she seems a bit funny or off her game tonight.'

Adie went on to confide that she was surprised the couple were even coming to the party. Her dear friend had been angry and upset with her husband for months now but wouldn't say why. To be fair to her, she didn't even seem to know why *herself*. She just seemed to be discontented in general, and he was a big part of that, but it wasn't easy for her – or for anyone else – to put a finger on why she had so little patience with him anymore. Adie explained that Mark and Kevin were good friends, and Mark had tried to get him to open up about things too, but poor Kevin was as baffled as everyone else about why his marriage seemed to have drifted into choppy waters.

'Maybe tonight a change of scene will help to diffuse a bit of tension between them.'

'Oh, dear,' Minty muttered quietly, as an all-too-familiar sinking feeling gripped her. 'That doesn't sound good. You know, I've seen it with my sister Fliss too, in France. She and Filipe went through quite a bad patch after she hit the menopause. I think it was a combination of him not knowing how to cope with her, and her being unable to tell him what she needed, and not knowing where she was going to end up or how she was going to feel at the end of the meno rollercoaster. She lost her libido, and I don't think she fully got it back. It's a tough time for a lot of women. Scary even, for some.'

Adie nodded. 'Everyone underestimates how much havoc it can play with your emotions and your sense of stability and self-confidence. Your whole life, in some cases.' She looked sad, now. She was clearly very worried, about Trudie, and Minty stepped forward, gave her a quick hug, and told her to try not to worry too much, that things had a way of working out the way they were supposed to if they were left to play out in their own time. It was the best she could offer, and she hoped it helped.

'You're right Minty, and I'm not one to gossip, especially about friends. But I do know that poor Trudie is feeling the march of time. I think every woman arrives at that point at some stage of her life; you know, wondering if this is all there is, what's the point of everything we've signed up for, and all that.'

Minty nodded. She understood, totally.

'Is there something better out there? A lot of women ask themselves that, and a lot do decide there is,' she admitted. 'Maybe Trudie's one of those. But I hope she sorts it out. She's a nice woman, and she deserves to be happy, whatever that means for herself.'

'Agreed. And what about you, Minty? Are *you* happier now? You seem to be. Is Marcel good for you? Is your new life what you hoped it would be?'

Minty was about to answer the questions when a knock at the kitchen door made both women look up. 'Come in,' Adie called, and Marcel came into the kitchen. He was a tall, heavy-set man with a thick shock of greying hair above a pair of twinkly blue eyes. He was impeccably dressed tonight in a navy shirt, dark denim jeans, and a navy and mustard-coloured checked blazer. Minty felt a small rush of attraction to him – the same one she always felt whenever he walked into *any* room.

Instantly, Adie sprang forward to shake his hand.

'Ah! You must be Marcel? Nobody in the world could look more 'French,' and I do mean that nicely! I'm so glad you're here! I've heard lovely things about you, and I've waited so long to meet you!'

'And I, you,' he countered, stepping forward and kissing her on both cheeks. 'It is nice to be here, to meet some of Minty's good friends. She has told me about you too, and her time here. Thank you for inviting me too, Aidee.'

'Well, you go with the territory,' Adie laughed. 'We wouldn't dream of leaving you out.'

Minty knew the rest of her conversation with Adie would have to wait, but she really did want to have it. Adie cared enough to ask, and Minty wanted her to know that she *was* happy, in her new life. She had healed a lot, over the time since she'd gone to live in France. She missed her kids, but Belle and Ethan were both adults who had both left home even before her marriage to their father had foundered. They were doing just fine, with homes, careers, and partners of their own. Belle was happy and settled with her long-term boyfriend Tim and Ethan was about to get married. They had been affected by her split with their father, but they'd recovered from the shock and moved on. Their own stability had helped enormously, with that. She didn't have to worry about them as much as she would have if they'd still been living at home, or struggling to get themselves established somewhere, when Leo had been exposed as a love-rat and a cheat.

Life *had* to move on, didn't it? Staying stuck in the river, on a raft of resentment and grief, wasn't an option – at least not for Minty Cartwright!

Who would want to live like that, if they had a choice?

Minty also knew that Fiona had worked hard too, to put her past behind her. She was still battling with her guilt and shame, and the inevitable loss of the people she had hurt. She was also still dealing with the aftermath of her cancer, which had turned everything on its head for her, Leo *and* Minty. Although she had found love with Minty's friend Stuart Thompson and had a new sense of purpose in her life, coming to terms with the kind of damage she had done to so many relationships and the turn her life had taken was still a work in progress.

But Minty didn't want her erstwhile best friend of forty years to be in torment over it, or anything else. Yes, Fiona's selfish actions had been horrible in the extreme, but she had suffered mightily too, and nobody deserved to have to pay for their follies by being miserable for their entire lives. Both women knew that there was no way they could ever go back to having the sort of friendship they'd had before. It simply wasn't realistic to pretend, or even imagine, that such terrible damage was repairable; that it hadn't changed the landscape of all their lives forever. But a line had to be drawn beneath it all. Both women wanted and needed that.

So, if there's anything I can say to her tonight that might make it easier for her to put this all behind her, I'll say it. I don't owe her anything, but I have forgiven her, and she deserves to know that. I'm at peace with it now, and she should have that too.

Adie's husband Mark came wandering into the kitchen now. He'd had a shower and shave, and was 'party-ready,' in a clean pair of jeans, a checked shirt that was open at the neck, and a pair of almost-trendy-but-not-quite fur-lined leather moccasin slippers. Minty grinned at the look of surprise on his face when he saw her and Marcel. She quickly embraced him hello, and introduced the two men. They shook hands, and Mark shook his head as he checked his watch.

'Ecky thump! Tell me I'm not late fer me own bloody party? Well, since yer't first in, I'd best get yer both a decent drink. What's yer poison, man?'

Marcel looked a bit bemused as Mark took him by the elbow and led him out of the kitchen. Minty giggled.

'I did tell Marcel about Mark's Lancashire accent! He might struggle a bit, until he gets the gist of it. But, to answer your questions; yes, I'm pretty happy Adie. It's not the life I ever imagined for myself, as you know, but I'm enjoying living and working in France.'

'And what about work? You told me you were always pretty snowed, when you worked as an A & E Consultant here in the UK. I know you're still working, but are things a little easier for you now?'

Minty nodded. 'Kind of. Did I tell you I've been called back to general surgery, though? I'm operating again, every Tuesday now, at a nearby hospital. It's good to be back wielding the knife but I don't want to do any more than just the one day. Between that and all the other stuff I'm doing, writing training programs and everything, it keeps me pretty busy.' She grinned, wryly.

'If I thought moving to France was going to mean a less busy life, I was wrong, but I don't think I'd change anything. Having Fliss and Filipe close by helps a lot, especially as I'm still getting to grips with the finer nuances of the language. They're always keen to correct me when I say something wrong, so I'm learning pretty well. And Marcel helps with that too. He's lovely. He's sweet and supportive, and he encourages me to be and do the best I can with everything. So, my life is all very different but it's better than what it was before I left.'

'Well, it couldn't have been much worse, as I recall, surrounded by saboteurs instead of encouragers! Things had to improve on *that* front at least, and I'm really glad they have.

You do seem settled and happy. So, is it a long-term thing with Marcel?'

Minty hesitated before answering.

'Umm… yeah, I *think* so. Neither of us is interested in seeing anyone else, put it that way. I don't think I'll ever get married again, or live full-time with anyone again, because I like having my own space too much. I honestly didn't think I *would* adapt so well to being on my own, but I find I prefer it. There's a lot to be said for being able to do everything on your own terms! I have a dog, but at least I'm not the dreaded cat lady who prefers the company of seventeen scratty felines to the solid comfort of a man like Marcel. When he's not in Paris working, we mostly spend the weekends together, usually at my place, or off exploring the countryside somewhere. I just appreciate the balance, and I'd like to keep it that way.'

'It's nice to feel independent, and to only have yourself to look out for, isn't it? And the dog, of course. Just as long as you don't exclude the possibility of getting all loved-up and snuggly with someone again. You're far too young to cut that side of your life off completely, unless that *is* what you really want.'

'It isn't. I don't want to turn into a stone. Marcel and I get on very well, and we have a good balance of time together, and time apart. The arrangement seems to suit us both, and it means the time we spend together isn't all caught up in 'discussions' about who forgot to unload the dishwasher or put the rubbish out. The expectations don't get out of hand, and we don't get to a point where we start taking one another for granted. I never want to end up down *that* track again!'

Adie grinned at her. 'Fair play to you for putting respect first. A lot of couples stop doing that and I think it's when the rot sets in. And, as the saying goes, 'if it aint broke, don't fix it!' By the way, speaking of rot and respect – I did warn you, didn't I, that Fiona will be here tonight?'

Minty nodded. 'Yes, you did, but please don't be anxious about that, Adie. As I've said before, she and I aren't in a bad or awkward place. In fact, I'm very happy that that she's finally got her life together. Stuart seems perfect for her, and she's a happier person for having real love in her life. I think it's what she always needed. We won't ever be close friends again, but we're okay. As good as we can be, under the circumstances. A lot of the love I had for her is still there. It's just changed. Different, and hard to describe, but I do want her to survive her cancer and have a good life. In some weird way I think she has earned that. It's hard to put it into words, so I won't even try, if you don't mind?'

'No, I totally get what you're trying to say. Human relationships are complex, Minty. Emotions aren't taps that you can switch off at the drop of a hat, and there's a lot of goodness to look back on, beneath all the layers of complicated crap that came later. It's important to appreciate what was good, in any relationship, instead of just focussing on the betrayals and what made things go bad. Keeping perspective on *all* of it is what allows you to heal, and I think you've done a pretty good job of that.'

'Thank you. It means a lot, that you've noticed that.'

I am in a much better place about it all now, but I have to admit, it's been hard to get here. I've certainly had my share of moments while I was 'putting it all to bed.' Nobody flicks the switch on forty years of friendship, or on twenty-six years of marriage, without having to do some serious spadework in figuring out how to live with what broke it, do they?

'Moving to France gave me something else to focus on until the dust had properly settled on everything, but I had a fair bit of time in a dark tunnel after it all caught up with me.'

'I'm sure you did. I don't think it's possible to outrun these things. They do catch up eventually, but hopefully not until the initial impact has receded at least a little bit. And what about Leo? Do you ever hear from him?'

Minty shook her head. 'Like you I suppose, with your ex, we talk very occasionally about matters concerning the kids, and he will be at Ethan's wedding of course, along with *his* parents, because they're Belle and Ethan's Nan and Gramp. But that's about it. It will be my first time, seeing Leo or his mum and dad, since he left me. I've no idea if he's seeing anyone, or if he'll be bringing a plus one. I haven't asked Ethan. I suppose I should have but, well … you know.'

She wasn't sure how to finish the sentence. She didn't much care if Leo had a new partner but – thinking about it now – she probably should have asked Ethan if his father was bringing someone. She still had time to do that and get herself prepared to meet a new 'squeeze' and not be taken by surprise over it.

'Wow!' Adie exclaimed. 'That's a big thing, then! And how do you feel about seeing him, and potentially with a new partner?'

'Well, Fliss and Felipe will be there to support me. I'll have Marcel with me too, so that will be a bit of a buffer. It will at least communicate the message that I have moved on like he presumably has. But I don't think Leo will make things awkward, Adie. For Ethan's sake, I hope not. I'm sure Belle's boyfriend Tim, and a few others – and even Marcel himself if necessary – will step in and stop any nastiness before it really starts. Nobody wants the day spoiled for the boys.'

Minty hoped with all her heart that Leo would behave himself. He was an asshole, but he'd have to be even more of one to cause a scene at his own son's wedding. It was bad enough that'd he'd thrown his wife over for his mistress, then abandoned the mistress herself as soon as she'd discovered that she had breast cancer. Nobody would have high expectations of him, but he would stop shy of making things uncomfortable, wouldn't he?

She brought her attention back to Adie, then startled a bit, as she remembered that the food she'd brought for tonight was still in Marcel's car.

'Oh, God! I've forgotten my contribution to tonight's supper! Let me just run out to the car and get it.'

She dashed out to the car and came back with her 'plate' – a gorgeous unbaked lemon-zest cheesecake sitting on a very large silver cake board and covered with cling-wrap. It was huge. She put it on the kitchen table and grinned as Adie beamed at it.

'Holy hell! Well, I'm glad *that* survived the journey! It would have been a criminal waste of epic proportions if it hadn't!'

Minty laughed. 'We had to pack it very carefully in the back footwell of the car. I can't even claim the credit for it, Adie. Belle made it this morning, to a double quantity, so it should be big enough to grace a few tummies tonight.'

'Sod that, Minty! I think I'm going to hide it, before anyone else lays eyes on it, and eat the whole thing myself.'

At that moment, the doorbell rang. Minty heard Mark open the front door, and she smiled when she recognised Peg Tripper's and Sheila Shalloe's voices.

Within half a minute, the two women had taken over the kitchen, filling every available surface with platters, bags, and plastic boxes, full of food. Adie and Minty both sprang forward to help, and the kitchen table was soon covered with sumptuous pies, deep-filled quiches and plates of home-made, succulent sausage rolls and trays of assorted sandwiches. Sheila had also brought two large boxes of gorgeous mini chocolate eclairs, and another two of her apparently quite famous Cointreau-laced Christmas mince pies.

Within no time at all, Sheila and Peg had unpacked all their boxes and bags and were starting to get everything plated up and ready to take through to the buffet table in the living room, later in the evening. Minty smirked, at Adie's lovely big kitchen being hijacked so efficiently that she didn't need to do very much, herself! Peg and Sheila were so well organised, and worked so seamlessly together, it was magic to watch them. Minty thought that a more coordinated pair of 'kitchen matriarchs' would be pretty hard to find.

Mark had left the front door ajar so arriving guests could just wander in. Minty looked up as a babble of excited voices filled the hallway, and then two very attractive young men came into the kitchen carrying casserole dishes. One dish had a lovely-looking chicken cacciatore in it, and the other was full of what looked like Jollof rice, made with chunks of lamb, vine tomatoes, red pepper, ginger, garlic, and other spices. Minty remarked on it and Adie told her that it was one of her son's wife's signature dishes, from her native Nigeria.

'Marie makes this dish a lot, for Matty and the kids. It's fantastic, and I imagine it'll be one of the first things to be attacked and polished off tonight, once the food serving starts! My chilli con carne, which I make every year to high demand, will be a close second. So, get your portions squirreled away now if you want the guarantee of any. Once the hordes descend you won't get much of a chance unless you're first at the table. It's never far shy of a bun-fight, to start with. Far better to get the inside scoop but for God's sake don't tell anyone!'

Adie introduced Minty to Matty and to her daughter's fiancé Chris. The men dropped off their food and promptly left again, clearly reluctant to get caught in the kitchen, and Minty wondered if it was going to turn into one of 'those' parties, where the women stayed in the kitchen all night while the men commandeered the living room. Adie seemed to be wondering too, and she quickly shooed Sheila, Peg and Minty out, and told them to get themselves a drink before coming back, and to get her one – a decent sized vodka martini.

'In fact, get Mark to make two. Miranda will probably be down in a few minutes, and she'll want one.'

Minty hung back. 'I'm happy to stay and keep helping, Adie. It's nice to have you all to myself, for one thing. Once everyone starts arriving and mingling, I'll be lucky to see you for the rest of the night, and we're heading off again in the morning. Belle and Tim have us all booked into a nice restaurant for dinner tomorrow night with the boys and Cal's parents.'

Adie nodded. 'Go and grab a drink and bring it back in here, then. But why don't you and Marcel come here for breakfast tomorrow? I know they'll be serving it at The Feathers but perhaps you could come here instead, before you guys head off.'

'Really? Yes, that'd be fantastic, thanks!'

Minty moved towards the kitchen door to get the promised drinks, and collided abruptly with Feen, who was coming in.

'Ooh! Hello, Minty! I thought I heard Aunty Sheila's voice a few minutes ago. I wasn't aware that you'd arrived too. How fab it is to see you! How is France?'

'It's good, thanks, yeah. Took me a while to get used to everything, but I'm as settled now as I ever will be, I think. Getting to grips with the language, and my sister helps a lot with that – and so does her husband of course, who's French. How are you, and your family?'

'We're all good. I've left Gavin upstairs twettling the sins. They've had a really full-on day, with everyone here. They had us up at quarter to bloody four this morning, would you believe, wanting to know if Santa had been. I've had to have a nafternoon ap!'

Minty laughed with delight, remembering Feen's funny penchant for Spoonerism, where she routinely transposed the first letters on a pair of words. 'My kids were the same. It nearly broke my heart when they stopped believing in Santa Claus. Something changes then, and you know you'll never get that bit of magic back.'

Feel rolled her eyes. 'Well, that's certainly coming, but I hope we have a bit more time before we have to deal with it.' She turned her attention to Adie.

'*Did* I hear Sheila, or were my ears traying plicks on me?'

Adie nodded. 'They've gone through to the living room to get a drink. I'm shunting Minty in to do the same, so why don't you go too, and chase up my and Miranda's vodka tonics? I'm bloody parched, in here, with all these ovens on.'

Chapter Three

After Minty left the kitchen, Feen glanced over her shoulder to make sure nobody else was in earshot as she handed Adie a drink. 'Just so you know, Gavin's gone a bit quiet tonight, and he might be like this for the rest of the time we're here. He's had some nerrible tews, that he didn't want to bring up over Christmas lunch, but he's really struggling with it. Some friends of his from America are missing, presumed killed, in that crane plash that's been on the news. You might have seen it? The private Gulfstream jet that lunged into the platlantic with nine people on board. Did you see or hear about it?'

Adie nodded, grimly. 'We did, yes. Mark actually mentioned how awful it was for that to happen right before Christmas. The plane was on its way to Edinburgh, wasn't it?'

'Inverness, actually. The passengers were all on their way to spend Christmas and New Year in some cancy fastle in rural Scotland. Three couples, two pilots and a steward were all on board. The plane apparently just rell off the fadar without warning. The authorities say it crashed into the sea about half an hour after take-off from Boston. They've found some wroating fleckage that identifies the plane, but no passengers as yet. They're all missing, presumed dead. But one of the couples was Gavin's friends. He found out last night that they were on it. He's really upset.'

Adie sighed, deeply. 'I know. He mentioned it to me this morning, but only briefly. He didn't want to elaborate on it, with it being Christmas Day and all.'

'He's still a bit shell-shocked and not quite sure what to think.'

'Well, that's understandable. It's horrific. It's the kind of thing you read about, or see on TV, but you never imagine it'll touch your own world. I'm sure poor Gavin is devastated. They were longtime friends of his father's, weren't they?'

Feen nodded. 'Yes, and *his!* I first let them in Mondon. Gavin's other step-dad, Mike, introduced me to them, not long after I'd met *him*. We all had dinner at the Savoy, in the city. They came to our wedding too, if you remember, and then they sent flowers after I ad my haccident, but we've only seen them a couple of times since, and only briefly.'

Feen's voice cracked a little, and she gave a short laugh, to try and deflect it, but Adie picked up on it and cocked her head on one side as she looked at her shrewdly.

'You don't seem overly upset yourself, about the crash? Didn't you see them as your friends too? I remember you sang their praises after you met them. I do vaguely remember them from your wedding. You had a funny name for them, but I don't remember what it was.'

Feen bit her bottom lip and lowered her voice again. She felt almost conspiratorial, talking like this, but she suddenly realised that she needed an ally. It felt important to let Adie know how she felt.

'Yes. Ratt and Mitch. And to answer your question, I *did* like them, very much, and I thought they liked me too. But I've since heard through the grapevine that they didn't think much of me at all, Adie. Their friendliness towards me was entirely fake, as it turned out. Behind my back they were actually quite mossipy and gean. They even said nasty things to Gavin himself about me! He was furious about that, and it changed their relationship quite a lot.'

'Well, I'm not surprised! Pulling a woman down, to her partner? Good Lord! That's not acceptable in *any* shape or form! No good friend would do something like that. It must have hurt *both* of you, that they did that.'

'Yeah. He kind of fell out with them a bit over it and they cadn't been in hontact since. So, he really has no idea how to feel about the fact that they're both dead! Nor do I, come to that.'

'That doesn't surprise me. What a horrible position to be in. Has their treatment of you caused any problems between you two? Please tell me it hasn't!'

'No, of course it hasn't! We both know where our loyalties lie. But what surprises *me,* about *all* of it, is my own failure to realise that their friendliness was fake! I'm usually pretty good at reading people, aren't I, Adie? But my own instincts let me down bigtime, over that. It's astonishing. I don't know how to feel about that either.'

'Yes, that *is* surprising. What do you think happened, there?'

Feen shrugged. 'I'm really not sure. It feels like I was somehow *shielded* from knowing, and I've no idea why! The guys were incredibly enthusiastic about a *lot* of things. I've met a few Americans, before those two, and since, and they've all been lovely. Genuine people, you know? Gavin's dad Martin also had a good friend from Seattle who came to stay a couple of nights with us last year. He was a gravelly-voiced paxophone slayer, and he was amazing. The loveliest guy *ever*, and his wife was sweet and funny; so real, and down-to-earth. A proper, genuine, no-bullshit couple. Ratt and Mitch were *full* of bullshit, now that I look back. I always knew they hammed things up a lot, almost to the point of being over the top, like certain people and places are *'udderly adorable'* or *'completely fa-yan-tastic,'* and that sort of thing.'

Adie tried not to smirk at Feen's dismal attempt at an American accent.

'I mostly just found it funny, Adie, but I somehow managed to miss the fact that they were being fake about *me!* My bullshit-ometer never went off once! As time went by though, it became ever clearer that they really didn't like me and probably never actually had. And the masks finally slipped.'

'Well, I guess if that was how they really felt it was only going to be a matter of time before it did. Nobody can keep up an act like that forever; not even clever people, and it doesn't sound like those two were particularly smart. But I'm sorry you've borne the brunt of it. It's outrageous, and so hurtful. There's nothing *not* to like about you, darling, for anyone who knows you well. I hope you do know that, in your own heart.'

'Thank you. It's sweet of you to say, and I don't think I'm particularly offensive. A bit bonkers maybe, in some people's books. But Ratt and Mitch hardly acknowledged me or the kids at all, over the last couple of years,' Feen confessed. 'You know, they recently invited Gavin to go and bisit them in Voston for as long as he wanted, but they made it clear that me and the kids weren't invited.'

Adie looked horrified. 'What? Are you *kidding* me? That's awful, Feen! What kind of morons try to get between a man and his family like that? And they called themselves *friends*?'

Feen rolled her eyes and shrugged, again. 'Yeah, it's not how you'd expect most normal people to behave, is it? I guess it was just some weird combination of them being gay and oversensitive, and ditchy and befensive with it, and me being what most people describe as a nit of a butcase that they really didn't understand and would rather avoid. We have a ton of gay friends and they're all incredibly cool, but those two? Well, let's just say that they were in a league of their own, on lots of levels. There was nothing cool about them.'

She shook her head and smiled, ruefully. 'How they treated me and the children was really no big deal to me, Adie. I let it pass over my head. As for Alder and Willow, well… they were too young to have noticed, I suppose, which is all for the best. They certainly didn't need role models like *that* in their lives! Hypocrites never teach anyone anything good, do they?'

Adie laughed. 'That's very true. Other than the lesson to avoid them as much as you can, I suppose.'

'Yes, totally. And, you know, I'm used to people burning their tacks on me. It's happened all my life, in one way or another, so it never bothers me much. Once I realised they were the type of guys I'd always need to alk on weggshells around, believe me, I was more than happy to disengage! But I *am* upset about the fact that they put poor Gavin in such a difficult position. He's known them for half his life. And, as he says, his dad would be grinning in his spave if he knew. I never knew Martin Black, but I'm sure he'd never have tolerated that.'

'I'm sure too. Honestly, I really don't know what it is that makes some people so mean. All I can think is that they must be pretty dissatisfied with their own lives if they can judge and meddle in other people's like that! I saw it all too often with friends of mine and my ex-husband's, back in the day. I felt it very personally too, the lack of tolerance, so I get what that's done to you. It blew your trust in them.'

She came and gave Feen, a massive hug, and she was grateful. She hugged back, tightly, and blinked back her tears.

'Thanks, Adie. You're one of the few people I can talk to about this, and how it affects me. Few other people understand how complicated this is, for us all. I could talk to Daddy, I suppose, but he's likely to say something to Gavin, and I don't want that. He already has enough swirling around in his head about it.'

'I can imagine. And all I can offer you myself is my own experience and observation, darling. Sadly, a lot of men – even so-called sensitive ones – just can't handle a woman they can't stuff into a box and ignore. Yes, it's archaic, misogynistic thinking, but it comes from a place of fear. Weak or scared men feel threatened in some way at the idea of their dominance being challenged, and their response is to treat strong women – or the ones they simply don't understand – with contempt.' She shook her head and sighed, impatiently.

'It's pathetic Feen, in the modern world, that some men would still rather hate you than try to understand you, but I guess they're lazy, and it's easier for them. Idiots like that don't want to do the work. But how they behaved is more of a reflection on who *they* were, not on who *you* are! Hold onto that.'

'I know you're right about all of it Adie, but it's always good to be reminded so thank you for that. You know, I actually felt a bit sorry for them. It must be awful, mustn't it, to live with such a big ship on your choulder? One of them – the more opinionated, bombastic one – had previously been in a hetero relationship that hadn't worked out, and he told Gavin that there were things about me that reminded him of her.'

Adie snorted with scorn; so loudly that it made Feen jump.

'Oh, for God's sake! Seriously? Was that the best he could do, in explaining himself? That really *is* pathetic! You're nobody's scapegoat, Feen, for any of the crap they haven't dealt with!'

Feen laughed. 'I know. I found that quite funny actually, but Gavin was fit to be tied over it. He more or less said what you just did. But it did all turn a bit icky for us both after that because I stuck up for myself and pulled the pin before they did, and I told the over-opinionated one exactly what I thought of him.'

She grinned now, remembering. 'He didn't like that at all! How *dare* I be so assertive, to dump them before they could dump me? Normally I wouldn't have bothered, because it's bad energy, isn't it? But when someone threatens to come between me and my husband, and doesn't seem to give a damn about putting my jamily in feopardy in the process, I will always stand up and roar. I don't think they expected that. It only seemed to make things worse, but I was past caring what they thought, by then. Oh, and in case you're wondering, their plane going down is not a jarmic kustice I requested.

'But I think *someone* asked for it,' she muttered as an afterthought, half to herself.

Randomly, and suddenly, a few days ago, she'd felt an overwhelmingly powerful connection to both her mother and her grandmother Alice. It had washed over her like a tidal wave, and she'd later realised that it had occurred at *exactly* the same time that Ratt and Mitch's plane had crashed into the sea.

The unexpected and profound presence of two powerful witches-in-spirit had almost knocked her of her feet, and when she'd realised the timing connection it had left her feeling shaky, and once more in awe of the forces that continually surrounded her that protected her from evil.

The stark truth was that no good ever came to anyone who crossed her, even though she never had a 'say' in it herself. Much greater forces than she could ever influence took care of everything, eventually. She never had to lift a finger. It meant that her conscience was always clear because, even if she did have any sway over karmic justice (which she didn't), she wouldn't have chosen negative outcomes for anyone – no matter what they might have done. She would simply walk away, put them firmly behind her in the 'forgotten' basket, and move on. But her mother and 'Anny Gralice' seemed to have a slightly different perspective on things. Feen never bothered to try and tell them off for whatever interventions they may have had a hand in because she knew it wouldn't make a blind bit of difference. From the spirit world they would do whatever they wanted, no matter what she might think or say about it. They would avenge her; in whichever way they saw fit.

Ratt and Mitch had turned out to be thoroughly ridiculous and ignorant, but they hadn't deserved to lose their lives – not in *her* book at least. The knowledge that spiritual intervention (or 'witchery' as some would undoubtedly call it) had decided otherwise was uncomfortable, but it was something she simply had to accept.

'Anyway, they're all dead on that plane, Adie. I know that beyond all doubt, even if nobody else is 'officially' sure, and even without knowing that people in that sea would last no longer than ten or fifteen minutes without a life jacket in December.'

'It didn't sound like they had any time to prepare,' Adie observed. 'Everything happened too quickly, by all accounts.'

'Yes, it did, and it makes me wonder what happened in all those people's lives that brought them all together, where they all had to forfeit at the same time.'

Adie stared at her. 'Seriously? Do you really believe that fate herded up a specific group of people that all had a karmic case to answer, and put them on the same plane to then cause it to crash? Sorry, darling, but that's a bit of a stretch, for me.'

'Well, it's a million times more complex than that, Adie. And, as mere mortals, we don't understand enough to be able to answer even a tenth of what goes into it. Even with my insight I can't articulate or even fully appreciate the vastness of it all. But yes, I believe that all of the people on that plane ried for a deason.'

She took a deep breath and tried to explain, knowing that nothing would be adequate. Imparting her knowledge was a challenge at the best of times, but when she was trying to explain something that she didn't fully understand herself, it made her aware of how inadequate her grasp still was, of much of what she 'worked' with.

'It's not our job to understand why, but let's just say that their deaths are having an impact on other people too and there are very likely reasons for that, which we also don't understand. We might see the notion as grossly unfair, that the innocent can be made to perish to punish the guilty, but ours is not to question the wharmic keel. We simply have to let the universe do its thing and trust the outcomes it provides, and respond with contemplation – and appreciation if we're able – for the lessons and guidance within it all.'

Adie frowned. 'That all sounds quite harsh, if you don't mind my saying so. Divine retribution at its finest, I suppose. Nobody wants to believe that exists, do they? But I suppose for someone in your position it's impossible *not* to believe it. I'm sorry for Gavin's loss, though. This must bring up a lot of stuff for him.'

'It does, especially around the death of his dad. He's not sure how to feel. He's very conflicted and I'm trying to be of as much support to him as I can be but I'm not quite as objective as I'd like to be, in getting him though this, after the way those cretins treated me.'

'Yeah, I get that. It's sad, that they were so intolerant. I find it ironic too, that a gay couple who probably struggled to find tolerance and acceptance in certain social circles themselves could be so intolerant about a different form of diversity! It feels quite incongruous. But you have a lot of good friends and family that do see your worth, Feen. Just concentrate on that. It's a far better use of your energy.'

'I don't think Ratt and Mitch saw my witchery, or my 'quirkiness' – for want of a better term – as a form of diversity, Adie. They weren't enlightened about very much at all, to be fair, and certainly not about that. They just found fault with everything I did and didn't say or do. You have to forgive that kind of ignorance though, from people who don't know any better.'

'A lot of people don't, I guess, but at least we can be thankful that most aren't mean or openly intolerant about it. And, as you say, they're gone now. The circumstances were unfortunate, but at least you can stop thinking about them and choose to let go of the hurt they caused you.'

Feen nodded, now. 'That's not hard. I don't really feel much at all, about the fact that they're gone. I'm quite good at turning my back when I need to, and disengaging without much of an emotional overhang. I'm not sure what that really says about me, but it is what it is.'

'Yes, you *are* good at pulling away, and for what it's worth, I think it's a good thing. It's an intuitive form of self-protection Feen, and I really envy your ability to do it. I don't find it easy at all to let go of people, even the ones who hurt me. I carried a lot of pain for a long time. Too long, really. I didn't know how to let go of it or the people who caused it.'

'It's easier if you can take a step back and see people for who they actually are, Adie. You know, what they've shown themselves to be, instead of who you believed or *wanted* them to be.'

Adie smiled, softly. 'That's a good bit of advice. I guess it comes down to not giving too much of yourself to people you're not really sure of and taking the time to learn as much as you can before you invest too much of yourself. I wish I'd done that, with a lot of people. Looking back, I trusted too many, too soon, with my heart and my generosity. It backfired a lot, and they were hard lessons to learn, every time. Painful.'

Feen smiled back. 'There's always more to a person than meets the eye, Adie, and always more than they want you to know. But time reveals the trueness of people's hearts in response to yours. Give them enough ribbon and they'll either wrap it around a nice gift for you, or they'll hang themselves with it before you become engaged enough to care. And I *don't* care, but Gavin kind of does, and I have to think about that.'

Poor Gavin. He really hadn't known how to feel, about Ratt and Mitch. He was hurt by their treatment of her, but the friendship went a long way back. He'd been sixteen when he'd met them. They were good friends of his father's, and they'd taken him to their hearts. He'd felt a lot of things, after they'd shown how intolerant they were; surprise, anger, sadness, and confusion too, that people who were already on the 'outside' of social circles that had no tolerance for gay people could be so intolerant themselves of someone else who didn't fit a 'mainstream' mould. Feen had been nothing but good to them, and yet all they could concentrate on were her faults. It baffled him that they did that, and it hurt him that they tried to exclude her from the contact they wanted to maintain with him.

As he'd said, himself; 'If they were real friends to me, they wouldn't be trying to come between us! I just don't understand in whose stupid world that would ever be okay, or why they would expect my loyalty to them to be greater than it is to my own bloody wife.'

He'd been a lot more upset by it than Feen had been, herself. What did upset her was the effect his so-called friends had had on *his* life. He'd been forced to acknowledge that they weren't who *he'd* always thought they were, either.

I know I'm not everyone's cup of tea, but it's one thing for people to decide they don't like me, and quite another to try and come between me and my husband. What were Ratt and Mitch thinking? That he'd choose them over me? We have children! We're a family!

They either didn't know what they were doing, or they simply didn't care. Either way, it was a huge disrespect.

Ah, well. They're dead now, so I suppose it doesn't matter. My only hope is that from where they are, still buckled into their smashed-up seats at the bottom of the ocean, they can know how much they hurt him.

It hurt Feen's heart, that Gavin was so bewildered. He deserved the time and space to mourn his friends, but that was only a part of the hodgepodge of emotions he was dealing with. Ratt and Mitch were responsible for all of them, and in a rare, quick stab of resentment, she was suddenly – but only briefly – glad they'd lost their lives. It wasn't something she was used to feeling, so it scared her, a bit.

Hey! Get a grip! Remember the fundamental ethic – wreak no harm! And when harm is done to me, step back from thoughts of vengeance, and let the Universe deal with it instead.

But she had to acknowledge, to herself at least, that harm done (or even just the threat of it) to those who were close to her heart was a very different matter in how she chose to respond. That quick flash, of being grateful for Anny Gralice and her mother's intervention, had surprised her.

I guess that's what happens when an enemy encroaches on your family. It makes you behave like a lioness with cubs.

She shook herself mentally, now, bit her bottom lip, and grinned at Adie.

'Well, I can't keep dwelling on all this, can I? It's over and done, and Gavin will come through it. We have so much that's good in our lives, and even though he has his grubborn, stumpy, and obstreperous moments where I seriously want to smack him hard with the rolling pin, he's very much an optimist. He'll square this away, in his *own* way, and life will go on. Did you know he's just scored a lovely contract with a new band in the States? They've given him the lyrics to a full album of songs, and asked him to write the music. He's over the moon about it.'

Adie beamed at her, now – clearly grateful for the chance to move something nicer to talk about. 'Yeah, he mentioned that too, and I think he'll soon be too busy to have time to dwell on the 'icky' stuff, as you put it. That's nice news, and I know how much he loves writing music.'

'He prefers it to writing lyrics, and you're right. Something to get his teeth into properly will be just the ticket. And he, Alder, and Willow have all started their chai ti lessons. The twins look so adorable in their little white suits! I'll show you some photos, later. Remind me. For now, though, I'd better go and check on the little monsters and make sure they're not tearing the place apart, upstairs.'

She left the kitchen, grateful for Adie's listening ear. Her stepmother was curious and open, about wanting to know more about the world Feen lived in, and how it impacted her. Feen had taught Adie much, over the past few years, and it was nice to have a new 'ally' in a world where so few people understood the strange and unfathomable one that Feen Raven-Black so often lived in!

Adie's such a loving, supportive presence in my life, I'm so grateful for her, especially now that Anny Gralice has died.

The loss of her beloved Grandmother, back in the summer, had been so hard. Alice Brierly had been a strong witch, and a magnificent guide for her, as her intuition was developing, especially after her mother had died from bowel cancer when Feen was fourteen. Gralice's passing had left a massive spiritual hole in Feen's life. Her mother, Beth Raven, had been a white witch too, but had more or less shunned her powers, preferring to live as 'normal' a life as possible without them interfering with the way she wanted to live it. She'd still been a gently insightful guide for Feen as she was developing her insights and spiritual strength, but it had been her grandmother who'd guided her the most. She'd always been Feen's rock, explaining everything well and encouraging Feen to embrace the spiritual side of herself and use it for good work. Thanks to Gralice, she had never grown up confused about her abilities or afraid of them.

Feen had found it interesting, that Adie Bostock (as she'd been when she'd first arrived at Teapot Cottage), had come into her life at the same time as dementia was tightening its grip on Gralice. The old lady was losing her mental faculties because of it, and the process had been wretched for all concerned.

Timing was everything, and although Adie wasn't endowed with the same kind of spiritual gravitas, she'd been willing to listen, learn, offer support, and do her level best to understand. That had meant everything to Feen, who often felt very alone and misunderstood in her 'weirdness,' as everyone who didn't understand it liked to call it. She never got to talk about her intuitive gifts much because they were far too complicated for most people to understand. The fact that Adie tried, and had in fact adopted a few of Feen's beliefs herself, meant that she really *did* have a new ally of sorts. It meant more to her than Adie would ever know.

In the hallway, on her way up the stairs, she literally banged into her stepsister Teresa (Tezzie), who was coming down. Tezzie grinned at her and gave her a quick hug.

'Hello, Steppy! I've just put Lewis down in Mum and Mark's room. Thank you so much for the use of one of your bassinettes! I've switched the baby monitor on. I take it the receiver is still in the kitchen?'

'Yes, it is, and the stupidly expensive babysitter will be here any minute, to oversee the kids. We'll all be popping up and down at different times too, so please don't worry about Lew. He'll be absolutely fine. I'm just going to check that Alder isn't pulling all the hair out of Willow's doll! He's a surreptitious tyrant. A proper little warlock in the making. Mutter wouldn't belt, when he's standing in front of you, but the minute you turn your back, he starts trying to tear things apart. He's the Voldemort of the family, I think.'

Feen was happy that Tezzie was home for Christmas. Last year, she hadn't been. She'd been away at her job as a war photographer, covering the conflict in Ukraine, and Adie had been seriously worried about her. Feen knew she didn't *have* to be so concerned; that Tezzie was safe enough there, and would be coming home unscathed. She also knew that Adie never wanted to be a nuisance by asking about it all the time, so Feen was always at great pains to reassure her, whenever she could, that she didn't have to worry about her daughter.

Now, Tezzie was on maternity leave and wouldn't be going back to work for another few months. She did intend to go back to the frontline, but she'd struck a deal with her employer to only do short assignments. She planned to only be away for a week, as a maximum, after she went back to work. Adie had tried to persuade her to properly give up her job and do something 'safer,' but Feen knew she was flogging a dead horse over that.

Tezzie hadn't meant to get pregnant. In fact, she and her fiancé Chris hadn't wanted to have children at all, but Mother Nature had had other ideas – as she so often does. Tezzie had given birth to Lewis just a few months ago. She and Chris were over the moon to be new (if unexpected) parents, but they were both determined that it wouldn't let it get in the way of the plans they had for their lives. They were slowly working out an achievable balance between their work and recreational passions, and parenting.

Tezzie wanted to continue working in conflict zones and Chris was keen to keep working too, and hardcore mountaineering and writing for an 'extreme travel' magazine in his spare time. They didn't want to compromise on the things that gave them so much joy, but having children had the potential to permanently derail the lifestyle choices that meant so much to them both. On the back of the 'oops' that had created their gorgeous little son, Chris had decided to have a vasectomy. It meant that Lewis would be an only child, but Tezzie and Chris were equally determined that they would juggle their commitments as best they could and apply themselves fully to his wellbeing. They adored him, and Feen knew that they were well on their way to working everything out so that nobody would have to make the kind of compromises that would inevitably lead to resentment or a sense of failure. She had no doubt that they would make their lifestyle work and that Lewis would always feel central to their lives. The baby had a big family to be part of too, so he would never have to feel alone.

'It's so good to see you, Tezzie! You were saying earlier, over Christmas lunch, that you're home for another six months or so. That must feel nice?'

Tezzie rolled her eyes. 'Yeah, like I said, it's okay. I'm permanently tired, and failing miserably at breastfeeding, so the poor little sod's on formula. He's putting on weight and thriving, and that's the important thing. I hate having to do it this way but sometimes you have to accept the inevitable. I seem to be the only one who's worried about it, so that's something, I guess.'

Feen was immediately sympathetic. 'I wasn't able to breastfeed the twins and I felt like shit about it too. But, like you say, you have to accept the inevitable and for what it's worth I don't think the so-called *experts* are right when they say that an inability to feed them yourself wets in the gay of bonding. So don't waste any time worrying about that! I'm as close to my children as any mother could be. I had to accept that I needed to do things differently and I just got on with it. I think you need to do the same.'

'That means a lot, Feen. It really does. Thinking about it always makes me emotional. Like I'm denying him, or something. I don't know…'

Feen was surprised to see tears welling up in Tezzie's eyes. She felt an immediate rush of compassion and jumped forward to hug her stepsister hard.

'Sweetie, I know you feel like a failure for not getting Lewis on the boob but honestly, it really *isn't* the dig beal a lot of people make it out to be! There's so much pressure, isn't there, to do this, or not do that, or whatever the hell it is? Just follow your instincts, and don't let those 'benchmark' idiots bet the getter of you. You and Lewis will both be absolutely bloody *fine*, if you can let go of other people's ridiculous judgements and expectations and just do things your own way!'

'Thanks, Feen. I knew that, I think, but it's nice to hear it. I didn't know you'd struggled too. I guess it's something that never came up in conversation because I was pretty sure I wasn't going to have any kids until Lewis came along.'

Feen laughed. 'I know, and I don't imagine you could have had a bigger bolt from the blue than Mother Nature saying 'well, bollocks to that, Miss Bostock, because I have quite a plifferent dan for you!' But you're doing just *fine*, Tezzie. Please believe that. So is Chris. You guys have this. Just trust yourselves, and one another, and everything will work out the way it's supposed to for all of you.'

She was surprised, but very pleased, when Tezzie moved forward quicky and caught her in a tight hug back.

'Thank you. You know, if anyone else had said that to me I'd think they were just offering me stupid platitudes by telling me what they though I needed to hear. But if my totally weird, white-witch stepsister equipped with the wisdom of *aeons* thinks we'll be fine, I'm pretty sure I can trust that!'

Feen winked at her. 'You can. Now, *I'm* pretty sure I have a doll and a distraught daughter to run up and rescue, before the screaming starts, so I'll catch up with you a bit later in the living room. The great thing about not breastfeeding is you can have a douple of crinks! Do me a favour and pour me a gin and tonic?'

'Sure thing, and I'll make it a double!'

Feen gave her a wink and a wide grin and headed up the stairs.

Chapter Four

Stuart Thompson watched his wife Fiona as she wandered through to the kitchen at Ravensdown House, with the heavy plastic box full of the fat, succulent sausage rolls she'd spent the morning making. They were one of her specialities, and she'd started making them about two years ago, after trying various different ones on offer in shops and cafes and deciding they weren't even close to what she'd been craving as a side-effect from her chemo. She used a combination of sausage meat, chopped onions, and a carefully measured selection of herbs to make the filling, and she wrapped them in the most mouthwatering pastry. They were three times the size of any others on offer, and each was almost a meal in itself. Stuart fancied hijacking the plate and eating them all himself, even if it made him feel sick. Fiona never made them often enough for him, but he'd managed to get her to make a double batch this morning, so there were some still at home in the fridge.

Peg Tripper would have brought some sausage rolls too, as she always did but, Stuart reasoned, you could never have too many at a party. They always went down a storm, didn't they? Fi's were the best though, and he'd still be fighting for one later when they eventually came back out of the kitchen.

He grinned to himself, as Gavin came wandering out of the living room, into the hallway. 'Hey, Stu, Merry Christmas dude! What are you grinning at? Share the joke, mate. I could seriously use one.'

'Nothing too funny, I'm afraid. Just the mouthwatering prospect of my wife's amazing sausage rolls. And Merry Christmas yourself! How goes it?'

Gavin pulled a face. 'Apart from a couple of friends being killed in a plane crash this week and having too much work to do and not enough time, I'm all good, thanks.'

He looked at Stuart's plastic carrier bag of gifts. 'Is that stuff for the Secret Santa sack? It's by the front door. You walked straight past it.' He indicated to a traditional, large hessian sack propped up behind the front door, with green tinsel wrapped around it.

'Ah! It looks pretty full already. You know, I love this bit of the party. Presents for under a tenner! Last year I got a small, framed picture of the Dalai Lama. It's officially the strangest thing I've ever been given, but Fi thought it was cute. She's hung it up in the loo. She got a shaving brush and a pancake of shave soap, so we swapped. It worked out pretty well, but I still don't know who they were from. Sorry about your friends, by the way. A plane crash is awful, and what rotten timing – right before Christmas. Were you close?'

Gavin grimaced. 'That's a bit of a complicated one to answer. Ask me again when I've had a few JD and cokes. Speaking of which, since the kitchen appears to have swallowed Fiona at least temporarily, why don't you come though and grab a drink?'

'It will have to be a soft-drink. I'm the designated minivan driver tonight.'

'Lucky you!'

Stuart followed Gavin through to the living room, where the fire was blazing, and a big dining table had been set up in the big bay window in front of the enormous Christmas tree. As in previous years, the room had been beautifully decorated, to the point where it simply wasn't possible to avoid feeling festive. In the centre of the table, as always, was a massive Christmas cake with sparklers sticking out of it. It was the 'piece de resistance' of Christmas supper, every year.

He saw Minty (McLeod? Cartwright?) over at the side of the room, talking to a heavy-set, grey-haired man. She caught his eye, and smiled, and beckoned him over.

She hugged him, briefly, and introduced him to her partner. His name was Marcel, and he seemed friendly. He was obviously French, but his English was impeccable.

'Oh, yes! I have heard about you, Stuart. You taught Minty to ride a horse, which was not without its problems, I believe?' His eyes sparkled, merrily, and Stuart decided he liked him.

'Yes, that's an understatement. I don't think she'll ever go near a horse again, but I'm glad she chose to stay friends with me, in spite of the fact that I nearly killed her.'

Minty laughed at him. 'No, you didn't! I nearly killed *myself*, all distracted and uptight as I was. If there's one thing it taught me, it's that when you're doing something you've never done before, with the constant threat of injury around it, you do have to give it your full attention. But how are the stables doing? Adie says you've had a busy year?'

Stuart nodded. 'Yeah, spring and summer were flat out, and we had more bookings this autumn than we had last year. It's all heading in the right direction. It's taken a while but we're turning a decent profit now, which means I can afford to hire some help, since my daughter Meghan is now at university and has less time to pitch in, at least until she finishes her degree.'

'How is Meghan, Stuart?' Minty enquired.

'She's great thanks! Busy with her studies, as you can imagine, and managing to have quite a good social life as well. She said she and her boyfriend might drop in tonight, if they can, on their way to somewhere – I don't remember where.'

'Oh, I hope so! It would be lovely to see her again!'

Marcel cocked his head on one side. 'Minty tells me you and your wife also buy old houses and fix them up? You sound like a busy man.'

'That's an understatement. The days when I had any time to myself are long gone. But I'm not one for sitting around doing nothing, anyway. Keeping busy is how I manage to relax, believe it or not.'

Fiona came into the room at that point. She hesitated a little, when she saw who Stuart was talking to, before moving forward slowly. His stomach fluttered, a little. This was the first time she and Minty would be seeing one another since before Minty had moved to France, after her husband's affair with Fiona had been exposed. He hoped things wouldn't be awkward, and he was relieved when Minty simply smiled gently and greeted Fiona politely.

'Hello, Fi. You're looking well. Married life seems to agree with you. This is Marcel Junot, my partner. He's a solicitor, based in Paris.'

Fiona smiled nervously and shook Marcel's hand. 'Paris! One of my favourite cities. Stuart and I were there last year, for a few days. There's a little hotel in the Latin Quarter, just across the Seine from Notre Dame, where I always stay whenever I'm there. One of my many 'haunts,' I suppose you'd call it. I know the city quite well. I've been many times. I'm so glad Notre Dame is open again after that terrible fire! Where is your office?'

'Near to the Boulevard Haussman,' Marcel answered. 'I too have 'haunts.' The city is like that. Parts of her speak to us, don't they? She calls us back, again and again, to the places we fall in love with.'

Stuart smiled. 'That's a good way of putting it, Marcel. I also have a haunt in Paris. The Church of Saint-Germain-des-Prés? I was there, years ago, when I got a telephone call telling me that my grandfather had died. I was close to him, so it hit me hard. I remember feeling glad about where I was, you know, in a really important place of worship. I'm not at all religious, but I lit a candle for him in there before I left, and each time I've gone back to Paris I've always called in there and done it again. It's our place – mine and his.'

'That's lovely,' Minty murmured.

Stuart excused himself to go and get himself and Fiona a drink. Her favourite tipple, Campari and soda, wasn't an overly popular drink but Adie or Mark knew she liked it and had thoughtfully provided a bottle.

He felt okay about leaving his wife with Minty, for a few minutes at least. They had a lot of bad history, but he didn't think any hostility would rear its head in the time he'd stepped away to pour a couple of drinks. Minty seemed polite, and Fiona was a lot more humble and self-accepting than she used to be. She'd made terrible mistakes, but she understood now what had driven her to make them, and it made a difference to how she interacted with people. She was softer, gentler, and less defensive. Her inflammatory breast cancer diagnosis had rocked her world and had thrown her into the biggest and longest imaginable fight for her life.

Stuart had fallen in love with her as soon as he'd met her and, as soon as he'd learned that she was in real danger of dying from the IBC, he understood that she would only fight for her life if she herself thought it was worth anything. At that point, she didn't.

She was crippled with guilt, fear, confusion, and defensiveness. He'd recognised that straight away, and he'd dedicated himself to supporting her through her double mastectomy and all of the subsequent treatment. He'd also encouraged her into therapy, to talk about the demons that had plagued her since she was in her teens. He'd believed in her, right from the start, and he'd encouraged her to believe in herself. It had made her strong, but in a better way – one that *encouraged* meaningful interactions, rather than spurning them. Fiona Winterson had become the compassionate, caring, competent and visionary woman she had actually been born to be, before the brutalities of being orphaned at a pivotal point in her development had set the new direction for a life of ruthless self-protection at any cost.

Stuart hoped that the changes in Fiona would be obvious to Minty. He knew the poor woman had had a tough time, coming to terms with the fact that Fiona had blown her marriage apart, and destroyed her daughter's trust too. But everyone deserved a second chance, and Fiona was no exception. She deserved to be forgiven for her mistakes, just like anybody else. Minty was a fair-minded woman, and if she could see the positive changes in Fiona, maybe it would put any last residual gremlins firmly in the past where they belonged.

As he got back to the little group and handed Fiona her drinks, he was relieved to see that everyone was smiling. Marcel was regaling the two women with a story about a particularly pompous client, and they were grinning with delight. As he closed out the story, Fiona caught Stuart's eye, and he gave her a wink. She nodded, ever so slightly, and he was reassured that her meeting with Minty hadn't caused her any problems. He knew she'd been worried about it.

Minty was talking now about her son's wedding. 'It's all organised. His fiancé Cal is from Toronto, and the whole family have flown in. It's going to be quite a 'do' by all accounts! It's all happening at the Mandarin Oriental, in Hyde Park, in London.'

She went on to explain that the young men had originally wanted to get married in Swindon, where they live, but they decided it was easier to do it in London, at an all-in-one wedding and hotel venue.

'With so many family arriving from Canada, it made perfect sense, because they couldn't get a place anywhere near where they live, to cater for the numbers! The Canadian contingent alone hits forty, even without my side of the family and all their friends they wanted to invite. Everything that might've fitted the bill in or near Swindon was already booked up solid for at least a year in advance. They couldn't get in *anywhere*. So, it's ended up in bloody London, with the price tag to match.'

She rolled her eyes. 'The cost of the entire thing makes me want to cry, if you want the truth, but it's what they want. Cal's family have contributed, and so have Leo and me. We've managed to cover it between us all, but I'm praying that when Belle's time comes, she'll want something a little more modest.'

Fiona spoke softly. 'I can't believe Ethan's getting married. I held him, minutes after you gave birth to him. He was so tiny. He and Belle both were. The years fly, don't they? They'll be having kids of their own, next.'

Stuart felt a rush of compassion for his wife. At one time, before the events that had torn their friendship apart, Fiona would have been a guest at Ethan's wedding. She'd probably have been somewhere close to the top table, if not actually on it, with Minty and Leo. She would be thinking about that now, and wishing she could be there. She still loved Ethan and Belle fiercely, even though the relationships were gone. He knew that she felt small and left out, now. Left behind. The fact that it was her own fault didn't make it easier to bear, that she would never have a place at *any* table, anywhere in Minty's family.

Minty clearly recognised the undertone behind Fiona's words, because her voice was just as soft, in return.

'I know. Sometimes I struggle to believe how far they've come. Independent adults. Imagine that. We couldn't, back then, could we? It all seemed too far away. But I'll send you a few photos, after the event, if you like? And maybe we can have a virtual coffee online together, sometime in the New Year.'

Tears sprang to Fiona's eyes. Stuart saw them, so he knew that Minty couldn't have missed them either.

'That would be lovely, Minty. Both things would. Thank you.'

Minty then asked her about her work. 'Are you back surveying, or still building up to it?'

Grateful for the change of topic, Fiona nodded. 'I'm back at the office on online comms, just as a consultant, two days a week. I do still hope to return to the job but obviously not back in Bristol! For now, they're happy to use me in an advisory capacity. When the time comes to return to work fully, I might look in Carlisle or even set up my own consultancy, but for now I'm doing okay with the part time stuff and working on the properties that Stu and I acquire as part of our investment portfolio.'

'How many properties have you renovated now?' Minty seemed genuinely interested, and Stuart was grateful to her for steering the conversation into safer territory.

'Eight. We're still working on a B & B over in Ravenglass, on the west coast, and getting that ready for sale. We already have a buyer for it actually; a friend of Feen and Gavin's, who wants to run yoga and dance retreats there.'

'Having that one pre-sold takes a bit of the pressure off,' Stuart offered. 'After taxes, we should still have enough capital to split between the retirement pot and invest in something else to work on. It keeps my team busy and employing them and other local contractors, as and when we need them, helps the local economy.'

'It sounds very interesting,' Marcel remarked. 'I always think it is a brave thing, to take on a difficult property and make it beautiful. But it sounds like you are well experienced, now.'

Stuart nodded. 'We're getting there. Learning a lot as we go along, and we've made a few silly mistakes, but we have an excellent team to help us identify certain issues. We take our sparky, chief chippy and plumber on viewings now to get their take on the scope of the work that might need doing. We trust them to tell us what's what. It's allowed us to walk away from a couple of prospects that would have ended up disastrous cost-wise, but mostly they do feel they can cope with what we ask of them.'

He was proud of what he and Fiona had achieved to date. Renovating derelict and sub-standard homes was a challenge, but it was one he relished. They'd sold a few, to buy more, but they had a nice portfolio now and, assuming that Fiona *was* going to live long enough to have a retirement, they were saving towards that too. Between that work, and his business of the Beaconsfield horse-trekking and riding school, Stuart was enjoying the projects he'd taken on.

Beaconsfield was in good shape now, and he no longer missed his days as a high-flying contracts lawyer at all, after falling from grace in the worst way possible; after too many lunchtime drinks, he'd got back behind the wheel of his car, and accidentally hit and killed a pregnant woman. It had turned into the stuff of nightmares for all concerned, and had felt like the complete ruination of his life, at the time. In retrospect, however, it had had been the making of him.

Certainly, the six years he'd served in prison hadn't been any kind of picnic, nor had putting himself in front of the dead woman's family in Bali, to offer them the chance to say their piece, but he'd emerged from it all as a more humble man; less cocky and arrogant. He'd got his relationship with his daughter back on track and flourishing, and he was looking forward to the time when she would finish her degree and join him at the stables, as a business partner and fully qualified Equine Therapist.

And his journey to the Lake District, to the gentle, healing space of Teapot Cottage and ultimately to Beaconsfield Riding School and Stables, to buy and resurrect that dying business, had enabled him to meet Minty Cartwright, which had led him to Fiona.

Stuart's wife and daughter were the best part of his life. His heart ached with love and pride for them both. Meghan had overcome huge hurdles to become the incredible, clever, and compassionate young woman she was now, and Fiona was brave in ways that most people couldn't even imagine having to be. Both women got up every morning with a clear sense of purpose, and a work ethic they could both be proud of. It was ironic to him that they both credited *him* for that, when he truly felt that the inspiration they were to him was more significant. It was, in fact, immeasurable.

He looked up now and was grateful to see his best friend coming through the door. Darren Davies was an inspiration too. He had his own terrible back-story, which had also involved doing prison time, and feeling responsible for the horrible death of a young friend when they were committing an acquisitive crime, but he'd turned his life around and was now one of the most well-respected newcomers to Torley. He'd gone on to study veterinary surgery and, as a partner in the town's biggest vet surgery, he was widely regarded as the most experienced and compassionate farm vet in the area. He looked after Stuart and Meghan's horses, and had set up a small equine clinic there, to treat and rehabilitate injured ones.

'Fi, I'm just going to say hi to Darren and Debs.' She caught the half-wink he gave her, and seemed to understand that he was offering her the chance to stay with Minty and Marcel on her own, or go with him to their friends.

'I'll come too. I haven't had chance to thank Debs for the orchid she sent over last week.'

She turned to Minty, to explain. 'Debby grows orchids in her little greenhouse at Appletree Cottage, and she sent me a beautiful one, last week. I know they're quite temperamental, so I need to ask her what I have to do, to keep the poor thing alive! Please excuse me? Perhaps I'll catch up with you a bit later. It's nice to meet you, Marcel.'

Minty and Marcel offered smiles, and Stuart gave one back, before taking Fiona's arm and leading her away.

'That seemed to go okay?' He murmured, quietly, and her response was just as hushed.

'I think so. No handbags at dawn. Not that I thought there would be, but it was a little more than just civil, so that was nice. It makes me feel a bit less stressed, about being in the same space.'

'Minty seems to have moved on. I know you two will never be bosom buddies again, if you'll pardon the terrible pun, but at least you know she isn't going to stab you with the cake knife now.'

Fiona laughed a little, which reassured him. 'I think we've gone past that. I imagine it's as good as it ever will be now. We'll talk, from time to time, and I'd like that. But I'm sad to be missing Ethan's wedding. At one time …' she trailed off, having run out of words to explain how she was feeling.

'I know. I'm sure it's really hard to think about that, after all those years of watching him grow up. But maybe you're better off *not* thinking about it, Fi. No good will come of you wishing for what you can't have.'

'You're right. But I wish things were better, even just to the point where I could at least send a gift, or a card. It would be a waste of money, as things stand.'

'Well maybe at some point in the future, you could reach out. But, for now at least, I think you must accept that it's not an option, sweetheart.'

Her face was sad, and he drew her close and hugged her. 'Meanwhile, back in the jungle … there's a friend of yours over there who I think will be very glad to have one of your special hugs. Debs loves you. Let's think about where we *do* fit in, around here, and concentrate on that.'

She hugged him back. 'Okay. And thank you, for being here, and being my rock. I couldn't have come tonight without you.'

'As if I'd even let you! A knock-out bird like you, floating around on your own, checking out the eye candy in the room? Forget *that*, young lady!'

Fiona giggled. 'I don't know where you get the idea that I'm a 'knockout bird,' for God's sake, *or* that I'd ever have eyes for anyone else? You're it, I'm afraid. And as for 'eye candy,' while I'm firmly stuck in that weird place of few prospects between the oldies like Mark Raven and Stan Walton, and the *real* eye candy like the gorgeous young Gavin and Chris, I think you're the best shot I have in this room tonight. Like it or not, you're stuck with me, Mr Thompson.'

'Well, that suits me, Ms Winterson. As wives go, you're not too bad a catch. And, since it's Christmas, I am going to find the nearest piece of hanging mistletoe and give you a bloody good snog under it. How about that, for starters?'

Chapter Five

'Forty-eight seafood skewers!' Wendy Whitelaw sang, in her lovely Welsh accent, as she wandered into the kitchen with a platter piled high with the most mouthwatering kebabs. They were made with king prawns, scallops, pieces of squid, and miniature octopus, interspersed with chunks of green and red pepper, red onion slices, and wedges of lemon. They were generous and incredibly colourful, but still raw and needing to be grilled. 'I was up at the crack of dawn this mornin' to prepare them! Christmas dinner had to go on hold until I'd finished!'

'Oh, my God!' Adie yelped with delight. 'These look incredible! But you *have* kind of put the rest of us to shame!' She looked at the skewers dubiously, clearly confused. 'What do I do with them?'

Wendy laughed. 'Billy's comin' in with a mini-grill. It's an Italian 'arosticini' thing. You fill it with charcoal and place the skewers on top of it. He can sit it on the aga, if there's room?'

'There probably is,' Adie confirmed. 'How long will they take to cook?'

'Probably about ten minutes, once the charcoal's hot, and it's all in mini pieces so it should heat up fast. I'm plannin' to make the skewers a feature for New Year's Eve. I'm openin' AyO for a special gourmet dinner. Limited, stupendously expensive tickets, so I'll need to offer them somethin' special.'

'And we're the guinea pigs, I presume, to test this idea first?'

Wendy laughed again. 'Yeah, kinda. But I think it's pretty cool. At least I hope it is, because I've bought twenty of them from a guy who makes them in Italy!' She set the tray of skewers down, in the one remaining spare space on the kitchen bench.

'Of course you have! And the skewers look fantastic, Wendy.'

'I've also made some seafood sauce to dip them into when they're done. You'll just need a little pot to put it in.'

'A little pot, I can do. But we'd better get set up soonish to cook those, because we serve the buffet around nine o'clock.'

'Billy's comin' in to get them underway. He's just settlin' Robin upstairs with all the other little ones. She's a bit grizzly, tonight. The babysitter – Lucy, is it? She met him at the top of the stairs just now, and she's helpin' him to get her snuggled down. I'm so grateful for you doin' this, you know, havin' a sitter to look after the kiddies. We couldn't have come, otherwise.'

Adie nodded. 'Babysitters are nigh-on impossible to get on Christmas night. Even if you did by some miracle manage to get one, the cost is hundreds of pounds. What they charge is shocking, but I guess it's understandable on a special night, when most sitters probably just want to be at home with their families instead.'

'Or at a party somewhere, havin' some fun.'

'Yeah, well, Lucy comes every year for us. She charges a lot, but it isn't ridiculous, and she's brilliant at keeping the children entertained so the ones who aren't sleeping won't wander down here and create havoc, or have to confront the horror of their parents staggering around under the influence.'

'Well, it's a fantastic idea, and we'll be happy to contribute to the cost. Just tell me how much, and I'll sort it out.'

Billy came into the kitchen now, with a table-top contraption that looked like a cross between a fish smoker and a long, thin barbecue. It had collapsible legs and a removable grill rack. He grinned at Adie.

'I take it the chef has explained? Let me just get this set up and filled, and let's get it lit.'

'You know, I think it might set off the smoke alarm in here, Billy. Why don't you set it up outside the back porch, instead? It's sheltered.'

'Good point. Somehow, I seem to have drawn the short straw, on cooking these damn things, while the actual Chef who dreamed them up gets to abdicate all responsibility for them, and go and mingle and get pissed. Not quite sure how that works, to be fair. I just wanted to bring a bloody carrot cake.'

Wendy tutted at him. 'Seefer, for God's sake! Its half an hour! And I'm breastfeedin' aren't I? There's no alcohol for me tonight. We can take turns keepin' an eye on these.'

Adie rolled her eyes. 'Well, I'm no Michelin starred chef, but I do know a thing or two about grilling fish. Just set it all up and leave these things to me. I'll cook them.'

Billy looked hopeful, and instantly brighter. 'Are you sure?'

Adiel laughed at his obvious relief. 'Yes, completely. Now, go! Get yourselves a drink and join the party.' She waved them both out of the kitchen with a tea towel.

Wendy was thrilled to see that the living room had been beautifully decorated for the festivities.

'Oh God, Billy! Look at that Christmas tree! And the cake, on the table, with all the sparklers stickin' out of it! That's massive, isn't it?'

She was enchanted. Someone – presumably Adie herself – had gone to a *lot* of trouble to make this room beautiful for a Christmas party, and it was stunning. Plush green garlands covered every spare surface, peppered with frosted pinecones and shiny baubles. Scented candles dotted around the room gave off a cosy glow and the aroma of cinnamon and other warming spices, and the Christmas tree itself looked magical. It stood a full ten feet tall, in her estimation, and was heavily laden with glass balls and other exquisite decorations that were obviously all antiques. A warm fire was blazing in the grate, and a holly wreath hung from the mirror above it.

'You couldn't be in here, and not feel Christmassy, could you?' she breathed. She felt like a child who had stumbled into a magical Christmas grotto. The room was like a picture on an olde-worlde Christmas card.

'Oh, the secret Santa gifts – are they still in the car?'

'No, I brought them in, and put them in the sack by the door, as the invitation said.'

'Good, okay, thanks, Seef. Now we can relax, and start to mingle.' She spied a large cabinet in a corner of the room, laden with bottles, glasses, a large bowl of olives, and another of lemon and lime slices, an enormous bucket of ice, and two cocktail shakers.

'That looks suspiciously like a set-up bar arrangement, to me. Can you get me somethin'? A nice cold juice or lemonade, please. I'll be minglin'.' She smiled cheekily at Billy, who grinned at her.

'Okay, but just so you know, it's the only drink I'm getting you. After that, you're on your own. Your big girl pants extend to getting your own top-ups.'

Wendy wandered further into the room, shuffling past a couple of groups who helpfully stepped aside, as best they could. She saw Teresa Bostock over by the Christmas tree, talking to her partner, Chris.

'Hiya! It's good to see you both. How's motherhood treatin' you, Tezzie?'

Teresa rolled her eyes, and laughed. 'Let's just say it's putting me through my paces. I wasn't exactly prepared for motherhood, as you know, but we've all adjusted pretty well, I think. It's not as freakishly awful as I once believed it might be. How's it treating *you?*'

'Honestly Tezzie, I don't know where the time goes. Robin'll be walkin' soon. I know you were pretty adamant about not havin' babies. When I heard you were pregnant, I was astonished! But you're happy, are you?'

'We are. Still feeling a bit blindsided, at times, aren't we Chris? But Lewis is lovely. I wouldn't be without him now. I do really miss being at my job, though. It seemed like I finally found my passion, got all excited about it, made it happen, and then had to step right back from it.'

Wendy *had* been astonished at the news that Teresa Bostock was pregnant. She had been crystal clear about babies never being part of her plan for life! Chris had been equally aversive to the patter of tiny feet but, on discovering that they were pregnant, they'd both rallied admirably and seemed to be thriving on being parents now.

'Well, I never thought I'd *ever* see you enthusiastic about babies!'

'No offence, but I'm still not even remotely enthusiastic about any, *other* than Lewis! And I never will be, so please don't ask the question as to whether we will have any more. That door has closed for good. I'm just working on not being one of those new mothers who walk around with a glazed, half-insane look of blind adoration on their faces and have literally lost the art of talking about anything other than the colour of baby poo. Battling away, not to turn into one of those!'

Chris almost giggled. 'She had me booked in for the snip so fast, it made my head spin. Said I could never go near her again, unless I had it done.'

'Yep. Faced with the prospect of sex being taken off the radar for the rest of his natural life, what else could a bloke have done?' Tezzie punched him playfully on the arm.

Wendy grinned. 'Fair enough too. But what does havin' Lewis mean for your career, Tezzie? Do you have to give that up, now?'

Teresa shook her head. 'No. I'm on maternity leave for the first half of the year, then I'm going back, but for shorter stints. They're actually recruiting another 'snappie' to interweave with my trips to wherever. It did take some wrangling but when they realised they couldn't sack me for being pregnant and unable to travel, or because I have a child that forces me to find a better balance between work and home, they had to come up with something. They've worked hard with me, to find the best compromise for all of us, I think.'

'That's lucky. They must think a lot of you, then! It must still be hard, though, the thought of leavin' him? Especially when you'll have to go away at short notice?'

'Yeah, it's a tough prospect, but I'll be in constant touch with Chris, and with whoever has Lewis while Chris is working. Usually that'll be Mum or the childminder we have lined up over in Keswick. She comes highly recommended for being flexible and accommodating. It would be a lot harder for sure, if we didn't have the support. But I'm pretty sure we'll manage to make it work.'

'The most important thing is that Lewis has a routine and some continuity, and he's not farmed out to a dozen different carers,' Chris explained. 'We'll make sure he has the stability he needs when he has to be with someone else, which hopefully won't be too often.'

'We're so lucky, in that respect,' Wendy replied. 'Robin is as good as gold, with Billy. He mostly works from home, but he can take her to site, if he has to go and I'm not on hand. He tries to make his trips to locations for the time of day when I can have her with me. It's rare that he has to take her with him but, whenever he does, he just has her in a papoose, on his chest. Everyone's used to him showin' up with her. It's a long-standin' joke now, that she's the youngest contractor he's ever employed.'

Chris laughed. 'I know. He stopped in recently, as he was passing a cottage we were working on. It made me laugh, that he had Robin strung around his shoulders like a necklace. She was so tiny, and sound asleep, bless her. Such a sweet little thing. He was saying that your mum is going to be spending a lot more time up here soon. That'll be helpful too, yeah?'

Wendy nodded. 'It will be. She gets up here whenever she can. She's been talkin' for a while about havin' a second house up here, so Billy and I are on the lookout for a little place for her. We've asked Fi and Stu to keep their ear to the ground too, for somethin' that might come about. They're always at the auctions, so Stuart said if a place pops up that's worth a look he'll see if I'm interested. Mum's given me permission to just buy somethin', and she trusts my judgement, so we'll see. We're happy to have her at AyO with us, of course, but she's been sayin' she wants her own space.'

'That's understandable,' Teresa observed. 'She'd probably be comfortable about staying longer, if she didn't feel she was underfoot. Her generation, they don't want to 'be any trouble,' do they? They always seem to they think they are, even when they're not.'

Wendy nodded. 'That's it, I think. She knows we all like our privacy, but she wants to be of more help. It will be great to have her around more, though. That way I'll also see more of my Godmother, Trish. We're close, and she'll be visitin' Mum up here a fair bit because they're always in each other's pockets, so I'll win on every count.'

'I don't think you'll have to wait long for a place to come on the market. Cottages are popping up all the time. They're a lot more expensive than they used to be, and you'd have to be quick off the mark to get a good one at the right price but, if anyone has their finger on the pulse, it's Stu and Fi. They'll see you right, and hopefully sooner rather than later.'

She grinned at Chris, grateful for him trying to reassure her. She *was* excited about the prospect of her mum being around more often, to help out with baby Robin, and to give them the chance to enrich their own relationship as mother and daughter. Gail was keen to make that happen too, and waiting for the right place to come onto the market was starting to get a little frustrating. The way the crazy, drawn-out house-buying process worked meant that it would be at least three months, even from when the right house was found and an offer accepted on it, to when Gail could hope to move into it. Nothing was going to change much before the summer, at best. They all had to simply keep watching, and waiting, and be ready to strike when the iron was hot.

Gail wanted a bit of a garden at least; something easy-care to potter about in and for baby Robin to enjoy, so a townhouse or an apartment was out. So was any property that needed a lot of work doing to it. Nobody had the time or the energy for big renovations.

Ideally, a house needed to also be close enough to Wendy and Billy for her to only have a short drive to and from the restaurant. They were looking on the outskirts of Carlisle, on the Torley side, and also at Torley itself, which Wendy thought might even be better, since Gail was already acquainted with a handful of the people there after meeting them at the opening night of Wendy's restaurant. It would certainly be an easier transition if there were at least a few people her mother was friendly with in the area, even just superficially, to start with. It was a question of 'rusting the tuniverse' as her dear friend Feen would say, for the right situation to present itself.

'How's Billy's work going?' Chris seemed to want to steer the conversation away from childcare arrangements, and Wendy thought it was probably a good idea. She hadn't meant for him to feel defensive about the plans he and Tezzie had for Lewis, but he had started to sound a bit that way. She seized on the opportunity to talk about something else. She looked over Chris' shoulder and saw Billy coming towards them.

'Ah, well it looks like he's finally headed this way at last with the drink I asked him for, thirty-six hours ago, so you can probably ask him yourself and get a better answer!'

Billy looked apologetic. 'Sorry, I got a bit waylaid, with Gavin. Needed to have a few minutes to chat with him.'

'Don't tell me – a natter about vintage sports cars, by any chance?'

'Not exactly. A couple of friends of his were killed in a plane crash, a few days ago. He's a bit cut up about it. It didn't feel appropriate to just walk off.'

'God, no, you're kiddin'? Poor Gavin! Were they good friends?'

Billy grimaced. 'Well, that's the whole conundrum. They had been, for quite a long time, but they'd fallen out recently. Something about them being mean about Feen behind her back. He was really upset about that of course, but it's left him a bit unsure how to feel. He's okay. I mean, he's not in a screaming, sobbing heap or anything. Just a bit quiet. Reflective. So, I needed to stay for that few minutes while he talked a bit, but here's your juice.'

Wendy smiled gently at him, as he handed her a gorgeous glass of orange juice, with an assortment of chopped fruit pieces floating on the top of it and a little translucent glass stick with a red heart at the end of it, poking out from one side. 'Seefer' could be incredibly sweet at times, and about the oddest things. It was nice too, that he'd lent a sympathetic ear to poor Gavin, just now.

'Chris was just askin' how your work is goin'. I'll let you fill him in, while I go and see if Adie needs any help with the seafood kebabs. I wouldn't want her gettin' into a pickle with them. I'll see you both a bit later on. Maybe we can see little Lewis, Tezzie, when we pop up and check on the babies later?'

She winked at Chris, and at Tezzie, before heading back towards the kitchen.

Chapter Six

Gavin looked up from his drink and saw Wendy coming towards him.

'Hey, Wendy the Wesh wonder! Merry Christmas! It's nice to see you. How's AyO doing?'

He and Feen were regulars at Wendy's restaurant, on the road between Torley and Carlisle. They always aimed to dine there a few times whenever they came to Torley for a decent block of time. It was lovely to have a place to go that was adults-only, where diners could enjoy a romantic evening without having it ruined by screaming kids who would tear around and destroy the ambience while their parents remained oblivious. It was a bugbear for many, and Wendy had taken a big chance on opening her restaurant to be child-free on every day except Sundays, when she offered a carvery lunch for families.

'Hiya! It's doin' well, thanks. Still standin' after just over a year, and we're actually turnin' a small profit now, would you believe?'

Gavin loved Wendy's sing-song Welsh lilt. It always made him want to laugh. She was such an upbeat person, it was hard to imagine her *not* being successful, in whatever she wanted to do. Opening AyO had been a huge gamble for her, off the back of being publicly pilloried for her refusal to cook a dangerous dish for someone, and losing her job as a result. But if anyone could pull off the concept of an adults-only restaurant – with all the potential controversy that came with it – it was Wendy Whitelaw. Instead of shying away from being controversial, she had embraced the past scandal and more or less told everyone they could think whatever the hell they wanted, because she was carrying on in just the way she wanted to, thank you very bloody much, and they could take it or leave it. Gavin admired her guts, and her tenacity.

'I'm glad! AyO was quite a punt, after that blowfish scandal. But you're quite the celebrity now, aren't you? I've seen you featured in a few of the magazines Feen gets, and you're always portrayed in a positive light. I'm glad the concept hasn't backfired on you.'

'No, it hasn't. I do still get a few internet trolls, and a few bad reviews, but they're always about the ethos, and never about the food. And, of course, I've been able to challenge a bit of that with the magazine interviews. I do think we're past the worst of it now. But what about *you?* Billy just told me about your friends, and the plane crash and everythin'. That's terrible, Gavin! I'm *so* sorry for your loss.'

Gavin felt his heart plunge, for the hundredth time, after hearing about the death of his friends Rich and Matt. He wondered when it would get easier, to accept that they were gone.

'Yeah, it was pretty unexpected. You can't prepare for something like that, can you? It's just hard to accept that I'll never see them again, or get the chance to get our friendship back on a good footing. It wasn't, and sadly it'll forever be a slightly tainted memory now. That's harder than you might imagine, to reconcile.'

He had to acknowledge that there was nothing he could ever do about how he'd left things with his friends. The way they had spoken about Feen behind her back when she hadn't been around to defend herself had made him furious, to the point where he'd been literally unable to respond to their attempts to connect with him after the fact. They'd backed off all contact after that, and he'd been *relieved* that he didn't have to deal with them until he was ready. It just hadn't occurred to him that when he ultimately decided he *was* ready to confront them, they might not still be around. It was true what he'd heard – that you never know when you'll see somebody for the last time.

Wendy laid a hand gently on his arm. 'Billy said you'd had a fall out. Something to do with Feen? Well, I don't know much about it, Gavin, and I'm not interested in pryin' into your private affairs. And I get that it's complicatin' your feelin's around losin' them, but let me just say that if anyone badmouthed Billy to me, I would go for the fuckin' throat, and he would do the same for me. So, if you're feelin' guilty about your first loyalty bein' to your partner, don't be. You didn't do anythin' wrong. *They* did. Protectin' one another's how it's *supposed* to work in any relationship. And I do believe that people who try and break that loyalty don't have much of their own.'

Gavin considered that, for a moment, and he realised Wendy was right. Someone who came between a man and his wife like that, whether they realised what they were doing or not, really *didn't* understand the concept of loyalty, or the sacredness of it, between partners. He wondered now, how Rich or Matt would have reacted, if he'd slagged one of *them* off to the other. He'd never find out now, would he?

'It's just sad, you know, because I met them through my dad and they were in my life for a long time. I'm not such a good person that I can just forget what went down and pretend it didn't matter. I'm not much good at taking the high road.'

Wendy smiled at him, sadly. 'Yeah. Me neither. But, you know, we all have shit to live with that we can't simplify or square away. We just have to find a way of livin' with it, even when it makes us question ourselves. And you will find a place for it, Gavin. Just give it some time, yeah? It's still a bit raw and fresh.'

She stepped forward and gave him a quick, strong hug, and then scurried off towards the kitchen.

A tap on his shoulder made him turn around, and he was surprised to see Tony Valley, grinning at him.

'Merry Christmas, mate! I hope you and Feen are around for a bit? We need to tee up a squash game, or at least all have a night in the pub.'

Josie Valley was Feen's best friend, and Gavin had hit it off well with her husband. He and Tony played squash at the Torley Sports Centre as often as time would allow, whenever Gavin and Feen were at Ravensdown, but they hadn't managed to connect before now on this trip.

'Yeah, Merry Christmas to you too, Tones! Long time no see! Feen says work's keeping you chasing your tail, and Josie's busy with her work too, and the kids?'

Tony nodded. 'It's been a crazy few months, that's for sure. I took on an apprentice a few months ago and he's a godsend. Still in the early stages of learning, mind, but I've been able to hand over quite a bit for him to get on with and it's meant I haven't had to turn work away. What about *your* stuff? How's life in the music industry?'

'Yeah, it's busy for me too. I've just scored a new contract with an American band, a full album of songs to write the music for.'

'Are they well-known? Would I have heard of them?'

'Maybe not. Quantum Ruin? They're emerging in the States, and trying to get into touring in Germany and the Netherlands.'

'Not the UK?'

Gavin shook his head. 'Nope. Too many financial challenges for them here, apparently. They're a little off-beat. The level of following their genre would have here doesn't make it viable, or so they said. I'm not sure they've done the right research on that, but it's their call. They'll probably still get airplay, if the songs are successful, but they may not have a high profile here. It's nice though, as an English muso, to be offered the work.'

'Only proper proof that you're one of the best in the business, mate. Nice win. Congratulations on going global, and hopefully this job opens the door to many more. I imagine there's a lot of work, and a lot of money to be made, from that side of the pond.' Tony lifted his pint in salute and Gavin raised his also.

Josie appeared and threw her arms around Gavin. 'Merry Christmas, you! Feen's just told me about your friends. I'm so sorry. Right before Christmas! What a horrible thing. Are you okay?' She quickly brought Tony up to speed about the plane crash.

Gavin closed his eyes, briefly. 'Not really, Josie, but I have to be, don't I? It'll take me a few days to get my head around it, I suppose, but life rumbles on like it has to.'

She nodded. 'Well, if there's anything we can do. I know everybody says that – probably as the only thing they can actually *think* of to say, but we mean it, don't we Tony? Anything. Just let us know. And I told Feen that you guys should all come and have dinner with us tomorrow night. Bring the kids, they can all set up in the spare room and watch telly until they all fall asleep. Do come! It's time we all had a decent catch-up.'

Gavin grinned. 'Well, if Feen says we can, we certainly can. I never know what's on the social calendar from one day to the next, to be honest. I just get told where we're going, what to wear, and what time to be ready. But that sounds nice, thanks. Otherwise, we'd all just be sitting around here, eating leftovers, and drinking too much, like every other Boxing night.'

He was so grateful for Josie and Tony. Their friendship was gentle and genuine, and their two little girls weren't much different in age to the twins. The kids all played well together, and one couple often had the other couple's over for playdates, when a bit of time out was needed. They were all gorgeous kids; sharp, intelligent, and playful, but they could be quite demanding. It was great to have friends who understood that and pitched in when you need to take a break for a couple of hours.

Feen and Gavin were blessed, especially while they were here in Torley. Adie and Mark were doting grandparents, and his own mother Carla, and her husband Dave, were also always keen to have the twins for a while. It was harder in London, where the family support wasn't available, so they relished their time in Torley. They went out more by themselves or with friends, without having to worry about whether or not the kids were in good hands. Alder and Willow were nearly always gleeful, in fact, at the thought of spending time with any of their grandparents.

Feen was an excellent mum, and she adored her family, but she was very much a free spirit who needed a lot of time to herself, to stay connected with her spiritual side. Gavin was conscious that her time spent in London didn't offer as much scope for that as she really needed, so they spent as much time as they could up here at Ravensdown, where she felt more in tune with the earth and connected to her ancestors. London was all he'd ever known, and he was used to the fast pace of life there, but he knew Feen struggled with it, at times. Calmness was in her DNA, along with her quiet ability to connect spiritually with forces Gavin couldn't even *hope* to understand, but respected, nonetheless.

Feen had been very much adrift after 'Anny Gralice,' her rock and spiritual mentor, had died. Alice had had a good innings before the dementia that had addled her brain finally claimed her. There was no disputing that, but the loss was hard for the granddaughter who had nobody else to guide her with understanding, through her own spiritual journey, especially when she was fearful of 'stumbling,' and getting things wrong. The big positive that came from the loss was Feen's ability to communicate with a 'fully intact' Alice through the portal she had to her loved ones in the afterlife. She didn't connect with *everyone* in her world who had died, just the few who she'd felt deeply connected to in life.

Gavin wasn't sure if that was a blessing or a curse but, either way, it was Feen's cross to bear, and all he could do was support her as best he could. He'd had to open his mind to that, in ways that he'd once never imagined. At one time, he'd have written Feen's particular capabilities off as a load of mumbo-jumbo. But he saw the evidence, time and time over, of the power of her gifts and talents, and how they helped people in crisis. She'd even worked her magic over *him,* when he'd first come to Torley, angry and wretched with grief after losing his father, and looking for belongings that had mattered a long time before. He hadn't wanted to connect with his 'half-mad' mother, and Carla Walton hadn't been happy to see him either. But, after being estranged for ten full years, they had finally been able to reconcile a few of their differences and reestablish a good mother-son relationship. Feen had been instrumental in enabling that. Without her intervention, he didn't think they'd have made it.

Carla caught his eye now, and beckoned him over. She looked lovely tonight, he noted, as he made his way across the room to her. She wore a heavy velvet knee-length dress with a sweetheart neckline that wasn't too low, and a fitted pencil skirt. It was a gorgeous shade of bottle green, and she'd pinned a large spray of frosted holly, berries, and the tiniest miniature pinecones to the shoulder. The dress brought out the sharpness of her gorgeous, glittering green eyes that he had been blessed with, himself.

'Hey, Mum. Merry Christmas! You look very festive. Quite beautiful, in fact.'

Carla glanced heavenward, good-naturedly. 'Thank you. Feen made this bloody brooch thing, and insisted I wear it. You do know how determined she can be at times, about something? Well, I said no at least three times over it, but she wouldn't take that for an answer. Apparently, I 'have' to wear it, because it goes with the dress. I feel like a bloody Christmas tree, and I'm wondering if I should swipe the angel from the top of the other tree and slap that on my head too, but I do have to admit that it's quite a lovely thing. I'll probably wear it every year from now on, but for God's sake don't tell her I said that.'

'I wouldn't dream of it, Mum. Heaven forbid she'd ever get to think she'd won a battle with you! Thanks, by the way, for the cashmere jumper and the Christmas socks. I did need a new jumper.'

'I asked Feen. I gave her a list of possibles, that I was thinking of getting you, and she leapt at the socks. I'm brilliantly imaginative, when it comes to buying highly original presents, as you know. It's one of my star qualities.'

Gavin laughed. He loved his mother's self-deprecation, and her sarcasm. She had long-since stopped being mean with it, and was now mostly just funny, *especially* when she poked fun at herself.

'Well, I really did need a jumper. Sometimes the less exciting presents are just as important, Mum. And you were certainly brilliant with Feen's gift! She was over the moon with your painted wooden box filled with every kind of herbal seed imaginable, and with the gift voucher inside it, from that store in London where she buys all her essential oils and creams and stuff. She was thrilled to bits with that. As soon as we get back, she'll be scuttling off to the shop with a list in her hand.'

'There you go. Acquisitive brilliance. I found that wooden box in the bottom drawer of a chest I picked up in Lancaster a month or so ago, and I thought it was worth sanding and painting. I'm glad she likes it, and what went into it. Dave got the best present of all, of course, but it's one you can take advantage of too if you want.'

Dave smirked, and puffed his chest out a bit. 'A pool table! Full size. Takes up half of one of the barns, but she's a beauty. A proper old-hall, vintage piece with slate top and legs to die for.'

'Steady on, you can't talk about my mother like that!' Gavin grinned and Dave winked at him.

'Ah, I've said worse about her, and she knows it. But seriously; come over, for a few games before you go back to the big smoke.'

'I will, thanks. But bloody hell, Mum! How did you manage to keep *that* a secret, or even get it delivered, come to that? Those things are bloody enormous, and heavy enough to sink an average freighter!'

'I was over at a house in Windermere, picking up a couple of vintage wardrobes and a matching chest of drawers, and I saw it in their garage. They agreed to sell it, and I arranged transport. It arrived a couple of days ago and I've had a *right* game, trying to keep Dave out of the barn until this morning!'

'She locked the bloody doors, and then said she'd left the keys at the shop. Kept dithering about going to get them, and wouldn't let *me*, and then eventually said there was a surprise in there and I'd have to wait until Christmas morning.'

'Only because you nagged the crap out of me and wouldn't leave me alone about it. Odd, how you don't go in that barn for weeks, then you only want to when you realise you can't.'

Carla grinned and rolled her eyes at Dave. 'Wah-wah, I want to get into the barn, even though there's no reason to, because there's absolutely nothing in there! Honestly. Your tantrum would rival a four-year-old's.'

She seemed to be on fine form tonight, as usual. Gavin was glad, once again, that he and his mother had managed to put their differences aside. He'd been very worried initially about contacting her again, but his fears about her desire to make things difficult for him had proved unfounded. It was actually pretty good, having her back in his life. Despite her incredibly prickly, frosty 'front,' Carla Walton-Holloway was a funny and generous woman, and lot kinder than she wanted people to think.

Letting go of the terrible demons that had driven her all her adult life and allowing the softer side of herself to show, had eventually led Carla to gaining some much-needed confidence and self-belief. She had gone from being a woman the Torley townspeople barely tolerated, to becoming a much-admired and important figure in the community. She very much championed other women to maintain or get started in business, in and around the town, and people genuinely respected and liked her now. Gavin was proud of her achievements, which included setting up her own little business, lovingly restoring old furniture. He was glad too, that she'd found the courage to let love into her life after too many years of being on her own and believing she was worthless. Dave Holloway was good for her, and Gavin liked him too – very much. Among a few things the men had in common was a love of classic cars.

Feen danced up to him, now. 'Hello, husband,' she twinkled, smirking.

'Hello, wife,' he responded kissing her lightly on the nose. 'Where have you been?'

'Kecking on the chids, taking drinks though to the captains in the kitchen, and dropping wearls of pisdom everywhere I go.'

'I'll check on the twins from time to time too, if that helps? You needn't be up there every five minutes. We'll all pitch in. Just enjoy the party.' Carla offered.

'That's sweet of you, thanks Carla! And the babysitter is actually having the time of her life up there right now. She's telling a rather complicated stairy fory, with every kid hanging off her every word. It all seems to be well under control up there.'

Feen put a hand gently at Gavin's back. 'How are *you* doing?'

'Honestly? I'm trying not to think about the plane crash much. A party's not the place for ruminating on shitty stuff, is it? I am a bit concerned about poor old Mike, though. He's gone to spend Christmas and New Year with friends in Romania. I bet the last thing the poor bastard felt like doing was getting on a plane, last night. I had a brief chat with him this morning, but he's taking things hard. I'll ring him again tonight.'

He briefly explained to Carla and Dave that he'd lost two friends in a plane crash earlier in the week, and that his other 'dad' Mike was taking it hard too. Predictably, they were horrified, and very sympathetic.

'I saw that, on the news,' Dave admitted. 'I know you probably don't want to dwell, so I won't bang on about it, but at least it was quick. They hit the water so fast, and with so much force, they wouldn't have had time to wonder what the hell was happening. There's that, at least.'

'I know. And they were excited, to be spending Christmas in the Scottish Highlands, or wherever the hell they were planning to go. So, I guess they died happy. It's the best you could hope for, I suppose, under the circumstances.'

Gavin pulled a face, hoping that the discussion would be left there. Carla was about to say something, when Feen quietly interjected, and took the focus off it for him.

'Daddy wants a word,' she said, gently. 'It's nothing to worry about. He just wants to ask you if you fancy a play clidgeon shoot somewhere in London next month; some chest-beating caveman thing he's been invited to by a business guy he's meeting down there. He wants to know if you'd like to go along.'

'Thanks, sweetheart. I'll go and find him.' Gavin excused himself from his mother and step-father, and went off to find Mark. It didn't take long. He found him in the opposite corner of the room, surrounded by a group of farmers' wives. He was happily holding court, and recounting a silly story that they all seemed to find enthralling.

That was Mark Raven to a tee. He had the broadest 'Lanky' accent imaginable, and he was – in his own words – 'as rough as a badger's arse' at times, but he sure knew how to make people laugh. He was well on form tonight too, dressed up in a newer version of the old favourite Christmas shirt he'd worn for more than a decade to every party, until Adie and Feen had finally managed to wrestle it off him and put it in the bin with its frayed collar and cuffs. He was telling his story with expansive hand gestures, no thought for the roughness of his tone or his language, and a twinkle in his bright blue eyes. If anyone was offended, they were making a very good job of pretending they weren't. But he was the host, after all, so they more or less had to be nice. Mark Raven wasn't above throwing someone out of his party or – at the very least – telling them what he thought if they were being rude. Nobody seemed inclined to want to upset him. He was hugely entertaining, literally the life of the party.

Gavin adored him. Meeting and marrying Feen had been the most amazing thing that had happened in his life, but 'inheriting' the Raven family had been a pretty good bonus! Mark was a scream, and as down to earth as you could get. He and Adie were the salt of the earth, and Mark's sister Sheila and her husband Bob Shalloe were similar. They were straight-up and honest to a fault, but they had hearts of solid gold.

Gavin knew that both Adie and Sheila were a great guide for Feen, and a steadying influence on her, especially since she'd lost her beloved gran, earlier in the year. Those two women knew the full impact of that, and they'd held her up – literally, at Alice's funeral – and helped her recover from losing one of the most important people she'd ever had in her world.

They were a great family, and he felt privileged to be a part of it. Mark was readily able to laugh at the world a lot more often than he'd let it get the better of him. His silly stories, which poked a lot of fun at life in general, were all astute and real. Gavin decided he could do a lot worse tonight, than listen to a few of them himself.

Chapter Seven

It was early, but the party was already in full swing, and the noise level was rising. Teresa checked her watch, and was surprised to see that it was only ten to eight. It felt later, somehow, but that was probably because she'd got Lewis organised earlier than usual, to bring to Ravensdown and get settled upstairs. The baby was still only a few months old, and she was ever-so-slightly paranoid about leaving him, but the babysitter was a certified nanny with credentials a mile long, and Teresa was grateful that Adie had managed to get her to come for Christmas night, to look after a gaggle of children ranging from tiny babies to older kids who needed a fair bit of entertaining. It was going to be quite a demanding night for the poor woman, but she seemed to be taking it all in stride. It must be costing an absolute fortune too, but with all the parents pitching in to help cover the cost, it was as near a perfect arrangement as anything could be. Adie simply wanted everyone at her sixtieth birthday party, and would go to any lengths to ensure it.

Teresa couldn't blame her. Her poor mum, with her birthday on Christmas Eve, had always felt like her special day was overshadowed by Christmas itself. Even her fiftieth had somehow got swallowed up and more or less cast aside, amid the family's typical festive focus. This time, Adie wanted it to be different, and even though it was a 'normal' Ravensdown Christmas party that happened every year on Christmas night (and had for decades, as one of the oldest traditions in Torley town) this year there would be a special part of the evening set aside just for her. She would have the focus on her, and get to open the many presents that Mark had asked people to keep a secret until the moment arrived. He planned for her to be overwhelmed with love, in that special moment, to mark her milestone birthday. A separate cake had been ordered and was sitting in the fridge down at Teapot Cottage, for Teresa to run down and fetch just before the lights got dimmed at nine o'clock and the spotlight fell on her mother.

Adie looked beautiful tonight. Trudie Sangster, her friend who owned the local boutique in the town, had managed to track down the perfect dress for her special night. Beneath the voluminous apron Adie was currently wearing as she raced around in the kitchen, was a waltz-length, fifties' style dress in shimmering turquoise satin. It hung beautifully, and flowed when she walked. The colour was amazing, and Teresa had caught her breath when she'd seen it on the hanger, in front of the wardrobe in Adie and Mark's room.

Adie had teamed it with pair of shoes with heels of an almost sensible height – something from the Irregular Choice or Poetic Licence range, by the look of it. They were cream satin, and embellished with turquoise flowers, pearl-coloured sequins, bits of ribbon, and various other interesting things. They set off the plainness of the dress perfectly. They were a birthday treat from Feen, apparently, and Teresa smirked. She knew that poor Feen always had a terrible time trying to find nice shoes that fit her own tiny feet. She usually had to resort to getting them made. Shopping for stunning shoes for her stepmother must have been a bittersweet experience for her.

Teresa caught a glimpse of her step-brother-in-law Gavin, and she made a beeline for him. She wanted to check how he was doing. He'd briefly shared, over Christmas lunch, that he'd lost a couple of friends in the plane crash in the Atlantic. Despite his goth-rocker appearance, and down-to-earth attitude to life, he was a highly sensitive soul, and she knew he was feeling the loss keenly.

'Hello, bro! How are you doing?'

Gavin's face lit up a little, at her breezy greeting. Teresa supposed that everyone had heard about the crash, and she didn't want to trivialise it, but she was keen to keep things light for him, if she could, especially if other people had been a bit sombre or heavy about it. It was a party, after all.

'Hey, Tezzie! I bet everyone's asking you how motherhood is treating you, aren't they? It's like me, with this plane crash thing. Everyone thinks they have to say something about it, when I really wish they wouldn't.'

'Yeah, I'm sorry again that you've lost your mates. It's bloody awful. I lost a friend a few years ago, unexpectedly, and it does take a while to get over the shock. I did find it easier to cope once people had stopped getting in my face about it, so I won't witter on with condolences and all that, but I'm here if you want to talk about anything. How's work? I didn't get the chance to ask you earlier, with everyone chattering nineteen to the dozen over Christmas lunch.'

Teresa was fascinated by Gavin's work as a song and music writer. She wasn't musical herself, in terms of creating it, but she did have a strong passion for listening to it, and she and Gavin had talked before – many times – about why music was important to her, and how certain songs enabled her to express herself more freely than just talking, which she wasn't always good at or comfortable about. When she and Chris had got together the power of the music she had used, to show him how she felt, had been instrumental. She would never be great at wearing her heart on her sleeve, but expression through well-chosen music was helpful to her.

'Good thanks, new work coming in, and wrapping up a few projects in time for the New Year. Got a song for Lewis yet?'

She giggled. 'Of course I have! Carrie Underwood. What I Never Knew I Always Wanted.'

'Ah, good song! Perfect actually. So, when do you go back to work?'

'In a few months. We're putting the infrastructure in place now, around Lewis, so I can go back and not have to worry about his welfare. Chris is off to Alaska in a couple of months with his friend Marcus, to climb Mounts Bona, Foraker, and Hunter. They've been on his list for ages, but he wants to do them before I go back to work. They're up to a week each, depending on conditions, so he'll be away for about a month.'

'Yeah, he mentioned that, earlier today. It makes sense, I suppose, for him to do it all now, but how do you feel about him being away so long, with Lewis being so little and everything?'

That was a good question. How *did* she feel? She hadn't really given herself much time to think about it, since they'd decided Chris should go.

'Ooh, you know, nobody's asked me that, and I haven't really thought about it! My mind's a bit mush, with Lew, and sleep deprivation, and all that. But I get why Chris wants to do it now, and I'm pleased that he and Marcus finally have the chance, because it's been on their wish-list for a long time. Finally making it happen; it's exciting for Chris, and I'm happy about that. Dreams are important, aren't they?'

'They are. And I don't suppose much will change with Lewis in a month or so, other than him putting on weight. And you can send videos and stuff, so Chris can stay in the loop. It's harder to be away when they start with the milestones, like walking and talking, and being contrary with their food.'

'That's right, and I've got Mum and Mark for support, and a handful of friends, and even my crazy father if it comes to a short enough straw! We'll be fine. I'm not worried about it.'

And Teresa *wasn't* worried. The arrival of Lewis had changed certain dynamics for them logistically, but none of that meant that she or Chris couldn't still do the things they wanted to do. They had to adjust their time schedules a bit, but they were working hard to ensure that Chris could continue with his passion for extreme mountaineering, and she could continue with hers as a frontline war photographer. They weren't reckless people by nature, but there were inherent risks involved with what they did, and they had to be a little more mindful now than they were before about the impact a potential accident either of them might have, on their son.

It didn't mean huge changes; just modifications to schedules and expectations. But Teresa and Chris had promised one another – and Lewis – that he would never be deprived or treated as second to *anything*, especially not hobbies and careers. If things had to change in a big way, they would make whatever changes were necessary. It was as simple as that.

'Adie sems to be chained to the kitchen.' Gavin observed.

Teresa nodded. 'Yeah. Same old, same old. I tried to offer help, but I got shooed out. She and Sheila and Peg have a well-oiled process in there. It doesn't pay to wander in and try to get involved. Mum doesn't usually get out of there properly until serve-up time, but Peg and Sheila are pushing for it to come out a bit earlier tonight because Mark wants to dedicate the night to Adie at nine o'clock.'

'Yeah, that's a nice thing to do. I can't believe she's sixty! She looks a lot younger.'

'She does, and she's always busy doing something physical, which helps to keep her fit. She's got good genes too, and I inherited *some* of those, so if I look that good at sixty, I won't be complaining. Here's hoping my father's less-than-lovable genes don't make an appearance too early. Anyway…' she trailed off, looked around, and frowned.

'I suppose I should keep mingling, but I just want to remind you that while we're all here I'd love to hear some of the music you're writing, if that's allowed? You're not one of those precious artists, are you, that refuses to let anyone hear a single note until it's finished?'

Gavin laughed at her. 'Not at all! Feedback is always good. If something is shit, I'd rather know before I get too far into it. I'd *love* you to have a listen. Maybe we could aim for tomorrow, just before lunch time? We're off over to Josie and Tony's for dinner tomorrow night, but I'll probably be working for a few hours until around midday.'

'Hangover permitting?'

He nodded, and grinned. 'Hangover permitting. I'm planning on not having one but of course, when it comes to the Ravensdown parties, it never takes long for good intentions to fly out the window, does it?'

Teresa grinned back. 'No, it does not. If I find you throwing up in the flowerbeds later tonight, I'll give you a slap and a splash in the face with cold water. How does that sound?'

'Fair enough, and I'll do the same for you. Catch you later, Tez.'

She wandered off towards the drink station set up in a corner of the room, and bent to pull a couple of logs out of the basket and throw them onto the fire as she went past it.

'Thanks, lass! I were just about to d'that meself.'

'Hi, Mark. Are we still okay for nine o'clock? Thanks for helping me with the washing up after Christmas dinner today, by the way. A mountain of food always means a mountain of bloody pots, and it's funny how everyone scarpers when it comes time for the clean-up. I thought I was going to get stuck with the lot, all by myself, while everyone else pretended to be asleep.'

'Aye, yer welcome, love. It were a grand lunch, weren't it? Adie always does us proud. Nice to have new little'un, this year. 'E seems as good as gold, Lewis.'

'He is. He gets a bit fractious when he needs a nappy change or a sleep, but all babies do, and he usually goes down without a squeak. I've been blessed with an easy baby. Considering I never actually wanted one, I think the universe has tried to make it as easy as possible for me to have him. He is adorable though, and I'm slowly getting used to things.'

'Yer doin' *grand,* lass! Yer a good little mam, and 'appen 'e's an easy bab because yer not a panicker yerself. They do pick up on things. An anxious mam always means a restless babby.'

'Thanks, Mark. That means a lot. Some days I'm not so sure I'm doing it right; other days it feels a piece of cake. Every day is different.'

'Yer know, lass, even if it in't perfect, it's still good enough. There's no blueprint. We all learn the ropes o' bloody parentin' as we go along, and we all make we're share o' mistakes along the way. Believe me, yer doin' fine. Don't doubt yerself.'

She gave him a quick hug, and he returned it. He was a special man, and she was glad her mother had found him. Mark Raven called a spade a spade, and nobody ever had to wonder where they stood with him. He was a fair and warm-hearted man, but everyone knew where his boundaries were.

Wouldn't it be nice if everyone was as honest and real, as he is? It's such a faff, trying to figure out what so many people really mean, or want, because they won't be straight about it. Some people will tell you anything, or nothing at all, instead of being honest. Mark doesn't walk on eggshells around anyone, and nobody has to with him.

Mark was a treasure; there was no denying it. Her own father was a monumental flake, in her eyes. He was a weak man, always having affairs and getting involved with people who tried to take him for all he had. Bryan Bostock had had a rough ride lately, but it was largely his own stupid fault, from making choices without weighing up the consequences, and losing all but the shirt off his back in the process. He never seemed to care much who *he* hurt, but he complained long and loud about the people who hurt *him*. He was nothing of a role model for Teresa or her brother Matty. Bryan was a presence in their lives, but only just, and they'd both had to make sure it was on their own terms, and not Bryan's. Mark was a far better example of what a man should be, as a husband, father, and friend. He wasn't perfect but he had integrity, and that counted for everything.

Teresa grabbed a glass from the big drinks cabinet and poured herself a pint of beer from the keg that sat spread between two chairs next to it. She looked around for Chris, with a view to pouring one for him too. She couldn't see him, but Fiona Winterson was coming towards her with a big smile on her face.

Teresa smiled back. Fiona was in a very long, hard battle with breast cancer, but you wouldn't know it tonight. She looked radiant with her blonde hair done up in an elegant top-knot, impeccably applied makeup, and wearing a plain black, jacquard A-line dress with at least a dozen gold and silver chains of assorted sizes, around her neck. Some were chunky, others less so, but the effect was stunning. Teresa assumed Fiona had put them together to draw attention away from her silhouette that showed her to be flat-chested after her double mastectomy.

'Wow! Look at you! I love that dress! It's dead plain, but the cut is amazing, and those chains, Fi! Nobody could pull that off but you. You look *fabulous*. Merry Christmas!' She stepped forward and gave Fiona a warm hug.

Fiona giggled lightly. 'Merry Christmas yourself! And thank you.'

'Please, Fi – don't ask me how motherhood is treating me. If you hear me screaming at some point, it will be because someone else has asked me. I swear to God, it seems to be all anyone is *capable* of asking! There's more to me than a simple failure to bloody lactate, for God's sake!'

She giggled, then. 'God, listen to me! A few weeks into motherhood and I'm already as defensive and neurotic as fuck.'

Fiona burst out laughing. 'Okay, well let me ask you something else, instead. How do you feel about taking on a bit of a job? You could bring Lewis with you, that wouldn't be a problem. I need someone to start taking footage of the properties we're renovating to sell. You know how you did the progressive shots of Wendy Whitelaw's barn as it was being turned into a restaurant? Well, this would be something similar. We've set up our own sales website now, and I need professional video taken of what we're putting on the market. Please tell me you're interested!'

Teresa thought for a minute. 'Hmm… well, I might be, depending on the time involved, and all that.'

'It's houses, Teresa. Nothing too big, just the same kind of thing you did at Wendy's but obviously a lot less intensive. Not progressive at all, in fact. Just a view of each in it's before-state, then a more detailed showcase after completion.'

She went on to offer an hourly rate that made Teresa blink.

'Cash in hand, of course, because I know you're on salary already. I can make that work, and I just thought you could do with some mental stimulation in the real world. Sadly, I never had a child myself, but I do know how frustrating it is when a career-focussed new mother can't get enough of a balance. Of course, I also appreciate how knackered you must be, so if it feels like too much ...'

Teresa jumped in. 'No. It wouldn't be too much at all. So, what are we talking, a few hours work a week?'

Fiona nodded. 'Yeah, sometimes not even that. We don't always have a fast turnaround, because some places need a lot more work than others. But if we could call on you, on an ad-hoc basis, I think it might run to that. And of course, there's the editing time, which you could do in your *own* time, as long as it didn't take too long. Just tell me how many hours it all takes you in total, and I'll pay you as you go along, if you like?'

'That sounds amazing! I did enjoy doing Wendy's restaurant. It's nice to see that video on AyO's website, and even nicer that she's credited me.'

'Well, I know it's a long way from the excitement of shooting footage in a war zone, but it might just keep you from going insane with suburban neurosis or something, especially since Chris has taken a full month's bloody leave from his work with us, thank you very much, and won't be around to offer you adult conversation. Let's talk next week, about when we can get you started.'

Fiona turned to leave, but then turned back. 'By the way, a failure to lactate is actually not a failure. It's just an unfortunate quirk of nature that isn't your fault. I don't know a lot about babies, but I do know that much. So, take a load off, okay? Don't beat yourself up over what Mother Nature has decided isn't right for you and Lewis. He will be fine, so let *yourself* be, over that.'

Then she melted into the throng of party guests, and suddenly Chris was standing in front of her. She startled, a little.

'Oh, there you are! I've been looking for you. Was going to bring you a beer before I got waylaid by Fiona, with a job offer, no less!'

'Yeah, she said she was going to talk to you about shooting some videos of the houses we're doing. What do you think?

'I said yes! It's random, but well-paid and cash in hand. I'd be a *fool* not to say yes! Why didn't you mention it?'

'Ah, she seemed excited about offering you the gig, so I didn't want to steal her thunder.'

'Oh, you sweet man! That's so thoughtful. Anyway, what's the evil nasty goss from your end?'

'What, apart from Gavin's mates taking a dive into the Atlantic? That's about as grim as it gets around here, I hope, with it being bloody Christmas and all. Nah, everyone seems happy enough, apart from that. There's the usual moaning and groaning about the cost of grain and livestock, but everyone seems keen to forget the bullshit for a night and let their hair down.'

'Fiona seems mildly miffed about you wandering off for a month, but I don't think it's a critical problem. If it was, she wouldn't have said yes to it, would she?'

'There's a quiet patch on the horizon, and they have a stand-by guy.'

'Of course they do! Fi and Stu are always going to have a back-up plan! It's why they're so successful. They keep all their bases covered. But I think Fi will be glad when you go back, after your trip. The construction team's a bit special, isn't it? And when one of the cogs is replaced, even just temporarily, I suppose it never feels quite the same.'

'I'm glad *you've* got something to get your teeth into, Tezzie. It's pretty low-key but it will get you out of the house now and then, and doing something you enjoy, even if it's only taking pictures of toilets.'

Teresa punched him playfully on the arm. 'And I shall see to it that they're the best *ever* pictures of toilets. It's nice to be wanted, isn't it? Being head-hunted to take pictures of toilets is still better than sitting at home suffering from 'nappy-brain,' and slowly talking myself into the idea that I'm a terrible mother for wanting to keep my job as a war-shooter.'

'Or telling yourself that I'm a terrible father for wanting to keep risking my life on mountains.'

Teresa shook her head. 'Nope. Not happening. We are never going to allow ourselves to feel bad about the choices we've made in life. Lewis was a surprise event, for sure, but we'll find a way to make this work. We absolutely will. We will find a way to be true to ourselves, and to him, and make whatever compromises are necessary that allow us to *keep* being true to ourselves.'

Chris looked at her, softly, and the love in his eyes made her catch her breath.

'You know, Tez, whatever journey life takes us on, as a family, we'll always have dreams to make and strive for. Maybe they will change, and maybe the landscape of our lives will end up looking different than what we planned. But that's not to say it won't be better. We will end up where we're supposed to, and wherever that is, it will be amazing, because it's you and me.'

Tears sprang to her eyes now, and she blinked them back. 'Promise?'

'Yeah, I promise. And, Mistress of Songs, I have one for *you*. Take a listen to that old nugget of Bon Jovi's; It's My Life. I'm not as eloquent with the messages as you are, but it's one life, and it's now or never. We're not going to live forever, babe. We have to live while we're alive. Do whatever we can, to live life on our own terms. We're Tommy and Gina, Tez. Lewis will be the child of brave, fearless people who grab life by the balls and shake it. A child could have worse, for role models.'

He lowered his voice, and made it gentle, because he knew that she was scared. 'We will make it work, Tezzie. We're going to have a great life. And one day, when we're sitting in our rocking chairs and trying not to dribble into our tea, we can look back and say that whatever compromises we made, they didn't take anything away from a bloody good life well lived.'

She turned to him, and felt his arms go around her as she buried her face into his shoulder.

'Hey, you can't be crying at a party! Mop up, have a good sniff, and I'll race you to the end of your pint. In fact, let's see if we can get a boat-races thing going in here.'

She laughed, now. 'What, and end up shitfaced before Mum's big moment? Not on your life. Get pissed after the fact, but not before. Mark would never forgive me, especially if I dropped her cake! And I won't be dragging you down to Teapot Cottage, later. If you can't walk, you'll be sleeping where you fall.'

'Maybe Matty can help you get me down the drive.'

'I will not be involving my brother either, thank you very much. Besides, it might be all *he* can do to walk, later.'

She looked over at Matty who was chatting to his wife Marie. She was Nigerian, and she was gorgeous, with smile that lit up a room. Tonight, she was turning a lot of heads, in her beautifully designed halter-neck jumpsuit in heavy gold satin. Its top was modest, and the pants were wide-legged, so it actually looked like a dress. Teresa felt compelled to go and compliment her on how stunning she looked.

'Gosh, look at you! Beautiful! You were still getting ready when we left you, down at Teapot Cottage, and now I can see why! It was worth the wait, to see you look so gorgeous.'

Marie rewarded her with the biggest smile imaginable. 'I was surprised about the dress code. 'Dress to the Nines' was the recommendation, so I did, and I'm just relieved not to be the only one! I do have a more modest outfit back at the cottage. If it turned out that I'd misread the directive and ended up overdressed, I'd have bolted back down to get changed! You look lovely too, Teresa. Burnt orange suits you, and I love the sparkle.'

'The pleated front on this cocktail dress hides what I still have, of a baby belly. All the sit-ups in the world don't seem to be shifting it as quick as I would like. I didn't put on much weight, as you know, but it all went on around my middle, and I hate it.'

Marie looked sympathetic. 'It doesn't look as bad as you think it does. I do mean that. And it will take time to go back to what you were, but you have an athletic frame, so you'll snap back soon, I'm sure. I was the size of a house, with Milly *and* Sophie! My bum is huge anyway, but I looked like a sumo wrestler, from behind!'

'I'm off to get another drink. Can I get you anything?'

Marie and Matty held up drinks that were still half full. As Teresa turned to go back to the bar, Mark tapped her on the shoulder. It was almost time to run down to Teapot Cottage and pick up her mother's cake.

Chapter Eight

After poking her head around the door to the back porch, to check that Wendy and Billy's raging arosticini contraption was finally cooling down and the charcoal was no threat to setting the house on fire, Adie noticed Trudie in the garden. She was standing off to one side, under the apple tree, and she was leaning against its gnarled old trunk with her shoulders heaving.

'What are you doing out here, Trude? It's bloody freezing!' Adie put her arm around her friend gently and pulled her close. 'Tell me what's wrong.'

Trudie shook her head and mumbled through her tears. 'I can't tell you, sweetie. At least, not tonight.'

'Why not tonight?' Adie asked her softly, but she thought she knew the answer. 'You know, it might be a party, and it might be my birthday to boot, but none of that matters. What does is the fact that you're hurting, and that's not okay. Please, just tell me. Stop suffering in silence, Trudie. Tell me what's going on.'

Trudie's voice was low, but ragged. 'I'm in a horrible marriage, Adie. I'm shackled to a man who never wants to hear me, who never wants to let me in. I'm irrelevant. I don't know what I'm doing hanging around anymore. My needs don't matter to him. What's important to me doesn't matter to him, if it isn't important to him too.' She sniffed hard, and her voice suddenly became too bright, and her smile became too brittle.

'But it's okay. It's shit, but I *am* getting out of it. I'm *definitely* getting out of it. I've made a few plans already.'

Adie sighed, deeply. 'I know you're unhappy, Trudie. But you and Kevin have been married a long time. Is this really not fixable, for you? It's fair enough if it's not, but you need to be sure, darling, that this is more than just a midlife wobble. We all have those. Well, most of us do, at least. For some of us, it's no more than that. But, if it is, you need to be *sure* that it is, before you do anything drastic.'

Don't throw the baby out with the bathwater.

'It's been shit for a long time, Adie. Years, now. Kevin wants to call all the shots, like only his life matters. I'm so sick of fighting to be relevant to him. It's years since I felt heard, or noticed, or desired. It's like living with my brother, Adie. Like being kissed by my grandfather. There's no passion, no sex, no *anything* that makes me feel like I matter. It's *years,* since I felt like I mattered.'

She was crying heavily now, and Adie felt at a loss.

What do I say, to any of this? Her pain is so huge, I can feel it myself. Is it menopause, haywire hormones, that's making her feel this way? Or is it something more profound? More deep-seated? She's in anguish, and I don't know how to help.

Adie felt inadequate. Wise words were sorely needed, so why couldn't she find any? Why was it so hard, to say the right thing that would help?

'Have you told Kevin how you feel?'

'I've tried, but it's just another thing he belittles, every time I try. I'm not allowed to have feelings that make him feel uncomfortable. I'm supposed to not have them, or hide them, at least. I'm supposed to keep stuffing it all down, and putting up with being treated like a nuisance or an irrelevance, for just wanting what's right and fair. I'm supposed to just keep swallowing down the hurt, and the anger, and frustration, and sadness. I'm *done*, Adie. I'm done with pretending to myself that I can carry on living like this. I'm starting to doubt my own sanity now, and that feels really scary.'

Adie nodded, finally feeling like she had a foothold. 'That, I understand. Having to carry on as if everything's okay because you don't want to admit to *yourself* how much pain you're in is the hardest thing of all, because you the start to wonder if the problem is *you* – if you're quietly going mad.

But trust me, darling; you're not. You've just woken up to the fact that you might have to make some really big changes to *save* your sanity. Have you thought about your options?'

'Yes. And I want to leave. I want to stand on my own two feet, start again, reclaim myself and be who I'm *supposed* to be' who I *deserve* to be, instead of living like some shadow attached to a man who doesn't understand or value me; a man who doesn't even seem to *like* the real me. I want to leave, Adie, so that's what I'm going to do.'

'Well, if that is your decision, tell me what that looks like, for you.'

Trudie took a deep breath. 'I want to move into the flat above GladRagz. Kevin's office. It's a proper flat, with a kitchen and a bathroom, and a couple of decent-sized bedrooms. I want to make that my home. He can find another office, somewhere in the town, because that's all he really needs. I want the flat, and the cat, and my independence.'

Adie chose her next words carefully. 'So, would that be temporary, like, until you decided if you really did want to split? Maybe take some time to decide for sure? I mean, you have such a history together, and you were happy for a long time. This arrangement could offer a bit of space, and time to decide if you really do want to transition, or if some time apart is all you need, to get to a place where you feel more confident in confronting the issues with Kevin and coming back stronger together. But, on the other hand, I know a lot of couples find counselling helpful, even if it's only to enable them to split well, if you know what I mean. Sometimes leaving *is* the best option, and therapists recognise that too.'

Trudie shrugged. 'I don't know, Adie. Maybe. I don't know if it's worth even trying to find a way forward. Maybe me and Kevin are just done. All I know is that I deserve better than to be living half a life with someone who doesn't really care whether I'm there or not. Kevin doesn't want to be challenged or even disagreed with, and I don't want to live a life that's dictated by someone else.'

'I get that. I *totally* do. And splitting might mean that at least one person ends up happy, after being in an unhappy union. But ending a marriage is a really big thing, and you need to take time to decide if it really *is* the right move to make. I don't know. Maybe you could suggest to him that he move out temporarily, and let you have the flat until you work out what you really want to do? You know, to buy yourself some time, until you're sure?'

'He'll just see that as an attack. Every time I disagree with him or want something he doesn't, he sees it as an attack. He's so defensive it's terrifying, and I just don't have the strength to keep going. I'm *so* tired, Adie. I'm mentally exhausted from walking on eggshells, or taking endless flak if I say how I feel instead. I just can't do this anymore.'

Poor Trudie did sound utterly defeated. This was a crisis, there were no two ways about it, but Adie wanted her to be sure, in her own mind, before she burned any bridges. Her idea of taking over the flat above the shop made a lot of sense, certainly in the short term. Kevin could probably work from home, or at least get a short-term lease on office space somewhere in the town, until he and Trudie worked through their marital problems. The gossip mills would rumble, as they always do in small towns, and nobody needed their private problems put on public display. But what was at stake here was far more important than a bit of idle gossip.

Adie would happily wager that most of the people in Torley would actually be *concerned* about Trudie and Kevin. They were such a well-liked couple in Torley, it was hard to imagine them being the target of malicious or gleeful gossip. If votes in the town were cast, Adie suspected that most would be in favour of them working things out and staying together.

But what did anyone else really know, about the state of someone else's relationship? Many couples bickered for years – sometimes viciously – but they'd never even *consider* splitting up, even while everyone around them was scratching their heads, wondering why the hell they stayed together. And what looked like the happiest marriage on the planet was often the most abusive, or miserable in other ways, behind the closed front door. Relationships only ever made sense – or not – to the people in them. Rarely did outsiders understand the dynamics that enabled them to work or not.

'Have you talked to anyone else about this, Trude? Are you getting any support from anywhere?'

Trudie shook her head, miserably. 'No. I tried to talk to my friend Stella. We've been friends for more than thirty years, but she doesn't get it. She *never* does. Whenever I'm in some kind of crisis, she's usually nowhere to be found. She offers the usual platitudes, something along the lines of 'oh, well, I'm sure you'll figure it out,' or 'don't worry, everything will work out for the best,' but then she scarpers, and I don't hear from her for weeks at a time. It's as if she waits for things to settle down before she comes back into my orbit, so she doesn't have to deal with anything heavy. She never offers me the same kind of support I've always given her.'

Adie rolled her eyes and nodded, knowingly. 'Oh, believe me, I know all about *those* friends! But the truth is, Trudie, that some people just aren't cut out to be the type of friend we need in a crisis. I have a few myself who I've learned not to bother trying to talk to, about personal or painful stuff, because they literally can't give me what I need. They're incapable. They'll gloss over my pain and almost *trivialise* it, which really hurts, but I don't think they mean it. I think they just don't know how to be anything more than what they already are.'

She pulled at her bottom lip with her thumb and forefinger, before carrying on trying to explain.

'People usually don't mean to hurt us; in fact, they'd probably be upset if they thought they had! But some just don't have the emotional capacity to be more than the jolly, night-out, shopping buddies they're comfortable being, to us. We also really need friends like that at times, just at different ones; like when we just need a bit of a pick-me-up, or a step away from working too hard, or to let off a bit of steam, or something. That's it. That's their limit. They're inadequate for offering more than that, and they know they are, so they step back. They simply can't handle being forced out of their comfort zone to do what they don't know how to do.'

Trudie sniffed hard again, and nodded. 'What you're saying makes perfect sense. We're all different, aren't we, with different capabilities and emotional tools? I was there for Stella, all through her divorce and moving away, and everything. I even drove sixty miles to her new house and helped her to unpack a load of boxes, because she had so much to deal with. I went to such a lot of trouble to let her know that she wasn't battling through everything alone, because it was a ghastly time for her, and it's the kind of transition that does make you *feel* alone and facing a mountain you've no idea how to climb all by yourself, to get used to that new life.'

She sighed, raggedly. 'I guess I was pretty dumb to assume she would do the same for me. I should have known better, Adie, because it was the same as years ago when I was told that my adenomyosis meant I'd never be able to have a baby. She couldn't be there for me then, either. She'd lost a baby, and then she had a much longed-for little girl, and I suppose I thought she'd understand how horrible it is, to be told that you're infertile and it can't be fixed.'

Trudie laughed, shortly, without a trace of humour. 'It seems I don't have the best perception sometimes, doesn't it, especially over things like that?'

Adie smiled, gently. 'You have a mountain of your own to climb now, my lovely. And Stella isn't there for you. That hurts, and I know that because I've been through it too with different friends, as you know. You and I have shared enough stories in the past about people we thought we could count on who let us down instead. But it comes down to expectations, Trudie, and we judge by our own standards. We expect people to be the sort of friend to us that we are or want to be to them. I've learned the hard way that some of them just can't.'

She took a deep breath, and carried on. 'I think it would help you a lot, if you can understand that Stella simply isn't emotionally developed enough, to have the kind of empathy you need, and it isn't her fault that she can't be more to you. But some of us can be, Trudie, if you let us. You know me. You know the fires I've been through. I get it, and I know how scared and bewildered, and daunted, and *lonely* you feel. If you want my support to get you through the decisions you're going to make, and what happens in the aftermath, I will be there for that. You don't have to go through this alone, but you do need the right people around you.'

Not everyone is a 'good' friend just because they've been around a while. Memories are great, and so are shared good times, but people who can't handle a friend in crisis are not the kind of people you turn to when you're having one! Save those people for the nights on the town, and the shopping sprees and spa days. Fairweather friends are important for when you need something light and fun, and even frivolous, but you have to know who actually can and <u>will</u> be there for you in the ways that matter more, when the chips are down.

'Thanks, Adie. You know, that means everything to me. I know I could have talked to you earlier about this, but I sometimes feel that your life is finally sorted now, after so much drama of your own. You don't need a basket case like me coming in and dumping a load of anguish on you. You deserve to have a nice life, without drama queens hovering around the edges, wailing, and gnashing their teeth.'

'Oh Trude! Come on, darling! You know me better than that. I'm a big girl, and I'm capable of maintaining my own happiness at the same time as helping you to figure out how to get some of your own. How could I sit there, all loved up in my own 'fancy castle' while you're on the ground somewhere in a panicking heap? I *love* you. I really do, and I'll do everything in my power to help you with whatever you need. Don't ever doubt that for a single minute. And you're not a drama queen. You're a woman in personal crisis.'

'Drama queens' are really only women who have too much on their plate and no real idea how to deal with it all. They don't need platitudes, or friends who fade into the woodwork. They need the kind of people who can get their sleeves rolled

up, who can and will ask; 'what do you need', or 'how can I help?' People who ask those questions and actually mean it. I can be that, to this lovely woman.

'So, tell me how I can help, Trudie. Maybe you don't know the answer to that yet, and that's okay, while you're still forming your decisions. But we can talk. I can be a devil's advocate, or a champion for your decisions, whichever ones you choose to make. I can even just offer tea and cake, or a place to stay for a few nights, or the use of my car, or help to move your stuff out of the house, help redecorate the flat, unpack boxes, go shopping for any essentials you might need. The list is long, I promise, of what I can do to help. Don't be afraid to ask.'

Money may be a little trickier, if she needs that, because that would mean me asking Mark, but I know he would never let a friend sit in a crisis either, for want of enough funds to get them out of it. It's only money, for God's sake! We can't take it with us, and if someone we care about needs help, Mark and I can find a way to make that work. It's a sticky subject, for sure, but I'm going to raise it with her.

'Trude, if you need money to make something happen, tell me that too, okay? I know lending and borrowing cash can change friendships, but it doesn't have to. I wouldn't want it to, and I think we are open enough with one another where it wouldn't. We can always talk about it, if it becomes an issue. So, if you are broke and that is all that is stopping you from getting out and standing on your own two feet, tell me.'

At that point, Trudie burst into tears again, and Adie was sure she wasn't going to be able to stop. She seemed completely inconsolable for a few minutes, but she eventually managed to get her sobs under control, and took a long, shaky breath.

'Adie, thank you. From the bottom of my heart, thank you for offering that. I don't need it, because Kevin and I have been financially sorted for years now. He's always taken his job as a financial adviser very seriously, and money isn't something I'll have to worry about, even if I do find myself on my own. But thank you. Most friends would never have the courage or the trust to offer that kind of help. The fact that you have means everything.'

'Well, I figured you *would* have the financial side of things covered, and probably have for a long time. Kevin is excellent at his job. He's made Mark and me a lot of money over the years. But I don't want to assume anything, and I want you to know that I *am* the kind of friend you can ask anything of. I'm not afraid, like a lot of people are, to be of real help when it's needed. Practical help - and that includes money if you need it, to get through.'

Mark and I are comfortably off too, but even if I didn't have much, I'd still offer it. There's nothing to be gained by hiding behind the sofa, trying to convince myself there are certain types of help I 'shouldn't' give. I'd rather be the kind of friend I'd want to <u>have</u>, in this kind of crisis. A woman should always have enough money to bankroll herself independently for a few months at least, if she finds herself in a position where she needs or wants to do it, but I couldn't just assume Trudie already has that. The fact that she has is great. It's just as I expected, but I wouldn't be a good friend if I didn't offer.

'Kevin would never see me struggle, Adie, even if I made it crystal clear I wanted to leave him. Money isn't something he'd weaponize. He sees it as a means to an end, and nothing more. He would give me what I asked for, and I do have my own business, which is never going to make me rich, but it's a living, in and of itself.'

'Well, that's good to know. But *you* need to know that whatever you need, you do have friends who will help.'

Trudie hugged her, hard, and Adie hugged back.

'Now, let's get you back inside, before we both catch our death of cold out here. It's freezing. We need to warm up, and I think a hot coffee with a decent slug of amaretto in it might be just the ticket.'

Trudie grinned, as she wiped away her tears with the back of her hand. 'Make that a hot chocolate with amaretto, and you have yourself a deal.'

Chapter Nine

The Ravensdown party was usually fairly predictable, Carla thought to herself, as she looked around the room. The same people tended to turn up every year, and the conversations were pretty much the same every time, but that was no bad thing. To some extent, it was comforting, that no seismic change had rocked the Torley community or anyone in it, since the last time they all chewed the fat. Sometimes 'boring predictability' had a welcome place.

It was hard to believe that a full year had passed, since they were all here for the last Christmas party. It was always a happy event that everyone looked forward to attending every year. Wittering about the weather and the challenges it brought to the farmers was fairly inane, but it was always reassuring. Likewise, the business community had its fair share of observations about trade and function in the town, and most business owners or operators shared the same or similar perspectives about it all.

Life in the Torley community was fairly steady, and it was nice to just chat about the non-heavy stuff. Nobody wanted to 'do' politics, religion, or other divisive subjects at a Christmas party! Dwelling on the state of the nation, which currently left a lot to be desired, would only frustrate everyone about things they didn't have the power to change. Chattering about upcoming crops or the January sales in Carlisle was far more positive and uplifting.

Dave handed her a glass of white wine. It was Chardonnay, her favourite, and it was nicely chilled. The Ravens set the bar up along the same wall of the living room every year, with well stocked fridges and 'tipples' to cater for most tastes. Adie had moved Mark along from providing simple beer and cheap wine, to something a little more upmarket, and offering a decent selection of spirits and mixers too. Guests brought drink contributions these days too, which helped keep the costs down. Mark Raven could certainly afford to throw a party, but most of the townspeople didn't want to take him for granted.

It was a long time now, since her first ever party here, when she'd had him firmly in her sights, trying to convince herself that they had a romance going. He hadn't been as interested in her as she thought he'd been, and it had become excruciatingly obvious as the night had progressed, that he was a lot more captivated by the newcomer, Adie Bostock.

At the time, it had felt humiliating to be so obviously usurped by an attractive, middle-aged, and apparently 'available' woman who had landed quite abruptly as a house-sitter at Teapot Cottage, at the edge of Mark Raven's land. It had been owned by someone else at the time, and they'd drafted Adie in to look after the cottage and their pets while they'd gone abroad. Adie been invited to the Ravensdown Christmas party, and had soon found herself to be the centre of attention, especially from Mark and Feen.

Carla hadn't reacted well to being openly sidelined. She'd done some shameful things, in retaliation. It still made her uncomfortable, when she thought about her actions, the court case that had followed her trying to poison the cottage owners' dog. Mark had got the police involved, which he'd had every right to do, and the hostility from the townspeople had been hard to bear. That had been excruciating, and humiliating in the extreme, even though she'd fully *deserved* to be pilloried and ostracised for a long time. She'd had to work pretty damned hard to turn that around, but she'd managed it. She'd finally earned the town's forgiveness, and then some, but she still found it hard to look back on that time.

Gavin coming back into her life had turned things around for her. She hadn't known how to react, when the son she'd been estranged from for more than ten years crashed back into her life without warning. That had been uncomfortable too, and even more so when he'd declared his intention to marry

Feen Raven, Mark's decidedly odd and unfathomable daughter. The two women hadn't liked each other at all.

But events had unfolded in ways that had compelled Carla to look at her life a little differently, and find the courage to mend the broken bits of it. Now, she was in a much better place. She had her son back, and had got to know Feen a lot better. She was a grandmother too now, to the couple's beautiful twins, Alder and Willow. She had a little business that was doing quite well in town now too, and she'd found a cause that spoke to her own heart, in championing the town's businesswomen. To put a cherry on top of all of that, she'd met a man who had melted the frozen part of her heart and enabled her to take another chance on love.

Dave Holloway was a pretty decent guy. He was honest and real, and he adored her. At the same time, he didn't allow her to be a prima donna about very much at all, and the result was a mutual respect for one another's boundaries and a deep appreciation all the great qualities each brought to the relationship. Dave could be a bit pedantic and 'picky' over details that Carla didn't see as important, but she knew she had her fair share of irritating habits too. She was probably no picnic to live with either, so she didn't have too much trouble biting her tongue when saying something would only make a situation worse.

He put an arm around her shoulders.

'Hello beautiful. What's your name?'

She grinned at him, and nodded over at Feen. 'My name's Darla, and you must be Cave.'

Dave grinned back. 'Ah yes, the spoony weeny Feeny has called us that, hasn't she? Well, I for one feel honoured to have made it to the ranks of Spoony couples, along with the famous Egg and Peric Tripper, Han and Stazel Walton, Bendy and Willy Britelaw-Wiggs and Ark and Madie Raven. Not everyone gets 'Feen'd' in such a way, do they? Anyway, my real question is, Darla, *darlin;'* d'you fancy coming home with me tonight?'

She grinned and put her head briefly against his neck. 'Oh, go on, then. As long as you really *have* stopped drying your socks in the Aga.'

Theirs had been a quiet romance. Not so much 'fireworks,' even at the beginning. More of a gentle 'enduring warmth' which, at this time of life, was a lot more reassuring and stable. Dave was a man to grow old with – a man she could rely on. If this was the best it was ever going to be, it was more than good enough for Carla, and it seemed to be for him too.

'I'm sad for Gavin tonight though, Dave. The plane crash is rotten news, right on Christmas. You never met his American friends. I met them at his and Feen's wedding. They seemed decent enough, as far as I remember, but it seems they somehow managed to fall out with Feen somewhere along the way, which very much complicates Gavin's feelings.'

Dave pulled a face. 'If there's one thing I've learned, it's that even if you don't like a guy's wife, it never helps to even *say* so, let alone show it.'

Carla nodded. 'Quite. And it's a tad ironic too, I think; condemning a woman just because you don't understand her, at the same time as moaning that people persecute *you* for being gay! Gavin's father Martin was gay, as you know, and he struggled with it for a long time before he came out, and even then, life wasn't easy for him. There's a lot of prejudice out there. Personally, I think people should be bloody grateful for the friends they do have, instead of moaning that they're not good enough in some way, like those guys did with Feen. I mean, I knows she's as weird as a three-pound note and everything, but she doesn't have a harmful bone in her. She really liked them, but that wasn't enough for them. I don't know why it wasn't, and I don't know what really happened, but those two hypocrites are dead and it's really no great loss to anyone, as far as I can see – except to Gavin of course.'

'The world's full of hypocrisy, Carla. And remember, it's not that long ago that you condemned Feen too, because you didn't understand her either.'

'I still don't! But I have learned a bit too, over the years! You don't *have* to understand someone but, if they're in your orbit, you pretty much have to figure out how to *accept* them, if you don't want to have ongoing problems – especially when it's your family. You have to let certain things go, because that person's heart is more important than their actions on a given day. You don't know what they might be struggling with. If all you care about is how their words or actions affect *you*, to the point where you lose sight of who they really are, and all the good that's there underneath a little bit of nonsense, it says more about you than it does about them, doesn't it?'

Dave nodded. 'It does. It's funny, isn't it, the human condition? You can do a lot of good for someone, sometimes over a long time, but the minute you fuck up they'll only see the bad in you. You're never respected for all the things you got right, only condemned for the one you messed up. And you might not even have messed it up! People will just choose to see it that way. I'm sure Feen didn't go out of her way to upset the Americans. They *chose* to see her badly. People always have choices, Carla. Sometimes they're simply too stupid or too self-absorbed, to make the right ones.'

'Poor Gavin. He hasn't a clue how to feel about it all.'

'No. I guess not. But he'll figure it out, love. He's a smart guy. He'll find a way to square this away. It might take him a bit, you know, but I really don't think you need to worry too much about him.'

Carla grinned, wryly. 'He's my kid. I *always* worry about him. It doesn't stop just because they grow up and get to start making their own decisions. When they hurt, *we* hurt, right? If I live to be a hundred and twenty, I'll still be worrying about my kid.'

Dave cringed. 'Yeah, and you'll be a pretty bad-tempered old bag by then, won't you? But I get it. It's the same for me with my sons. All we can really do is be there for them, when they stumble or screw something up, or find themselves at a crossroads. We just have to walk with them on whichever path they take.'

'That's a nice way of putting it. I'm sure Gavin *will* be fine. It's just the shock, right now. Once the dust settles a bit, he'll find his way forward. His feelings are tied up with the loss of his dad, too, so that complicates things even further, for him.'

I hate to see him grieving and bewildered like this. Those bloody morons! What were they thinking, putting him in such an awful position? If they didn't like his wife, that's one thing, and I kind of get why they didn't – because they were just like too many other people; simply too ignorant to see how good she is, in spite of her weirdness. They never saw how pure her heart is. But to <u>tell</u> him they didn't like her, and to tear her down behind her back, to him? That's a monstrous way to behave. It's unforgivable. How <u>do</u> you balance the hurt that brings, with the years of love that preceded it?

Dave nudged her gently out of her private thoughts. 'You've guzzled your drink, in record time. Do you want me to get you another, and indulge this bender you seem to be starting on?'

Carla shook her head. 'No, I'll go. I want to talk to Feen about all this, if I can.'

She started to make a beeline for her daughter in law but was quickly intercepted by Debby Davies.

'Ah Carla, hi! I haven't seen you in ages. How are you? My shifts and the kids keep me busy and whenever I do seem to be free all the shops are shut, including yours! Your window displays are always gorgeous, and I'm longing for the chance to get in again for a decent poke around, especially now you've extended! How's that going? It must be lovely to have more space?'

'Yeah, it's all going pretty well, thanks. The shop next door came vacant back in the spring, so I snapped it up and we took out the wall between to make a bigger space. It also means my workshop at the back is bigger too. That helps a lot, because I've started taking on projects for other people, to restore their pieces. Right now, I have a Victorian bedroom suite to strip back and fix for its owner. There's a huge three-piece wardrobe, a massive chest of drawers, a dressing table and mirror, and two bedside cabinets to do. It takes up a lot of space, but at least now I have room to move things about and store the finds I'm always stumbling across on my travels. I'll go somewhere to pick up a sideboard and end up with other stuff people don't want. One time, a guy virtually chased me down the street to ask if I'd take an old oak table off his hands. Said he hated it. Begged me to just take it, so I did.'

And I sold it a month later for a hundred and seventy pounds!

'Does that happen a lot?' Debby laughed.

'Not all the time, but more often than you'd think. Sometimes the pieces on offer aren't worth having, but the ones that are, well... I'll never turn down a free piece of furniture I can make a profit on. That would be bonkers, wouldn't it? If there's room in the van, I'll always take what's worthwhile, or arrange to go back and collect it if I have to.'

'It's a lovely business, Carla, and congratulations on winning the Laketowns Businesswoman of the Year award, by the way! You've earned that, with your own business and championing the ones of other women in the town. They have a good collective voice now, thanks to you. I don't think anyone would dispute how deserving you are, of the award. It was quite an event too, wasn't it? Didn't they hold it at The Beeches?'

Carla nodded. 'They did, and it was horrendous, of course. Terrible food, thoroughly obnoxious people, God-awful surroundings. It was absolute torture, but Dave and I managed to endure it.'

Debby doubled up with laughter. 'So, you enjoyed yourself, then? Did a little acceptance speech, and some wiggling on the dance floor after all that horrible food and drink?'

Carla grinned. 'I did. It was the poshest do I've ever been to in my life, to be honest, and I felt like a bit of an imposter – you know, like I didn't have the right to be there. Little Carla Walton from Torley? I wasn't surprised to have been nominated though. That sounds conceited, and it isn't meant to be – I was tipped off earlier in the year by someone in the know at the Chamber of Commerce that I might be in the running. But I *was* surprised to actually win it. I thought the nominees were all excellent. They *all* deserved to win. But how are things going for you? How's your therapy group going, for childless women?'

Debby grinned. 'It's not exactly a therapy group. It's more of a quiet get-together every Tuesday night, to talk about the issues so many women are facing, in trying to fall pregnant, or come to terms with the fact that they maybe never will. It does encourage some of them into therapy though, and that's important because a lot of women do need that extra support, above what the group provides.'

'Validation is important, isn't it, when you're dealing with something that tough? I remember you saying how much you went through yourself before you and Darren got Ruby and Thomas. You're the best person to steer a group like that, Debby. But it's a lot, on top of part time nursing and two demanding kids. Not to mention the husband. If he's anything like mine, it's almost like having another child to take care of, sometimes.'

Debby closed her eyes briefly and grinned again. 'Definitely. Darren certainly has his moments, when I wonder whether he's pushing towards fifty or fifteen! But to be fair, he's mostly pretty good. Quite self-sufficient too in a lot of ways. He even does his own laundry, and he's the best father *ever* to Tom and Roobs. I wouldn't change much about him at all, if I'm honest. Soft git, he is, under all those tatts and that piercing stare. The only thing I *would* change is his tendency to bring stray pets home, then moan about the mess they make. You wouldn't believe the menagerie we've got now!'

Carla smirked at her. 'Oh, I think I would. One of the hazards of being a soft-hearted vet, I suppose.'

'He's as soft as butter. We've got at least one of almost everything you can think of, now. And he even has me feeding the food scraps to the foxes in the wintertime. I do know the poor things struggle when it's cold.'

Debby cocked her head on one side, and closed her eyes briefly again. 'Truth is, Carla, I don't mind much, really. We've enough space, and resources, to help out with whatever we can. A lot of the wildlife on the edge of town is only hanging around because their land got taken up with development. They have to live and find food from somewhere, don't they? They've as much right to exist as we have, so we've decided that working with them is better for all of us than trying to keep them away. Although we have had to reinforce the henhouse to stop the poor old chickens being preyed upon,' she added, half to herself.

'I'm sure the kids enjoy the wildlife. Your place is lovely; all nestled into the edge of the woodland and invisible from the road. It must feel like a proper little haven.'

'We do love it, yes. The kids are enchanted by the birds, mostly, especially since Darren put a handful of different-sized bird boxes up. There's all sorts nesting in the garden now. There's a badger sett not far from our place too, and Ruby keep asking to go spying on them at night. She and Thomas are both too young for that yet, but eventually we'll take them, when they'll be able to keep still and quiet enough.'

Carla glanced over Debby's shoulder. 'Ah, there's Feen, and I really need to talk to her! Can I catch up with you later, Debby? Maybe arrange to come down to the shop sometime soon and unlock it, so you can have a mooch, if we can find a time that suits us both? It's nice to see you, by the way.'

Debby nodded, and stepped forward to give her a hug, which she returned with equal warmth.

Chapter Ten

Debby stepped back to let Carla go, and cast her eye around the room. It was beautifully decorated for the party, and everyone seemed to be very jolly, and enjoying themselves. She recognised a few of the 'outliers,' as she called them; people who nobody saw very often. They were mostly farmers and their wives, many of whom lived on the edge or outskirts of town on farms that weren't even seen from the roads. She didn't really know any of them but Darren did, professionally, as their veterinary surgeon. He would probably introduce her to a few of them as the night wore on. For now, she was keen to take a quick look upstairs to see how the kids were getting on. It was already way past their bedtime, but she knew they'd be too excited to sleep. They'd both had a decent nap in the afternoon, straight after Christmas dinner, so that was something, at least.

The babysitter seemed competent and cheerful, and Ruby and Tom had warmed to her straight away. There was no reason to be worried, but she decided there wouldn't be any harm in popping up anyway, to check on how they were.

When she poked her head around the door, trying to stay unseen, she saw the babysitter sitting on the floor, surrounded by rapt, attentive children. She was animatedly reading a story about a boy and a girl who were heading faster down a river than they should have been on a raft they had made, while their parents on the riverbank were running alongside, trying to tell them how to slow it down. Debby giggled quietly to herself as the babysitter assumed all the different voices in the story. The kids were all hanging off every word, so she decided they were in excellent hands, and tiptoed away again.

It had been nice to have a quick chat with Carla Walton-Holloway, who was always good fun. Her sarcasm always amused Debby, and she'd been genuinely pleased to hear that Carla had won the coveted business award she'd been nominated for, but she was surprised to learn that she hadn't expected to win! Carla always seemed so confident on the surface, almost *hard* even, to those who didn't really know her. But her confession had hinted at a deep insecurity. She hadn't felt that she deserved the accolade.

I suppose we all feel like imposters in our own lives, at times, and I know she's had some trouble in Torley in the past. I'm glad she got past all that because whatever her faults might be, she really cares about the businesswomen in the town.

Carla genuinely wanted Torley's women in business and senior management to be successful, and she had even set up a networking group for them. Tall Poppies had grown into an impressive force for the town, in enabling the women in business and higher positions of management to express their concerns and have them fully heard and considered. They had some great ideas and the collective meant they were taken seriously now, with full consideration, for what might enhance the profitability of the town. Sixty seven percent of Torley's business owners were women, so they were in fact the majority. Carla had seen to it that they were no longer swept aside as if their perspectives didn't matter. Debby had been invited to join the group, because of her own support group for women who were struggling to conceive, but she hadn't found the time to get to a meeting yet.

I think that should be one of my New Year's resolutions – to go along, and meet some of the other amazing women who are doing such a lot of great things for the town I live in.

Back in the living room, Feen was standing on her own again now. Carla had evidently moved on from chatting to her. Debby managed to catch her tiny friend's eye and smiled when Feen beckoned her over and gave her a surprisingly strong hug.

'Merry Kissmas, Mrs Davies!'

'Hey, witchy-woo! Merry Christmas to you too! We haven't spoken for a week or three. How are things? I love your gorgeous dress, by the way.'

Feens' dress *was* gorgeous. It was a full-on, voluminous vintage taffeta ballgown, probably from the 1980's, in the most divine, shimmering shade of Airforce blue, with a square neckline and short, puffed sleeves. She had teamed it with a pair of black leather ballet flats and an intricate black choker, studded with black crystals. A headband with a cheeky black feather poking out at the top completed her endearing, quirky look. In a rather strange example of fashion defiance, the huge dress somehow *complemented* her tiny size-six frame, instead of swamping it.

Debby felt faintly ridiculous standing next to her, in her dark-red sequinned cocktail dress and gold heels. She'd felt pretty good in her outfit when she, Darren, Barbara, and Pat had left home. They'd all raved about how lovely she looked. But somehow, standing next to Feen, she *always* felt a bit frumpy. She tried to shrug it off, knowing how crazy it always was to try and compare yourself to anyone else. Feen Raven had the kind of style that most women only ever dreamed about having. Aspiring to that was something that most would never achieve, so the effort involved in trying seemed like a total waste.

'How do you always manage to look so bloody incredible? *Wherever* did you get that dress? It's stunning!'

Feen grinned. 'I got it from an antique stothing clore not far from where we live, in Mayfair. The woman in there knows me quite well, after all this time. I do spend rather a lot of money in there, for one-off pieces. This dress came in, and she called me straight away. She knew I'd want to lake a took at it. And the minute I did, I lost my heart. Apparently, it was worn for about twenty minutes once by some wildly amous factress; I don't remember who. But it is nice, isn't it? One of my favourites, now. I plan to wear it as often as I can.'

'Well, you absolutely should! I would wear something all the time that made me look that good, if anything ever did.'

'Oh, don't be silly! You look fantastic tonight! That shimmery shade of red suits your colouring, and the gold heels are gorgeous. Tell me they're not Louboutin's or something!'

Debby laughed. 'I wish! They're Steve Maddens, but that was expensive enough! I plan to get a lot of wear out of these. Someone once told me that the penny per wear cost of something should equal zero before you get tired of it. I'll have to wear these shoes about a thousand times to get them down to zero, but I'll give it my best shot. It might include trips to the supermarket and the dentist. Before I know it, I'll have a solid reputation as a chav.'

Feen looked aghast. 'My God. Penny per wear down to zero? Tell me; do decades in a coffin count? I'd have to wear this every day for the next yeventy sears at least, for it to even *head* towards zero! Then I'd have to wear it until I turned to grust in the dound.'

'Or pass it to little Willow, so she can carry on trying to get it to zero.'

'That's a very sensible point. I hadn't thought of that. But it's ludicrous, isn't it, how much we clend on spothes? Gavin would go mad if he knew what I'd paid for this, and he *knows* he would, so he doesn't even ask. Denial is his hafest sarbour, sometimes. Anyway, how are you? I get a sense that you're a bit tired. If you have any time off over Christmas, I think you could use a few days in front of the fire, burled up with a cook.'

Debby nodded. As usual, Feen's radar was bang on the money. 'I *am* tired, and a roaring fire and a good book sound sublime. Pat and Barbara are lovely to have around but sometimes I just want to close the door and not have to worry about whether they're comfortable, or have everything they need.'

Feen nodded, sagely. 'Houseguests are fine for a few days, but even the easy ones that can fend for themselves a bit do become wearing, after a time. Are they still using the caravan, or are they in Appletree cottage with you?'

'Caravan,' Debby confirmed. 'We decided not to get rid of it after we'd finished the renovations and moved properly into the cottage. It's such a useful resource. It's hooked up to the mains, so they're as warm and cosy as toast in there. It does take a bit of the pressure off, especially since it has its own bathroom, of a sort.'

'That does make it easier. It's hard to have people underfoot when you only have one loo, even when it's family.'

Debby looked fondly over at Darren's mother Barbara, and her partner Pat, who were chatting to Stan and Hazel Walton. They were great in-laws, and she knew how lucky she was to have good ones. Poor old Darren hadn't dropped so lucky with *her* parents! Don and Carole Cameron weren't the easiest people to have around. Carole could be cold, and critical to a fault about the most ridiculous things, and the first few years of Debby and Darren's marriage had been sorely tested at times by the fact that Carole hadn't liked Darren and had made no secret of the fact. But, after working through a few issues of her own, she'd come to realise that her dislike had been misplaced, and she'd worked hard to be a better mum and mum-in-law. She was a pretty good grandmother too, now; much warmer and more generous with her time than she'd ever been as a mother to Debby and her sister Jayne. Don and Carole stayed in the caravan occasionally too, but they usually went home instead, after a visit. They lived just a couple of hours away now in Lytham St Annes, after moving from Devon to be closer to Debby, and to Jayne who lived in Manchester.

Feen looked at her kindly, then pulled a cheeky face. 'You *are* lucky, with Bat and Parb. I've got Carla as a mother-in-law.'

Debby laughed. 'Well, there is *that!* She's alright though, isn't she? I actually really like her!'

'Well, I do too, as a fatter of mact, but please don't ever let her know that. We've certainly had our moments, especially in the beginning, when we didn't like one another at all. I thought she was a grazy cold-digger, and she thought I was just crazy, *period*. But when I became the mother of her premature grandchildren, after that accident on the rain moad into town, she decided to make a decent effort. It's fine, now. We get on pretty well these days, and I also have my adorable grandparents-in-law. Han and Stazel are amazing, and as a set of grandies you simply couldn't design a better pair. But I think most people have a rocky time with in-laws at the start, don't they, on one side or another?'

Debby nodded across towards Hazel, as the old lady stood chatting to one of the local farmer's wives. 'She's lovely. Really elegant and genteel, and I just love her wry and insightful wit at times, especially when she turns up at one of Adie's infamous Friday coffee mornings and shares her view on the state of the nation and its people.'

'Yes, it's easy to see where Carla gets her wit from, isn't it? Hers is a lot sharper, of course. Stan is equally sweet but he's more quietly earnest about life. He's very much a pragmatist, which is also probably why Carla's similarly inclined. She got the best of both parents, I think.'

'Stan's very typical of his generation – quite dismissive of any kind of mollycoddling! I remember he came to the hospital once, to see an old friend. I'd been on the team to reattach the poor man's severed fingers after an incident with a drop saw. Stan bumped into me, and said something like, 'well, if he *will* operate the damn thing without a safety guard, he can't expect much else, can he? He'll recover well enough, I expect. He's made of strong stuff, is Barney Browning.'

Feen doubled up with laughter. 'Oh, my God, you sounded just like him, then! If you ever get nired of tursing, find a career on the stage, would you? But you're right about Stan. He's a pragmatist, and no mistake.'

Stan Walton's easy dismissal of his friend's mangled hand had set Debby on the back foot for a second or two, until she'd realised that while the observation had been almost cheerfully made, Stan had done it with a twinkle in his eye. He'd cared, enough at least to come and ridicule his old friend while the poor man lay in his hospital bed.

She nodded at Feen, now. 'Yeah, I think you and I are both lucky with the in-laws we have. I guess maybe a lot of people do find it a challenge, to assimilate them. Darren had a right palaver with mine; especially my mother, if you remember? But they're okay now too. You don't just marry the person, do you, in spite of what you might think, or what you promise yourselves? Animosity does leak through and spoil things if you don't get it nipped in the bud. It took us ages to come right with Mum and Dad, but we got there in the end.'

Feen nodded. 'A lot of parents simply can't mind their own business, when it comes to their children's choices. We have friends in London who haven't spoken to their in-laws for over yen tears. The in-laws don't even want to know their own grandchildren. Imagine that! It's plainly ridiculous, and all because their daughter married a man they didn't like. And it's not like he's ever hurt her, or their children, or ever would. He's just a regular working-class, clue-bollar guy, and her parents wanted better for her. Yarda, yarda. It doesn't matter to them one jot, that she's happy.'

Debby grimaced. 'That sounds familiar. It was the same with my parents, with Darren. They didn't even try to get to know him before writing him off because of his criminal record, and his tattoos. They eventually came around but the ones who can't, or just refuse to; maybe the families affected are better off *without* that kind of opinionated nonsense or interference.'

Feen nodded. 'I have a friend who made the choice to divorce her parents and not let them see their grandson. They were so nasty to her partner, and to her for getting together with him in the plirst face, *she* ended up drawing the line, to keep the toxicity away! Nothing will change that now. That poor family is broken forever. The pamage is dermanent.'

'People who can't back off, or mind their own business – it never has a happy ending, does it?'

Feen's face was grim. 'No, it really doesn't. I know my lids are only kent to me. I don't own them, and I can't expect them to live the life *I* want for them. They'll find their own path, and maybe I won't agree with it, or whoever they choose to end up with. And I might even make my feelings known, out of a genuine concern, but I certainly wouldn't allow myself to be alienated from them because of how I chelt about their foices. It would never be *my* choice to cut the cords. That's just stupid.'

She smiled sympathetically at Debby. 'On a different note, I know you're being a bit knocked around by peri. Is there anything I can do to help? Maybe make some elixirs that might provide a bit of relief? If you let me know your specific symptoms, I can make something to target those, and give you some respite.'

Debby allowed her shoulders to sag, a little. 'That would be great, Feen. Thanks. It's the normal stuff, from what I understand; irritability, periods all over the place with lots of cramping and heavy bleeding, then nothing for months. Feeling anxious all the time about stupid things, flaky patches of skin in random places, and a complete lack of interest in sex, which is going down like a lead balloon with Sir Rampant. I feel like some alien force has crept in and taken control of my mind and body. Darren is trying to understand but he's frustrated, on more than one level!'

Feen chuckled. 'Yeah, I get that. It's a tough time, and the symptoms aren't like a broken leg that you can see, are they? I know that a lot of women are accused of being over-dramatic in peri, which is really unfair of course, but you can understand why people not 'in the know' don't get it. They don't tend to understand what they can't actually see.'

'I'm lucky that a couple of other theatre nurses I work with at the infirmary are going through it too. It's treated with a bit of sympathy there at least, by managers who understand the mechanics of the biology and what effect it all has. But it's a lot, all at once, with an already full plate. I do feel a tad overwhelmed, at times.'

Feen bit her lower lip. 'One of the hazards of late conception and delayed motherhood is the onset of peri at exactly the same time as you're trying to get a pandle on the harenting as well as everything else you have to deal with in your life. It's a bit of a bitch, I think.'

'You know, Feen, I think *any* time it happens is a hazard. My mother went through menopause at the same time as my sister Jayne and I went through adolescence. *That* was hell, for the entire family! We didn't know which way was up, for *years!* I don't think there is an 'optimal' time for it to start turning you upside down. Whenever it comes, it's like a freight train blasting through your life and leaving you sitting on your arse, wondering what the hell is happening.'

'Can you talk to your mum about it? Can she be of any support; you know, with her experience, I mean?'

Debby pulled a face. 'Well, she's as sympathetic as she's capable of being, which isn't much. It's certainly not enough. She was at the back end of the queue when they were doling out compassion, remember? She does try, but…' Debby trailed off, knowing she didn't need to say anything further. Feen got it. Of course she did.

'Well, I can certainly put a few things together to help with the cranxiety and the amps, at least. Let me do that, sweetie. I'll drop a few remedies off in the next week or so. One of them might taste foul-to putrid, but do persevere with it, if you can.'

'Thanks, Feen. I appreciate that. I'm nearing the time when I have to decide about whether or not to start HRT, and I just don't feel ready yet. I know Adie went through her menopause without having to take it. I'll start on it if I have to, but I *would* rather find another way, if there is one. I'm not such a hard-boiled 'medic' that I can't appreciate the benefits of complementary therapies. I do think they have a lot to offer.'

Whether or not they'll be of any help to me now, and when menopause starts properly for me, it would be a bit short-

sighted not to give them a go, at least. It's better that than to pump myself full of fake hormones, in an attempt to delay the inevitable.

Feen looked at her keenly. 'You know, HRT isn't delaying the inevitable, Debs. It just makes the transition easier, for the women who decide to take it. I'm not a dran of the fug route, as you well know, but women have to do what works for them, it's as simple as that. And some do find that it's the right answer for them.'

Debby laughed. 'I see your radar is working. No thoughts are safe around you, are they? But thanks for clearing that up. HRT is still a bit of a mystery. As I say, I don't feel ready to look at it yet, but if things don't improve, I'll have a chat to my doctor and see what she recommends.'

Feen looked at her speculatively for a moment. 'You know, I'm in two minds about whether or not to say something, but I think I really should, so I will.' She took a deep breath before continuing.

'I know I've overstepped the park with you in the mast, even though it was done with the best of intentions. I waded in where I shouldn't have, before you got pregnant with Ruby and I often wonder if that was a mistake.'

Debby shook her head. 'Categorically no. As outrageous as it felt at the time, it wasn't a mistake. I didn't want to hear what you told me, but I needed to! You *saved* me, Feen. You saved me from going insane and losing my marriage. I'll never be able to thank you enough for that, so whatever it is you want to tell me – please just go ahead.'

'Okay. There's a window, Debby. It's a short one, and it's closing fast. If you want to have a third child, stop with the birth control, and do it now. My estimation is that you have about four months to decide. If you do want to pall fregnant again, it's very likely that you will. If you do, your baby *will* be fine, even at this late stage in your fertility. But, once that window closes, the choice will be gone.'

Wow! Debby blinked, as she tried to digest what Feen had just said. That was as heavy as things could really get, as conversations went! But her little friend had been right before, in saying that after endless failed rounds of IVF, it was still possible for Debby to get pregnant naturally. She had, and not just once, but twice! It had saved her marriage when it was literally about to fold under the pressure of ongoing infertility and the deepest desolation imaginable. Debby and Darren had been at the end of their rope when they'd come to Teapot Cottage, to try and figure out what kind of life they were going to have as 'failed' parents, and indeed whether they even had a future at *all* together. Falling pregnant while staying there had turned their lives around so completely it was hard to believe now, looking back, what they had gone through and survived.

'Umm… well, okay then,' she giggled. 'Time to have a think! We said we'd have to stop at two for economic reasons, but maybe we could still have good lives financially with three kids. I would *love* another one. I've never made any secret of the fact. I'm just not sure how I'd make it work, with my job and everything. That means a lot to me too. I love it so much, and I did work pretty hard for my career.'

Feen inclined her head. 'I know you did, and I understand how important it is. And I do have to say that a lot of parents make it work very well with three or more kids. Yes, they need more support, but research clearly shows that it's the *quality* of the time you have with your children that matters, not how *much* of it you have.' She chewed the inside of her mouth for a moment, before ploughing on.

'For what it's worth though, I think you'd fanage just mine. But sticking with two is just as good a choice for your lives. All I'm saying is that your fertility window is about to slam shut again Debby, and it would be horrible to feel cheated just because you took too long to decide. I would hate for you to go through any more anguish over your ability to have children. God knows you've been through enough of that.'

Feen's voice was gentle, but firm, as it always was when she was imparting her drops of wisdom. Debby knew and loved her well enough to understand where she was coming from with her advice. Her intentions were *always* good, and seldom was she ever wrong about anything that really mattered.

'Well, Darren and I have discussed it a few times, but not so much lately. I guess we'd pretty much decided to call it quits at Ruby and Thomas, even though we've never actually *said* as much. It's not exactly unresolved, more kind of just, I dunno, *left?*'

'And it's absolutely fine if you discover that you *have* decided on the lovely neatness of Ruby and Thomas! One of each is what everyone prays for, isn't it? I just wanted you to know what I'm seeing for you, sweetie. Two clear choices, both equally fine and comfortable, but one choice needs to be made very soon, if that's to be the one.'

Debby sighed. 'Maybe Darren and I could talk about it again. Thomas is still young enough to be a good, close sibling to a new arrival, and Ruby would be a slightly imperious older sister, but still fine, I guess. Age gaps are alright up to a point, but I wouldn't want a new baby to feel or be treated like an afterthought or an unwanted nuisance by its brother and sister who'd got used to life without it. Time *is* running out, I guess.'

I worry so much more, about so many more things, nowadays. Is that the menopause approaching? Is it simply motherhood and the juggle of daily life, with the job I love and the husband who needs me more than he'd care to admit?

'It's all of those things and more,' Feen said quietly. 'Age and wisdom come with strings attached, I'm afraid. I'm a bit behind you age wise but believe me, you'd be *gobsmacked* at the things I worry about. And *I* have the benefit of guides to reassure me! Mere mortals like yourself must find it impossible, at times, to see the wood for the trees.'

Her startlingly blue eyes twinkled with mirth, and she placed a reassuring hand on Debby's arm.

'Like I say, your life is going to be just fine, with two kids or three, and you really *don't* have to worry so much about all the things you think you do. Remember, I'm always on the end of the phone, if you ever want to talk about what's bugging you. I'll drop some remedies off for you in a few days, once we've got Christmas over with.'

Debby looked up to see Gavin trying to catch Feen's eye.

'I think your husband is looking for you!' She nodded in Gavin's direction, and he winked his thanks as Feen turned to look at him, smirked, and rolled her eyes as he motioned her over to him.

'Yes, he seems to be! Again, bless him. I'm sure whatever he wants is critical. Again. I'll catch you in a bit, Debs.'

She winked and was suddenly gone, as if she had simply evaporated. Debby couldn't even track her before she was standing in front of Gavin! Feen moved like mercury. In so many ways she was a completely unfathomable enigma, but she was a good and solid friend, and Debby was grateful for their chat.

I'm only in my mid-forties. A lot of women have babies well into this decade, without any problems. And we're comfortable, financially, aren't we? No mortgage, Darren earns a good salary, and mine's not too shabby for part time theatre nursing. We could comfortably afford support and, just like everybody else, we'd figure out the details of managing everything as we went along. I would love another child! I know Darren is a little more on the fence, but he hasn't said he definitely doesn't want to go down that track again. We do need to talk again.

'Penny for them?' Darren was suddenly beside her, with a cheeky grin. Clearly, he'd had a few pints already, and was well on his way to being tipsy. Happily, he was a loveable drunk; funny and sweet, and he often said surprisingly 'gooey' things – the kind he'd never normally say when sober. He leaned forward and kissed her forehead.

'That looked like a heavy chat you were having just now with her Right Royal Feen-ness! Anything I should worry about?'

Debby grinned at him cheekily. 'Not really – only that if we were going to have another baby, we need to get on with it before the eggs dry up for good in four months' time.'

He gaped at her. 'Seriously? *That's* what you were talking about? Here, in the middle of a party?'

Debby chewed her bottom lip, nervously. 'Umm… yeah. It popped up randomly because we were talking about the perimenopause and the fact that it heralds the start of the fertility window closing. And I just wondered, you know, if maybe we could consider it again? We haven't talked about it for a long time, but I think we're in a pretty good position now, if we did want to have a third. Not sure what your take on that is and I'm also not sure this is the best place to be discussing it, as you say, but you did ask…'

Darren's eyes sparkled. 'I did, didn't I? So, is it up to me then? If I said yes okay, would you?'

She grinned. You *know* I would! In a *heartbeat*, babe! I know it's probably the least practical thing we could ever do, with our lives set up so well now, but …'

She trailed off, not sure about how to continue her train of thought. They *had* talked about having a third baby, and often enough to have covered all the ground several times about the implications. There wasn't much more to be said about it, really, other than to make a firm decision, one way or the other.

'Well, okay then. Let's do it.'

She stared at him, and he stared back, making something of it, shaking his head ever so slightly and boring his stare into her eyes.

'Are you serious? You'd better be serious if you say that, because it's a cruel thing to say if you *don't* really mean it.'

He laughed out loud now, and a few people turned to look at them both, smiling, before turning back to their own conversations.

'Look, if you want a third rugrat, jut fucking have one. It probably is the last chance, and I don't want to live with regrets, Debs. I don't want *you* to have them either. I can't see myself ever regretting having a third kid, but I *could* potentially see myself regretting the fact that we didn't, at some later stage, if it upset the applecart in some way. So, go.

You've got the green light. Condoms in the bin, and off we go, babe.'

She squealed with delight, and literally jumped into his arms. She looked over his shoulder to see Feen with her steepled hands in front of her mouth. She was smirking, and she gave Debby a wink, and a thumbs up.

'Well, okay then! Whew! That was easier than I thought it would be, but I guess I'd better get my quota of wine under my belt now, while I still have the chance. From tomorrow I'm on the wagon, back on the folic acid tablets, and getting plenty of sleep.'

'And plenty of sex. I know you're struggling with all this hormonal stuff, but we have to keep doing the dance between the sheets, in order to get pregnant. You have remembered that bit, I hope?'

She laughed. 'God yes! Let's have plenty of sex! Better stock up on oysters and scented candles. You might have to work a bit harder to get me in the mood, because of all this 'hormonal stuff,' as you put it. But this really is our last chance, Darren, if Feen's predictions are as true as usual.'

'Just don't be too disappointed if it doesn't happen, Debs. We're okay with Ruby and Tom, so a third would be a bonus. I don't want us to be under pressure for it. Can we just see how it goes?'

She nodded. 'Of course we can. Let fate decide. We'll have what we should have in life. I'll be okay if it doesn't happen, but if it does, it will be amazing. And thank you. I love you *so* much. Thank you, for agreeing to this. I know what a massive thing it is.'

'I'd love a third child too. I'm grateful for the two we already have; after thinking we weren't going to have any at all, but I always did wonder if a third might be nice. There's more than enough love to go around, isn't there?'

'Yeah, there is, you soppy sod. You're a great husband, and a great dad. Did I ever tell you that?'

'Not often enough. Tell me again, and I'll get you another glass of wine, and you can get shitfaced tonight as the last night off the wagon for a while. I'll carry you home and have my wicked way with you later.'

'Maybe we should book into Teapot Cottage for a night or two, you know, to kind of seal the deal?'

Darren shook his head, but his eyes were still dancing. 'We don't need to do that. Mother Nature has us in the loop. If she thinks we're due another baby, it won't matter where it's conceived. I'm a bit excited, now we've decided to throw our hat into the ring again. Is it okay to say that?'

'Yes, it is, and I'm excited too!' Debby hugged herself tightly and allowed herself to feel a small thrill of anticipation.

We might get lucky. But we're already lucky enough, so if it happens, it happens, and if it doesn't, it doesn't. But at least there's a chance. It's more than I had this morning, so I'm taking it.

Chapter Eleven

The front door of Ravensdown House was ajar, so Meghan gave it a gentle push. It swung properly open on well-oiled hinges, and as soon as she and Parker had made it into the hallway, the smell of Christmas hit them like a warm wave. She dug into her little carrier bag and pulled out the two wrapped gifts she'd brought for the Secret Santa sack, and popped them in. They might not still be here when the presents were handed out, because this was a flying visit. They were due at her friend Jayde's place in less than an hour, for a late supper. She figured she could ask her dad to make sure there were two secret Santa gifts set aside for her and Parker. She'd probably get them from him tomorrow.

Just as she was about to head into the kitchen to drop off her tray of veggie lasagne, Debby Davies came barrelling out of the living room. She saw Meghan and threw her arms around her.

'Oh my God! You made it! Adie will be so thrilled! You're just in time for the big presentation!'

Meghan hugged Debby back. 'We can't stay long – we've somewhere else to be in half an hour or so, but I didn't want to miss this. Where's Dad and Fi?'

Debby jerked a thumb back towards the living room. 'They're in there. Go and get yourselves a drink and I'll catch up with you in a minute. I have some really exciting news to tell you – potentially anyway. I'm just off to the loo.'

Meghan went through to the kitchen with her lasagne, and giggled when Adie's face lit up like an actor's mirror.

'Meghan! Parker! I'm *so* glad you're here! Put down that yummy-looking dish, and come and give me a hug!' She held out her arms and Meghan stepped into them, and the two women hugged for a good few beats before Adie stepped back and held her at arms' length.

'I haven't seen you for *months!* How have you been, darling?

'Good, just busy with uni, and the part time work at the stables. We're finished for the semester of course but I have a ton of academic work to do, in spite of that. My friend Jayde is having a quiet Christmas night supper, and she asked us if we wanted to come. Her mum died a few months ago, and I think she's really feeling it, with it being Christmas and all, so of course I said yes. I haven't managed to see her since the funeral, and I've been feeling bad about it, so this means I can kill two birds with one stone and catch up with everyone here too! Merry Christmas Adie, and Happy Birthday!'

Adie beamed at her. 'Well, I couldn't ask for a better present than to have you here, even if it's only for a little while. Supper will be coming out in a few minutes, so I'll just quickly microwave this, and get it out with the rest of the food. Go and grab yourselves a drink. Your dad and Fiona are here.'

'Yeah, I know. I saw Dad's truck outside.'

In the living room, the fire was blazing, and the room looked very festive with its huge Christmas tree and other beautiful decorations. Meghan spied her dad, chatting to Darren, and she bounded over.

'Hiya. Flying look-in, on our way to Jayde's but wouldn't miss being here for Adie's presentation. Thanks for the heads' up on the time. We literally have to fly, straight after, so let's get the hugs in now before the everything starts.'

She hugged Darren hard. He was one of the rocks of her life, and he wasn't just her dad's best friend – he was one of hers too. Years before, he'd gifted her the other great love of her life – her beautiful, part Palomino horse, Astro. Meghan had been in a bad place back then, full of anger and self-doubt. She'd lost her way – bigtime – but meeting and forming a bond with Astro, who'd been in the field next to Teapot

Cottage when she and Stuart had been staying there, had turned her life around.

Meeting Astro had shown her the way to a new and better life. Darren had given her the opportunity to work with the horse, who he was rehabilitating at the time. Astro was as damaged and sad as Meghan was herself, back then, and the two became close very quickly. They were unshakeable now, in their love for one another. Two hearts had mended, over the time, and when Darren had gifted Astro to her for her sixteenth birthday, it had been the best day of her life.

She adored Darren. He was a combination of a big brother, an extra dad, and a bomb-proof friend, all rolled into one. He'd not only saved her from going completely mad, but he'd also rescued her after she'd been abducted by the crazy ex-partner of a woman who was working for Stuart on the barn conversion at Beaconsfield. Keith Brockett had somehow got it into his head that his ex-wife was sleeping with her new boss. Nothing could have been further from the truth, but Brockett would not be appeased. He'd abducted Meghan on her way home from school and had also tried to murder Stuart *and* Caroline – the wife he'd abused horribly for years before she'd finally found the courage to leave him.

Darren had come to find Meghan, on a backroad behind Torley after Brockett's accomplice had managed to talk him out of raping her. They'd dumped her at the side off the road, traumatized and bleeding, and left her to fend for herself. The experience had been traumatic in the extreme, but Darren had found her, and he'd also rescued her father from an almost certain death. Darren and Debby (and others too) had rallied around Meghan and supported her through that terrible ordeal. They were as good as family now, and she couldn't imagine life without them.

Darren hugged her back, twice as hard. 'Hey babe, hi Parker! Merry Christmas to you both. I'm surprised to see you here, but I'm glad you made it. Have you seen Adie yet? I think she's still in the kitchen.'

Meghan nodded. 'Yeah, I've seen her. She's wearing the most amazing blue dress. I can't wait to see it without her apron over it. Is Trudie here?'

On cue, Trudie came up behind her and tapped her on the shoulder.

'Hello, stranger! How lovely to see you! Merry Christmas, sweetheart. How long has it been? It must be a year since you last worked in my shop. I miss you. So do a bunch of GladRagz clients. Some still ask after you.'

'I miss you too! I loved working in your boutique! I just had to stop, with all the study. It's pretty heavy, to be honest.'

'Are you enjoying it though?'

Meghan closed her eyes briefly, and grinned. 'I'm *loving* it! I never knew that psychology could be so interesting! I used to think it was a scary thing, but it's fascinating, actually. The more I'm learning, the more I *want* to learn. It was once described to me as going into a room full of doors, and choosing one but instead of finding yourself just in one room, you find that's got loads of doors too. And it's true! It's a labyrinth of learning, and I'm having a lot of fun with it. Statistics drives me crazy though,' she admitted. 'I'm crap at numbers, so I struggle with that, but it's compulsory so I have to tough it out. Parker helps me a lot with it, being all left-brained and all.'

Parker rolled his eyes at her. 'You just need to concentrate, instead of letting yourself be distracted by everything else when it comes time to work on it. Classic avoidance, in psych terms?'

She laughed. 'Yes, that's it, in a nutshell. Ooh, look! There's Doctor Cartwright – or is it McLeod? I forget which way round it is, since she got divorced. Has she had a row with Fi, by any chance?'

Stuart smirked. 'No, Minty and Fi have had a chat, and it's all been quite civilized.'

'I didn't realise she would be here, Dad. I must go and say hello to her. Come on, Parker, I'll introduce you to the woman who broke her shoulder on a trek, not long after we started the business. I think I told you about her.'

Minty turned around as Meghan made her way towards her, and beamed at her. 'Meghan, hi! My goodness, you've grown into a lovely young woman! How old are you now?

'Nineteen. I'm at uni now, studying to be an equine therapist.'

'Yeah, your dad told me! It's so lovely to see you! And this must be … Parker, is it? Sorry, Stuart did tell me, but I'm rubbish with names. It is Parker though, right?'

Parker nodded and grinned at her. 'It is. I'm pleased to meet you, Minty. Meghan has told me about you, and I think Fiona has mentioned you a couple of times, in conversation.'

'Where is Fi, by the way?' Meghan looked around but couldn't see her stepmother.

'She's probably in the kitchen,' Minty replied. 'I think they're about to start bringing the food through. The presentation will start in a minute, for Adie's birthday. It's nice that you're here for it. I'm sure she'll appreciate that.'

'We do have to rush off straight after, but I didn't want to miss it.'

Debby came up behind her and tapped her on the shoulder. 'I know you have to dash off soon, but I wanted to share some news with you, before you go. Darren and I have decided to try for another baby, while I might just still have the time.'

Meghan laughed and clapped her hands.

'Debs, that's *great* news! I'm really pleased for you! That's pretty exciting, isn't it?'

Debby shrugged and looked pensive. 'Well, it will be, if it happens. Feen has had a word, and told me that I'd better jump to it before time runs out. So, we'll see. If it happens it happens, and if it doesn't it doesn't.'

'Well, I really hope it does! You're such a great mum, and how cool would it be for Tom and Ruby to have a little brother or sister? I think it's awesome news. Can I organise your baby shower, when the time comes?'

Debby laughed. 'Let's not get too far ahead of ourselves. We wouldn't want to jinx anything! Do you and Parker want to come over for dinner one night in the New Year? We'd love to have a proper catch up with you. It seems like we hardly ever see you now, with all the studying you're doing. We're so proud of you, but we do miss having you around. Does Astro miss you too?'

Meghan shook her head. 'She doesn't have time to miss me. Whatever spare time I do have, I usually spend with her.'

Darren says she's doing well.'

'She is! She's doing great, and she's still my first real love, and always will be. Sorry Parker, but you already know you'll always come second to a horse.'

Parker shrugged. 'Such is my lot in life. But I adore you as much as you adore her, so I'm going nowhere.'

Meghan put an arm around him and kissed him. 'I love you. You'll never *really* be second to a horse. But you do have to settle for being equal. She was here first.'

She gave him another squeeze, and he held her close for a few seconds and kissed the top of her head. Then she looked around and realised there were more people in the room she needed to say hello to, as quickly as she could. Once Adie's presentation was over, they would have to bolt for the door, and it might be a while before she saw any of them again.

Life as a student was demanding. Her studies ate up most of her time, but her time with Astro was equally important. She was lucky that Parker was also fully committed to his studies. He wanted to be a civil engineer, and the courses he was doing were heavy and time-consuming too. Many a time, they simply stayed in at Beaconsfield or at Parker's mum's house, and studied.

She'd taught Parker to ride, as a way of getting some 'downtime,' and he'd become quite a good rider. He often sat on the railings at the edge of the ring while she trotted Astro or groomed her. He was gentle, a kind and patient man, and he supported her in everything she wanted to do. She couldn't imagine life without *him* either. A few people had been worried, at first, that she and Parker were getting too serious too quickly. Her dad, in particular, had expressed his concern that she should be 'playing the field' more before settling into a meaningful relationship.

But that wasn't what she wanted. And, as she'd pointed out to him, it was better that she was with someone like Parker Truman than some rake who would string her along and break her heart. She didn't want or need to kiss a bunch of frogs. She already had her prince! Parker was handsome, sweet, funny, clever, and patient. He made her laugh. He put up with her when she dithered about silly things. He encouraged her to achieve her dreams. She didn't *want* to play the field. She was in love with Parker, and he was in love with her, and everyone had now got used to the idea, and nobody gave her a hard time about it anymore.

She looked up at him, as he held her. She felt safe with him, and secure, loved and supported. In return, she gave him the very same. They fitted, somehow, and his quiet maturity was something she valued and cherished. If he was to be her 'forever' man, she wouldn't be arguing about it.

Chapter Twelve

The last of the food trays were leaving the kitchen, now. Peg, Sheila, Feen, Fiona, Minty, and Matty's wife Marie had all pitched in to move the food quickly, from the kitchen to the dining table in the living room. Serving up had gone like clockwork, as usual. It was now almost nine o'clock, and the buffet was about to start.

As she wiped down the kitchen table, Adie allowed herself a huge sigh of relief. It was always a marathon, getting to this point, even with solid help in the kitchen. Wendy Whitelaw-Briggs' plateful of seafood kebabs had taken a lot of attention that was also sorely needed elsewhere. Billy had left her to it, after she'd foolishly insisted on him doing that, so she'd been managing that on her own as well as working with Peg and Sheila to get everything else prepared.

Others had popped in and offered to help but the three of them knew, from hard-earned experience over many years, that they were the most efficient combo in the kitchen by themselves. Anyone trying to step into their seamless framework simply got in the way and held things up. Wendy's kebabs had turned out fine, but it had meant running backwards and forwards between the kitchen and the porch, to keep checking they weren't burning. More than once, Adie had bitten her tongue about how inconvenient that was.

But they were done now, and it was time for her to get her apron off, mop her sheeny brow, run a comb through her hair, and get out the kitchen herself, and have some fun. She didn't mind being chained to the catering for the first couple of hours of the party, but this was her sixtieth birthday, and it was definitely time to relax and enjoy it!

Just as she was getting herself organised, Mark put his head around the door.

'A'reet, lass? Spread's lookin' good on't table as ever but yer needed in't party room, quick-smart.'

Adie raised her eyebrows at him, and he gave her a wink, and held out his arm. She grinned and took it, and allowed him to escort her into the living room, where a small space had been cleared just in front of the fireplace. Everyone was standing around, beaming at her, including some of the older kids from upstairs. Adie caught Meghan's eye, and smiled at the thumbs up she gave.

Miranda was standing in front of the fire, beaming, and Adie felt a pang that she hadn't actually managed to see or speak to her before now. Miranda had wisely kept well out of the kitchen, but she held out her arms now, as Adie approached. She looked stunning in a pleated sheath dress in the most gorgeous shade of emerald-green, which she'd teamed with gold sandals and a simple rope of red tinsel strung across her body like a beauty pageant sash. She had done her hair in a high, elaborate and almost-retro beehive and wound another thin strand of tinsel around it. She looked amazingly 'Christmassy,' and the effect made her a commanding presence. She knew how to work the stage in a West End theatre, so 'working a room' was no effort for her at all. She owned the space here now as if it had always been hers to own. The room fell quiet, in a hush of expectation.

'Here she is! The woman of the hour! Adie, darling, come and stand by me.' Miranda then turned to the crowd.

'For those of you who don't know me, my name is Miranda Quirk, and Adie has *always* stood by me! She has been my friend for virtually our whole lives, and I'm so thrilled to be here tonight to celebrate her sixtieth birthday. She has spent most of the night so far, slaving away in the kitchen so we can all have a lovely party with food to die for. She's also pulled together the best people in the world to celebrate with, tonight.

'And just look at her! Isn't she gorgeous? She's party ready, finally, and looking as lovely as ever. This woman is beautiful, inside, and out. She is the kindest, most generous woman I know, and I just want to say how much I adore you,

Adie, and I know that everyone here appreciates and loves you too. So, let's all raise a glass to Adie Raven, for being who she is to us all. Happy sixtieth birthday, darling!'

Adie suddenly felt herself overheating violently and hoped it wouldn't show. *Bloody hell! This really is <u>not</u> the time to be having a post-meno hot flush!!!*

She had no choice but to grit her teeth and smile through it, as Miranda handed her a glass of champagne, and everyone toasted her birthday.

Then Mark cleared his throat. 'I've summat to say too, but I know yer minds are all on't buffet, an' yer worried about food goin' cold, so I'll keep it short. Adie wandered into me life about eight an'alf year ago now, an' turned it on its 'ead. I've not been't same man since I first clapped eyes on 'er, and although she knocked me for six and I'm still on me arse in a lot o' ways because o' that, they're *good* ways. The best ways a man can *be* knocked over. She's changed me. She's brought me the kind of 'appiness I never thought I'd 'ave again, after Beth died. Beth were me first wife, for those who don't know. Fer those of you that did know 'er, I think you'll agree that she'd be 'appy for me, that I've got someone as lovely as Adie to see out the rest o' me days wi'.

Mark stopped, cleared his throat, and took a couple of beats before carrying on.

'I thank God every day, for this woman, an' for the big family she threw me into, that keeps on growin'. I started out wi' just one beautiful daughter, an' I've lost count of 'ow many I've got now, and extra sons, and grandkids to boot. I'm too owd to do't bloody countin' but it doesn't matter, does it? I'm as 'appy as a pig in shit, wi' me life, and that's the bit that counts.'

To Adie's surprise, Mark sounded a little choked up. She grabbed hold of his hand, and gave it a quick squeeze, as he took a deep breath and carried on.

'I've learned to be a better man, because of Adie, an' she might be sixty, but she makes me feel thirty. So, let's 'ave another toast to Adrienne Raven, pillar o' the community, mam, grand-mam, friend, and the best wife a man could ever 'ope for. I love you, lass, like nothin' on earth.'

Adie blinked back tears as Mark raised his glass and encouraged everyone else to do the same.

Then he stepped away, and Matty, Teresa and Ruth came forward. All three hugged her, and Teresa grinned at her, and handed her an envelope.

Matty spoke for all three. 'Mum is sixty. Can you believe that? I once thought sixty was so old it couldn't even be contemplated, yet here she is, looking forty, and acting like twenty-five. But she has the wisdom of sixty and more, and she has always offered that to me and to my sisters, in ways that really help us to get through the crap life often throws at us. Mum isn't perfect. She's made some big mistakes, but so have we, as her kids. We've let her down, many a time, but here's the thing; she has never *once* not been there for us when we've needed her. She's never once failed – to steer us through choppy waters when our boats were threatening to capsize, or pull us from the water when they did.

'She's the rock of this family, and Tezzie, Ruth and I, and our own families, are all thrilled tonight to wish her a very happy sixtieth birthday.'

All three hugged Adie again, and she did start to weep a little now. It had been a long time, since events of the past had torn this little family apart. At the time, she hadn't been sure if she could pull things back together; if she'd ever have her family back the way she'd had it before. She'd been in anguish over it for a long time, as she'd tried and failed to make connections with the kids after hurting them terribly, in a shocking act of cowardice and omission that had caused her first marriage to founder. But, over time, the bonds with Teresa and Matty had held true. Her bond with Ruth, her first-born, adopted-out daughter, and her wife Gina and *their* daughter Chiara, had also strengthened and grown. They'd all survived the worst fire, and they wore the scars to prove it, but they were a real family now.

Standing here, being hugged by her children, was the single best moment of Adie's life.

'Open your envelope, Mum,' Teresa urged her. 'We all clubbed together for this, so we hope you like it.'

Adie felt uncomfortable opening a present from her children in front of a crowd of people, even though they were all friends. Being under scrutiny for something so personal felt uncomfortable but, if that's what the kids wanted, she'd go along with it. She gasped, when she saw what was inside. She looked up at a sea of expectant faces and laughed at how everyone was hanging on what she might say.

'It's a two-week cruise for two, to Scandinavia.' And at that point she openly burst into tears.

Someone had listened – and it had been a long time since she'd mentioned, just in passing, that she'd love to see Scandinavia. It was back at a time when everyone was sitting around at the kitchen table, dreaming about what they'd do if they ever won the lottery, and what was on their 'bucket lists.' It had never come up in conversation since, but the kids had remembered. Adie was literally lost for words.

She stepped forward herself, now. With wobbly knees, she gave a little speech of her own. It hadn't been at all prepared, so it felt a bit ham-fisted, but these people were her friends. She knew they wouldn't judge her.

'You know, I've spent years, like most mothers I guess, worrying about my kids and gnashing my teeth over the fact that they never listened to a word I ever said. But here's the proof that they did, at least once.' She waved the envelope.

'This was a dream; one I thought I'd never get to have. There's always some reason, isn't there, to put things off; to say 'oh well, at some time in the future, maybe…? But it would appear that Mark and I are finally off to Norway.'

Someone in the crowd piped up, 'better take out a mortgage then, or you'll be able to have a beer or a burger, but not both.'

Laughter rippled through the crowd.

'Well, speaking of food, I'd like to thank my sister-in-law Sheila Shalloe and my darling friend Peg Tripper, for all the work they do, every year, to bring the most sumptuous food to the table, and this year I think they've outdone themselves. Thanks to *all* of you actually, for bringing what you have. Your amazing contributions always make the buffet extra special, and it's lovely to have you all here, especially on this extra special night for me. Mark and I love you all, and we're glad you're with us tonight. So, without further ado… please get stuck into the food now, and no elbows or fisticuffs please!'

Mark took the envelope from her that had the cruise tickets in it, and put it in the sideboard drawer.

'This is a damn good prezzie, in't it? There's a table set up over yon, look, wi' a few *more* gifts on it f'yer.'

Adie looked across and saw an occasional table piled high with beautifully wrapped presents, some with very pretty ribbons and bows on them.

'God, are they all for me? I asked people not to make a fuss, as I recall!'

Mark chuckled. 'Ah, well. 'Appen they didn't think it were a fuss, lass. 'Appen they just wanted to make it a bit special f'yer. Because it *is* special, love – like you say. 'Appy birthday, Adie. You'll not get my gift until tomorra mornin', but I think you'll be 'appy wi' it.'

Adie grinned. 'I'm sure I will be. Anyway, get yourself some food. I'm just going to have a chat to Mand.'

As everyone stampeded towards the dining table, picking up cutlery and plates from the sideboard as they went, she managed to locate Miranda, who had in fact gone through to the kitchen. She was standing in front of the freezer with an ice bucket in her hand.

'Ah, you're out of ice, darling, I was just getting more for the bucket. Lovely speech, by the way. And didn't the kids do well? A cruise to Scandi, no less, you lucky thing! I went, years ago, with a very delicious young man called Jordan Pickle. I don't suppose you'd remember that? He was a lovely artist, who'd offered to paint me, and then wouldn't take any payment. Well, not outside of the bedroom, at least. But I wanted to do a Scandi cruise, and I didn't fancy going alone so I asked him to come with, and he said yes. We only did a week, the Norwegian fjords, but it was lovely and so was he. I had to push him back into the woodwork not long after we got back, but it was fun while it lasted.'

'Jordan Pickle. No, I don't remember that name. Did he *have* a nice pickle, by some chance?'

Miranda smirked, cheekily. 'He really did, darling! But he was a dalliance, and nothing more. Far too intense, and trying far too hard to become the next Vincent Van Gough. He'd have cut off his own ear if it would have helped. But he'd have driven me bonkers if he'd hung around. I think we both knew it was a fling and nothing more. He went, without a bleat of protest.'

Adie giggled. Miranda's colourful and ever-so-slightly outrageous past was peppered with strings of lovers young enough to be her sons. Her tally was impressive, but that lifestyle had eventually started to leave her unfulfilled. Thankfully, she had settled down in recent years by marrying Max, who was a thoroughly nice (and incredibly wealthy) man closer to her own age.

'Is everything okay in your room? Do you and Max have everything you need up there?'

'Yeah, thanks darling. By the way, I have a gift for you.' She reached into her sheath dress (which apparently had pockets as an added joy), and pulled out a long, slim box wrapped in silver paper and tied with silver gauze ribbon. She handed it to Adie with a flourish and one of her trademark cheeky grins.

'Don't tell me off. But sixty is diamonds, so that's what you get.'

Adie opened the packaging and was stunned to find a leather Tiffany box inside, in a colour that matched her dress. Shakily, she took the lid off.

Inside, nestled against black velvet, was a necklace so beautiful it made her catch her breath. It was a simple flexible platinum band, but it had tiny oblong-shaped, platinum-encased diamond baguettes hanging from it, all the way across the front.

They glittered and flickered like fire under the lights in the kitchen.

'Are these… are they real? Are they real diamonds, Mand?' Even to Adie's own ears, her voice sounded incredibly tiny, and far away. She felt like she could hardly breathe.

Miranda chuckled. 'Yes, they are. I hope you like it. It's a one-off piece. It's interesting that the box is the same colour as your dress, which is beautiful by the way, and get a load of those *shoes!* Mad, but perfect. Perhaps you'd like to take off your pearls and wear the necklace now?'

'Oh, God! I'm almost too scared to, but yes, I really think I should.' She giggled nervously as Miranda took off her pearls and fastened the diamond necklace around her neck, before stepping back to appraise her.

'Yes. Perfect. By the way, you know I'm not one to shout out loud, about money, but please will you get this necklace insured before you leave the house wearing it?'

'Umm… yes, of course I will. I can probably add it to the policy that covers my engagement ring. But how much should I insure it for?'

Miranda's voice was low. 'Thirty thousand pounds.'

Adie gaped at her. 'Are you even halfway serious? What are you, *insane?* That's a *ridiculous* amount of money to spend on me. I…'

She trailed off, usure of how to even say that she didn't feel she deserved something so expensive and magnificent.

But Miranda shook her head. 'No. Don't you *dare* tell me you can't or shouldn't accept it. I won't have that. For one thing, darling, it's a simple tax dodge. But this is your sixtieth birthday, and you mean twenty times more to me than this little frippery is worth, so this is actually quite a *small* token of my love, and the value I place on our friendship. And let's face it – every woman should have a few decent diamonds in her jewellery box, shouldn't she?'

'Jewellery box? This will be going in the bloody *safe*, Mand! Kept under very tight lock and key.'

'Yes, well I *was* going to suggest that, but you're a sensible girl. The clasp is quite intricate, so it should never fall off, but there's a lot of peace of mind in making sure any loss is properly covered.'

Adie nodded. 'I'll get right on to it the day after tomorrow. I'm not sure insurance companies work on Boxing Day, but I'll get it covered as soon as I possibly can. My God, Miranda. This is the most incredible gift I've ever had. I feel so humbled, over it. Thank you.'

'No problem. You deserve it. You mean the world to me, Adie. I can't imagine how I'd ever have managed to navigate the sometimes-appalling vagaries of life, if I hadn't had you by my side, for all these decades. You've always given me great courage, and so much love, support and, well… *joy* over the time. I'd rather stop *breathing* than lose you from my life.'

Adie rolled her eyes, and laughed. 'God, you're such a diva! It's made you rich, and I've loved seeing how your life has developed, but best of all – it hasn't made you insufferable! You've always had your feet on the ground, haven't you? You've managed to keep it real, for all this time.'

Miranda laughed back. 'It might surprise you to know that I am, in fact, a *shocking* diva. A total brat, backstage. If things aren't the way I want them, I can be about as easy as a bloody razor blade, to get along with. I'm certainly no saint, darling. Many a stagehand or makeup artist has quit, because of me. I'm quite the bitch, in creative circles.'

'But you're not a bitch to *me!* Or to my kids, or to the friends we still share. You're one of the kindest and most enduring rocks of my life, and you always have been! I judge people by how they treat waiters, and how they treat me and my family. I don't care what others think. That's playground stuff. I *know* you're no saint, but you're *my* saint, and I love you to the moon and back.'

'Saint Miranda. That does have rather a nice ring to it. It appeals to my ego, which is the size of a small continent of course, after decades of having people pandering to my every whim, but you're right, Adie. No matter where we are in life, we have to keep at least *one* foot firmly on the ground, don't we? If we don't have that stability, who knows where we might end up? Nowhere good, I suspect. Thank you for being my anchor. If I've kept it real, it's because you would never let me get away with being the complete cow I've so often wanted to be, at times.'

At that point, Mark poked his head around the kitchen door, pulled a face at them both, and growled.

'I thought we'd got you *out* o't bloody kitchen! There's a couple o' vodka martinis wi' yer names on 'em, out 'ere, wi' their ice meltin,' and for God's sake, *eat* summat!'

Adie burst out laughing. 'I've been picking at the food all night while we've been getting it ready, like I always do. I'm full to the gunnels with it all. Mand has just given me the most incredible birthday present, Mark! Come in and take a look.'

Mark's eyes widened. 'By 'eck. That's summat special, in't it? Real diamonds, I take it, given that yer eyes are shinin' just as bright? Suits *you,* missus.'

He turned to Miranda. 'Yer've stolen me thunder, a bit. My present's probably not goin' to excite 'er quite so much.'

Miranda pulled a face. 'Sorry, Mark. But I needed to do this, for her. I hope I *haven't* stamped all over your toes.'

He winked at her. 'No, y'aven't. It's a beautiful thing, an' she deserves *all* beautiful things.'

'Oh, stop it, the pair of you! You'll have me in tears again. Anyway, I need to dash to the loo, so I'll see you both back in the party, and we can grab those vodka martinis. *Everyone* get out of the kitchen! And Mand, you do need to eat!'

'Are you kidding? Your Christmas lunch was *insane!* I haven't eaten that much in bloody *years,* darling! I don't think Max has, either. I might have a pick at the cheeseboard later, but I think that'll be my limit. No limit on drinks, however,' she added. 'So, let's get going on that. I'll bring the ice through.' She smirked at Mark. 'No objections to me getting rat-arsed tonight, with your good lady?'

He shook his head. 'Nope. Yer've not far to crawl up't stairs, an' I'm sure Max can do a decent fireman's lift, if it comes to it.'

Chapter Thirteen

After hugging Meghan goodbye, and shaking Parker's hand, Darren Davies found himself alone, momentarily. He blinked, to himself, as he cast his mind back to the conversation he'd had with his wife, before Adie's presentation.

Holy shit! What the fuck have I done? Under the influence of drink, I've somehow managed to tell my wife that she can have another bloody baby!

He knew he couldn't *really* blame the drink. He wasn't that drunk, at least not yet. His only hope was that he wouldn't get so shit-faced that he'd say something to her, like he wanted to have a rethink. She was excited now. He couldn't ruin that, could he? She'd never forgive him, and he'd probably never forgive himself. Besides, there was every chance it wouldn't happen. If Feen Raven was right, and Debs' window on fertility was starting to close, they may not have enough time for her to 'fall' before it slammed shut for good. As he'd said to her - and he *had* meant it – if it happened it happened, and if it didn't, they could be content with the two kids they already had. God knows, they'd been through enough to get them.

You shouldn't be greedy about these things, especially when you knew – as Debs did – how many women would never get to have a baby at all, no matter how hard they tried. Her support group for women who were struggling to conceive kept her own feet firmly on the ground. She'd said she'd be okay if a third pregnancy didn't eventuate, and he just had to hope she meant it. A return to the pre-Ruby and Tom days, where every unwanted period spelled yet another IVF failure and sent her into a total meltdown, was something he never wanted to face again. It wasn't fair on either of them, to be in that state. And, of course, the last thing their children needed was to feel like they somehow weren't enough, in the midst of some crazy hysteria Deb might fall prey to, over failing to conceive again.

But Darren was feeling a bit like a rabbit in the headlights, over this latest development. Three kids were going to be a stretch, financially and timewise. They currently had a good balance with Ruby and Thomas that they'd worked pretty hard to achieve. What would a third child do to their routine? Would there be a big adjustment?

Only time would tell, and he resolved to try and put it all out of his mind for tonight. If he had the chance to talk to Stu about how he felt, maybe he'd say something, but this wasn't the night for heavy convos. It was Adie's sixtieth birthday, and Christmas as well, so the last thing anyone needed was to be thrown a conundrum to wrestle with that wasn't even their own.

He checked over towards the dining table, and saw that Fiona was loading her plate with something that looked like a rice dish. He wandered over to her, and peered at her plate.

'That looks good. What is it?'

It's something called Jollof rice, apparently, with lamb, tomatoes, garlic, peppers, and spices. It looks amazing, doesn't it? And it smells *divine*. You should grab a plate and get some food onto it before all the best stuff goes.'

'I'm like Stu – I'm a sucker for Adie's chilli con carne, so I might grab a plate of that instead, and if there's any jolly rice left after that, I'll give it a go. It does look nice.'

'*Jollof* rice,' Fiona chuckled. 'It's Nigerian. Adie's very beautiful daughter-in-law Marie is Nigerian. She made it. It's a native dish from her homeland. But are you okay, Darren? You look kind of shellshocked – like someone's just dropped a bomb on you or something.'

He chewed his lip for a moment, debating on whether to say anything to his best mate's wife. He settled for something that hinted at the truth but didn't quite spell it all out.

'Oh, nothing to earth-shattering, Fi. We're thinking about having another baby, that's all. You know, while there's still time. I've just been contemplating the implications.'

He grinned as she gaped at him. 'Seriously? Well, that is actually pretty major! And you look scared *shitless,* if you don't mind my saying so.'

'Is it really that obvious?'

Fiona grinned and shook her head.

'No. Only to me because I know you so well. Meghan and Parker have scarpered, by the way. I think she plans to drop into Appletree Cottage soon and properly catch up with you and Debby and the kids. They're off to some late supper thing at her friend's house. I'm glad she made it here, for a few minutes at least.'

Stuart drifted over now, with a plate full of chilli con carne and rice, and told Darren to get in quick if he wanted any.

Darren's stomach rumbled. Relieved that Stu had offered him a reason to sidestep a burgeoning conversation with Fiona, he excused himself with a grin and went to pick up a plate. As predicted, he got there just in time to scoop up the last of the chilli con carne.

This was always such a great party. It was nice to socialise a little, with some of his clients. Most times, he saw these farmers professionally as their vet, at times when they were a bit anxious about something, usually the suffering of one or more of their animals. They always wanted good news and a quick remedy, and sometimes it was tough to try and manage their expectations when the problem being faced wouldn't have the solution they wanted. He always did his best for them, and they always knew that to be true, but sometimes driving away from a farm where he'd had to put an animal down or diagnose something that was going to mean a long recovery was hard.

Tonight, there was none of that. Even if one or two did have an issue they wanted to discuss with him (as had happened at previous parties), they never let it dominate the evening. They merely alluded to the need to talk to him soon about something. Everyone seemed to respect everyone else's right to have some time 'off the clock,' to simply enjoy a party without anything getting heavy.

It had been great to catch up briefly with Meghan too. He loved his 'surrogate' little sister and always enjoyed spending time with her. Watching her blossom from the moody, belligerent teenager she'd been when he'd first met her, to the lovely young woman she was now, had been one of the joys of his life. Meghan Thompson would go far in life, and he was proud that part of the reason had been down to him, and his faith in her, way back in the day when she didn't have much to cling to or be happy about. Meeting his horse, Astro, had been the turning point of her life – especially when he'd entrusted her with training the animal, after it had become clear that they'd formed an uncannily swift and profound bond. They were two lost souls that sensed the need to connect. He'd never seen anything like it, and probably never would again.

Meghan was at university now, studying to be an equine therapist, and she was looking forward to being a full partner in Stuart's business when she graduated. Darren knew she'd be a huge asset to Beaconsfield. How well things had come together for her and for Stuart had been remarkable, but it was proof that if you let things take the course they were supposed to take, without too much pushing and shoving, you generally ended up where you were supposed to. At one time, Darren would have thought that to be a load of actual horse shit but, after experiencing the 'magic' of fate for himself and his wife, in events that brought them to settle in the Torley valley after moving from Exeter, and witnessing how Stu and Meghan had been similarly affected, he was more inclined now to believe the predictions of witches – well, one in particular: Feen Raven. She'd gently woven her spells around them all, to encourage them to create lives they once only dreamed of having.

His chat with Debs tonight, about having a third child, had been brief but seismic. They'd touched on it, and agreed on it, but they'd shelved it until they could have a more meaningful discussion later. She was ecstatic tonight, and he wanted to keep it that way. He wanted to be happy *himself,* about the decision, even with its weighty implications. So, when Stuart wandered up to him again and raised the fact that Fiona had told him about it, he was quick to shut him down.

'Yeah, we still have a bit to talk about, and it won't be for a day or two, but I think we're fairly sure it's what we want, you know, to see what might happen there. Have you and Fi had a nice Christmas Day? It was pretty cool to see Meghan, if only for a nanosecond.'

Feen came over to him now. 'Hello Darren! Merry Christmas! I've just kecked on the chids. They're all fast asleep, horing their sneads off. It's very peaceful up there now. I think even the babysitter has nodded off, not that I blame her! It is a very comfortable sofa, and she's had a full-on night with them all.'

Darren couldn't help himself; he had to mention Feen's conversation with Debby.

'You've stirred the pot a bit tonight, haven't you? It would appear that we may be dragging a third kid with us next Christmas, or expecting one, at least.'

'Feen grimaced. 'Eek. Me and my big mouth. You know what I'm like, Darren! But I didn't think it was fair to know what I know and not say something, especially after all you've been through. I couldn't deny you and Debby the bance for another chaby if that was what you wanted, only to find out that you'd left it too late to decide to try. I hope I haven't waded in again where I'm not wanted.'

'No, seriously, you've probably done us a favour, once again. It's been the elephant in the room for far too long, now. And besides, it may not even happen, right? There's just a chance and, given Debs' history, it's impossible to say which way it will go. We're keeping an open mind. We won't be too gutted if it doesn't come to pass. She isn't monitoring her hormones anymore, so this was a bit of a bolt from the blue.'

'Yeah, I get that. But whatever will be will be and, as I said to her, whichever way it goes, you'll all be more than fine.'

'As one of the weirdest but most reliable sources of information I've ever met, I do trust you on that. How are you and Gavin? I heard something about a plane crash, involving some of his friends? That must be hard, since it's Christmas and all.'

Feen shrugged. 'It is very sad. But I didn't like them much in the end, to be fair, and they didn't like me at all. So, I guess you could say he's on his own with the grieving. It will take time, but he has lots of new work to get his teeth into, so he'll be fine. I know Daddy says you've been busy with working too, especially with the farm stuff. And I do think you've reached your limit, with your good wife, about bringing waifs and strays home. Your place is bulging with critters, now. Enough should be enough now, don't you think?' Her voice was firm, but her blue eyes were dancing with mischief.'

Darren laughed. 'Don't push your luck, lady! You've cornered me into being a father again to a human critter, so don't you dare try to deny me the furry kind!'

She laughed back, and winked at him. 'Fair do's. I can only advise. As for railroading you, I'm sorry but I'm not taking the blame for that one. You're a big boy. You're certainly capable of saying no if the mood takes you, even to the stupendously beautiful Debby. She looks gorgeous tonight, by the way. I'm so glad there's a dress code at this party. It's wonderful to see everyone all nessed up to the drines. I'd *kill* for her shoes. They are gorgeous.'

'They need to be. They almost broke the bloody bank! But you're right. She's a hard woman to say no to. All I want is for her to be happy and if another snot is what it takes, I say let's just do it. We'll find a way to make it work.'

'If it happens, it won't be as hard as you think. I can promise you that.'

Darren gave her a quick hug and let her go. Within seconds she had melted away from him as if she hadn't been there at all. He couldn't even see where she'd gone.

Chapter Fourteen

They were a cheerful bunch, Billy decided. In his experience, Christmas either brought out the best or the worst in people, but a party seemed to make most pretty happy, and this was one of the better bashes he'd been to, of late.

He'd heard a lot about the Christmas party that was held every Christmas night at Ravensdown House, but he hadn't known – at least before yesterday – that it was Adie Raven's sixtieth birthday too. Wendy had somehow forgotten to mention that little nugget, even though she was adamant that she'd told him, well ahead of time. He was equally adamant that she hadn't. Either way, it had left him scrambling with the task (on the back of her 'reminder') to pick out a decent birthday present for their hostess.

Nappy-brain. All new mothers had it, apparently. In Wendy's case it amounted to forgetting all kinds of important details that she then tried blaming him for not attending to. He'd lost count of the number of times she'd been frustrated with him for forgetting something she hadn't told him about, even as she was adamant that they'd had the conversations. He was constantly uneasy about what else she might have convinced herself she'd got him in the loop about, but hadn't. Was a bailiff going to come knocking over some bill she thought she'd asked him to pay? Was her car out of its MOT because she thought she'd told him to get it renewed?

As Billy quietly contemplated how many things could potentially come and bite him on the arse that he hadn't been 'in the loop' about, and yet would have to bear the brunt of, he pulled himself off that train of thought. It was heading into a dark tunnel that he wasn't sure he'd see light at the end of. He was tired too. Newborns were a challenge, and he shared as much of the schedule as he could with Wendy, when his own work permitted. But he was busy with Rockliff Ridge, the housing development up towards Gretna Green, which had been delayed several times now, and was finally pushing ahead. He was on site more than he wanted to be, and the timing of the delays meant that Wendy had more to do on her own, which had never been the plan. As much as he longed to be able to do it, he couldn't put a large team of construction contractors on hold for the needs of a newborn baby.

Wendy's ongoing forgetfulness wasn't helping with the pressure. Her omission about Adie's birthday present had sent him skittering into the city to buy something suitable, and having to make excuses for being late, to everyone hanging around waiting for him up at the Ridge.

It's easy to be frustrated with her, but I can't be, can I? Her hormones are all out of whack, not to mention her sleep. She's knackered with this mothering malarkey and trying to run the bloody restaurant too. I can hardly lose my rag over a few missed details, can I? I need to be more on top of things myself, even if it means nagging her to make sure I know everything I should. I can't just leave it to her to be responsible for everything, and I don't need to be caught out with stuff that puts me under pressure to resolve at the eleventh hour.

Billy was doing everything he could, to help Wendy. Robin was his baby too, and he felt just as responsible and devoted to her upbringing as Wendy did. But his wife had always been independent – almost to the point of being stubborn. She never found it easy to ask for help or admit she needed it, and that made it hard for her to accept it, even when it was readily available from the most obvious person: her own husband and the father of their child! Billy was a hundred percent willing and committed to sharing the load. He'd told her, many times, that she didn't need to tackle everything on her own, but she usually went ahead and tried anyway! He knew it wasn't because she didn't trust him. It was simply who she was – to be independent and to manage things herself. The fact that she'd asked him to get Adie's present was an admittance that she couldn't easily manage to do it herself. That was important, and Billy couldn't let her down. It just would have been nice to not have been scrambling at the last minute, to get it. Last minute crises derailed him, especially if he had his mind focussed on something else. It added to the pressure he was under.

Wendy had given the seal of approval, though, to the gift he'd chosen for Adie. A sixtieth birthday was a big deal, and it had him racking his brains. He hadn't been raised by a mother himself, and his knowledge of older women was minimal. He had no *idea* what they might want, so he went into a bit of a tailspin, to start with, about being tasked with something so important. But he'd met an incredibly helpful shop assistant in a gift store in Carlisle and had thrown himself on her mercy. She'd asked a few key questions, and together they'd come up with the idea of a beautiful little music box, in the shape of a quaint cottage, with crystal windows and the most beautiful, intricately woven thatched roof. It had a handle at the back, and when it was turned it played a beautifully toned rendition of 'River Flows in You,' by Yiruma. It was German, apparently, and incredibly unique and special. It was also hugely expensive, and had been kept in a locked cabinet behind the shop's counter.

It had made Wendy cry. Billy had a lump in his own throat when he listened to the music with her, as they sat quietly with baby Robin (who had quietly fallen asleep straight after her feed), and they both agreed that it was the perfect gift for Adie.

So he was off the hook, and had earned a substantial brownie point. Adie wouldn't be opening her presents tonight, so he wouldn't get to see her face when she saw the music box for the first time, but he was pretty sure she'd love it. It was the kind of gift you passed down through your family as an heirloom. He'd love to buy one for Wendy, now that he knew how enchanted she'd been with it, and he decided that he would go back to the shop as soon as he had a chance. They could probably order one in for him, and it might be a nice 'eternity' present, to mark Robin's birth.

'Hey, you!' A voice pulled him out of his daydream, and he grinned to see Feen standing in front of him.

'You were miles away! What were you thinking about?'

He smirked at her. 'Don't you know?'

'She laughed. 'Well, I don't sense everything, Billy. Imagine the state of my poor head, if I did? I guess it wasn't critical, or I probably *would* have picked up on it. But how are you? Merry Christmas, by the way. I've said that so many times, today and tonight, I forget who I've said it to, but I know I haven't talked to you yet, so I'm safe to say it without pounding like a demented sarrot. This time, at least. I looked in on the kids a bit ago. Baby Robin – my God, that child is beautiful! She is going to be creative, just like her mother.'

'Well, better that than ending up a crashing idiot like me. with two left feet that both fit into my mouth. I'm all for her having more of Wendy's genes than mine. To answer your question, I was actually thinking about notes. Not the musical kind – the post-it kind; the sort you stick on fridges and doors to remind you of what needs doing. I think I have to get Wend some.'

Feen closed her eyes and giggled. 'Don't tell me – she's gone all forgetful, post-partum. I was the same. This too shall pass but, until it does, notes are an excellent idea.'

'Are you guys okay? Gavin mentioned about the plane crash, involving some of your friends, and we had a bit of a chat about it. He is still here, isn't he? I seem to have lost sight of him.'

'Yes, he's around, but he's having a few quiet minutes by himself upstairs. The crash has hit him hard, and I think he's finding all the attention a bit weird. I know people can't *not* ask about it! It would feel rude and uncomfortable for you all, to *not* offer condolences or support, but he's a bit overwhelmed. It's a gromplicated crief, and I'm sure he will tell you more about it if you ask him, when he comes back down. But don't worry about him. He'll be fine.'

'What about you? How are you feeling about it?'

Feen shrugged, lightly. 'Well, it's a sad thing, of course. There's no denying that. But I'd already fallen out with them over something really stupid, so I won't wiss them like he mill. Anyway, why don't I get you a fresh drink? That beer looks a bit flat. And please do get some more food while there's still something decent on the table.'

She grabbed his glass and rushed off with it at lightning speed. He hadn't finished his pint, but it *had* been going flat, and he had the distinct impression that she really didn't want to keep talking about the death of Gavin's friends. She was too polite to say that, outright, but it seemed fairly clear. He'd wandered into uncomfortable territory in touching on the subject with her, especially when she'd more or less had to confess that she'd had a disagreement with Gavin's friends.

Feen Raven-Black was an odd little thing. Billy always felt slightly wary around her, but he did like her very much. She had given him some life-changing advice back in the day, when he was staying at Teapot Cottage, trying to figure out how to move forward after finding out that his father had sold the land Billy expected to inherit. It had scuppered his plans for developing it, to stave off a looming bankruptcy, and had thrown him into a panic. He'd split up with his girlfriend of the moment too, which had been inevitable but still more painful than he'd wanted to admit. He'd been in a strange place, angry and resentful to the point of being belligerent in public, and Feen had set him straight on a number of things. She'd helped him to see his life for the mess it really was, and that had been instrumental in him finding the courage to turn things around.

She was a nice woman, and he loved her quirky way of talking. He hadn't realised that Spoonerism was actually a 'thing,' but he'd been gently amused by the way she routinely swapped the consonants on a pair of words, without even realising she was doing it.

'Here you go.' She was back, already, and she handed him a fresh pint, with a decent head on it.

'That's a better one than I poured for myself, earlier.'

'Ah, well, I've been doing this for a few years now, so if I can't pour a decent pint after this long, there's definitely something wrong. How is fatherhood? Are you up all slight and neeping all day?'

'God, I wish that were the case! I'm up all night and *working* all day! To be fair, it's not horrendous. Wendy and I share the bulk of it, but I can't breastfeed, obviously, so she has to be up through the night more than me. I have to take Robin to work occasionally, to let Wend prep for dinner in the restaurant or get a bit of shut eye, but we're figuring it out. She's a good baby, mostly, which helps, although she has a proper set of lungs on her when she needs a change or a burp.'

Feen giggled. 'They all do! I had two at once, and their bowels and bladder weren't in synchro, so I sometimes felt like my life was passing in a blur of nitty shappies and screaming.'

'I thought twins did everything in tandem?'

'Nope, not the pitting and shuking. That, my friend, is shockingly random. They might share a lot of DNA, but they're as different as chalk and cheese in more ways than they're similar. They're fraternal, so it's to be expected. But if you think *one* baby keeps you on your toes, try two at once!'

'I love being a dad. It's early days, but so far, so good. From the second Robin was born I'd knew I'd die or kill for her. I would for either of them, really – her *and* Wendy. Babies might be tiny, and screaming and shitting and puking all the time, and kids might be annoying as fuck at times, but we wouldn't change them for the world, would we?'

'God no! Not for a nanosecond! Alder and Willow are the light of our lives, and Willow is taking after me with the witchery. She is going to be just like me. Alder is going to be more like his father – musical and a little more pragmatic about life in general, but he does have a few warlock tendencies, so let's just say that it's an interesting journey with them both. They're doing chai ti, to help focus their minds. Gavin is doing it with them. It gets him out from underfoot, one night a week, so I can have a bit of time to myself in the house, which I rarely otherwise get.'

'Has he bought a vintage sports car yet? I know he was talking about it.'

'Yes! He dithered for quite a while over a Ferrari Dino, which was absolutely beautiful, and I could see why he was tempted. I wanted that one myself! But I'm afraid I had to lean on him to go for something with four seats, so he could still have a play by himself when it suits him, but we could take the kids out when *that* suits. He's not a young, see, fringle man anymore with only himself to please! He's a mamily fan now, so we had a long chat about it, and he opted for a very beautiful 1966 ragtop Mustang, with two back seats. It's beyond gorgeous, and he's very happy with it.' She frowned, suddenly.

'As you've probably figured out, he's not on his best form tonight. He won't be for a while, I suppose, until the dust settles on this crane plash thing. Here was silly me, thinking Christmas would be peaceful this year! There's always something to throw a spanner in the works. Last year the chimney was all but blocked, and we just about got smoked out on Christmas Eve, and had to drag the poor swimney cheep out on Christmas morning to get it sorted in time for the party. This year it's Gavin getting to grips with a hard bereavement. I wonder what next year will bring?'

'Well, if you ever get bored, you could write a book,' Billy offered.

'Bored? Fance would be a chine thing! I've had to employ a tart pimer now, to help me get Gina Gordano's jewellery orders done in time these days, for her accessories line for GinGio. That's her clothing brand. Demand is so high for that, I barely have time to make stuff for my *own* website! And the twins are full-on, and so is Gavin, when he puts his abstract head on and forgets the world while he's working. If I only had time to *read* a book, let alone write one, I'd be thrilled. But it's a nice thought.'

She stepped forward, and gave Billy a strong hug. It surprised him.

'You know, you've turned into a very good, capable, and successful man. I know you were successful before, but surely you must seel more fettled now that your personal life is sinally forted. You're where you're supposed to be, Billy Briggs. And you're better and happier for it.'

'Thanks, Feen.' Billy barely had time to get the words out before Feen smirked at him, gave him one of her trademark winks, and danced off into the crowd.

She's right. I am in a much better place, and I do feel settled, and content, in a way I once never imagined I could. Wend and Robin have changed everything. I was adrift before, and all that stuff I felt; the frustration towards my girlfriend Paula, just for trying to be a good partner, the anger I had towards my dad, for trying to be a decent one but putting his own needs first like he should at his age, and Wendy herself, who made me mad enough to want to kill her when we first met. I was a bit of a bastard, back then. Defensive. I didn't understand myself.

It's funny how life pushes you forwards to a better place if you let it. I think Adie, or Feen, or someone said that to me while I was staying at Teapot Cottage, baring my teeth at the world. I've come so far, this past year. Life isn't a bed of roses, but it's a hell of a lot better than it was, and I have my beautiful wife and my gorgeous baby daughter to thank for all of it. And the Ravens too. How they put up with me is anyone's guess, but they did, and that's what served as the catalyst for change. They'll never know how grateful I am to them, for giving me that chance to prove myself.

'Oh, my Goodness, Seefer! You look half insane! What the hell is on your mind, to be lookin' into space like a loon, like that? You look like a bloody halfwit, man!'

Billy shook himself, as Wendy sidled up alongside him. She was grinning.

'You make me laugh at times. It's a party, Seef! Time to whip off your serious head and park it. Think about the heavy stuff tomorrow, and come and dance with me, before I tear upstairs to give Robin a feed.'

'I don't dance. You know I don't.'

'You do tonight! It's Christmas, and it's Adie's birthday! We need to have a shimmy. Your moves aren't so terrible. You're not exactly a dad-dancer yet! You'll probably embarrass the hell out of our daughter, one day, but not tonight. C'mon!'

She dragged him over to the cleared space in the living room to join a few other dancers. One pair were 'Egg and Peric' Tripper. Eric's moves weren't bad, for an old guy, and Peg was twirling and twisting like a woman twenty years younger.

Someone had changed the vibe a bit, after supper, by putting on a few fifties songs. As he vainly tried to pull off some kind of twisty-jive thing with Wendy, a slower song came on. She moved close and put her arms around his neck. He pulled her to him and buried his face in her hair as they swayed gently to the music.

'If you really want to know, I was thinking about something I'd said to Feen, when we were chatting. She was asking about how my life feels now, and I told her I'd kill or die for you and Robin. Obviously, it wouldn't be my first choice. If there was another way around it, I'd go for that first but, if push came to shove, and I had to lose my life so you could keep yours, I'd let it go in a heartbeat.'

'Oh, you soppy git, *cariad!* What are you like? You're never goin' to have to die for either of us! But I do know what you mean. I would do the same for you.'

'I love you, Wendy Whitelaw Briggs. Or, Bendy Britelaw-Wiggs, as Feen is so fond of saying. I love you and Robin to the moon and back. There's nothing I wouldn't do. You know that, right?'

'Of course I do, Seefer. I know everythin' about how you feel about us. I love you too, like fire, and I thank God for you every day. We're alright, aren't we, our little family? We're doin' grand, it's all comin' together, Rockliff Ridge is underway, your new project at Hesket after that has had the green light, and the restaurant is doin' well. Sunday lunch is always overbooked and so are the Wednesday theme nights. Baby's thrivin,' our love is thrivin,' Mum's on her way here for good, and look at the friends we've got! I keep pinchin' myself at how well our lives are turnin' out.'

'As long as you're happy. That's all I want.'

She looked softly at him, and lightly kissed his nose.

'I *am* happy, Billy Briggs. Happier than a happy thing. Now, I need to go and feed our child before my boobs explode. Can you please make sure to save me a piece of that Christmas cake if its sparklers are lit and it's all cut up before I get back down here?'

'Of course I will. And a piece of birthday cake too, because that looks pretty decent. More like a wedding cake if you ask me, with six tiers. One for each decade, apparently. Someone said it was red velvet. That happens to be my favourite so, if you do take a while, remember that the bit I save for you might actually be gone before you get here.'

'I'll live, if it is, but do try.'

She kissed him again, this time fully on the mouth, And, as she started weaving her way through the crowd towards the door, his heart sang loud enough to lift the roof.

Chapter Fifteen

The encounter with Minty had gone a lot better than Fiona had been expecting. She'd been dreading walking into the party, tonight. It wasn't that she imagined Minty would go for her with flying fists or anything. Her erstwhile best friend was well above that. But it had still been hard to steel herself for what she expected to be an awkward or even frosty meeting. The two women had talked on the phone a couple of times, since Minty had moved to the South of France. Minty had rung once, to see how Fiona was recovering after her double mastectomy. They'd talked again a few months later, when Fiona herself had called to offer an update. She wasn't sure why she'd done that, but she supposed that part of her still wanted some kind of connection, even if it was an awkward one.

Both calls had gone well, but that was a different matter entirely than being in a room together. The relative safety of a thousand miles of distance was now reduced to the perilous prospect of a couple of yards at best. Minty had been cordial though, and almost warm in her greeting. That had been a welcome surprise, but Fiona still found it hard to look her in the eye.

She seemed pleased to see me, although I don't imagine she really meant that we should hook up over Zoom or something, for a virtual coffee. People often say things like that, don't they, as social fillers in a conversation? I've lost count of the times people have told me I should come over for coffee, or go out for dinner with them or something, but even as they're

Fiona recalled now that before she'd finally bought her house in nearby Bampton Rissell, just outside of Bristol, she had rented a little place in a quiet cul-de-sac in the city itself for a while. Not long after she'd moved in, she'd invited every neighbour in the cul-de-sac to a barbecue at her house. Almost everyone had come, but she later learned that they'd really only come to be nosy. They'd merely wanted to suss her out. Not a single one had ever reciprocated by asking her over to their house for a chat or a cup of tea, ever since. When the moving truck was parked in her driveway for an entire morning, a year or so later, none of her neighbours came out to wave her off, ask her where she was going, or wish her well.

Sometimes, neighbours could be a funny lot. For an entire year, she'd lived alongside people who simply didn't care whether she came or went. Her hospitality had never been returned there. Bampton, by stark contrast, had been welcoming to a fault. There was often a quiet get-together at one neighbour's house or another and sometimes, on a summer evening, someone would pull an impromptu barbecue together and invite everyone over. Fiona always had a few things in the freezer that she could quickly defrost and take along on occasions like that, and they always turned out to be fun times, with nice food, good wine, and interesting conversation. She felt like she *belonged* in her neighbourhood, in Bampton.

Selling the house had been hard, but she'd needed a fresh start, and after she'd fallen in love with Stuart and his adorable daughter Meghan, the future began to write itself. Stu had met her just as she was about to undergo her mastectomy for IBC, and he was beside her all the way through that and her subsequent treatment. She'd moved up to Carlisle, to be with him. The cancer was being held at bay, for now at least, but she knew it would probably storm forward again at some point. For now, she just wanted to live the best life she could.

Recent advancements in treatment were enabling her disease to be managed as a chronic illness, with a focus on prolonging her life and maintaining a good *quality* of life. One of the things she needed to do was avoid high levels of stress.

Being in a room with the woman whose husband she'd had a torrid, two-year affair with was not what anyone could call a low-stress event! But even as she'd been incredibly nervous, Fiona had been keen to test the water with Minty, face to face. It was only going to go one way or the other, but she needed to know where she stood, in a way she could never have gauged over the phone.

After tonight's conversation, she was quietly confident now, that Minty had got past the worst of the hurt and betrayal, and resentment and rage that Fiona had caused. She was relieved that her old best friend had been able to move on, at least enough to find a new love interest. Marcel was a decent guy. He seemed solid and dependable, and he'd given Fiona the impression that he'd always tell someone the truth about something if it was in their best interests to hear it, whether they wanted to or not. Minty deserved that. Fiona believed that Marcel was a better man than Leo McLeod had turned out to be. Leo had cheated on his wife, without a shred of guilt or remorse, and then he'd swiftly abandoned 'mistress' Fiona as soon as she'd got sick. He'd turned out to be a weak, cowardly, self-serving man, and the realisation had hit both women hard.

Forty years of friendship had been a lot to gamble with and lose, and Fiona would never be at a place in her life – however long or short it was going to end up being – where she could justify her actions. She'd deliberately embarked on an affair with her best friend's husband. The affair had torn that family apart, blown Fiona's friendships with Minty and Leo wide open, and destroyed her relationship with their children, one of whom was her goddaughter, Belle.

Minty's son Ethan was getting married next week, and Fiona felt the pain keenly, of not being invited to the wedding. She wasn't surprised, of course; there was no way she could ever have expected to be included. But it was sad to know that the baby she'd held just minutes after he was born, and looked after many times, who had grown into a wonderful young man, was now about to be married to the love of his life. Fiona hadn't even met Ethan's fiancé Cal. Now she probably never *would* get to meet the man that had captured Ethan's heart.

I'll get to see some pictures, at least, if Minty is true to her word. She said she'd send me some. Maybe she did mean it when she talked about a virtual coffee. She'd have no reason to say something like that if she didn't. She's never been the type to 'throw someone a bone.' So maybe I will get to 'see' Ethan on his wedding day, and find out what his new husband looks like.

Maybe at some time in the future, she could risk sending a card to the couple. She still loved Ethan, and always would. She wanted him to know that.

Adie came over and beamed at her. 'Hello, Fi! Are you enjoying the party? You look beautiful tonight. The 'little black dress' never dates, does it? And with all that bling, you look fantastic. Very Audrey Hepburn, in fact. A-line suits you perfectly.'

'Thank you, Adie! And Happy Birthday! And Merry Christmas! God, it must be a pain having the two together. Were you one of those poor kids who only ever got one present at Christmas, to cover your birthday as well?

Adie chuckled and rolled her eyes. 'Yes, I was, and I had to suck that up for a long time. But as soon as I was old enough to insist on two presents, I did start getting them.'

'I actually got this dress in a charity shop, would you believe? I was in Carlisle a few months ago, having a mooch, and I ran into Feen, of all people. She dragged me off for a coffee and we somehow ended up 'doing' the charity shops, which is something I've never done in my life before! It's not that I'm a snob, or anything, but it's just never *occurred* to me, to poke my head into those places before. I didn't realise how much fun it was. Feen spied this, in one of them, and demanded that I try it on. The shop didn't have a fitting room though, which was really annoying actually, so we had to buy the dress then go to a proper dress shop and use their fitting room to see if it fitted. Happily, it did, and it looks okay. It's not aways easy to find things that look or fit nice when you've got no tits.'

Adie nodded, knowingly. 'I can imagine. And lack of fitting rooms certainly doesn't help the matter, does it? After Covid, most charity shops just never reopened their fitting rooms. Apparently, they get a lot of theft.'

'God, really? You'd have to be pretty hard-nosed to steal from a charity, wouldn't you?'

'Some people are. It's outrageous, that the charities have to protect themselves by denying *everyone* the ability to try anything on, because of a criminal few. Every other shop in the country that sells clothes provides a fitting room, but the charities feel they can't. Feen spends a lot of time in those places, and it really frustrates her that most don't have changing rooms anymore. She often has to take things back, and it's all time and inconvenience, of course.'

Fiona laughed and rolled her eyes. 'Yes, I know. She made no bones about telling the poor shop assistant how she felt about that. But it's a sad sign of the times, isn't it? Just another opportunity that a few selfish people spoil for the masses. But I do love this dress. Feen has a really good eye. I had it dry-cleaned, and it came up beautifully.'

'The simple lines are the best, especially when we get to a certain age and the waistline starts disappearing.'

'Yep. I'm adding menopause to the list of what's wrong with me, now.'

Adie looked sympathetic. 'I'm sorry. It's inevitable, for us all, but it can be a bit wretched. I've been there. Any time you want to talk about it, just give me a holler. And Feen can be of help too, if you want to keep an open mind. Her holistic remedies helped me a lot while I was going through it. How's the cancer treatment going? Are you feeling well-managed?'

Fiona nodded. 'Yeah, as well as I can be, I guess. I'm back at work virtually, via video link. It's just two days a week, but it feels good. It's progress.'

She nodded over at Minty. 'That went okay too, coming face-to-face with Minty. I was dreading it, but it was fine.'

'I think you've all moved on a bit, from what happened. I was talking to Minty earlier, when she first arrived. She helped me in the kitchen for a bit. She seems pretty happy in her new life. She doesn't seem to bear any animosity towards you. That must be a relief.'

'It's incredible,' Fiona admitted. 'I couldn't blame her if she hated me for the rest of her life and stuck pins in a voodoo doll every day. But she's a bigger person than that. I still miss her, such a lot. My actions cost me dearly, didn't they? I never imagined I'd ever end up looking at her from the other side of a room, trying not to cry for the mess I made of everything, and wishing things were still the way they used to be.'

'Minty has forgiven you, Fi. Maybe it's time you forgave yourself.' Adie's voice was gentle, and low enough that only Fiona could hear it. She was grateful for Adie's empathy and tact. She laughed, lightly.

'Oh, I have, mostly. I do understand where my neediness came from, and why I was the way I was, for so long. Through therapy I've managed to become reacquainted with that lost girl who took the wrong path, all those years ago. I've worked through her pain and grief, and I'm in a good place with my lost little self, now. I'm not lost anymore, Adie. But when you know how much you've hurt someone you've loved your whole life, it's not an easy thing to sit with. Especially when they're in the same room with you, and they've shown you yet again how good they are, and how much they didn't deserve what you did to them.'

Adie stepped forward and hugged her. It surprised her a lot, and she was grateful for it.

'Fi, you made big mistakes. There's no denying that. But, as the saying goes, good people sometimes do bad things, and anyone who really knows and loves them knows that there is a lot more to them than the things they did wrong. Minty's a smart woman. You'll never have the kind of relationship you used to have, but there's no reason why you can't reconnect, if you both want to, to preserved what was good about those long years of love and friendship.'

'She said she does want to keep in touch. She suggested a virtual coffee, later in the New Year, and she's offered to send me some photos of Ethan's wedding. Hopefully, she'll include some of Belle, her daughter. My goddaughter.'

Fiona felt a rush of sadness so deep it made her catch her breath, and she found herself blinking back tears.

'I miss them all *so* much, Adie. It's like a little hole in my life now, that I guess I'll always feel.'

Adie tightened her hug. 'I know. But maybe, eventually, you can figure out how to be thankful instead that you had the time that you did with them all. A lot of people never experience that closeness to friends. You had something rare and wonderful, for a very long time. Maybe that's worth something. Maybe there's some comfort to be found in that, as a memory. I don't know.'

'Better to have loved and lost than never to have loved at all? Is that what you mean? I'm not sure about that.'

'I'm not, either. But where there's life there's hope, to quote *another* cliché.

Fiona laughed. 'Well, you know, cliches always come from a point of truth, don't they?

'They do, and on that happy note, the next one is 'bottom's up,' because I need another drink, and I'm sure you could do with a fresh one.'

Fiona drained what was left of her Campari and soda. As the two women wandered over to the makeshift bar, Mark intercepted them.

'Well, if it in't Fiona! 'Ello, love. Yer look like an Egyptian goddess, wi' all them chains around yer neck. Merry Christmas, lass.'

He smirked at Adie. 'It's time fer me to go an' get ready fer't secret Santa. Can yer gimme five minutes an' then start the music?'

Adie grinned. 'Sure thing. The usual? Rockin' Around the Christmas Tree?'

'Aye, that's the one. Five minutes.'

He quickly headed for the door. Fiona knew what was coming. Within five minutes, Mark was back in the room, dressed as Santa Claus, and handing out the secret Santa gifts from the hessian sack that had been placed inside the front doorway for people to pop their contributions into, when they arrived.

Secret Santa was lots of fun, and Mark being dressed up, and gyrating round the room, dancing to the music as he handed out packages, was always a riot. It was the one time most people saw him truly out of his shell. Everyone laughed and clapped him along the way, as he made sure that they all got a gift.

He handed one to her, with a twinkle in his eye, and she looked up and caught Stuart's eye as he was given one too. She crossed the room, with her fresh drink in one hand and her gift in the other, to stand beside him, so they could open their presents together. The general rule was that if you recognised the gift you were given as the one you'd brought, you'd put it back in the bag and accept a different one. Happily, Fiona and Stuart had both received unknown gifts.

Stuart unwrapped his. It was a rolled-up fabric open-fronted bag, designed to be hung with a coat hanger on the clothesline to hold pegs. Fiona recognised it as being from one of the trade stands at the Saturday Farmer's Market, where pot-holders, trimmed tea-towels, quilted oven gloves and other crafty things were sold. She laughed with delight, at the bafflement on her husband's face.

'Oh, I know what that is, Stu! It's a peg bag! Look at how beautifully that's been made! Does this mean you'll be doing the laundry, from now on?'

'Umm.. right, well, okay then. A peg bag. So, come on, open yours! I want to see if it's going to be another case of trading a shaving kit for the Dalai Lama.'

She giggled at him, and put her drink down. Her package had been wrapped so tightly it seemed to take forever to get the Sellotape off it. When she finally did, she burst out laughing.

'Two balls of string and a Stanley knife! Go on then, let's trade!'

She looked around the room at others who were opening their presents, with various reactions. Most were smiling or laughing, but a couple looked a little deflated, especially the six-foot-four farmer who found himself holding a pair of pink floral gardening gloves and a trowel with a matching handle. They looked like miniatures, in his huge hands. Knitted beanie hats, tasselled scarves, Santa socks, scented candles, Pyrex measuring jugs, boxes of chocolates, pillowcases, and all sorts of other interesting things were waved about, as people showed off their secret Santa gifts.

The music faded as Mark came to the end of his giving. There was just one present left in the sack, and he took it for himself, as the last person to receive a gift. Everyone stood around expectantly, waiting for him to open it. Fiona already knew what it was. It was *her* secret Santa gift, tonight.

Mark unwrapped the gift, and he did it gently because of the little tag attached to it that said 'fragile.' Beneath the wrapping, and nestled within a few layers of tissue, was a beautiful little crystal clock, in an art deco design. She had seen it in the same charity shop where she'd found her dress for tonight. The minute she saw it, she knew she wanted to give it as the secret Santa present at the Ravensdown Christmas party. She'd replaced the battery, and given it a polish, telling herself that it really wouldn't matter who received it. The clock was exquisite, and nobody except Fiona herself would ever know how important it was for anyone to receive as a present. To a woman battling cancer, nothing was more significant or poignant than time.

Mark cleared his throat, as everyone fell silent. Some were no doubt wondering about the oddness of the gift. Other might be envious that they hadn't received it themselves. Others were probably just waiting for Mark's reaction. Fiona deliberately kept her face blank.

'Well. I don't know who's put this into't sack tonight, but it's lovely. It's the nicest secret Santa gift I've ever 'ad, an' I don't want to know who's given it, but thank you. Time's important, an' we all have to be mindful of it, in different ways, fer different reasons. Every Christmas, we all feel the march of it, and the loss of it, and the need to use it well, to make the most of it. I'm goin' to find a good place fer this little gem of a thing.'

He looked up and twinkled at everyone. He really did look very sweet, dressed as Santa Claus.

'So Merry Christmas, one an' all, and thank you fer't generosity o' yer givin.' It's a special part o't night, an' I 'ope no bugger's too disappointed wi' what they got. It's just a bit o' fun, in't it, after all?'

The music started again, another upbeat Christmas song, and Mark left the room, carrying his empty sack and cradling the little clock in his other hand.

Fiona was absurdly happy that Mark had got her little clock, and that he'd understood and talked about the significance of it. What a lovely outcome.

People were dancing again now, and at the end of the next song Adie stepped forward and declared that it was time to light the sparklers on the Christmas cake. Everyone gathered around, and Mark came back in, dressed normally again, and wielding a fancy igniter. The sparklers hissed and roared as he lit them, and the cake was suddenly brought to life, illuminated in all its glory. It was another highlight of the party, every year.

Fiona looked across the room and caught Minty's eye. Minty pressed her lips together then smiled, gently, tentatively, and Fiona smiled tentatively back.

In that moment, standing there next to her husband, with his arm around her shoulders, she felt safe, and loved, and hopeful, that for however much or little time she had left, she could be a little more at peace. Minty's small smile was the perfect Christmas gift, whether she knew it or not.

Chapter Sixteen

Christ watched as Adie stifled a yawn and checked her watch, as surreptitiously as she could. He was pretty sure that she didn't want anyone at the party to think she was bored, or ready to call it a night, but she was clearly starting to wilt a little, and he felt a bit sorry for her. Everyone was still enjoying themselves, and she wouldn't want to be a party pooper – especially at her own event, but she'd been up since dawn, doing the Christmas lunch for everyone, and then she'd swung directly into getting prepared for tonight. It was ironic that it was her birthday party, yet she'd done most of the work in getting ready for it. She was a trooper, and no mistake.

He crossed the room to go and stand beside her, and just as he did, a seat on the sofa near to where she was standing became available. He gently guided her to it, and she smiled at him, gratefully.

'No offence, but you look dead on your feet.'

She laughed at him, as he perched on the arm of the sofa.

'None taken, but it has been quite a day. I hope it's not too obvious that I'm ready to fall in to bed, as soon as I get the chance.'

Chris shook his head. 'It's not. But I know a bit about exhaustion these days, so I can recognise the signs. I'm a kindred spirit, longing for the night when Lewis sleeps all the way through.'

Adie smiled sympathetically. 'It's hard with a newborn. It's so great that you and Teresa are able to share the night stuff.'

'Yeah. He's on formula so we can do relay in getting him fed and changed. We're better off than a lot of parents, in that respect. Both of us get a reasonable block of sleep, but it's still exhausting.'

It was true. Chris hadn't even had an inkling of how much responsibility came with parenting, particularly as Lewis had been completely unexpected. The baby was living proof that all the birth control in the world was still only ever as effective as Mother Nature wanted it to be. She would have her way, come what may. Fatherhood had never been in Chris' plans, and when he'd got together with Tezzie and learned that she didn't want to have children either, it seemed like all his prayers had been answered.

But here they were, parents to a healthy bouncing baby boy, and finding themselves making all kinds of random adjustments to their habits and plans, as life seemed to insist on steering them down the very path that they'd been adamant they'd never wanted to go down. Lewis was beautiful, and Chris knew that neither he nor Tezzie would change a thing now, so the adjustments hadn't felt like much of a sacrifice, in the end. But to say that Tezzie falling pregnant was a surprise was the understatement of the millennium!

Feen danced up to them now, grinning from ear to ear. She'd clearly had a few drinks and was well on her way to being tipsy. She grabbed Adie by the hand and tried to pull her up off the sofa.

'Come on, old thing! I saw that yawn you just tried to smother. I'm not having that. It's far too early for you to fade away. It's your night, this time around. We're all just peripherals this year.' She looked at Chris with a twinkle in her eye.

'She's the one who shets to gine tonight, isn't she?'

'Indeed, she is. I'd dance with her myself, if I could summon the energy but I think me still being awake this late tonight is a feat in itself, Feen.'

'Ah, the sleepless nights of new fatherhood! I don't envy you. But you and Teresa are doing a fantastic job, especially since you're still working full-time too, with Fiona and Stuart. How many hours' sleep are you managing to survive on?'

'About six, on average. It's not that bad, to be fair. I do need to get more though, and that's a bit of a challenge, because I've got a mountaineering trip coming up – three weeks of serious climbing, and I need to *not* be sleep-deprived when I go to Alaska.'

Adie shook her head. 'Don't worry about that. I've already talked to Mark about it, and we're happy to pitch in with Teresa to cover Lewis' needs so you won't have to get up through the night for the week before you go. She's going to move in here for that week. You can come too, of course, but you can keep sleeping through the nights and going to work from here, until you leave for Alaska. I will get up to tandem with Teresa, and we can have Misty here too, of course. She's fine with our dogs. Teresa, Lewis and Misty can stay with us while you're away'

'God, Adie! That would be fantastic! I've been so worried about it all. I've been on the verge of pulling the pin, but I didn't want to let my mate down. Marcus has been dying to do these Alaskan peaks for years too, just like I have. Pouring cold water on someone's dreams isn't really my style. And I know Tezzie really wants me to go. I've been so torn about it, I haven't known what to do, but you've come up with a *great* solution, and I can't thank you enough.'

'That's what families do, darling. You're important to us, and we want to support your dreams as well as Teresa's. If you want this, and she wants it for you, we're happy to pitch in and do what we can to enable it. So that's *one* thing you don't have to stay awake worrying about.'

'Fiona is gnashing her teeth about me being gone for so long. She's worried that my temporary replacement won't be up to the job.'

That's not your problem though, is it?' Feen observed.

'No, I suppose it isn't, but I don't want to leave and have her worried for the whole time I'm gone. They're so good to me, you know?'

Adie nodded. 'I know they are. But you work hard for them, and you need a break, and they understand that. They'll be fine without you. Contrary to what we'd all like to believe, none of us is indispensable.'

Chris knew she was right. He did need a break. The team had gutted and renovated five houses, back-to-back, and he'd only had three weekends off in as many months. It wasn't just a new baby that had left him exhausted. Mountaineering, in the way he did it, required massive concentration. He needed to be in top shape, mentally and physically, to do it safely. Trying to do those peaks on the back of months of sleepless nights wasn't just a recipe for failure – it could be a recipe for fatality.

Billy wandered up to them now, and clinked glasses with him. 'Merry Christmas, Chris. How's dadhood going? Tezzie says you guys are off to Ireland next week, in time for New Year's.'

Chris nodded. 'We're doing okay for a sleep-deprived pair, I suppose. We're going to spend a week with my sister Suzanne and her family. Haven't seen her since my father's funeral earlier this year.'

'Oh, condolences! Were you close?'

'Nope, not for most of my life. It hasn't affected me as much as my sister. Jack wasn't a great dad, and we hadn't been in touch for years, so it didn't make much of a dent, really. Life just carries on as normal for me. Suze has needed a bit of time to come to terms with it all, though. He wasn't nice to her either, but she hasn't been able to let go of the baggage in quite the same way as I have, so it will be good to catch up with her and see where she's at. They haven't met Lewis, either, and it's time they did.'

'So, just a week, is it? Back to work after that?'

'Yeah, and I'm starting my engineering degree with the Open University in February so I need to get mentally prepared for that.'

Billy looked impressed. 'Wow! That's a big thing. All part of some future plan, I take it?'

Chris shrugged. 'Well, I don't just want to be a sparky for the rest of my life. I want to do better for my family. I'm doing a tailored degree that's focussed mostly on electrical engineering, aiming towards consultancy eventually. Before I met Tez, I was happy enough in my trench, but she and Lew have changed the way I think. It feels more important now, to do better. I have money thanks to my previous fiancée's life insurance policies that kicked in after she died, but I'm not the type of guy who can sit around and do nothing. Providing meaningfully for the family and being an example to my kid – it feels important, you know?'

Billy nodded. 'I do. I get it. Family changes everything, doesn't it? Turns your whole life on its head. Well, fair play to you. It's a pretty full plate you're taking on, but I'm sure you'll do really well with it. Cheers!'

He clinked glasses with Chris again before draining his glass. Then he winked at Adie, poked Feen in the arm, and wandered off towards the bar for a refill.

Chris chuckled. Billy Briggs was an interesting guy. He and Chris had never really talked much. They were acquaintances who sometimes bumped into one another in the pub, or they'd nod to one another if both happened to show up for some reason at the same building sites. Chris and Tezzie had been for dinner at AyO a couple of times while she was still pregnant with Lewis, and Billy had been hovering about in the background, but he'd never been much of a conversationalist. In fact, tonight was the first time he'd shown any real interest in Chris, and it seemed to be polite, rather than friendly. He hadn't given Chris a chance to ask him anything about himself.

But everything big had to start with something small, and they might end up being friends eventually. Billy always seemed to have his mind on half a dozen different things at once, so it never felt like any one thing or person ever got his full attention, but he was nice enough, and he seemed pretty straight. Chris had the impression that you'd always get the opinion you'd asked for from Billy, and maybe one you didn't ask for at all, if he felt inclined to give it to you, but he wasn't deliberately offensive.

Adie turned to him now.

'So, you're really okay about your dad, Chris? I know you didn't get on. He wasn't much of a father to you, or to your sister, but sometimes these things can catch up with you after the fact. I know I had issues with my mother, and I thought I was fine about them, until she died. Then I realised there were things I still needed to square away. It's normal, if you do feel weird about him dying without any opportunity to set some records straight.'

'Ah, I did have the opportunity, Adie, but I chose not to take it. I decided he'd hurt me enough. I didn't need to see him again, to fee all that pain again, and I don't think he was in his right mind well enough to talk about anything meaningful that would have helped me feel any better anyway. I grieved for him a long time ago, well before he got old and started dying. I'm good.'

And Chris knew that he was. Nowadays, Jack Darcy was just someone he once knew, who he had a simple biological connection to, and nothing more. He didn't have any real feelings about Jack anymore. The man had lived and died on his own terms, without much of a care for the impact of that on his family, and Chris really didn't have anything to mourn anymore that he hadn't already processed years before. Tezzie herself had supported him to come to terms with what was left of his animosity towards Jack, and his sister Suzanne had been helpful too.

They all knew what kind of man Jack Darcy had been. Not the kind of man you'd grieve for, although Suze still had a few things to 'square away,' as Adie had put it. Maybe he could be of some help with that, in the same way that Suze had helped *him* when she'd popped in for a night at Teapot Cottage when he'd been staying there. At the time he'd been trying to come to terms with the death of Daisy, his previous fiancée, who'd died in a climbing accident the previous year. He'd still been angry and frustrated about his father too, back then, but Suze had helped him to come to terms with a few things. In that process, they had reconnected after years of only sporadic contact, and he was very much looking forward to seeing his sister and her husband, and his two nieces in a few days' time.

As he looked around the room now, at his new extended family on Tezzie's side, he felt lucky that he'd landed on his feet so well. Falling in love with Tezzie Bostock had been unexpected and scary, while he was still grieving the loss of Daisy, and the surprise of impending fatherhood had terrified him even more, but this was a rock-solid family that held him safe and secure within it. He had a place here, and the feeling of finally belonging somewhere, and being a part of something much bigger than himself – well, you couldn't put a price or even a description on how reassuring that was. Everything Chris had started off thinking that he did or didn't want or need had been turned on its head, but he felt at peace with all of it.

His baby boy – the child he was once in abject horror of having – had done exactly what Billy Briggs had described. It had turned his life *completely* on its head. Chris hadn't known just how profoundly he could love another human being, until Lewis arrived. Yes, he loved Tezzie with all his heart, but the love he felt for his child was on a whole different scale. There were times when he had to fight back tears, at the beauty of his son, with his already-wiry hair, chocolate brown eyes and latte-coloured skin. Ten perfect fingers, and ten perfect toes, all with the most incredible little nails. Lewis was perfect, and Chris couldn't find the words to say what it meant to him, to have created such a magnificent miracle with Tezzie.

Adie reached over and grabbed his hand, and gave it a quick squeeze. She winked at him, and he winked back, knowing that as mother in laws went, he couldn't have hit a better jackpot. She was warm, caring, gentle and wise, and he found himself once again counting the many blessings he now had, that he once never dreamed of having. He knew that whatever life threw at him and Tezzie, this family would be there to see them through it, and they'd rejoice in the good stuff too.

'Are you having a good night, Adie? Feen's right. It is your night, so I hope you're enjoying being the centre of attention. I know you're knackered but you might have to dig deep until the landslide of home-going commences. For what it's worth, I'm ready for bed myself, so I might get Lew, take him home and get him settled, and let Tezzie stay here for a bit if she wants to. I'm not usually a party-pooper but I'm whacked. Sorry to call it early.'

Adie nodded. 'Don't be! I'm not so old that I can't remember the early days of a new baby and never seeming to get enough sleep. You go, and get your head down. I'll tell Teresa, and she can make her own mind up about what she wants to do.' She leaned across and gave Chris a kiss on the cheek.

'Thanks for being here. I *have* had a wonderful night. And I think I have an hour or so left in the tank before I literally fall asleep on my feet.'

Feen smirked and grabbed hold of Adie's hands and pulled her up off the sofa. 'Best get you up on those feet then! As I said, it's your shight to nine, so you can do a twirl on the dance floor with me. Excuse us Chris, I have to try and keep Adie awake at her own party!'

Chris grinned and nodded. 'Take her away. I'm off to find Tez, and get my son home to bed. Goodnight, ladies.'

As he stood, Adie and Feen both gave him a hug, before dancing off into the crowd.

I can't believe how lucky I am. Two years ago, after Daisy died, I didn't think my life was worth living. Now, I'm in a place I once never imagined for myself, with my sister back in my life, with her husband and my nieces, another family to be a part of, and I've got my own kid. The best job I've ever had, a pretty decent house, and the chance to study to do a lot more in life.

Chris' life was a million miles away from what he once ever thought it could be, and while a lot of things weren't perfect, they were more than good enough. He and Tezzie still had much to figure out, but none of it was insurmountable, and he suddenly had the strong, unshakeable conviction that if he just stepped back from worrying about the little things that bothered him, life would continue to take him and his family exactly where it wanted them to go, and that would be more than okay.

Chapter Seventeen

'I thought I should haul you up, Adie, since you're in very real danger of falling asleep and Daddy appears to be too knackered to dance with you at your own birthday party! He did a great turn as Santa again though, didn't he?'

'He certainly did! And I think he was quite overcome by his own little present, at the end. Did you see that crystal clock? It was gorgeous. I hope he doesn't put it in the workshop. I'd quite like to look at it myself, and I think I have just the place for it, if he'll let me put it there.'

Feen laughed. 'I'm sure you do, and I'm sure he will! The giver of the clock is very pleased that it's he who received it.'

Adie rolled her eyes. 'I don't suppose I get to know who that was?'

'Adie! Shame on you for asking! Secret Santa shall remain exactly that. There's nothing to be gained by foiling the spun, or miluting the dystery. You'll have to keep wondering, just like *he* will.'

'Oh, you're no fun, sometimes!'

Feen smirked. 'Maybe not, but I'm not about to rain on the giver's parade. You should know me better than to ask me to.'

It was Adie's turn to smirk. 'I do know you better. I was just testing you. Even *you* can slip up at times. Rarely, but it does happen One of these days I'll catch you out over something. I'm just biding my time.'

'Bide away, my all beans. Gosh, you know, this year's crowd is even more interesting than usual. I think it musts be the mix of the Ceapot Tottage lot and your other friends, and the 'usual suspects,' as Daddy always calls them. I'm glad Bat and Parb tag along every year. I was talking to Parb earlier. Darren's mum. She's a nice woman, isn't she? She works part time in a centre that helps melocate rissing people, and she's an interior decorator as well. Bat's interesting too, very much involved in his local community down in Exeter. One of these days we'll have Don and Carloe, Debby's parents. That *will* be interesting, if it ever happens.'

'Yeah, I know Debby and Darren are heading down to Lytham to see them tomorrow for Boxing Day. Debby's sister Jayne is going over too, apparently. It's hard fitting everything in, over Christmas, especially when family is spread around, like hers is.'

'Are you having a lovely time though, Adie? Your special night – is it what you hoped it would be?'

Adie nodded, as she danced gently. 'It is. I can't believe how many people have made a special effort to come, tonight. I know we had everyone squashed in a bit, for Christmas lunch, but it would have been unthinkable for everyone not to have been here.'

'I agree. It's lovely to have so many family and good friends under one roof. I don't know when it will happen again. It's such a shame that Ruth, Gina, and Chiara are leaving first thing in the morning, though! I wish I had more time with Gina to go over the spring and summer jewellery designs and finalise the colourways. We have to do that via zoom call next week instead.'

Adie pulled a face. 'I know how annoying that is. But they promised to have New Year with Gina's family in Sorrento, and the day after tomorrow was the only time they could get flights. New Year seems to be a big thing in Italy. Gina always works hard not to miss it.'

Feen's face became serious, now. 'Trudie's not okay, is she?'

Adie shook her head. 'Nope. It's not my place to say what's wrong, but you can probably guess. She is going to need a lot of support in the coming months, Feen. She has some very big decisions to make. We must do everything we can, to help her.'

Feen nodded, sagely. 'We will, Adie. Daddy was taking to Kevin earlier, out in the hallway. It seemed a bit heavy, but as you say, it was their conversation to have. I don't prean to my, but if there is anything I can do to help, I hope you'll ask. For what it's worth, Trudie will be okay. She will have to battle through some choppy water, but this time next year, her life is going to be quite different. She will be happier.'

Well, without pushing any further, and finding out all that Feen can see or sense, I guess that has to be enough, for now. I don't want poor Trudie to have to battle through choppy water, but if she ends up happier at the other side of it then maybe it's worth it. And she will not be battling alone. I hope what I said to her earlier has helped. I'm here for her, every step of the way.'

She looked around now at her guests. Some were dancing, and a few were deep in conversation. Gina and Fiona were probably talking about fashion, because Fiona was a huge fan of Gina's designer clothing brand, Gin Gio. A while ago, Gina had sent Fiona some headgear made from factory offcuts, to cover her bald head while she went through her first round of chemotherapy and radiation, and it had developed into a lucrative line for GinGio, with a good portion of the profits going to cancer charities. Gina referred to Fiona as her 'muse' and Fiona was happy to be such an inspiration.

Some of the guests were still hovering around the edge of the buffet table, snaffling up the last of the food. It didn't look like there would be much in the way of leftovers this year, but Adie didn't mind. Some years, they couldn't get through it all before it went bad, and had to be thrown out. This year that didn't look like being a problem.

Her women friends were a lovely lot. People like Miranda, Peg, Trudie, Sheila, Fiona, Hazel, and Debby warmed her heart. They were good women, and it felt like a privilege to her, to be in their special circle. Carla too was a treasure, in her own prickly way. She, Ruth, and Debby were all over at the bar, chatting, and topping up their drinks. Ruth and Debby were trying not to laugh while Carla was talking to them, and Adie knew she was probably saying something sarcastic or self-deprecating, like she so often did.

Mark was standing in a group with Dave, Gavin, Billy, Tony, and Darren. They were all laughing and nodding their heads, and Adie guessed that they were probably talking about classic cars. Stan was cuddled up to Hazel, in a slow dance, and Darren's mum Barbara was dancing too, with Pat. Bob and Sheila were sitting holding hands at one end of the sofa, and Sheila had her head resting on Bob's shoulder, as he was trying not to fall asleep. Miranda and Max were on the sofa too, and Max actually *was* asleep, while she was murmuring quietly to Sheila. Stuart and Fiona were deep in conversation with 'Egg and Peric' Tripper. Teresa, Josie, and Wendy were in one corner, having a giggle about something (probably the consistency of baby poo and most women's inexplicable need to talk about it), and Marie and Matty were chatting to Trudie and Kevin, and Minty and Marcel. Adie wondered if Chris had asked Marcel anything about French mountains, and which ones would be the most interesting to climb.

The 'usual suspects' mingled among them all, and chatted to one another. Julie Evans, one of the farmer's wives, was talking too loudly about the fact that she wanted to wring their rooster's neck, at the same time as trying to drink what was probably her sixth or seventh glass of white wine. Hugh Garter, a longtime friend of Mark's, who had a farm adjacent to Bob's on the other side of the Torley Valley, was repeating himself a lot about the latest weather forecast, and what it meant for his parsnip harvest.

I am so blessed, to count these people as friends. I can't believe it's been eight years since I first turned up here, bewildered and suffering, and not knowing a single soul. The people here have all taken me to their hearts, and they've all earned a place in mine. Even the ones who are not here tonight; Fiona Frost, my lovely friend and florist, Cat Marshall from Cat's fish chippy, Maddie Murphy, my stalwart hairdresser, and other friends who never come to the Ravensdown Christmas party because of their own family commitments.

The first party here, eight years ago, was one of the best nights of my life, but this tops it. At that party, I had to contend with a spiteful, green-eyed (in more ways than one) Carla Walton and the stares of everyone who knew I was a stranger. Who could have known that night, that I'd end up calling this my home, and all of these people friends? I left that party walking on air, not even realising that I was already attracted to Mark, or that I'd come to love him, and Feen, and this place, and all these other people, so much.

This night, this culmination of so many milestones and so many wonderful friendships formed, is the new 'best night of my life.' I hope things never change. I wish we could stop the clock, right here and now, and let life be as good as this, for the rest of it. It doesn't get much better than this. I wonder what I ever did, to get to be this happy?

Mark looked over and caught her eye. He excused himself and came over to her.

'What yer doin' on yer tod, lass? 'As every bugger deserted yer?'

She laughed, 'No. They're just being party animals in their own way. I was just thanking my lucky stars again, for how wonderful my life is. And, as much as I hate to admit it, I feel sixty, tonight. I'm thinking about my bed. I know I shouldn't be, but ...'

'Well, yer've 'ad a full-on day, cookin' Christmas lunch fer't family and then again tonight, getting' prepared fer't party. Yer've not 'ad a minute to breathe, lass. I know you're probably buggered, and I don't think any folk'll blame yer fer bailin' early. But just before yer do, can yer come outside wi' me fer a minute?'

She gaped at him. 'What, *now?* It's really late, darling, and it's pitch dark outside, and freezing cold. What do you want to go out there for? If it's a bit of slap and tickle you're after...'

He grinned at her. 'Well, I wouldn't turn owt down, if it were bein' offered, but no, love. There's summat out there I want yer to see.'

She shrugged at him, in resignation. 'Well, alright then. If that's what you want.'

She allowed him to lead her by the hand, over to the door and through it. As they went, Feen stepped back to allow them to pass, and she winked at Mark. Mystified, Adie allowed herself to be led to the front door, and just before Mark opened it, he cleared his throat and said, in a low voice,

'I were goin' to wait till mornin, but I 'ad a rethink earlier, an' I think yer should 'ave a first look at it tonight.'

Mark then opened the door, and escorted Adie around the side of the house to the parking bay at the side, which couldn't be seen from the front door. She was amazed to see that the bay had been lit by hired floodlights. And under the floodlights, with a huge gold bow wrapped around it, was a brand-new, sleek, and utterly beautiful white Mercedes sports car.

Adie gasped. She was lost for words.

''Appy birthday, lass. She's like you; classy, elegant, and powerful. She's not as beautiful, mind, but yer do need to shine a *bit* brighter than she does, as the owner-driver.'

Adie fought back tears of shock and disbelief. She and Mark had seen the ads on the TV for the Mercedes, and she'd remarked more than once how gorgeous she thought it was. But never in a million years did she ever think she'd get to have one of her own!

'It's the second-generation Mercedes-AMG GT Coupé. This is the two-door V8 version, with plug-in hybrid powertrains, and you've got all-wheel drive as standard, active rear-axle steering, and AMG active ride control suspension.'

Gavin spoke from behind her, and she laughed.

'None of that makes any sense to me tonight but thank you for the description. My God, I don't believe this! It's the car of my dreams!'

Miranda stepped forward and grinned. 'Sorry, darling. It already has a few hundred miles on the clock. I collected it for Mark and drove it up from London. Max followed me.'

'Well, I'm not at *all* worried about a few hundred miles, for heaven's sake! It couldn't have been in better hands, Mand, but my God! Mark!'

Adie couldn't find any more words. She gave in to her tears instead, and when she turned to look back into the hallway of Ravensdown house, she was amazed to see that all of her friends were standing behind her, beaming from ear to ear. Miranda put a glass of bubbly in her hand, and everyone cheered as Mark stepped outside, looked inward, and raised a glass in a toast.

'To Adie. It's all been said, already, but this is a fittin' gift for a woman who deserves the best of everythin'. Once again, love; 'appy birthday. 'Appen yer'll need these.'

He placed a pair of carbon-look key fobs, with the AMG logo on the front, in her hand.

'But no spinnin't wheels tonight. Yer under the influence! We can take 'er fer a strop in't mornin.'

He pulled her into a bearhug, and held her close. Overwhelmed, she just stood and let him hold her.

'Are y'appy, lass?' His voice was soft, in her ear.

'Yes,' she sobbed. 'I've never been happier. I don't know if it's even possible to *be* any happier than this.'

'Well, that's okay then. Let's get back inside, before we all catch we're death o' bloody cold. I think it's time fer a few 'ot coffees or summat sustainin', before every bugger starts thinkin' about 'ittin' the road fer 'ome.'

I love how he protects me, and the family, and everyone he cares about. If this is my life, here with this man, I'm more than happy to take it. I wouldn't change a thing.

Part II

Chapter Eighteen

When Adie got off the train and made her way to the entrance to Euston station, she couldn't see her friends. It occurred to her that they hadn't actually arranged how to meet when she arrived! That had been an oversight, and so she wasn't sure if Mand or Max (or both) would be standing waiting, or sitting in a car across the street or around the corner.

Luckily, she didn't have to worry. As she looked around her, she heard Miranda's voice behind her; 'Good God! Adie Raven, you must be as blind as a bat!'

She spun around, and gaped. Miranda was standing in front of her, but she looked like a completely different woman!

'Oh, my Lord! Did I just walk straight past you? I did, didn't I? Why didn't you tell me you'd gone grey?'

Miranda laughed, as she ran her hand through her newly-styled hair. Her jet black, lovely locks which for decades had been long and always put up in a messy bun or secured with a jewelled clasp, were gone. In their place was a light and swishy, steel grey jaw-length bob, expensively done, with platinum highlights that gave it the most glorious texture and light. She looked beautiful, but Adie hadn't been prepared for such a radical transformation. She'd literally walked straight past her oldest and dearest friend without recognising her!

'You did just ignore me, but I forgive you,' Miranda laughed, as she threw her arms around Adie and hugged her tightly. 'My overhaul appears to have been successful!'

'My God, Mand! The hair is *gorgeous!* You look *stunning!* Unrecognisable, but not in a bad way at all! What on earth's made you decide to do it?'

Her friend gave an elegant shrug, and an equally elegant wave of her perfectly manicured hand. 'It needed to be done, darling. I was getting bloody fed up with dyeing it every five minutes! When the menopause started, it went so thin and lank, like yours did before you had it all cut off. I was in a never-ending battle trying to keep it looking even halfway decent! Then I had to wear a grey wig for a play I did recently – just a short stint in a local theatre, for a fortnight – and I felt kind of comfortable with the look. It was literally a case of waking up one morning, taking a *decent* look at myself in the mirror for once, and deciding that enough was enough.' She pulled a face that made Adie laugh.

'I was *horrified,* Adie! Utterly appalled! I looked like mutton dressed as bloody lamb, and I realised it was time to bow to the inevitable and admit it. 'That's it', I told myself. 'I'm giving up the fight.' And here I am darling, all grey, and hopefully now just decent-looking mutton.'

'Well, I think it's *incredible!* You know, in some weird way, it actually makes you look a bit younger. Your face looks fresher, I think.'

Miranda grinned. 'That's what Max says. You *both* know how to say the right things, don't you? But he likes it, and I'm getting used to it, so I think I've done the right thing. It's meant that I've had to tone down my make-up a lot, but I went to see the most amazing style consultant, and she gave me a few pointers. She gave me a proper talking to, about looking like a plastered clown. I struggled, not to be mortally offended, but she was right. And it was a ridiculously expensive exercise too because it more or less meant a whole new wardrobe, with her in tow as personal shopper. But I have to admit, it was worth every penny. She was worth her weight in gold, as it turns out, and I'm pretty happy with the result.'

'And you should be! You look fab, and I love the softer make-up. Your foundation is perfect and flawless, and that pinky lipstick, lilac and silvery-beige eye-shadow combo, and the gorgeous soft eyeliner; it's all just perfect for you.'

Miranda nodded. 'It does feel a little gentler. It was time to leave the harsher stuff behind, Adie. It really only belonged on the stage, but somehow, I never quite ditched it for the real world. I *had* started feeling a bit like a 'painted lady,' and it *was* beginning to get on my nerves. I found myself craving to *simplify* things, I suppose, including the time it took to get ready to go out anywhere and feel halfway decent when I did. Something had to be done, and so it was.'

'But my goodness, Mand! Going grey? It must take a lot of courage, to make that decision, especially when you've been in the spotlight – *literally* – for most of your life!'

'Well, there are wigs darling, for stage work.'

'Yes, of course there are! I'm still on the fence about letting the grey come through, for myself,' Adie confessed. 'I do have a great hairdresser; Maddie Murphy at Torley Tresses. She works wonders with me, but I know how you feel. It's like I'm down at the salon more and more these days, trying to keep it looking nice. Maybe I'll take a leaf out of your book and go grey gracefully.'

I just have to talk myself into it, that's all...

'So, what's the plan? Where's Max?'

'Cruising the neighbourhood, keeping an eye out for a parking spot or to see us, whichever comes first.' Miranda shook her head. 'This place is a zoo. Come on, let's get to the road and find him, or let him find us, and we can head on over to The Ritz. They can get a bit funny if people show up late. I'm glad your train was on time.'

'*I'm* glad you told me about the dress code! I was going to wear my usual jeans, jumper, and loafers for the journey, but when you said we were coming straight here, and they expected the men to wear a jacket and tie even just for afternoon tea, I thought I'd better spruce myself up a bit! I hope this dress is okay?'

Adie looked down at her maroon cashmere wrap-dress with black satin edging. It was a limited-edition designer piece; a Christmas gift last year from her daughter-in-law Gina Giordano, from her GinGio winter collection. It flattered her figure and gave her something of a waist. She'd teamed it with a black Burberry trench coat and a pair of mid-heeled black patent knee-high boots for today. It wasn't quite in the same league as Miranda's stunning, heavy silk Dolce and

Gabbana trouser suit, in the most incredible shade of purple, but she hoped it would pass muster.

'Darling, you look fabulous! That's a GinGio dress, isn't it? So pretty, and so perfect for you.'

She looked up as a horn tooted, and Max glided his sleek grey Maserati Quattroporte GT to a stop next to her and Miranda. Within seconds they were in the car, with Adie's suitcase next to her on the back seat, and pulling away from the kerb.

'Hey, Adie! Nice to see you, and you look lovely. That dark red colour really suits you.' Max caught her eye in the rearview mirror and gave her a wink. She grinned back at him.

'Good to see you too Max, and thanks. Gosh, this is a treat, isn't it? Afternoon tea at the Ritz? I've never been there before. I'm really excited.'

He rolled his eyes. 'Personally, I think it's a bit bloody pretentious. But it's Madame's choice today, so us lowly plebs will just have to tough it out. I do hate ties, you know. They drive me crazy.'

Adie laughed. 'Mark hates them too; in fact, I think most men do. But it's only for an hour or so, right?'

He nodded. 'Right, and I think I can just about manage that.'

He then turned his attention to the hair-raising process of driving through London traffic. When they arrived at the hotel, the valet took charge of the car, and they all went inside.

The Ritz was stunning. Adie caught her breath as she looked around at the gorgeous big dining room with its marble columns, mirrors, gold fixtures and fittings and elegant palms. It was ornate and opulent in the extreme, and she felt a small thrill, at the thought that she, who'd grown up in a decidedly working-class family who'd never had much more than two pennies to rub together, had made it to the Ritz in London! That felt like something. She turned now, to her best and dearest, oldest friend, and spoke in a hush.

'Mand, this is incredibly generous of you, to invite me here for this. I've never seen *anything* like this place. It's something you hear about, where the 'posh' people go, and you never really think you'd have the chance to go there yourself. Gosh, we've come a long way, haven't we, since we were kids? I never imagined, back then, that we'd be doing something like this now. It's amazing, being here. Quite unbelievable, really.'

Miranda smiled, and she had a twinkle in her eye. She dismissed Adie's thanks, with an airy wave of her hand. Her fuchsia pink fingernails cut a fabulous flash of colour.

'Max is right. It is *thoroughly* pretentious, and ostentatious and every other 'acious' you can think of, but what the hell! You only live once, and it's been on my list of things to do for ages, just to be able to say I've done it. I've lived in London for forty years, and I never made it here, so I decided it was time. And who better to be all 'acious' with than my bestest-ever friend? I wouldn't dream of doing this *without* you, darling!'

Max grinned. 'It was you coming to visit that gave her the idea in the first place. Her birthday isn't for another fortnight, but this felt like too good a chance to pass up, to do it with you. When she suggested it, I was all for it. Ridiculously expensive for a plate of silly little sandwiches and another of cake, for Christ's sake, but there *are* twenty-odd teas to choose from! We must look at the positives!'

Miranda smiled broadly. 'Shut up, Max. Stop being the bean counter, will you, just for today?'

Max held up his hands and shrugged. 'Far be it for me to moan about what you spend your money on, sweetness. It's probably worth every penny, actually. You can't put a price on memories and good fun like this, can you?' He winked at Adie again. 'Miranda is footing the bill for the afternoon teas, but I'm treating us all to the bubbly. It's only half a million pounds a bottle, so quite cheap by comparison.'

Adie was completely stuck about which tea to order. She thought Max had been joking when he'd said that there were twenty to pick from. In the end, she settled for simple Earl Grey with a slice of lemon.

Max was great company. He regaled her with stories about his time as a hedge-fund manager, while Miranda rolled her eyes, and he talked about his new project helping to establish a new golf course in Fiji. His son was involved in different areas of expansion for tourism, and Max was getting in on the action.

'It's not a huge thing for me; just a bit of a dalliance, really, but Tim needs a bit of support. It's also a daddy-sonny bonding thing, I suppose. A bit of fun, and I get to go out there when it opens, and schmooze with the local dignitaries while someone cuts the ribbon.'

'That does sound like fun,' Adie admitted. Fiji sounded exotic and far away. She said as much, but Miranda didn't seem all that keen on the idea of going with Max.

'I'll only go if I can be left alone to lie by a pool at a decent hotel somewhere. I'm not interested in traipsing around a putting green with a bunch of sweaty men, and risking being hit in the head by a golf ball. If I want a concussion, I don't have to fly halfway around the world for one.'

'No,' Adie giggled. 'All you have to do is fall off a stage somewhere in the city, hit your head, and end up in hospital.'

'Precisely, and I don't intend to do *that* again either. Once was enough, and I *did* hit my head, and I *did* end up in hospital! The newspapers had a field day with that one, didn't they? Pissed-up leading lady lands in the theatrical equivalent of a mosh pit. But that experience taught me to watch my step. That, and no more vodka martinis before getting up and treading the boards!'

'I would have said that you're the *last* person who needs 'Dutch courage.' You nail your part, every time.'

'Adie, trust me – some nights it's bloody hard to get up there, especially when what goes on in your personal life won't allow itself to be put in a box for the night. When that incident happened, I'd just lost my dad to cancer, and the boyfriend of the moment had dumped me because he'd been shagging someone else on the side and the silly cow had gone and got herself pregnant. I wasn't in a great place, to be playing a convincing dramatic heroine.'

Adie grimaced, remembering. Miranda had been in a pretty *bad* place. Her dad dying had been a terrible time, and not just for Miranda herself. Reg Quirk had been a delightful man, and his loss had been keenly felt by all who knew him. Adie had loved him very much. And as for the 'boyfriend of the moment,' he'd been twenty years Miranda's junior, and lacking the maturity to understand that a 'cougar' like Miranda needed to be let down gently. She used to love running with her toyboys, but she never quite managed to take it on the chin quite as bravely as she'd have liked, when they inevitably saw a younger piece of skirt they liked the look of, and raced off after that instead.

For all her 'in-your-face' bluster and bravado, Miranda had always been chronically insecure about many things. Ageing and being left alone were just two.

When Maxwell Kennedy ('the Third') had arrived on the scene, Miranda had reached a time in her life when she knew her time was running out for indulging herself with men who were half her age. She was losing her allure, and she knew it. She'd quickly realised that Max was the one man who could help her overcome her insecurities and take a chance on love.

Accepting his marriage proposal had been the biggest decision of her life, but it had turned out to be the best. She'd been afraid that Max would try to change her; that he wouldn't be happy with who she was, because on some level she didn't think she was worthy of *anyone* mature and serious, let alone *him!* But he let her be exactly who she wanted to be, and he adored her for it. They were the quintessential devoted couple, and it would be hard to find another as happy. Adie was thrilled for her best friend, that she finally had what she deserved – a lasting love with a thoroughly decent man.

Afternoon tea was gorgeous in the extreme, with melt-in-the-mouth sandwiches, exquisite cakes, and a rather excellent champagne – and the service wasn't obsequious at all! There was nothing pretentious about it, in the end. It was simply a delightful, memorable experience that Adie was thrilled to have, with the adorable, effervescent Miranda and her sweet, generous husband.

A couple of hours later, they arrived at Max and Miranda's new home in Stoke d'Abernon. Miranda showed Adie to a gorgeous guest room and then gave her the 'grand tour' of everything, and told her to treat the place as her own. Adie wanted to yelp with delight, at how amazing the house was. Miranda's kitchen was like something out of a magazine, with every conceivable mod-con, and yet it managed to look traditional, in keeping with the age of the house. She said as much, and Miranda nodded.

'The previous owners lived here for twenty-three years, and they gutted it and refurbished a lot of it, over that time. They planned to stay for probably another twenty or more but then the marriage broke, and other things happened, so the place got put on the market. We were lucky because we found out about it before it became common knowledge. Max has a few friends in good places, and we got a quiet tip-off. Paid the asking price – stupendous, to be honest, and I'm still actually feeling so guilty about it that I can't even utter the amount we paid, but let's just say that it was more than halfway to eight figures, and leave it at that.'

'I wasn't going to ask,' Adie murmured, grinning. 'And for God's sake, woman, if anyone has earned the right to something this nice, it's *you*, so stop feeling guilty, right bloody now! And that's an order!'

Miranda rolled her eyes and gave Adie a mock salute. 'Right-you-are then, sergeant.'

Mand's rich and successful but by God has she earned it! She has worked her arse off, for decades. Max has done well too, and they're such nice people, genuine and unaffected by their wealth. Why would anyone begrudge them what they have? But, oh, to have that kind of money!

'Come on, there's a couple of vodka martinis waiting for us in the conservatory. Max put them out, before he left to go and spend a couple of hours with Tim, going over the plans for this Fijian golf course. They've got the bit between their teeth, and Tim's wanting to crack on. Max will be home about half past seven, with a Chinese takeaway dinner from the very excellent place we've found in Cobham. So, we have a few hours to relax and unwind and catch up before he comes back. There'll be plenty of time for you to have a nap, swim, soak, or sauna if you want one.'

'Oh, I definitely want to do *all* of those things while I'm here, and maybe have a game or two of tennis with Max, if he's up for it, but not right now. All I want, for now, is to have that vodka tonic and sit and catch up on everything we haven't talked about lately.'

Miranda grinned at her. 'That was the right answer, and if you want a bit of extra joy, you'll meet the puppies later. Luna and Shadow. We've finally got them housetrained, so they're fit to go visiting, and Max has taken them with him to Tim's place, for a puppy playdate with his family's dog.'

Settled in the lovely big Victorian conservatory, with its ornate embellishments, black and white tiled floor and gleaming glass, Adie felt like she'd stepped back in time.

'You and Max have done well, with this place. It's totally gorgeous. You seem happy, Mand. Are you? Is married life what you hoped it would be?'

Miranda nodded. 'I am, and it is. Mostly. Obviously, getting married for the first time in my fifties has been an eye opener. I didn't know how set in my own ways I'd actually got, until I had to start compromising! That's been a challenge, in more ways than one. But it's good to shift your focus, I think, otherwise we all just become self-absorbed and unable to see or appreciate another's perspective, don't we? I was heading that way, and it took marrying Max to wake me up to the fact.'

'Not too many hiccups, then?'

'No, not too many. Nothing earth-shattering, and Max is gorgeous, but he's a slow burn, if you know what I mean? And, after decades of roaring passion with the twentysomethings, taking things at a slower pace has been a big adjustment for me.'

'You mean the sex? It's slower with Max? I suppose it's to be expected though? At our age it starts all becoming more about comfort and companionship than fireworks, doesn't it?'

Miranda pulled an easy-osey face. 'I suppose so. I didn't really feel quite ready to say goodbye to the fireworks, though. I do miss that, if I'm honest, but not enough to want to go back to it being all about that and nothing else. Am I making sense?'

Adie laughed. 'You totally are. What you're saying is that you'd just like a bit more of a balance. A bit of passion, to counteract the slightly more sedentary approach.'

'Yes. And I suppose I should talk to him about it, shouldn't I?'

'Yeah, of course you should! I'm surprised you haven't already! He'd want to know, Mand, if you weren't entirely happy. What's stopping you from saying anything?'

'That's a very good question. I dunno, Adie. Not wanting to seem ungrateful, maybe? I mean, look at all this!' Miranda gestured around at the house and garden. 'I couldn't have achieved all this on my own, could I? I'm wealthy enough, in my own right, but this would've been a stretch too far, by myself. I wouldn't have *wanted* it, if it was just me, on my own. This place is far too big for one person. In fact, it's almost too big for the two of us! Thank God for the dogs, who'll fill it up a bit more.' She shrugged gently.

'But all my dreams have come true, Adie, and it's mostly because of Max, and I adore him for that and everything else he is and does. I don't know; somehow, in the face of everything else being wonderful, the sex thing feels a bit nitpicky.'

'But if you're not fulfilled in that way, you do need to talk about it. Sex is a big part of a marriage, especially a newish one like yours,' Adie offered.

Miranda shook her head. 'It's not that I'm unfulfilled, darling. Far from it. I never have any complaints about the end result. It's always lovely, but it's kind of 'snuggly,' for want of a better term. I just miss the 'big bang,' so to speak. That's what I meant about compromise. I've had to adjust my expectations, and I guess I wasn't expecting *that*. I don't know *what* I expected, really. But Max is an amazing human being, and I know I can't have everything. So cosy, 'snuggly' sex is a compromise.' She thought for a moment, and bit her bottom lip. 'But it's okay to be a teeny bit wistful about how it used to be, isn't it?'

'Yes, of course it is! Just as long as it really *is* a compromise you're happy to make, and you're not spending all your time trying to *convince* yourself that it is.'

'No, I don't think it's an allowance too far. I'm grateful that he wants to do it at *all*, sometimes, when I look at what I'm turning into. Post-menopausal hair sprouting in weird places, and lumps and bumps where I once thought I'd never have them! Going soft in the middle in spite of all the Pilates and swimming. We really did get the short end of the stick didn't we, as women? It never ends, does it, the hormonal stuff?'

Adie shook her head. 'Nope, it never seems to. I'm more or less through it now, although I do get the odd symptom, still. What I'm left with is stuff like dryness. I never thought I'd be buying KY when I was pushing sixty!'

She laughed when Miranda's grin widened. 'So, it's all still good with Mark, then?'

Adie felt herself blushing. 'It's *great,* with Mark! And, before you ask, yes there are a few fireworks, but only now and then. It's snuggly at times, and sometimes it's just plain hilarious, when he gets impatient with his own lack of performance and starts effing and blinding and gnashing his teeth. He's such a scream when he gets into a tizzy. Then things go from bad to worse in the 'rising' capability, and it makes him even worse. The giggles take over, and we have to abandon the idea.'

'Good, God! How often does *that* happen?'

'Oh, not often at all. It's been, like, three times in the last two years or something. Not enough to be of concern, except to him of course, and I don't think it's going to get any worse.

At least I hope it isn't! I'm nowhere near ready to let that ship sail off for good, even though I usually need half a gallon of lube to get going. No, we're definitely on the same page about the importance of intimacy.'

She took a swig of her vodka martini and continued, 'But everything started drying up when the menopause kicked in, even the skin on my face and body, and my moisture levels have never come right since. It's bizarre, but it is what it is. I am a walking Sahara! That is something *I've* had to learn to accept.'

'Well, thank God for KY and moisturiser in general,' Miranda remarked wryly.

'Amen to that. I've found a great moisturiser, actually, that I can use on my face and body. It doesn't cost a fortune, and it doesn't over-promise what it delivers. And God love the expert pedicurists that have the ability to turn crusty lumps of dinosaur scales back into decent looking feet! Let's drink a toast, to our lovely, love-filled sex lives, that we never imagined, years ago, we'd still be having in our sixties.'

Miranda lifted her glass. 'Yes indeed, and cheers to a lot more of the sex. You know, darling, I remember being young enough to be utterly horrified at the idea of *anyone* having sex in their sixties. I once thought that was nothing short of obscene! The fact that I still want to have it myself, with someone who *actually* wants to have it with *me*, is a miracle and a half.'

'Oh, Mand! You're still completely gorgeous and you know it. Yes, okay we're past our best, but so are our men, and I think we're all just grateful that we've found happiness with one another. Not a lot of people get a decent bite at that apple, do they? Especially not a second time around, like me and Mark.'

'That's true, and I remember how worried you were, about your wedding night. I always thought it was a bit bonkers to 'wait' at your age, for God's sake, but it worked out okay for you both. I can't imagine what would have happened if it had been an utter disaster or a crushing disappointment. Luckily, it wasn't.'

'Yeah, I didn't have to be nervous at all, in the end. We were up at the Tor, and it just kind of happened. There was no big preparation, like closing the door and getting into bed, cringeing, and hoping for the best. It all just happened very naturally, and it's been that way ever since.'

'Ooh! I have some juicy gossip for you, Adie! Do you remember Rhonda Evans, the woman who used to come along to our big girly lunches sometimes, back in the day?'

Adie searched back through her memory. 'Oh, you mean the Welsh woman? The tall, blonde one with an obsession with black poodles, of all weird things?'

Miranda laughed. 'Yes, that's the one. She had three, at the time, so Lord knows how many now! Well, she's just run off with someone else's long-term partner. And you'll never guess whose.' She leaned forward conspiratorially, and grinned naughtily.

'Ok, put me out of my misery. Whose?'

'Penni Pickett's.'

Adie gaped at her. 'What? *Simeon?* She's hooked up with Simeon? *Penni's* Simeon?'

'Yes, the very same.' Miranda was laughing with glee now, at their old friend, who had turned out to be no friend at all, in fact. Miranda thought that Penni losing her man to another woman was hilarious.

'But Simeon and Penni were together for *years.* More than a decade, wasn't it?'

'Something like that,' Miranda nodded. 'They were engaged but he would never agree to marry her.'

'I've never seen the point of getting engaged if you're not going to go ahead and get married,' Adie observed.

'Quite. And rumour has it, among the ever-growing hordes who have decided *they* don't like her either, that she pushed him into getting engaged, and he agreed – to keep her off his back about it – but he never had any *intention* of marrying her. She liked to tell people she was engaged so she could show the evidence that someone actually wanted her. Except that he doesn't, anymore.'

'Doesn't he have Asperger's or something?'

'Yes, he's on the spectrum with *something,* I think, and I know Penni used to get very frustrated with him. She banged on about it for years after he was diagnosed, if you remember? She trotted that out as the reason for everything that wasn't going the way she wanted it to, in the relationship.'

'I've been cheated on myself, as you know, and I'd never normally wish it on another woman, but …' Adie trailed off, unsure how to finish her sentence.

'But that bitch deserves it?' Miranda offered.

Adie nodded, slowly. 'Well, I hate to say it, but she kind of does. She never had any patience with Simeon, and was always making excuses about one thing or another that happened to her, or to them both. Everything was always his fault, as I recall.'

Miranda barked a laugh. 'Everything was always *someone* else's fault, according to her, and I think poor old Simeon just ended up sick to death of being her handy little scapegoat.'

'Well, she treated him very poorly. I do know that. No wonder he took a better offer.'

'The funny thing is that she's apparently reinvented herself yet again. She's a relationship coach, now. Boom-boom-tish.'

Adie collapsed with laughter. 'Oh, my God, how ironic is that? She doesn't know the first *thing* about how to help someone else in a relationship! She can't even keep one of her own!'

'The woman has no idea how to even *listen* properly, let alone offer any constructive support. She has enough knowledge to be absolutely bloody dangerous, and that's the sum total of it.'

'Maybe she'll learn from this,' Adie mused, half to herself, and Miranda snorted.

'Of *course* she won't. The idiot's a lost cause, darling. I think Nincompoop is still hanging in there with her; not that she was much better. Neither one of them has a loyalty gene to split between them. They probably stick together because nobody else wants them.'

'Well, I'm not sure that's true,' Adie countered. 'Nincompoop, as you love to call her, just wants everyone to like her, and she won't rock a boat to save herself, but I don't think she's vindictive, or short of friends.'

'She's just too superficial, Adie. Too wishy-washy, and you don't need *anyone* in your life who still hangs around with people who hurt you, and doesn't stand up for you instead. They don't qualify as having earned your friendship or loyalty if they can't show enough of their own.'

Adie nodded, and sighed. 'It's all in the past, now. I don't really think about either of them anymore, until someone else mentions them, and you're probably the only person I still see from that old crowd. I heard on the grapevine somewhere that Nincompoop became a grandmother, which is nice for her, but I don't miss being in her orbit.'

'She was a wimp, and Pickitt was a ruthless bitch who fully deserved to lose the lovely Simeon. I hope he'll be happy with Rhonda. Put it this way, I don't think he'll be any *worse* off. At least he'll be getting a decent shag, now!' Miranda crunched her olive and grinned.

'You're terrible!' Adie giggled.

Trust Miranda, to always tell something the way she saw it, and her perspective was always funny, and usually very true. Penni Pickitt was insufferable, and probably no picnic to live with. Evidently, the long-suffering Simeon had had enough, and jumped to a better-looking ship. Adie was happy for him, and hoped that at least now the man might be with someone who actually appreciated and loved him. Pickitt was only really capable of loving herself.

A couple of hours later, after she and Miranda had indulged themselves with a swim and a sauna, then a hot shower and another lovely vodka tonic, Max arrived back with the promised Chinese takeaway.

The next few days passed quietly, with plenty of time for catching up and relaxing, and Adie enjoyed a couple of trips out, to the beautiful Painshill Park, shopping and a visit to the Brooklands Museum in nearby Weybridge. They also went out for dinner, a couple of times. She'd had a lovely bit of time in between, with Matty and Marie, and her sweet granddaughters. It was great that they'd managed to move their chronically busy schedules around, to spend some quality time with her.

When it came time to get the train home, she was ready, but she was grateful for having seen her son and his family, and for having such a lovely, gentle, relaxing time with Miranda and Max. They'd waved her off from Cobham train station with a bag full of lovely home-made sandwiches and cake, and a flask of coffee, and a promise to catch up again soon.

*   *   *   *   *

As she got off the train in Carlisle and made her way to the station entrance, Adie checked her watch, only to find that it had stopped.

Damn! That's annoying! I guess the battery went flat! Might've been nice to have some warning, but hey ho. Maybe we can stop by a jeweller after Mark picks me up, so we can get a new one put in.

Outside, there was no sight of Mark's Range Rover. She was surprised, because he was normally always ahead of time to pick her up or meet her somewhere. He prided himself on his punctuality, but he'd probably got stuck in traffic somewhere, and was running a few minutes late. He would no doubt be cursing, and worried about leaving Adie stuck on a street corner, wondering where he was.

She hoped he wouldn't be much longer. It had been a whirlwind trip, to see her friends and family, and she'd really enjoyed it, but all she wanted now was to get home and put her feet up and have a good hot cup of tea.

201

She wondered if Mark had messaged to say he was running late, and she fished around in her handbag for her mobile phone. When she opened it, she was astonished – and immediately terrified – to see seventeen missed calls, all from Feen. Nothing from Mark, but seventeen calls from Feen, all within the last two hours.

There was only one text: also from Feen.

FFS ADIE, CALL ME!

Shaky now, and scared, Adie called her. Feen pounced on the call on the first ring.

'Adie, thank God! Why haven't you been answering your fucking phone?'

Adie caught her breath at Feen's demanding, terse, and abusive tone. The younger woman had never spoken to her in such a way, and it left her feeling unsure of how to respond.

'Er... umm… I think I must've knocked it onto silent, and the reception probably wasn't great on the train either. Why? What's happened? Is Mark all right?'

'No, he isn't. If you're at the station, stay there. Gavin is coming to get you. Daddy has had a very ad baccident. His combine ran over him and crushed him this morning. He's lighting for his fife. We're at the hospital now. Gavin will come and get you and bring you here.'

Adie's blood ran cold. Mark? Again? Another farm accident? *Again?* Her mind scrabbled to make sense of it.

'No, tell him to stay put, with you. I'll get a taxi. It'll be faster.'

'Whatever. See you when you get here. We're in the ICU.'

With that, Feen abruptly hung up.

White noise descended and enveloped Adie like a hostile fog. Feen hadn't given her anything more than the bare bones of what had happened, but the rage in her voice indicated how panicked and upset she was.

Frantic, she managed to find a taxi and set off for Cumbria infirmary. Mercifully, it was only a ten-minute drive, but the minutes were the longest of her life.

When she got to the ICU, Feen and Gavin were pacing the floor. Feen saw Adie first, and she flew at her.

'There you are! My God, Adie, I've been trying to reach you for hours! You bastards and your BLOODY phones!'

Her voice was shrill, and Adie could see that she was trying hard to keep her fear in check, and not doing the best job of it. Bewildered, she looked to Gavin, and he took up the narrative.

'Mark's been very badly hurt by his combine, Adie. He's being operated on now. They were very keen for you to get here. He's having lots of surgery. It seems very serious. They said someone will come and talk to us as soon as they have any news. He was out in the field in the combine. Feen tried to ring him, to tell him that someone had turned up at Ravensdown wanting to see him, but he wasn't answering his phone. She had a bad feeling, so I went to find him, and...'

His voice trailed off. Clearly, he didn't know how to describe what happened next, but Adie pressed him.

'Tell me. Gavin, please. Tell me. I need to know.'

He wiped a hand across his face. He looked weary, and defeated, and his voice was deadpan.

'The combine was running but it wasn't moving, and he wasn't in it. I ran up to it and saw him on the ground. He wasn't conscious. At first glance, I thought he was dead. As soon as I realised he wasn't, I called 999 and they sent a chopper.' Gavin's voice broke, at that point, and he swallowed hard. He wasn't able to say anything more.

Feen stepped up beside him now. 'It seems that the machine ran him over. We don't know why he wasn't in it. All I can think is that he got out for some reason, and it moved. We've really no idea what happened, or how. When he wakes up, hopefully he can tell us more.'

'I'm sorry I didn't pick up the phone! I checked the settings, after I called you. It was on silent. That's not something I did, or would *ever* consciously do. All I can think is I must've bumped it, somehow. It never rang once, that I heard or felt, and the trains are notorious for intermittent reception. It never even occurred to me, to check it.'

Feen said nothing, but she looked away, with her lips compressed into a thin line.

Gavin found his voice again and shook his head. 'Adie, it's okay. It's just one of those things. It happens all the time. It wasn't your fault.' He glanced over at Feen, and lowered his voice. 'It's just really hard to handle, when the person you're frantic to speak to doesn't pick up the phone, even after a dozen calls.'

Adie nodded. She felt cold and shivery, as she fought back tears of panic. 'I'm so sorry, to both of you. I'd never let you down on purpose, about anything, ever, at all. I hope you both know that.' She looked over Gavin's shoulder at the door to the ICU. 'Will they let *me* in, do you think?'

He grimaced. 'I doubt it. He's still in surgery, and I suppose they'll want a full picture of where he's at before they have to deal with any of us. But they wanted you here, so I guess there's no harm in asking.'

Adie rang the bell at the door. A nurse arrived and told her that she, Feen, and Gavin would all be advised as soon as there was something to report. Mark was, apparently, still being operated on, and there was a lot to repair. It was going to be some time before they could say much at all about his condition. His body had taken a massive trauma, and they were still trying to establish the extent of it. The nurse spoke quietly but with good authority, and Adie was comforted a little, by her tone and sense of purpose. Mark was in the best possible hands, and once they had determined the extent of his injuries, and repaired what they could, they would be able to talk more about next steps.

All she could do now was wait.

'Where are the twins?'

Alder and Willow were not here at the hospital with Gavin and Feen. Adie was glad about that. They were sensitive children, and the fraught circumstances here would probably have bewildered them. Feen was like a cat on a hot tin roof, and they' have picked up on that, and they'd have been worried and upset.

'They're with Josie and Tony. I dropped them off on my way through. Feen came here in the chopper with Mark.'

Adie was relieved that her grandchildren were with the Valleys. Josie and Tony were close friends, in fact Josie was Feen's *best* friend, and had been since their school days. Alder and Willow couldn't be in a better place right now than with the couple, and their two daughters, Nelle and Erin.

Feen spoke quietly. 'Darla and Cave will go and get them at dinner time and take them back to theirs for the night. I don't expect we'll be going home any time soon. I don't plan to, anyway.'

'That will be good for them,' Adie offered. 'A bit of normality, and stability.'

Gavin nodded. 'Yeah, that's what we thought. Mum took her van down to Preston this morning, on a furniture buying trip. Some auction, or other. I couldn't get hold of her for ages either, but she's coming back soon. The kids often spend a night with her and Dave, and I think it's important for them to have as normal a routine as possible for now, because we don't know what's going to change for them, or for *any* of us really, with all this.'

Gavin ran his hands through his hair. He looked as if he was about to burst into tears. Feen was trying very hard not to give into panicked hysteria, and Adie simply felt numb.

It was far too soon to speculate about what had happened, or what it meant for Mark and the family. Feen was saying nothing about what she might have felt or sensed, either before the accident or after it. Adie tried to concentrate on the fact that they'd been here before, and they'd come through it intact. Mark's last accident, when he'd fell through the rotten mezzanine floor in the barn and torn his liver and fractured his neck, had been the catalyst for them declaring their love and building a life together. He'd recovered, and although he had to take things easier than he had before it had happened, he was still in pretty good shape for his age. The farm kept him as fit as a butcher's dog, according to his doctor.

Adie thought about her sister-in-law and her husband. 'Have you contacted Sheila and Bob?'

Gavin looked tired, drawn, and defeated. Finding Mark must have been traumatic for him. It was only a few years since his father had died, and then Feen's terrible accident had put him through the wringer, here in this very hospital, while her and the twins' lives had hung in the balance. Since then, two of his friends had perished in a plane crash. He'd been to hell and back enough times already. Mark's accident must have thrown a lot of emotions back up, for him.

'Yeah, we called them straight away and they met us here for a bit, but Sheila had a doctor's appointment she couldn't miss. They said they'd get back as soon as they can.'

As the hours ticked by, and no news came, Adie started to feel a quiet dread settle into her body. She looked across at Feen, who also now looked defeated and sad. Her shoulders had sagged, and the expression on her face was one Adie had never seen before. It was impossible to describe, but she sensed that her stepdaughter was feeling every bit as bleak as she looked.

She knows something, and she won't share it, even if I ask. I can't expect her to give us the kind of news we're dreading. That wouldn't be fair to her at all, but her body language is telling me that maybe this time we're not all going to bounce back like we did after Mark's last accident. Maybe be this one is going to be a turning point in all our lives. It's certainly starting to feel that way.

Bob and Sheila came back about half an hour later. Her doctor's appointment had taken longer than she'd hoped.

'Afternoon appointments always start later. They lose time all across the morning, and by the time your 'alf past three slot rolls around, you can't get in until 'alf past four. My blood pressure's up a bit, apparently, and I needed to have some bloods done. All routine, but important, I suppose. I 'ave to take some tablets, lose a bit of weight, and eat fewer carbs as a starting point. Is there any news?'

Adie shook her head. 'Not a peep. But they haven't come out to tell us the *worst* news, so that's something. Mark's hanging in there. We're still hoping to hear something positive, hopefully soon.'

'The amount of time it's taking should tell you *all* something,' Feen muttered, half to herself. 'And there's *nothing* positive about it.'

She sounded angry and bitter, and Adie felt at least partly responsible. Her consistent failure to pick up the phone every time, when Feen was trying to reach her, certainly wouldn't have helped. She'd felt let down, and possibly even abandoned, at her time of greatest need. That was still smarting, along with everything else she was feeling but couldn't bring herself to say.

Adie had no idea how her phone had ended up losing its ring and vibration, but things like that happened a lot, didn't they? And the number of times when someone calls with catastrophic news are probably quite few, compared to the overall number of 'regular' missed calls or messages to a phone that was misbehaving. Gavin had been philosophical about it. '*It happens all the time,*' he'd said, and Adie knew that to be true.

Feen would eventually come to appreciate that, and the fact that the last thing *anyone* would want was for her to feel unsupported! But, for now, Adie had to tread carefully with her.

At least Gavin was here with her. She wasn't alone, like she'd been when she'd found Mark unconscious and bleeding in the barn, all those years ago. She'd been panicked and terrified that her father was going to die right there on the ground in her arms. Adie had shown up and taken command, and that incident had led to the two women forming a strong bond. That bond felt a little fragile right now, but Adie was sure it would hold. Emotions were running high, and the normally composed Feen was not in a good place in her own head. That would feel alien to her too. She felt a rush of compassion, and stepped forward to wrap her arms around her.

She expected Feen to shake her off, but she didn't.

'I'm sorry,' Adie whispered. 'I'm sorry I wasn't there for you, for all the times you called. Please forgive me.'

Feen hugged her back, and her voice was low.

'Adie, there's nothing to forgive. Gavin's right. It was just one of those things. But I'm scared. I'm scared for Daddy, and I'm scared for all of us. None of what's happened or happening is clear in my head, but my mother is here, which means she knows I need her support. That scares me. I know it shouldn't, but it does, because there's so much I feel, but so little I can see, about what's going on. Mum never comes unless its serious.'

'Beth is in the ether, and I am here in the flesh. Neither of us is going anywhere. I'm right here, darling, to give you what your own mum can't, and she is here to give you what *I* can't. Between us, we've got you.'

Feen's smile was watery and wobbly, but she hugged Adie again, and left her surprised once again, at the strength in her tiny body, to hug as hard as she always did.

We're all scared. The more time goes by, the more we have to face the seriousness of this. Whatever has happened, we just need to know! Why is nobody telling us anything? This is crazy. We've been here all afternoon, and it looks like we'll be here for half the bloody night. How hard would it be, for someone to just come and tell us <u>something</u>?

Another hour passed, and nobody spoke much, except to offer the occasional coffee run. It felt as if the life forced had been sucked out of all of them. It was close to midnight when a doctor finally came through, and spoke to them. He introduced himself as Mr Campbell-Hawkins, the lead surgeon whose team had worked on Mark since he was admitted.

'Mr Raven sustained catastrophic trauma from his accident with the combine, and I'm sorry that it's taken so long for us to come and talk to you. We've had a lot on our plate, and we wanted to wait until we had the full picture so far, before telling you anything.'

He turned to Adie and smiled gently at her. 'Your husband needed immediate surgery, which has been complex. His pelvis was crushed, which led to significant internal bleeding. We've managed to get that under control and stabilise his pelvis. He also sustained some severe lower limb fractures and crush injuries – both of his femurs have been shattered, and these required surgical stabilisation too. There were some vascular complications; some damage to his femoral arteries, and some ruptured vessels, which we've had to bypass. We performed surgery to repair a ruptured bowel and bladder. The good news is that his kidneys and intestines are intact, but your husband's legs swelled so much after the accident that the muscles were being crushed from the inside. The casing around the muscles doesn't stretch, so the pressure built up fast. We needed to act quickly to avoid the blood supply being cut off and the tissue dying. We performed a fasciotomy.'

Adie felt confused. 'What is that, exactly?'

It's where we make long cuts along his legs to release the pressure. It looks dramatic, but it was the only way to save what was left of the muscle. The wounds are open for now, but we'll manage them carefully and, later on, he may need grafts or further surgery to close them. The injuries are extensive He will need a lot more surgery, but we've done what we've needed to, for now, including removing some damaged tissue to stop infection. We've stabilised him, and his blood pressure is holding, but this is only the first step.'

Adie's heart lurched, then sank, at the phrase *only the first step*.

'He's critical, but alive,' Mr Campbell-Hawkins continued. "Right now, that's what matters. We'll need to go back in once his body has had time to recover a little. We'll keep him in intensive care tonight, and we should know a lot more in the next twenty-four hours. He won't wake up, and you won't be allowed to see him, so I suggest that you all go home and get some rest, and try not to worry too much. He has a long road ahead of him, but he's strong, and fit, and that will go in his favour for getting safely through this critical period.'

Adie nodded, but she couldn't trust herself to speak. None of them could. They all just stood around, staring helplessly at the surgeon, as the magnitude of what Mark had suffered started to sink in. *Alive.* That was the one word she and the family could cling to.

He asked them if they had any questions, and none of them could respond. It was all still too much, to have to take in. He seemed to understand that, because his next comment was to invite them to ask anything they wanted to later, when they'd had time to grasp the full implications of the news he'd just given them.

Gavin stepped forward and shook his hand. His voice was husky with emotion.

'Thank you. And thanks to your team, for pulling him through.'

'He's not out of the woods yet. But he's in the best place, and we won't take our eyes off him. The minute there's any change, we'll know, and we'll deal with it. And we will call you if we have reason to, but there's nothing to be gained by waiting here tonight. Please, go home and come back tomorrow when we'll know more and we can update you. He's not alone, far from it, so don't worry about that.'

He left the waiting room, and everyone stood exactly where they were. Nobody seemed to be able to move. Finally, Gavin cleared his throat and spoke up.

'He's alive.' Then, he simply burst into tears, and Feen put her arms around him, and led him to a chair. She looked up at Adie as he sobbed, beside her.

'Delayed shock. We're *all* still in shock. I want to stay here, but I sink the thurgeon's right. I'm sure none of us will sleep, but we can at least get some rest. Daddy will need all our strength, so we need to offer him as much as we have, and that means taking some kind of recharge, whichever way we can.'

Everything in Adie's heart railed against leaving the hospital.

I want to stay here too! I don't want to walk out of here and leave my husband fighting for his life alone. But Feen's right. We have to be strong, and hanging around in here, in this miserable place where so much bad news is given to so many frightened people, it isn't helping. The negativity has seeped into the walls. I can feel it! We need to be in the comfort and safety of our own home – in a place we love and trust and feel supported – to process all this.

Adie invited Bob and Sheila to Ravensdown, but they needed to get home to their own farm. They promised to come over in the morning, once they'd got the most important chores out of the way. Some things couldn't wait, but they'd leave what they could and come back to the house, and they would all travel to the hospital together.

It was going to be a long, hard road to recovery, for Mark. This was no small accident. As catastrophic as his earlier one had felt, at the time, it wasn't a patch on what he was facing now. His injuries were horrific, and life-altering. Adie knew, deep in her heart, that their lives had irrevocably changed today. Nothing would ever be the same again. The future now – *with* Mark if he recovered, and *without* him if he didn't – was impossible to fathom. Her brain was running at a hundred miles an hour, and she knew she had to somehow try and slow it down, or go mad.

I never knew what numbness felt like, until this. I've had shocks before, and I thought I was numb after them, but nothing has ever felt like this. I am literally numb with fear.

The terror, the desolation; it was like someone had reached a hand inside her and flicked a switch. The ability to breathe was all she could focus on, for now. When Miranda's text came through asking her if she'd got home safely, and she remembered that she'd promised to let her know, she simply looked at it with no idea how to respond. Instead, she gave her phone to Gavin and asked him if he could call Miranda and tell her what was going on.

'I know it's probably the last thing you feel like doing, and I'm sorry to ask, but I want her to know what's happened. I just can't face a conversation about it, myself.'

'Sure thing.' Gavin put the call through to Miranda, apologised for the lateness of the hour, and brought her up to speed. At the end of the call, he handed Adie's phone back to her, and told her that her best friend would be at Carlisle Infirmary by lunchtime tomorrow, to meet her.

*　*　*　*　*

Chapter Nineteen

As Adie mentally prepared herself to walk into Mark's hospital room for the first time since he'd properly woken up, she was full of both dread and anticipation. She was desperate to reassure him that the family were all still here, and waiting to talk to him. She was also desperate to see for herself how he was doing. For a full week, he had steadfastly refused to see anyone, and she braced herself for a 'bumpy' reception, after a nurse intercepted her when she arrived on the ward to finally see her husband.

'He's angry and resentful, and very snappy, Mrs Raven. He can't be polite to save himself right now, so be prepared for that when you see him. He may not respond well. Try not to be too upset, if he doesn't. Don't take it personally if you can avoid it. He is struggling to come to terms with how his life is going to be from now on. That's going to take a while, so be prepared for a rough ride. It's not unusual at all, in cases like this one, but it can be a bit difficult to navigate.'

'And just how exactly *is* his life going to be, from now on, or is that information still not relevant for us to hear?'

Adie realised immediately that she'd been rude herself, to the nurse, and the poor woman was probably heartily sick of being snapped at. But Adie was fed up too. She was tired of nobody telling her anything concrete. A big round of tests had only been done this morning, and the doctors were all probably still waiting for the results. Mark's injuries were complex, and the team had to fully understand the challenges to his recovery, to build the most appropriate treatment program to overcome or at least manage them. She understood all that, but her patience was wearing pretty thin now, with all of it.

Contrite, she tried to explain. 'God, I'm sorry! Please forgive me. It's just … well. Being so in the dark like this, and for this *long,* is starting to take a heavy toll on the family. We've made call after call, and nobody ever seems to want to tell us anything. All we need to know is what we're up against. We're all ready to move forward and get on with what's required, but we need to know what that actually is; what we have to do, and prepare for, you know?'

The nurse nodded, and reached out and briefly squeezed Adie's arm. 'I know. Believe me, I do. I've been in a similar situation to yours, with one of my kids, and it is hard not knowing what's really going on. And I'm sorry Mrs Raven, but I don't have the knowledge or the authority to fill you in. I'll see if I can page one of the doctors attached to Mr Raven's case to come and have a quick word with you both together, now you're here, and tell you what they can.'

'Please, will you call us Mark and Adie? The stiff formality is a bit daunting, on top of everything else…' She trailed off, unsure of how better to explain herself. The nurse nodded curtly and offered a small smile, before turning and heading back to the nurses' station, in the middle of the ward.

Adie took a deep breath and opened the door to Mark's room, hoping against all hope that his overall belligerence wouldn't extend to her. Her hopes were swiftly dashed when he simply scowled at her and turned away without a greeting. She smiled anyway, as brightly as she could, and tried to sound upbeat.

'Hello, darling! I've been hanging out, to see you! I came in this morning, but they turned me away, because they had a bunch of tests to run.'

'Sorry to be such a fuckin' inconvenience,' he muttered, at the wall.

'Not inconvenient at all,' she replied as smoothly as she could, even as her heart sank. Clearly, she wasn't going to be an exception. He was going to be rude to her as well.

Don't take it personally, remember?

'I got a few errands done in the city while I waited, so it's all good. I'm just glad to finally see you! I've brought you a pizza. It's your favourite; meat feast with fresh tomato. It's probably a bit cold now, but it should still be nice.'

'I'm not 'ungry. Mebbe yer should eat the bloody thing yerself.' He was still addressing the wall, and Adie bit her bottom lip, as she bit back a retort. She forced a measure of patience into her voice and tried not to sound patronising. She also didn't want him to know how thoroughly *terrified* she was.

'I'm not hungry either. Perhaps I'll just leave it on the table here, so you can pick at it later, if you've a mind to.'

Mark shrugged. 'Please yerself.'

'I've just spoken to a nurse. She can't give us any info, but she's paging a doctor who can. Someone should be here fairly soon, and then we might know what's going on.'

'I already fuckin' know what's goin' on. I know what they're gonna tell me. Me life's over, as I used to know it. Yer 'usband's not the kind of 'usband yer ever gonna need. Not anymore.'

'Don't talk like that! You don't have all the answers! At least wait until they offer their assessment before you right yourself off, and our marriage, and God knows what else.'

She fought back tears of fear and frustration. It wouldn't help either of them if she dissolved into a screaming heap.

'I'm fuckin' paralysed, Adie. From the waist down. I can't move a fuckin' thing, and I reckon if I were gonna come back from that, I'd 'ave 'ad some indication by now.'

'You *don't* know that! Just wait, until they tell you something reliable, if they even can, yet! They may still not know themselves, how this is going to pan out.'

Mark shook his head, and looked at her now, for the first time. She had never seen such fury and bewilderment in his eyes, and she had no idea what to say. All she could do was offer her own perspective, which seemed a bit pathetic, and verging on patronising, but it was all she had to give.

'Well, I'm sorry, but I'm not giving up on the best possible outcome even if *you* are. Until someone in good authority tells me otherwise, I'm going to keep believing that you're going to get back on your feet. Yes, it will probably mean some rehab, and yes, it's going to be painful and hard, and long. But I refuse to accept that it isn't possible, until I'm categorially and irrefutably told it isn't. And shown the evidence.'

Mark shrugged again. 'Believe what you 'ave to. But it's *my* body, and *my* numbness - to the point where I don't get a scrap o' fuckin' warning before shittin' or pissin' the fuckin' bed, and it's *my* understandin' of what's possible an' what's not.'

His voice had no fire in it. He sounded utterly defeated, and that made Adie panic. She'd never heard him speak like that before, not all the years she'd known him. Even after the last accident, he'd mostly been pretty upbeat. He always found a way to see the positive side of disaster. Always. He'd even said, once; 'even after a plane crash, you can still recycle the metal.'

She opened her mouth to speak again but realised it was futile. There was nothing she could say that would make Mark any less angry or confused. The only people who could do that were the experts and, even if they *did* have anything positive to tell him, they'd have a hard job getting him to believe it.

She looked up as the door to his room opened, and a doctor stepped in. He looked young; some might say too young, to have the future of a much older man in his hands. But he came forward, and introduced himself, and shook Mark's then Adie's hand with a surprisingly strong grip.

'Hello, Mr and Mrs Raven. I'm Peter Chukwu, and I'm on the team that's overseeing Mr Raven's recovery and treatment. Nurse Forbes has asked me to come and have a chat. I believe we need to clarify the situation for you, and I'm sorry you've been kept waiting. We're currently very understaffed, for different reasons, and the junior doctor's strike isn't helping.'

Adie nodded, gently. 'I understand. We'll be grateful for some clarity. It's been a horribly anxious time.'

'Of course. And I'm sorry I don't have better news. Mr Raven, you sustained an extremely serious abdominal crush injury from the combine harvester, which left you with some very complicated injuries. I know they have all been explained to you, along with what we've managed to do, to repair a lot of the damage to your body.'

Dr Chukwu fell silent, at that point.

'What's the bad news?' Mark's voice was still deadpan.

Adie steeled herself for what was coming next.

'You ended up with what we call Compartment Syndrome: which is muscle swelling, where the build-up of pressure restricted blood flow. We were able to alleviate some of the pressure to some of the nerves and muscles that sustained considerable damage, but we weren't able to reduce it fully. That has led to significant spinal cord damage, which I imagine you already suspect. I'm sorry to say that the tests that were done this morning show no improvement in motor function below the waist. On the basis of that, we feel it is highly unlikely that you'll regain your lower limb function. I'm so very, very sorry. I know it's news you didn't want to hear, and believe me when I say that we did everything we could to avoid this outcome, but the damage you sustained was just too great.'

The room felt silent, and all that could be heard was the quiet beeping of a monitor and the muffled sound of traffic passing by outside the window far below. Tears sprang to Adie's eyes, as the full implications of what Dr Chukwu had told them started to sink in.

Mark would never walk again.

Dr Chukwu spoke again, more softly this time. 'I really am so sorry. You've no idea how much I wish I could give you better news.'

'So, there's not likely to be any improvement at all, on the status quo? None? Even with rehab, and everything?' Even to her own ears, Adie's voice sounded tiny and far away, like it was receding, dragging with it the life she'd come to know and love. Something inside her started to crumble.

'There may be some marginal improvement, but it's not going to be significant enough to enable full mobility again.'

He turned his full attention to Mark. 'Once you've healed up enough from the other injuries you've suffered, we can look at a rehabilitation programme that will maintain your strength as far as possible. We'll also look at methods of mobility, where there have been some very impressive technological advancements, and we can discuss how your home environment might need to be adapted to accommodate your new way of life. You've a long road ahead of you, but we'll get you there.'

Mark had tears in his own eyes now, but they weren't tears of sadness. They were tears of outright rage. He didn't want to believe that this had happened. Everything in his mind was railing against it. Adie could see that, and she also could see that Dr Chukwu understood it too, and he'd probably been expecting it. He didn't add anything further, to 'poke the bear.' Enough had been said, for now.

'Why didn't you bastards just let me die? D'yer think this is better than that?'

Dr Chukwu bit his bottom lip. He was struggling to answer Mark, but he lifted his head and looked into Mark's eyes, and caught them before Mark looked away.

'I know that right now you feel as if you'd be better off dead. But you can still have a good, rich life – even without the use of your legs. Please, try to trust me when I say that in time you will adjust. You *will* find a way to make the best of this.'

Mark refused to look at him, or answer. He kept his gaze firmly on the wall.

The doctor stood to go. He smiled softly at Adie. 'I'm sure you still have a lot of questions. I'm going to leave you for now, to talk things through, and I or one of my colleagues will come and have a chat with you again as soon as you're ready, to explain further and to answer any questions you have. There are information sheets, with explanations, illustrations, internet links for more information, on various elements of this, and so on. I'll make sure you get those.'

After he left the room, Adie and Mark just stared at one another. Neither had any words to convey the horror and the shock of what they'd just been told. Mark compressed his lips together and stared out the window. Then he looked back at Adie, and uttered just one word.

'Farm.'

She shook her head. 'Don't worry about the farm. We've been here before, remember? We got a manager and a farmhand in, back then, and we'll just do that again.'

''Ow long for?'

'For as long as it takes, until we get things figured out. Maybe Eric can step in again, or he might know someone competent who can. I'll contact him over the next day or two.'

Her mind was racing, now. Eric Tripper had come to Ravensdown Farm to manage it temporarily, nine years ago, after Mark had fallen through rotten floorboards up on the mezzanine floor and ended up tearing his liver and fracturing his neck. Eric had brought a farmhand with him, and the two men had run Ravensdown like clockwork until Mark had got back on his feet again.

By all accounts, he wasn't going to get back on his feet again after *this* accident, but that didn't have to mean he couldn't run his farm again. He'd need a lot more support, but he wasn't going to be entirely useless. His brain and his upper body were still in good shape, although heaven only knew what kind of emotional toll this life-limiting accident might take on him until he could 'right his own ship' and look forward again.

Adie had no idea yet, how to manage the situation beyond the practical, so she concentrated on that. Eric Tripper was a close family friend now, after meeting and marrying Adie's friend Peg Wilde, as she'd been at the time, at Ravensdown Farm. Peg had been coming to the house every Friday night with a takeaway and a bottle of wine, while Adie and Feen had been working the farm until Mark recovered. One thing had led to another, and the widowed Peg and the divorced Eric had found love again in later years. They were as close to the Ravens as anyone could ever be who wasn't actually family.

Eric wouldn't see them struggle. Neither would Bob and Sheila. They were the salt of the earth. They would put their shoulders to the wheel and be instrumental in making sure that Ravensdown Farm stayed in good hands and continued to prosper. Short term, they would all be in crisis mode, but Adie was confident that over time, a way forward would be found to keep things ticking over.

For one thing, they had plenty of money, to pay for good support. Thanks to Kevin Sangster's careful management of Mark's assets over many decades, paying for help on the farm wouldn't be a problem for however long they needed it. Adie was thankful for that at least.

Money had never meant much to her, in and of itself. She was grateful that she and Mark didn't have anything to worry about financially, but that was all that mattered to her where money was concerned. She never felt the need to have a top-of-the-range 'this,' or the most expensive 'that.' Appearances never mattered one iota, and she wasn't a spendthrift. If anyone had ever asked her, she'd have told them; 'all I need is enough to ensure I don't have to worry.'

They certainly had that, and plenty more besides, and it was hugely comforting now, as they found themselves bobbing around in a choppy sea with no idea where solid land might be. At least they could pay for a life raft. Not everyone had that luxury.

'Eric's retired now, of course, but I don't think he'll mind stepping up for the foreseeable. He's still incredibly fit and able, and it's not like this is a new gig for him. He already knows Ravensdown like the back of his hand. And at least he's local! He can just jump in his car and drive home for dinner, at the end of the day. It can simply be a temporary job if he wants it.'

Eric Tripper would be worth his weight in gold if Adie and Mark could persuade him to come on board. Right now, he looked like the family's strongest lifeline. It was all Adie had to cling to so far, in terms of keeping the farm steady. Bob and Sheila were rock solid too, but they had their own farm to run. Bracefields kept them busy, and with spring coming they'd be strapped to the wire to keep things on an even keel if they had to take on Ravensdown as well. They ran sheep, at Bracefields. Spring was their busiest time, by a country mile.

I have to keep believing we can make this work. I have to call on every available source of support, no matter where from. This is not the time to be precious or proud about what we need. Even if people are busy themselves, I will still take whatever help they can offer and I won't let myself feel guilty about it, because without it we might sink.

She took a deep breath. 'Okay, so there's a lot to talk about now, about how we navigate the future. Do you want to do that right now? It's okay if you don't.'

'I wanna be on me own fer a bit, if yer don't mind, Adie.'

Mark's voice was tight, but quiet. Adie knew that he had the biggest of all mountains to climb now, in his own mind, in trying to come to terms with a vastly altered future. It felt a bit like he'd just closed a door in her face, but she understood that he needed the time, space and solitude to fall apart on his own terms, while he got his head around the implications of being wheelchair-bound for the rest of his life, and what that actually *meant* for his life, and the life they had together.

He was only sixty-two. There was plenty of life left to live, but it wouldn't matter how many people tried to tell him that. He needed to come to that realisation by himself, no matter how long it might take. Adie hoped it didn't mean he would shut her out, in the process. Her life was going to be altered forever by this too, and they would need to work *together* to get through the trauma and adjust to the changes. Now wasn't the time to point that out, but they would need to talk about it at some point.

It wasn't going to be an easy discussion for Mark. To Adie, it was simple enough. Whatever changes were needed, they would be made, and they would find a way to keep going, with the solid support and nurturing of family and friends.

'Okay. I'll head home, then. I'll stop by the café, and have a quick chat to Peg, and see if she thinks Eric can step in.'

I could do with a little support myself. I think she's the best person for me to talk to, right now.

Mark nodded, but he didn't look at her. She picked up his hand and kissed it, but he didn't react. She leaned over him and kissed him on the forehead, and whispered, lightly; 'Bye then, my darling. I'll see you tomorrow.'

She was out in the car park when she remembered that she hadn't asked Mark if he wanted or needed anything bringing from home. Instead of texting, she decided to quickly run back up to his room. There was enough time left on her parking.

When she got there, she was astonished to find him weeping. He didn't say a word, or even try to cover it up. He simply kept looking into the middle distance, with the tears streaming down his cheeks. The look of desolation on his face was more than she could bear. She rushed to his bedside and put her arms around him, and drew him close.

'Darling, please.' She mumbled, into his shoulder. 'This is horrible, I know. But we'll figure things out! We *will*. We *absolutely* will! It means a new way of life, but we'll manage. We'll be fine.'

He pushed her away, gently but firmly. 'Leave me, Adie. Please. Let a man 'ave at least a shred o' fuckin' dignity.'

Stung, she stood up. She suddenly felt defensive and, after so much time biting her tongue, about her own fear of the future, she decided it was time to let *him* know how *she* felt about it all. She tried to keep her voice even, as she countered his attempt to dismiss her.

'It's got nothing to do with 'dignity,' Mark. We're married, in case you'd forgotten, so this affects me too. And I am as scared as you are, about what it all means; for you, for me, and for the farm. But mostly, I'm terrified for *us*, and our life *together*, if you shut me out of this process. I know you have a big job ahead of you, in coming to terms with everything and finding the way forward. But so do I, and you slamming the door in my face won't help us to work through this together which, I believe, is what we have to do.'

The silence grew, between them. Mark's face was set, as if in stone. He wasn't giving her an inch.

'Look, Mark, I know it probably seems a little selfish, me talking about how your accident affects me. I'm sorry if it does. I guess I'm trying to say that I still need you, and I hope you still need me, as we navigate this.'

He blinked, slowly, and drew his gaze back from the middle distance, and rested it on her left shoulder. He was obviously finding it too difficult to look her in the eye. She had no idea what that meant, but it hurt her heart, to acknowledge it.

'I dunno what to think, lass. But right now, I can't give yer what yer need, an' I guess the really big question is whether I ever can again. All I do know is I need a bit o' time, to work that out. An' I need to do it by meself.'

'You're still my husband, Mark. I'm still your wife, and there's no reason why there should suddenly be *any* question tied up with that.'

He snapped, then, and it made her jump.

'For fuck's sake. Don't yer get it? I'm not gonna be the man I was, Adie. Think about it! I can't even control when I shit and piss! I can't fuck anymore. So, you'll have to go and find a man who can, or buy yerself some sex toys or summat, if you want to stay wi' me, because my rod doesn't fuckin' work anymore and it never will again.'

'Oh, my God! Is that all you're worried about? Sex? For heaven's sake, Mark! There's a lot more to our marriage than just sex!'

'But it's a pretty important part of it, right?'

Adie felt flummoxed. How was she supposed to answer that question? Of *course*, sex was important, but it wasn't the be-all and end-all! A lot of couples were perfectly happy together in celibate marriages. Some of her friends had lost their libido permanently after menopause, and their marriages had survived, and a couple of those had actually flourished. She pointed this out to Mark now, but he shook his head.

'It's too much for you to have to give up, Adie. I know 'ow much you enjoy it.'

She shook her head, in frustration and bewilderment. 'I enjoy it because it's you! I would still want to be with you even if we never had sex again! Don't you get it? It's you the *man* I want to be with, not what you can do with your bloody willy!'

'Well, I can't do *owt* wi' it, can I?'

'That doesn't matter to me. Not in the way you think it does.'

'You say that now, but it's a long road, a lot o' years, to be doin' wi'out.'

She tried a different tack now. 'Look, there are still way we can be intimate. There are still things we can do – maybe a little more of what we *already* do! And it means exploring different options, I know. It'll be unfamiliar territory for us both. It probably won't be without its little failures and silly embarrassments, as we figure out what's possible, but that's the whole point of a marriage, isn't it – finding ways forward *together*, when a challenge strikes? Working *together* to get back on solid ground?'

'I need yer to go. I've asked yer, and yer keep ignorin' me. I know why yer doin' it, an' I know yer tryin' to 'elp. But right now, I don't need it. I don't want it, Adie. Not right now. Leave me alone, will yer, please? I'll not keep askin'. Don't force me to beg for a bit o' bloody peace.'

Adie realised she'd come to the wall, for now. There was no way forward, not today. Mark *did* need time, to come to terms with everything, and she *wasn't* helping by trying to reassure him about anything, before he was ready.

She stood to go. 'Ok, I'm going. But not without saying a couple of things I need you to know and think about. I love you, Mark. Nothing will ever change that. I would walk through a mile of fire for you, no matter what. I would burn before I got out, if that's what it took, for you to be okay. Please don't forget that. I'm not going anywhere. I would rather die than live without you, no matter what it meant for us to stay together.'

She let her tears fall, and she let him see them. There was no point in either of them trying to hide anything from one another anymore. This situation was the most heartbreaking and terrifying thing any couple could be tested on. If they were to survive it, she needed him to know that she meant every word of what she'd said. Her need, for him to want to try at least to stay close in whatever ways they could, would have to wait a while. In the meantime, she could talk to her friends about how she was feeling. It wasn't enough, but it would have to do for now.

She felt like she was standing on the edge of the abyss. She simply had to hold on, as hard as she could, to the fact that nobody who cared about her would let her fall into it. It was time to go and talk to Peg.

'I'll see you tomorrow. I actually came back to ask you if you needed me to bring anything.'

Mark shook his head. 'Don't come tomorra. Leave it a few days lass, please.'

Adie bit her lip. 'Okay. I'll ring the ward then, to see how you are. Please let me know when you'd like me to come back. I won't force myself where I'm not wanted, even by my own husband, but I will want to see you, whenever you see fit. That won't change. I won't be deciding I'd rather not, so whatever nonsense you might want to tell yourself, don't make that part of it.'

She left the room without another word. She felt a bit childish and foolish for biting at him when he was hurting mightily, but she was hurting mightily too, and she'd gone past the point of being able to pretend she wasn't.

As she left the hospital it started to rain, which perfectly fit her sombre mood. She got into her car, and left the hospital car park, but she didn't get very far along the main road for home before she had to pull into a layby. It was similar to the one she'd pulled into, heading in the opposite direction, nine years ago. She'd been on her way *to* the hospital that time, after Mark's horrific accident in the barn. She'd realised that she'd fallen in love with him, and imagining that he might lose his life before she could ever get to tell him how she felt had literally forced her off the road and into a space where she could safely fall apart.

She allowed herself to fully melt down again now, after their conversation. In the midst of the most crippling grief, fear and confusion, the irony wasn't lost on her, how cruel life could sometimes be, when it came full circle.

A rap on her window made her jump. She looked up to see Billy Briggs staring in at her, with a face full of concern. He was standing in the drizzle, with his and Wendy's dog. She couldn't remember its name. She opened the window, and sniffed at Billy. Then she started crying again, and realised she couldn't stop. Her body heaved with sobs, and she couldn't even feel embarrassed about it.

'Adie. Come with me, over to the restaurant. Wendy will make you some tea.' His voice was gentle, and it only made her cry all the harder. She shook her head.

'No, it's okay. I just need a moment. I'll be fine.'

'I have no doubt that you will. But, for now you're patently not, so I'm not asking. I'm *telling* you. You need to get out of this car, come over to the restaurant, and let us take care of you, for a few minutes at least.'

She nodded, and wiped her face. She grabbed her handbag and got out of the car. Billy immediately took her elbow, in the same kind of old-fashioned way Mark always did, and it made her cry even more. He guided her gently to the opposite side of the road, and they walked towards AyO, Wendy's restaurant, where she and Billy lived. He gestured at the beagle, on the end of his leash.

'You know, I hate going out in the rain. But Jake needed a poo and a wee, and he likes the walk to the stream. He whines and whinges and eventually starts that horrible beagle-howl if

I don't take him at least once a day. It's easier to just do it, before all that bullshit starts. He's worse than Robin, for crying. I always thought dogs were easier than babies. Can't remember which idiot friend of mine told me that, but if I ever do, I'll hunt him down and double-kneecap him.'

Adie smiled at him, as best she could. He was trying to deflect her misery a little, in a gentle way, and she was grateful.

He opened the side door of the big barn that Wendy had converted into a home and restaurant, the previous year. It was the direct-access door to the kitchen, and she felt the welcoming warmth as soon as they entered. Billy called out to Wendy, who came through from the annex that separated the kitchen from the dining room. As soon as she saw Adie's tear-streaked face, she immediately looked alarmed.

Adie sniffed, hard. 'Sorry to crash in. Billy insisted.' She gave them both a wobbly smile, and Billy smiled back, before turning his attention to his wife.

'Adie needs some hot tea, and possibly a bit of a chat. I'm going to dry this dog off, and I'll be back in a few minutes.'

Wendy stepped forward and gave Adie a strong hug, then guided her gently back into the annex. Her laptop was switched on, and there was a spreadsheet open on it.

'I'm sorry. I don't want to keep you if you're working.'

'Oh, don't worry about that! It's nothin, that can't wait a while. Sit down, *cariad*. Let me get the kettle on, and you can tell me what's happenin'.

Within a couple of minutes, she was back with tray. She set down a pot of tea and a milk jug, some mugs, and a plate full of tiny and decidedly uneven-looking chocolate biscuits that resembled chocolate-covered rocks. Billy came back into the room, and he and Wendy sat either side of Adie, and both of them picked up and held one of her hands.

She was still weeping, but more gently now. Neither Wendy not Billy spoke. They just sat, holding her hands, and waiting for her to speak, or not. She knew it wouldn't matter if she didn't. They weren't the sort of people who would pry, or offer unwanted advice. They were content to just sit, and 'hold' her while she felt what she had to feel. It felt wonderful, and safe. She realised now that she hadn't felt safe since the moment she'd heard about Mark's accident. The white noise was still there, in the back of her mind, but at last it felt safe to cry, and be in her anguish, without having to explain herself or pretend she wasn't drowning in terror.

'Mark will never walk again,' she mumbled, through her tears.

'Ah, *cariad*. Do they know that for certain?' Wendy's voice was soft, in response.

Adie nodded. 'The test results from this morning have confirmed it. There's nothing more they can do to improve things, other than rehabilitation to maintain muscle strength.'

She felt Billy squeeze her hand, and she was surprised to see tears in Wendy's eyes.

'Adie, I'm so sorry. This must be devastatin' for you both.'

'Mark is *enraged*, Wendy. He's more upset than I've ever seen him, over anything. He's really struggling, but he doesn't want to talk to me.'

'Maybe it's too soon. Maybe he needs time, to get his own head around it, before you can talk about it together,' Billy offered quietly. 'I know that doesn't help, but it's important that you understand his reaction probably isn't about you.'

Adie nodded, and sniffed. Wendy reached into her track-pants pocket and handed her a small, travel packet of wet-wipes.

'I know. It's a lot, for him. But he threw me out of his room at the hospital just now, and I'm scared that he won't let me back in. He seems to want to go through this alone, but that means I have to as well, and I don't know if I can.'

Wendy shook her head. 'You won't have to do that, *cariad*. We're here, and a lot of other people who care about you are here too. You will absolutely *not* be goin' through this alone. Don't think that, not even for a moment.'

Her lovely Welsh lilt warmed Adie, a little. 'I'm scared,' she admitted, 'and it's kind of tough to say that out loud.'

Billy squeezed her hand again. 'You're safe to say anything you want to, in here. And of course you're scared. You're terrified, and facing an uncertain future. But Wendy's right. You won't have to face it alone. No matter what, we're here for you.'

'I hate seeing him so angry, and … I don't know, kind of *defeated*. Like someone tore the life force out of him. It's hard to explain, but he seems already like a shadow of the man he's always been. And the way he is talking, about us and our marriage; it scares me to death. It really does.'

Wendy let go of her hand, and poured tea into the three mugs. She handed one to Adie.

'Could you please do me a bit of a favour and try a chocolate biscuit? They're my own. Kind of an experiment. I'd like an opinion other than Billy's, because he will tell me they're incredible at the same time as someone else will be spittin' them out.'

Adie grinned, in spite of her anguish, selected one of the small, uneven cookies and took a bite. She chewed for a moment, then nodded.

'They're good.'

'Salted caramel cookies with a layer of caramel, then chocolate. Very indulgent. A bit rich, which is why they're so small. I'm thinkin' of servin' them with after-dinner coffee.'

'You should.' Adie reached for another, to prove the point.

'You know, that's a small thing that you've done for me Adie, but it means a lot. And it's partly to make the point, that certain elements of your life can and should go on as normal, in spite of this terrible thing. If you can, try to avoid it consumin' you?'

Billy nodded. 'Wendy's right. It sounds dismissive of how big what you're struggling to comprehend really is. It's not at all trivial, but I think what she means is that there are parts of your life that should and *can* go on as normal, even in the midst of a nightmare. Focussing on those might stop you from going a bit bat-shit over it.'

'Billy!' Wendy snapped at him. 'You can't say things like that!'

Adie shook her head at them both. 'No, he can. We're friends who *should* be able to say what we all think, and he's right. I have to pay at least some attention to what I can control in my life, otherwise I *will* go bat-shit, and not just a bit! Probably utterly and completely. I have to try to find a way to keep functioning, even though I want to crawl into a dark hole and stay there.'

Wendy blew the air out from between her teeth. 'I suppose he *is* right. He just has a terrible way of sayin' things, at times. But we *are* friends, and you do get him, so I guess it's not offensive.' She turned her attention to Billy again.

'It amazes me how many punches in the mouth you always manage to avoid, Seefer, for the way you say things.'

Adie laughed a little, at that. Wendy and Billy were a hilarious couple. They bounced well off one another, and she realised that she couldn't have ended up in a better place, right here, right now, than with these two hugely heart-centred people. One spoke with the kind of voice that always made you smile, no matter how horrible your world might be feeling. The other one's crashing inability to be tactful only revealed his kindness, which made it impossible for any sane person to take offence.

'Life goes on, doesn't it? You know, when my parents died, time kind of stopped for me and my brother Raymond, for a brief time. I remember coming out of Dad's funeral and seeing a couple of girls on bicycles, laughing, and chatting as they rode along, and it seemed incredible to me, at the time, that while my life was in this weird state of temporary suspension, everyone else's life was carrying on as normal.'

She sighed, deeply. 'I know that it does, and it has to, even for me as far as possible. But it's hard to just do the 'keep calm and carry on' thing when I've got so many questions. Like, will I have to take the responsibility for running the farm? If I do, how long will it be for, and will it actually be permanent? Am I going to be thrust into the role of decision-maker now:

dealing with livestock, crops, planning, finances, and God knows what else? Am I going to be the one who decides what modifications need to be made to the house for Mark? I've always supported him, but now will I be in charge? Will I *have* to be, if he decides to stop caring? And if I do end up running everything, is he going to be ready for that, or even accepting of it? Will I even be capable?'

Wendy grimaced. 'Yeah. I expect it's pretty hard to look at *anythin'* in your life in its 'normal' context with all that goin' on in your head! But maybe you don't need to find all the answers straight away. Maybe let the dust settle on this big news today, and then break it down into manageable chunks to tackle.'

'That's how you eat an elephant.' Billy offered. 'One bite at a time.'

Wendy rolled her eyes. 'Helpful as ever, Seefer.' She reached out and took Adie's hand again. 'But he's right about that too, in his own ham-fisted way. This is all overwhelmin', and I get that, but I think if you *can* break it down into smaller pieces, smaller elements to focus on resolvin' piece by piece, it might help to feel you're gettin' some control of it all.'

'Yes, you're right. I think the key to finding my way through the fog is to clear one obstacle at a time. I just don't know what to tackle first; Mark's attitude towards the future of our marriage, or the practicalities of keeping the farm running. I guess everything else will fall into place in its own way.'

Billy cleared his throat. 'For what it's worth, I'd say try and leave Mark to it, for now. He has to reach his own point of acceptance, in his own time, over what's happened to him. All you can do is wait, on that score, and don't try to influence him. I imagine that's pretty hard, if you feel like you have to fight for your relationship. But maybe just trust him, to find his way back to what's important, once he figures it all out?

I'd happily bet my shirt that you'll be at the very top of that list, once he's processed everything.'

Adie smiled at him, gratefully. 'Thanks, Billy. You're probably right. Our marriage has always been strong, and this is the biggest test of it yet. But I hope I'll still be what he really wants, once he comes to terms with how much else he's lost. Maybe he *won't* want to lose me too.'

'I'm sure he won't,' Wendy offered, gently. 'You're the best thing in his life! But he's a man, Adie, and they're crap at being soft, even when they want to be. Give him time, to find himself again. His world has been rocked to its core, but he's still the same man, inside.'

Adie burst into tears again, but this time it didn't feel desolate. She was grateful, for Billy and Wendy's belief in all that she held dear.

'I need to go. I have to talk to Peg, at the café, before it closes. Eric managed the farm last time, when Mark fell through the barn's mezzanine. He's very capable. I'm hopeful he can step in again, even just for a bit, until we find a more permanent solution.'

'See? You're already taking a bite of the elephant! I don't know Eric well, but I'm sure he wouldn't let you struggle. He sounds like a good guy to have on side, to help you in any number of ways, even with contacts for ongoing management.' Billy smiled encouragingly.

'Yeah, and when Mark has come through his own fog, he'll have ideas too, about how to make things work. You *will* get through this Adie; you and Mark together.' Wendy gave her another hug. 'Let me get you an umbrella. It's properly hosin' down out there now.'

Billy hugged her too, and Adie smiled when the baby monitor cracked into life on the sideboard behind him. 'Sounds like someone is awake!' Their infant daughter Robin had evidently been having a nap, upstairs.

He nodded. 'She probably needs changing, so I'll go. We'll see you soon Adie. Remember we're here, for anything you need.' And then he was gone, and Adie heard him climbing the stairs to their home above the restaurant.

'Thank you so much. I'm sure this won't be the only time I fall apart, but I'm glad it happened on *this* road today, near your house, and that Billy rescued me from myself.'

'We are always here, *cariad*. Don't bear this load alone. Share it with the people who care about you, and maybe everythin' won't seem so bleak.'

Wendy hugged her again and walked her to the door. 'Mind yourself on the main road, and send me a text when you're safely home. I know you're stoppin' off at the tea shop, but let me know when you're back at Ravensdown anyway, no matter what time it is. Okay?'

'Okay. And thanks again.'

As Adie arrived back at her car, shook the rain from the umbrella, and sat back in the driver's seat, she felt a small shift, in her heart. It was small, but it was significant. She realised that her time with Billy and Wendy had been exactly what she needed; to steer her clear of the cliff she was teetering on the edge of. They had been empathetic but pragmatic, and had helped her over that horrible hump of panic and uncertainty. Things would be what they were, and getting on with what could be done; that's where her primary focus needed to be, now. Billy was right; she had to allow Mark the time and space to come to terms with his accident and the changes it would mean for his life.

I can't let myself wallow in fear and self-pity, while the farm goes to hell in a handcart. I have to step up for him in that way, at least. He may not want me around right now, but the farm means the absolute world to him, and to lose that too, or to see it in jeopardy, would only make his situation seem more hopeless. He might have lost the use of his legs, but I can see to it that he doesn't lose anything more than that.

It was time to talk to 'Egg and Peric,' and see how they could help.

Chapter Twenty

Chukwu said it, plain as fuckin' day, like 'e were telling me the price of a tank of piggin' diesel; 'You'll never walk again, Mr. Raven. Sorry, an' all that.'

'Ow d'yer respond to that? What d'yer say to it?

Fuckin' nowt. I couldn't say a word to 'im. I suppose that's what 'appens when someone wanders int'yer world an' kicks it in. You don't scream, or cry, or wail. All of a sudden, yer reelin,'wi' a shitload of stuff goin around in yer 'ead, but yer can't get any of it out. You can't find nowt, to say. You just go fuckin' numb. I were numb, even in the parts the fuckin' combine 'adn't taken care of. I just stared at the wall. It were the only thing I could bear to look at.

Part of me expected it. I mean, I've not been able to feel me legs since the accident 'appened. Yer sit up in bed fer too long on yer own, contemplatin' what that actually means, and it doesn't feel 'alfway good. And, when they waltz in sayin' stuff like 'significant spinal cord damage,' you know what's fuckin' comin.'

But still.

It's a bit bloody 'arder when they say it out loud. When it becomes a fuckin' sentence, made up of proper words, not just a 'maybe an' let's 'ope not,' in yer 'ead.

It's not just me legs, me bowel and me bladder that've gone. It's me routine! Me whole fuckin' life's routine. Me mornin's; The click o't barn door. The weight of a bucket in one 'and, an' the keys to't quad in the other. The way the dogs all know me whistle.

That's who I am, who I've always been. At least, it was. Now? Who the fuck am I now? How I'm supposed to be a man if I can't stand up and do owt? If I can't even shag me own wife?

They're sayin' I can adapt. There's big advances in mobility technology, yarda fuckin' yarda. They'll get me physio, equipment, support, an adapted car, an' this, that an' the next bloody thing.

But no one's talking about the things they can't replace — like the feel o' wet mud under yer boots, or the smell o' hay when you're liftin' an' stackin' it wi' yer own two 'ands.

I've always been the one who knew 'ow to get summat done. Now I've got to let someone else get me showered an' dressed, while some other bastard runs me farm for the rest o' me fuckin' life?

That's a man I don't know 'ow to be.

I've walked me land for more than thirty years. I know every inch o' Ravensdown better than the back of me 'and. The 'um of the quad bike, the feel o' me boots, 'eavy wi' clay.

And now I'm sat 'ere, bein' told 'this is it, man. Yer life as yer knew it is over. Yer future will now be in a wheelchair.'

I built Ravensdown wi' me 'ands. Worked through blisters an' broken fuckin' bones, flu, storms, a torn liver, and a fractured neck, an' the death o' me first wife. I've shed blood sweat and tears in those fields fer fuckin' decades. And now I'm supposed to let someone else feed me stock? Deliver me ewes o' their lambs? Fix me fuckin' fences?

I saw that look in Adie's eyes. 'Er brave little smile, all full o' love and worry. She said all the right things: that we'll get through all this, that she doesn't care that I can't make love to 'er anymore, that we'll be as right as rain. But I don't want to be summat she 'as to fuckin' 'get through;' summat she 'as to put up wi,' just because she made a bloody vow to do it. In sickness and in 'ealth. All fine an' bloody dandy in principle, but the reality's a bit different, in't it?

I'm less than I was, an' there's no denyin' it. Important bits o' me are gone. Important bits o' me marriage are gone wi' 'em. She can't pretend that doesn't matter. If she tries to pretend, she's lyin', and I know why she's doin' it, but it's not right. I don't want 'er lookin' after me. I want her as me equal. Me partner. Not me fuckin' carer.

If I can't see the man I used to be, 'ow can she?

An' I know she's right in sayin' that I've weathered storms before. I buried me first wife, an' friends an' family since. I've come back from a previous accident that bloody near killed me.

I've started again more than once.

So maybe I'll find summat else to build a life around. Summat else to put meanin' into me life. But me 'ead can't go there yet, an' I'm not sure when it can.

Maybe that doctor were right in sayin' that I'm still alive fer a reason, and maybe he were right in sayin' I still 'ave more to do. I'm just not sure what that is, now. I don't know who I can be, from now on. Al I do know is that I can't think about any o' that yet. I first need to grieve the man I was, fer 'owever long it takes. I'm not one fer feelin' sorry fer meself, but this is a bit of a fuckin' doozy. As 'urdles go, this one'll take some fuckin' jumpin'.

When I'm done wi' some o' that, maybe I can work out who I might become. But I can tell yer right now, it doesn't look like a farmer.

Or an 'usband, come to that.

*   *   *   *   *

Chapter Twenty-one

The house was quiet, for the first time in a week, and Adie relished the peace that now prevailed. She'd had the builders in, to modify the doorways throughout the house and make other important changes that would guarantee Mark better access to all areas, and the hammering, banging, and shouting between floors had been relentless. A stairlift had been installed and ramps had been built at the front and back doors, and to the barn doors too. Her and Mark's bathroom had been extended into some of the space of an adjoining bedroom. The bath had been replaced by a walk-in one, and the shower had been changed for a bigger one with easier access. An extra handbasin and mirror had been installed too, at a lower height. Grab-handles had been added, in various positions in the bathroom and throughout the house, so Mark could hoist himself into and out of different places, to maintain a degree of independence.

A couple of weeks before, a very nice pair of occupational therapists had come to look over the house and barn, and other outbuildings, to determine what changes would be needed. Their inspection had been very detailed and immensely helpful, and Adie had gone ahead with every one of their recommendations. The cost had been outrageous, but worth every penny, in her eyes. It wouldn't have mattered to her if the bill was ten times higher. All that *did* matter was that Mark would be as comfortable as possible in his own home, with the challenges to optimal functioning kept to an absolute minimum.

His motorised, state-of-the art wheelchair was on order, and arriving in about a week. The downstairs store-room at the back of the house had been converted into a mini gymnasium, with weights, barbells, ropes, and every machine that had been recommended to ensure Mark could keep an optimal level of strength, at least in his functional upper body. With the right equipment, he could still maintain good power in his arms, chest, neck, and shoulders.

The workbenches in the barn had also been lowered, so that he could sit in his wheelchair and still work on things, and his beloved quad bike had been converted to full hand-controls. Gavin had arranged for one of his friends down in London, who was a motorcycle mechanic specialising in vintage machines and unusual modifications, to come up to the farm and make the necessary changes. It had been, apparently, a relatively simple thing to do. The quad didn't have a clutch; only a throttle and brakes that needed to be converted, to be hand-controlled. Gavin's friend had made the necessary changes very quickly. He'd also fitted a form of stirrup to each of the footpegs, to keep Mark's feet in place, and he'd fitted a loud alarm to the quad, with a button that Mark could press, to emit a noise so ear-shattering it was probably capable of alerting people two towns away, if he got into any distress.

He wouldn't be able to go out by himself on the quad, at least initially, in case he tipped it over or had some other difficulty that would cause him to be unable to ride it, but at least he would be mobile on it again. Adie had purchased another quad bike, so that she or someone else would always be able to accompany him on trips around the farm.

He'd been terribly upset at the thought of having to be chaperoned, but he'd recognised that being mobile again was more important to him than the fact that someone had to make sure he was safe. As Adie had pointed out, if he could prove himself competent, over time, the day would come when he could go out on his own.

Everything had to go slowly. Progress was going to take time. Mark understood that, but he wasn't a man blessed with much patience, and Adie knew there was a bumpy ride ahead, as everyone – including Mark himself – adjusted and learned to accept the changes.

She was determined that he would still have as much independence as humanly possible. She had changed their bed, for a bigger one. The new super-king comprised a zip-link mattress so they could both sleep together but independently. She knew there would be nothing worse for Mark than to lie beside her, trying to sleep if she tossed and turned, which she did more often now, post-menopause. Similarly, she didn't want him keeping *her* awake if he himself had a restless night. The linked but separate mattresses offered important reassurance for them both, that they'd both get a decent night's sleep without causing too much disruption to one other.

Adie was trying to cover all the bases. She knew that more adjustments would be necessary, as they learned to live with the reality of their new way of life. What they needed would be under constant review, at least to start with, but she was cautiously optimistic that solutions could – and would – be found for every conundrum that presented itself.

She hadn't as yet sorted out a hand-controlled car for Mark. She wanted to wait until he was home, and had adjusted to at least a few of the other big changes, before talking to him about it. She wanted it to be his choice, what kind of vehicle he wanted to drive. She knew how much he loved his Range Rover and would no doubt be keen to have a hand-controlled one. When the time came, they would consult a mobility-specialist dealer to see what his choices might be, for a model where the functions of the accelerator and brake pedals could be changed to hand-operated controls that would be mounted on the steering column or elsewhere in the vehicle. She hoped that choosing a new adapted car would be something for him to look forward to.

She was as satisfied as she could be now, that most of the practicalities were covered as far as possible until new needs emerged, and that was a good feeling.

What wasn't so great a feeling was the trepidation she felt, at the prospect of Mark coming home as her *husband*. Mark Raven 'the man' was easy to sort out in practical terms. But

Adie still feared for her marriage. He had flatly refused to discuss the matter of them being unable to have sex anymore, at least in the way they always used to.

Whenever she'd tried to broach the subject, she'd done it in ways that were designed to reassure him that she wasn't going anywhere, that it didn't matter to her if penetrative sex was a thing of the past. Tentatively, she'd tried to remind him that there were still things they could do that would offer a good degree of intimacy and potential satisfaction. She'd had a good chat with the family doctor, in the aftermath of Mark's accident, and he had reassured her that yes, a paralyzed man *can* still experience sexual pleasure. It was likely to be very different from what he'd experienced before his injury, because his physical sensations might be significantly changed, but a lot of men with lower-body paralysis did still find ways to experience intimacy and sexual satisfaction. Many discovered new erogenous zones, or found that certain areas of their bodies were more sensitive than before, offering new ways to experience gratification and pleasure.

Adie had tried to point out to Mark that sexual intimacy was a lot more complex and nuanced than simple physical sensations. Emotional bonds were important too, to the sense of closeness and fulfilment, and sexual enjoyment and satisfaction. The good news was that such bonds could be maintained and even strengthened, after an injury left a couple without the ability to have sex in the usual way.

Mark was not yet ready to listen. He was hostile whenever she tried to bring it up, but she knew it troubled him greatly. Their mutual desire had always been strong, and connective, and she knew he needed time, to come to terms with the apparent loss of what had been a central part of their marriage. She understood how afraid he was, that they had lost that. But he was astonishingly – and frustratingly – black and white, in the way he thought about it. It was going to take time, for him to come around to the idea that sex was still possible, but it would have to take a different form from what he'd previously considered 'normal.'

Adie was willing – *more* than willing – to experiment with whatever was achievable for them, to keep the intimacy that was such a big part of their life together. All that mattered to her was the ability to stay connected intimately, in whatever way they could. There were things they already did, that they could certainly do more of, and the opportunity to explore was one she was looking forward to if the opportunity came. All she could do, at this stage, was hope that Mark would eventually become more open to different possibilities too.

She checked her watch. It was nearly time to go and pick him up from the hospital. Feen was going with her, while Gavin stayed at home with the twins. She called up the stairs to Feen, to remind her to keep an eye on the time. Her stepdaughter came clattering down the stairs straight away, in a pair of bright red wooden clogs. Adie raised her eyebrows at them, and Feen grinned.

'Scholls. I've got fallen arches, apparently, and the doctor recommended Scholl footwear. Trouble is, most of their stuff looks like it's for little old ladies. No offence, by the way. These were the closest thing to funky that I could find. They're kids' ones, of course.'

They did look quite nice, Adie conceded, but she *did* take offence at Feen subtly suggesting she was a 'little old lady' with her own Scholl shoes. To be fair, they weren't at all 'funky,' so Adie decided it was probably better not to make anything of Feen's throwaway comment. Instead, she bit her tongue and let it slide.

Maybe I could fasten some fake flowers onto them, or something.

Feen looked at her own watch. 'We've time for a cuppa, if you want, before we set off? Maybe you'd like another chat? I know how nervous you are about Daddy coming home. I am too. Maybe we can talk about that again, here and in the car.'

Adie nodded. 'Yeah, I am still really jittery about it, and a quick chat over a brew would be great. I'll get the kettle on.'

Feen sat down at the kitchen table. 'Adie, as I've said before, you're not going to be alone with Daddy, not for quite a while anyway. We will stay here for as long as you need the support. Gavin has everything he needs here, to keep working, and the twins are able to go to school here in Torley again. It's no problem at all for us to stick around for as long as you neel you feed us.'

'That's very kind. I appreciate it because I do feel a bit overwhelmed.'

'I know. I've been sensing that very strongly, which is why I want to grab a few minutes now, to try and reassure you again. It's not just kindness for *you*, though, Adie. It's Daddy, and I want to be as much a part of supporting his recovery as possible. I'd feel terrible, being miles away in London while so much adjustment is having to be made up here. It's as much for my own meace of pind as anything else.'

She looked sympathetically at Adie. 'This is tough on all of us, but particularly on you. I know you're anxious, and I know what about. But trust me when I say that everything will work out the way it's supposed to. It's going to take time, and it's going to be a bit rocky, at least initially. He's a grumpy old bear when he wants to be. But he loves you, Adie. He absolutely adores you. Just hold on to that, as things pall into flace.'

'I'm so scared, Feen. I have no idea what the future holds for us. I know he is still coming to terms with everything, and the reality of his new life will hit him hard once he leaves the hospital and comes home. There won't be any avoidance of anything then, will there? He told me he feels very small, like the world has moved on without him and he's watching it all through a window. I tried to tell him that he still has a valid place in the world, but he didn't want to hear that. I guess he's just not ready.'

Mark had brushed her attempts at validation away like swatting an annoying fly. Every time she'd tried to get him to see things in a more positive light, he seemed to dig his heels in still further. He seemed determined to wallow; to feel sorry for himself. Adie had no idea how to get him out of his funk, and she had a strong suspicion that things would get worse before they got better, after he came home.

Feen sighed heavily. 'He's a proud, independent man. He always has been, and he had to pull himself up by his bootstraps after Mum died. He had to take care of whacky little oddball *me*, which was no chall smallenge, and he had to run the farm. He's used to doing everything by himself, and even after you came along, he struggled to let you lare the shoad for quite a while, if you remember?'

Adie did remember. Mark had been slightly resentful at her taking over the running of the house. He *wanted* her to do it, in *principle*, but the reality of significant changes, such as having someone else decide what was for dinner every night, what food was bought on grocery day, or when the sheets got changed, had taken him by surprise. He'd endorsed Adie's decision to redecorate the jaded, faded living room after she'd first moved in, but it had taken him some time to be comfortable with a change in his surroundings. He was a creature of habit, and he never took kindly to change – no matter how small or nice it was.

Those and other general household matters (both large and small) were all adjustments he'd needed to make after deciding to share his life with someone again. A few of them had put him on the back foot for a while, but they hadn't forced him to make compromises because of his own lost independence – his own significant loss of choice! This time would be very different. Adie knew it, and she felt sick to her stomach, with nerves.

I hope I can do this. I hope I have the patience I'll need to have with him, while he goes through this horrible period of adjustment. I'm so grateful for Feen and Gavin, that they're sticking around for a while. I'm not sure I could do this alone, right off the bat. I need support too, but at least I've rallied the troops.

Peg, Sheila, and other friends had promised support, and she knew they meant every word. Once the true extent of Mark's injuries became known throughout the valley, they'd had an *avalanche* of messages, calls and cards. Help had been offered on every scale imaginable, and from some very surprising places. Mark was so well liked and respected, *nobody* wanted to be left out of the support loop.

Adie knew she wouldn't be stuck, or left to struggle to cope alone, but she still felt queasy at the thought of Mark coming home. There were certain things that nobody else could help with, or even be privy to, that they would need to iron out between them. She was desperate to have him home again, but shaken to the core with doubt about how he would behave while he was getting used to a new way of living.

'Adie, you have to stop being so anxious. Daddy might surprise us all. He's nothing if not pragmatic. It's not going to take him long before he realises he has two choices. All I would say is don't take any nonsense from him. Stand your ground, and let him know where the boundaries are. We all have to do that. Yes, he's going to be rumpy and gangry at the turn his life has taken, but he'll come to terms with it, and life will go on.'

'What kind of life is it going to be for us, though? As a married couple, I mean?' Adie blurted the question out before she had time to check herself.

Feen looked uncomfortable, but only for a beat or two. Then she shook her head resolutely.

'I know what's bugging him. And I know how that's affecting *you*. He's not able to think laterally yet, about the more intimate side of things. You've certainly got some work to do, on that front. But I would recommend theeing a serapist - preferably together; someone who specialises in recovery from life-changing trauma, and needing to find a way forward.'

'You mean a sex therapist? I don't feel comfortable talking about this, certainly not with you, and certainly not to some random stranger.' Adie was acutely embarrassed now, at Feen having wandered into her very private thoughts!

'I get that. I totally do, and of course I'm the last person you want to be talking to, about your sex life with my father!

But I know that you and Daddy do have one, or at least you did, and I know that you need to wind a fay to maintain what you can of it. And I know that you can do that, with the right support. All I'm saying is don't throw the baby out with the bathwater, Adie. Don't accept his refusal to talk as final. Right now, it all feels insurmountable, but believe me when I say it's not. *He* will get to a point where he knows it's not.'

Adie nodded. She did want to believe Feen – desperately. There had never been a time, in all of her recall, when her stepdaughter had been wrong with *any* of her predictions. If she couldn't see a way forward with something, she always said so. She wouldn't give anyone false hope, or a bum steer.

It was all Adie had to hold onto right now, so she took it, in the spirit in which it was offered. Feen had her own feelings to process too, over what had happened to her dad. It was no easy thing for her either, to see Mark so decimated, emotionally, and physically. But she was strong, and visionary, and she had tried to tell Adie not to worry. That was as good an endorsement as anything could be, that they would get through this as a family. Feen drained her cup and jumped up.

'Well, drink up, lovely. It's time to go. We don't want to poke the bear still further by showing up late, do we? Let's aim to get on as good a footing with Grister Mumpy as we can, from the get-go.'

Chapter Twenty-two

'Please don't start this conversation by tellin' me everythin's gonna be fine. That in't goin' to 'elp, because we both know it's not.'

Adie didn't seem particularly surprised that Mark had wasted no time in getting the first word in, as they sat in the kitchen. He'd said virtually nothing on the journey home from the hospital, as he'd tried to brace himself for arriving back at his home in a vastly altered state from when he'd left it, nearly three months ago. He'd left the house, that fateful morning, with no inkling that by nightfall he'd be fighting for his life in intensive care with only a 50/50 chance of pulling through.

It was still so frustrating to him, that he couldn't remember a single thing after closing the front door behind him. Obviously, he'd gone to the barn, unlocked it, opened the big doors at the other end, climbed into the combine, started it up, and driven it into the field. But he couldn't remember any of that. If he only could, it might perhaps unlock the memory of what followed – why he'd got out of the cab, and how the machine had come to run him over. The sequence of events, from leaving the house, stayed tantalisingly out of reach. He knew that he would, at some point, have to accept that those memories may never come back at all and, in continuing to try and force them to, he'd probably drive himself mad.

But now – in the comfort of his own home – he felt more able to say what was on his mind. It was early evening now, and Adie had just put a shaved-beef stew with dumplings in the oven. It was one of his favourites, and he hoped that by the time it was ready he'd be hungry enough to at least eat some of it.

He guessed that she'd wanted to start a conversation gently, about how the first few days were probably going to look and feel. On the way home from the hospital, she and Feen had explained the changes that had been made in and around the house. He hadn't managed to find a word to say, about any of it. He sat mute, in the back seat, like he'd lost the ability to talk as well as walk.

A pot of tea was sitting on the table, now, along with the usual accoutrements. Adie poured him a mug and set it in front of him.

'I can pour me own bloody tea, lass. I 'aven't quite lost everythin'.

She stared him down, and he immediately felt uncomfortable. He knew he'd put her on the defensive, which wasn't a good start, but he had no idea how to be less combative. He wasn't himself, anymore. He wasn't the man he used to be anymore, and he was scared to death about just how much of himself he had permanently lost.

It wasn't as if the accident had happened yesterday. He'd had months now, to come to terms with things. Admittedly, it still hadn't been long enough to accept that his entire life as he knew it as a walking man was over. But it had been long enough to accept that the situation was what it was, and being a prima donna back at home, as the main guest at his own private pity party, wasn't going to get him very far with his family. He wasn't going to be allowed to quietly drown in a well of self-pity either. Right from the start, he had to appreciate where everyone else's boundaries were. He'd pushed at the edge of one just now, and he knew it.

His heart felt heavy. If they had to start his homecoming with a row, so be it, but he knew Adie would rather they had a civil discussion where she could outline her expectations about communication and respect. It was what he wanted too, deep down, but he couldn't seem to stop himself from being snappy and belligerent. It was just the way he felt about everything, now.

But she was glaring at him in a way that compelled him to finally look her in the eye.

'I just poured the tea, Mark, like I always do. Are you going to be picking up on every little thing I do, from now on, including the stuff I've *always* done, like pour a mug of tea, or do your washing? It's going to get pretty tedious around here if you're going to be hell bent on interpreting every gesture I make as one of pity, or from an assumption that you can't do something for yourself?'

He sighed, deeply. 'Sorry,' he muttered, but couldn't think of anything further to say.

Rain lashed the kitchen window. It had started halfway home from the hospital and had got progressively heavier. Getting out of Adie's car at the end of the journey, in the deluge, hadn't been a picnic, and he'd felt vaguely humiliated over how much help he'd needed. But they were here now, and there was tea on the table. Dinner was in the oven, and Feen had given him a hug and a kiss and quickly left him and Adie to have a little privacy. Gavin had briefly poked his head around the door after Adie had got Mark settled in his wheelchair at the table, offering a simple 'hi, and welcome home.' Clearly, he was determined to act as normally as possible around his father-in-law. They probably *all* were, and he suspected they'd had a big talk about it and assumed it to be what he would have wanted.

They weren't wrong. Normal life, as he'd always known it, was over, but he couldn't have borne them pussyfooting around him and feeling like they had to walk on eggshells.

In truth, he still didn't know how he really felt about any of what had happened, so it was probably fair to say that nobody else did, either. It was going to be an adjustment for all of them, not just for Mark himself. He tuned back in to what Adie was saying.

'Dinner will be about an hour. D'you fancy a snack in the meantime? I can rustle up some chips and dips, if you like?'

'I'm fine.' He wasn't, and he knew it, but he didn't know what else to say. He had the very real feeling that if he tried to say anything meaningful, he would simply burst into tears.

Adie poured herself a mug of tea and sat down across from him. He tried to ignore the long pause, and the ticking clock. The silence weighed a lot heavier than anything he'd ever felt before in this kitchen. Then Adie tried again.

'The physio people rang. They want you to start going next week. I said yes to Tuesday morning. I hope that's okay.'

'I told yer; I'm fine, Adie. Let 'em give that appointment to some bastard who'll walk out of it.'

Adie's response was firm, but gentle. 'Please, Mark, don't do that.'

'Don't do what?' He knew he sounded confrontational, and probably peevish and childish too, and he hoped she wouldn't escalate it into a full-blown argument. He simply didn't have the stamina for that.

'Don't shut me out. Don't pretend you're not scared or hurting, when I know damn well that you are. For what it's worth, so am I, but I want to make this work, in whatever way we can.'

Mark didn't look at her, or answer. Instead, he clenched his jaw and looked out through the window, over her shoulder, into the pouring rain. The silence lengthened. She seemed determined not to break it. She wanted him to speak, instead. Eventually, he gave her what she wanted.

'Yer don't get it, do yer? This in't a bloody bad back or a broken arm. This is the end of everythin' we 'ad, Adie. Forever. Me, in this fuckin' chair. For ever.'

'I know you're angry. I know that it all feels hopeless. But it's not, Mark! It's just the beginning of a new chapter in our lives that we have to write as we go along. Just like we always did before.'

'Don't bloody trivialise this! An' 'ow could yer possibly understand? You married a man who could fix an 'undred yard fence in rain worse than this! I could drag a bloody lamb out of a breach birth an' save its life, an' then go on an' plough a fuckin' field till way beyond dusk. Now I can't even put a pair o' boots on! There's no bloody point, is there? And as fer 'avin' sex? Forget it.'

Adie reached across and took his hand, gently. He steeled himself, not to pull away. But he didn't squeeze hers back like he normally would. He wasn't ready to concede anything yet.

'I didn't marry your boots. Or your legs. Or your ability to have sex. There's a lot more to this marriage than that. I would like to think so, anyway.'

'But that's who I were, Adie! That's 'ow I showed up fer you; a capable man wi' two good legs! I showed up like that fer me 'ole family. Fer *this* place.' He gestured around the kitchen. 'I'm useless to't bloody lot o' yer, now.'

Adie shook her head, and smiled softly.

'You're still showing up! You're here, aren't you? And you don't have to prove a single damn thing. Not to me. *Ever*. By the way – you're not useless. You're angry, and grieving, and you're allowed to be fully human in that. But you're still *you*, darling! You're still the man I'm madly in love with, who peels me off the ceiling when I lose the plot, or all good sense of perspective. You're still my rock and compass that I couldn't do without. I still need you in all the ways you *can* show up.'

Mark looked down at his rough, calloused hands. He didn't know how to respond.

'Look, can we just start with one thing? One step? Not physio, not anything big. Just… let's sit together here for a bit, holding hands. No planning, no pretending, no brave face? Can we do that?'

She was pleading with him gently now, and it hurt his heart that he could give her so little of himself; so little of what she needed now. He knew he had to make more of an effort, to bridge the chasm that was already growing between them. He didn't want to lose Adie too, on top of everything else but, as yet, he couldn't see how trying to keep her would be fair to her.

He shrugged. 'If yer want, lass. I suppose I can at least do that.'

'You can do *so* much more than that, but it's all I want, right now.'

Finally, he squeezed her hand, just a little. She needed some reassurance, and he understood that, but that little squeeze was all he could give her, for now.

'Adie, I know I have to say goodbye to the man I used to be. But so do you, lass. You have to let go o't version o' me that I was before this 'appened.'

He wanted Adie to understand, how altered their lives would be. He couldn't bear her continuing to pretend that nothing significant had changed. *Everything* had changed. She needed to understand that, and he needed to know that she did.

But she shook her head, resolute. 'You're still my husband, you silly sod. In whatever way our lives have been altered, that still holds true. I can accept *whatever* version of you shows up. Just don't shut me out. I can't be alone, coming to terms with what I have to. We need to do that together, so we keep strong *together*. There doesn't need to be any conflict between us about it. Let's just sit, for now, and tap into our combined strength. Please? That will be enough to guide us forward.'

She sounded convinced, and half-way convincing. He couldn't poke the bear anymore. She needed him to do what she asked; just sit, and be, and keep his terror to himself, while she lent him some of the strength and conviction she had in herself, that they would get through this.

Feen too, was struggling. He knew that. It was hard to get it out of his head, her face, full of anguish and confusion. She'd been to see him while he was in the hospital, a few days before he was due to be discharged, and she'd tried to cheer him up a little, but it hadn't worked very well. It hadn't taken long for the conversation to come around to Feen trying to understand what had happened; how he'd come to be outside a running combine harvester to be run over by it in the first place. Even though she'd grown up on the farm, and had a good appreciation for how dangerous the machinery could be, actually being faced with the results of a life-changing accident had knocked her for six.

He'd never been anything to her, other than the strong, capable father – the man who could and did do everything required to run the farm efficiently. In the early years, while she was growing up, he'd run the house too, until she was old enough to take some responsibility there. He'd been her superhero for her entire life. He couldn't imagine how tough it must be for her now, to see him like this; vastly diminished and dependent on support to do even the most basic of functions.

Feen's grievin' the loss o' me capabilities, but she's angry an' all, about 'ow fate's allowed this to 'appen. She's angry wi' me, for takin' the risk I took, even though I can't remember 'ow I ended up outside the machine. It's all a blank. I got out of the cab, that much I do know, but I don't remember why. It's not summat I'd normally do! An' I know she's feelin' guilty for bein' angry about it. That poor lass 'as to deal wi' all this too. It's not just me, or Adie. It's me daughter, and Gavin. That poor bugger found me. I'd probably've died if he 'adn't, and right now that's the outcome I'd have wished for, if I'd 'ad the bloody foresight or the choice. This is no life to be livin', no matter who says what.

The new reality was going to be a challenge for them all. Gavin was dealing with it in his own way, but Mark understood what a hell of a thing it must have been for him, to have found Mark in such a terrible state.

He knew that Feen wanted to be strong for him. Gavin was strong for her, and she was incredibly strong and resilient within herself, but this was a massive curveball for her to catch and run with. They didn't have to worry financially – that was one blessing – but the emotional rollercoaster was going to be a long one. Mark knew that everyone in his family was fully committed to helping him find ways to adapt, find a life purpose again, and keep the family together. He needed to want to do it, but right now he couldn't. He understood their frustration, but they had to be patient while the biggest loser of them all in the process – Mark himself – came to terms with what was and wasn't possible anymore.

After a time, Adie gently released his hand and looked up at the kitchen clock.

'I think an early night might be a good idea? It might take bit to get settled and everything. As I said, there have been some modifications made. The bathroom is bigger, and you'll notice a few other things that have changed, or been modified, to make it easier for you to get around.'

'That's a lot o' trouble to go to, lass.'

Adie shook her head at him. 'It wasn't. It was all very straightforward. The builders did everything. There's a chair in the shower for you to sit on, and a hand-held shower rose for you to use.'

Mark grunted. 'Well, at least I can wash me own bits in private.'

Adie laughed at him, with a twinkle in her eye.

'I was rather hoping I could have the joy of doing that.'

'It's not gonna be like it was, Adie. You won't get it to do anythin'. It'll never stand up again. I'm dead from't waist down, remember?'

She shook her head. 'I like to play with your bits because they're cute. They don't have to stand up, or do anything, for me to enjoy messing about with them. And you can still mess about with *my* bits, any time you want, without pressure to do anything more than that.'

'I'm not sure when I might be ready to look at that side of things, Adie. I don't know if it's just gonna make me feel worse, fiddlin' wi' summat I can't follow through on fer meself. I know I could get *you* to where you need to be, but I don't know 'ow not bein' able to get anywhere meself is goin' to make me feel.'

She nodded and smiled at him so gently it nearly broke his heart.

'I know what you're trying to say. But there's no rush to get to *anywhere*, with all this. If and when the time feels right, we can look at ways for you to feel positive about the intimacy, and achieve a tangible pleasure from it. We'll get there. But there's no pressure, Mark. None at all. Let's just navigate the waters as we sail them. Boats change course all the time, don't they? We are going to be fine.'

He wasn't able yet, to believe her. He wanted to trust that their marriage would survive, but he had no idea how it could, even if it was what they both wanted. Adie *said* it was what she wanted, and she probably believed it herself, but it was early days. What if she decided it was all too much? Or not enough?

This wasn't what she signed up for. She said in sickness and in 'ealth, were't vows she's appy to stick to, but the idea's a lot different from the reality, in't it? Time'll tell, I suppose.

*   *   *   *   *

A fitful night's sleep followed, for them both. In the morning, Adie made coffee and brought it back to bed, along with a plate of bacon sandwiches. Bless her, she knew all too well, how fond he was of bacon.

'It's a one-off,' she warned him. 'Don't get used to being waited on, or to having bacon butties for breakfast. This is a welcome-home treat, and that's it. We're back on the toast and cereal wagon from tomorrow.'

She helped him prop his pillows up and then got back into bed herself with her coffee and sandwiches.

'Breakfast in bed! When did we last do this? Maybe we *could* make it a more regular thing. We're getting older, and it might be nice to let a few luxuries become the norm now. What do you think?'

Mark grunted. He wasn't sure whether or not she was simply trying to be nice. He didn't know what to say, so he shrugged and mumbled, 'I suppose so.'

She finished her first bacon sandwich, then turned to him.

'It does feel odd, right now. Being in bed as we normally would be… I keep thinking you're just… chilling. That any minute you'll swing your legs off the bed, throw on some clothes, and head out to do some fencing.'

Mark blew out a sigh, and shook his head.

There's no fencin' in my future.'

'Don't say that.'

His throat tightened. 'It's the truth, lass. My farmin' days are over. Me days of being an adequate 'usband are over. God knows what the point of me life is, now.'

'C'mon, Mark. I know you're scared. I don't know who wouldn't be, faced with all this. But you're still… you. Still the man I married, in all the *really* important ways.'

'Doesn't feel like it.'

She moved closer to him in the bed and put her arms around him.

'Then let me remind you who you still are. Until you can feel more like you again.'

Mark blinked hard and tried not to cry. Adie picked up his hand and kissed it, and he gave her fingers a light squeeze.

'You are the man who took a chance on me, after everyone else had given up on me. You opened your home to me, then your heart, then your whole life, and you accepted me and mine. You have loved and supported me, and been right behind me, in everything I've done ever since. You make me laugh. You reassure me when I worry too hard about silly things. You remind me of what matters and what doesn't, whenever I get wound up about something. You know when I'm too tired to do much. You know when something's happening that I'd love to be a part of. You make sure I have everything I need, and most of what I want, and you love me and champion me in *all* of the ways that matter.

'And you're a wonderful dad – not just to Feen but to Gavin, and to my lot too. You're a magnificent grandfather, with more love inside you for the little ones than any other man I know. You're a great brother to Sheila and to Bob, and a true friend to a lot of people in this town who value you so very, very much for the man you are. I'm not talking about the man you were, Mark. I'm talking about the man you still are.'

Adie's voice was soft, and it made his heart ache. He probably still was that same man, to everyone she talked about, but who he was to *himself* now – who was *that* man? How was *he* going to show up, for all those people?

He sniffed, hard, but said nothing. Adie hugged him again.

'You don't have to be strong, here in this room. I know how afraid of the future you are, right now. But let me tell you something. I am *not* afraid. I am ready for *whatever* this new life brings. Yes, there will be frustrations, and every other emotion in existence, until we figure things out. But I'm ready for it. I'm ready to take this ride with you. I'd rather be on the ride than trying to live without you. That would be a thousand times harder, for me.'

'It won't be't same lass. It can't be, can it?'

He choked on the words, as if they were being forced out of him. He didn't want to have this conversation again, but clearly she did, and he owed her that.

'No… but maybe I don't need it to be. Maybe we can adapt to the new normal, whatever that turns out to be, and discover one other all over again. Maybe we need to take the time to figure out who we *both* can be now. Together. Love isn't about staying the same, Mark. It's about staying, *full-stop*. Figuring out how we can make things work and still be happy together. That's all I want – for us to be happy together. If you want that too, forget about assuming you know what I may or may not be happy with. Give me the chance to show you how things can be, between us.'

The silence stretched out, until Mark felt compelled to say something. He said the first thing that came into his head.

'I *am* scared, lass. Fuckin' terrified. I don't know 'ow to be anythin' other than what I've always been.'

'Then you learn. I learn, we learn together, who we can be as a couple from now on. I'm not going anywhere, darling. So, get used to that fact, and find a way to work with me on this. I don't care how long it takes. I know we can get there together.'

'I don't want to have to rely on you for everything.'

'You *won't* have to rely on me for everything! Just for the bits your legs used to do. The rest of you's still here. You're still stubborn, opinionated, bossy, and funny, and charming, and gorgeous with all of it. But mark my words young man – the time will come where you will be expected to step up and do everything you *are* capable of doing, and that will be a lot. The free pass will run out around here just as soon as you get your strength and your resolve back, and get fed up of telling me what to do and find a way to do it yourself.'

She kissed him on the back of the hand.

'And I'm not doing anything *for* you. I'm doing it *with* you. We're a team, Mark. A lot of things have changed, and will continue to change for us, but that won't. We will still be the team we've always been, and if we need support to keep being that team, we'll go ahead and get it. Whatever we find we need, we'll sort it. And I am fully expecting to be repeatedly left in the dust, in the quadbike racing, by the way.'

'Yer can't just let me win owt! That's patronisin,' an' a bit pathetic, if yer don't mind me sayin' so. Not on't quadbikes or owt else! All contests 'ave to be fair an' bloody square.'

'I would never *dream* of 'letting' you win, at anything! I expect to be beaten fair and square. That's the first challenge I set for you. Quadbike racing. And I've been practicing, so don't make the mistake of imagining I'll be any kind of walk-over. You will have to put up a fight, to win.'

He chuckled a bit, in spite of himself, and he felt the tension between them ease, just a little. It occurred to him that it was all of his own making, and he resolved to try, at least, to keep things as light as possible while the dust settled.

Chapter Twenty-three

As the months passed, Mark started attending his physio and rehab appointments and spending more time in the home gym. He decided that he wanted to keep his upper body as powerful as possible, so that when he did feel confident in heading outdoors to look at what he could achieve out there, the parts of him that still worked would be ready for action. His confidence increased a lot when he realised that he could still do certain tasks, like lift fence posts, fix engines and other equipment at the newly-lowered bench in the workshop, and sit in his wheelchair at the edge of the field next to the house and work the dogs to round up a mob of sheep. He still wasn't ready to get onto the quadbike and go far, but the experiment with the sheep in the adjacent field proved to him that once he could go further on the farm, some of what he used to do was still possible for him.

The frustration still bubbled over, a lot, and Adie often found herself biting her tongue at the fact that on some days (she called them the 'pity-party days'), he didn't seem to want to acknowledge his progress and preferred to complain about all that he had lost instead.

It was inevitable, she supposed. It was always going to be a bumpy ride. Mark's loss was like every other kind of grief. There were days that went well, and others where it was almost impossible to find the will to even get out of bed. She had those days herself, but she'd never let Mark see her in the throes of self-pity and resentment, so the opportunities for indulging herself were few and far between. She was strong, but there were times when she longed for someone take the load off her; to be free of it, just for a little while.

Feen had helped a lot, in the early days of it all, when every morning was a lottery, in terms of what mood Mark might wake up in, or lapse into, and how he could be managed. But she and Gavin had to go back to London eventually and, on the morning they finally left, Adie was surprised to feel a peculiar mix of fear and relief. It was going to be scary, without the support she'd had from the outset, but it also meant that she could establish routines with Mark, without having someone else to consider. Part of her was craving that opportunity, for the two of them to be truly alone, and able to figure out how to live life on their own terms. Feen and Gavin were due back at Ravensdown in a few months, but Adie was confident that by the time they made it back here, she and Mark would be 'running' like a well-oiled machine.

Feen stepped forward, and hugged her.

'Don't be worried. I'm only a call away, and of course if there's an emergency I can get a flet to jy up here at very short notice. You're going to be just fine, the pair of you, and I know that us being here has been as much of a hindrance as it has been a help, but I didn't want to leave until the rime felt tight. It does, now. Daddy is getting stronger, and he has more fositive pocus, and you are finding your feet with him quite well, in his new situation.'

'Some days it doesn't feel like that. Some days, I still feel like I'm making a complete hash of everything.'

'I know you do. But trust me; you are doing *brilliantly*. You *both* are! And now it's time for us to leave you to it. Please just keep me in the loop. You know I don't see or sense everything, and I would never want to intrude on you if you're struggling but *don't* want to share that. But, if and when you ever do, just call me, okay? I want to be a jart of this pourney. Don't let the distance convince you otherwise.'

'I won't, and thank you for everything. It's been great, having you all here. The twins have been such a tonic for Mark, and for me. I don't think we could have got this far without you all.'

Feen hugged her again, so tight that she almost lost her breath.

'I'll text when were safely home. See you in a few months' time, or earlier if you need us.'

She bent down and hugged Mark, as he sat in his wheelchair on the driveway.

'Bye, Daddy. Don't give Adie too hard a time, or those poor rehab ladies. Be nice, okay?'

Within minutes of that, they were all gone, and Ravensdown House suddenly felt unnervingly silent. Adie set about making some soup and sandwiches, while Mark made a pot of tea.

Later that evening, the farmhouse still felt surprisingly quiet. Even though Feen and her family weren't noisy by nature, things seemed a little off kilter, now they had left. The energy had changed, and she felt it keenly.

It's going to take a while to get used to that too, I guess. They've been part of the 'new normal' just by being here, ever since Mark came home. Now we have to find <u>another</u> 'new normal.'

Adie decided to have a soothing soak with some lavender bath crystals one of her friends had dropped off a few weeks ago, as part of a 'care package' of gifts to pamper herself with. Rain tapped against the window as she came into the bedroom after her bath. Mark was sitting up in bed, propped against pillows, reading the Sunday papers and he looked up and smiled softly as she in, with damp hair and wearing a slightly scruffy old cotton nightie. She winked at him.

'You're still awake. Anything interesting in those papers today?'

'Not really, but I've 'ad too many thoughts rattling about in me 'ead. Reading all this rubbish takes me mind off other things.'

Adie kicked off her slippers and slid under the covers beside him. They lay in silence for a moment, listening to the rain.

'Weather's bloody shyte, int it? Farm 'ands'll 'ave a right game tomorra, tryin' to plough that bloody field. They'll be up to their knees in muck, at this rate.'

Adie suddenly felt a rush of love. 'Can I snuggle up to you?'

She felt Mark tense a little before dropping his shoulders.

'Aye. That'd be nice, lass.'

She shifted gently against him, laying her head on his shoulder. His arm moved around her, awkward at first, then settling as muscle memory returned.

'I were worried you wouldn't want to anymore.'

'I've been scared of breaking a boundary or three.'

To her immense relief, he laughed quietly, but his laugh was choked with emotion.

'We're 'usband an' wife. We should be able to 'ave a cuddle at least. I've missed that.'

He turned, as best he could and they lay facing one another, with their foreheads touching gently.

'You're still you, you know,' she whispered.

'Sometimes I forget that.'

Adie kissed him; slowly, tentatively, then with more certainty. His hands cupped her face, and she could feel them trembling. She kissed him again, more lingering this time, and rested her palm over his heart.

'We'll find our way. It might be different… but it can still be us.'

'I do want that, love. I really do. More than anything. I just don't know what I can be.'

He put his arm around her as she lay there, and he pulled her closer. They folded into each other, like they always had before, but it wasn't happening with a passion or an urgency; it was a soft and gentle connection, with a new exploration of trust, and rediscovered desire.

Half-nervous, and half-longing, Adie pushed him gently back against his pillows. Then she leaned over him and kissed him deeply – still gently, but with a need to communicate how much love she had for him.

'I miss you. So much.' Her voice was barely a whisper, and she tried not to cry at how delicate everything was, right now, in this moment, like a wrong word or action could shatter the fragile advances she was trying to make, and her even-more fragile heart along with it.

Mark swallowed hard. 'I miss you too, lass… more than I can tell yer.'

She brushed her fingertips down his arm. He shivered slightly, under her touch, but not from the cold.

'We can still be close, darling, if you want to.'

'I want to. I just don't know if I can.'

Adie leaned forward again and kissed him softly, silencing the doubt. She allowed her lips to linger, slow and searching, and Mark let out a low sound in his throat. As her hand traced down his chest, over the familiar lines of him, he trembled. She felt his muscles tighten, but he let her explore. She slipped her nightdress over her head, baring her skin to him in the lamplight.

He was crying, quietly. 'You're so beautiful, Adie.'

He lifted his hand, and cupped her breast. She wanted to weep with the familiarity of it, with longing for things to be the way they'd been before the accident. She desired him so deeply. His rough, calloused thumbs stroked her nipples gently and she gasped. His touch was hesitant, careful, but so, *so* familiar.

She moved up and straddled his hips, kissing his mouth, his jaw, and his neck, letting her tongue blaze a trail of fire over skin that hadn't been touched in far too long. Mark gasped at the sensation, and he slid his hands over her waist, and back up to her breasts. He leaned forward and took one of her nipples in his mouth. He sucked it gently, and she moaned softly.

'Oh, God, that feels so good. I've missed you. I've missed *this.* But let's go slow. Let's just feel. Just us. Just… what we are to one another. Let the love guide what we do.'

She moved against him, as his hands moved over her body, and down between her thighs. They kissed again, more deeply now, their breath mingling, as the familiar rhythm between them slowly came to the fore. Again, there was no urgency, only tenderness, the urge to rediscover one another, and the *need* for each other, that pushed forward.

Mark moved his fingers gently in familiar places and Adie allowed him to continue until a gentle, sweet climax filled her, and left her whimpering and breathless. Then he clasped his hands around the small of her back, and they moved together. It wasn't like before, in what felt like aeons ago, but it was beautiful for them both, to feel the heat of each other's skin, and rediscover the spark that still existed between them.

When they finally collapsed together, Adie laid her head on his chest, and he wrapped his arms around her and held her tight.

He was crying again, and his voice was ragged.

'I didn't think we could still 'ave this.'

'We never *lost* this! We're still what we've always been to each other.'

Mark reached across and switched off the lamp, and they lay there in the dark, listening to each other's breathing, and feeling each other's warmth.

The next thing Adie knew, morning light was spilling through the bedroom curtains. The air was soft and still. They lay tangled together beneath the quilt, her head tucked beneath his chin. The world felt quiet, suspended, and neither of them wanted to change that.

She looked at Mark, lying quietly with his eyes closed, and whispered, softly; 'Are you awake?'

'Aye. Been awake fer ages. Too comfortable to move. I don't want this to end.'

She smiled against his chest, and let her fingers idly draw little circles over the hair on his chest.

'Well, there you are, Mr Raven! I found you again.'

'I think we found each other again. I were scared it were gone, Adie. That part o' me. Of us.'

She lifted her head and looked at him. His eyes were soft, and vulnerable in a way she hadn't seen before.

'It's not gone, darling. We just had to learn each other again.'

Mark brushed his thumb over her cheek.

'Thank you for bein;' so patient wi' me. I know it's taken us a while, to get 'ere.'

She pressed a soft, gentle kiss to his mouth. 'And here we are. And we'll continue to find new ways. There's more to being close than just what willies can do. I think we've already established that, don't you?'

They laughed softly together. Outside, the farm's cockerel was waking up his chickens and the rest of the world. Other sounds started filtering through. Mark gently cleared his throat.

'I know yer said that bacon butties were the exception, but…'

His voice trailed off, and Adie laughed at him.

'Is that all I have to do, to get your attention? Wave a bacon butty in your face? Well, that's an easy thing. Let me see what I can rustle up. But not for a few minutes yet. I'd like to stay cuddled for a bit, of you don't mind?'

'Aye, we can do that, lass. But only until me stomach starts 'moanin' that me throat's been cut.'

They lay quietly together for a few more minutes. Adie rejoiced in the feel of Mark's heartbeat, steady against the side of her face. Then she got up, mindful that one of the most maddening things about getting old was the bladder's refusal to let her stay in bed for long after waking. She knew that Mark needed some privacy to get himself to the bathroom too, to sort out his own hygiene needs. It seemed logical to pop downstairs while he did that, and make some breakfast, to take back to bed again.

Maybe we <u>should</u> do more of this. Maybe bacon sandwiches shouldn't just be a weekend thing. We've earned the right to a few indulgences, haven't we?

Down in the kitchen, as she made breakfast, she found herself humming. She and Mark were a long way from having the lives they had before the accident, but at least now the fear of intimacy was no longer a challenge to be faced. Mark hadn't rebuffed her last night. Instead, he'd been willing – almost insistent even – to offer her pleasure, and allow himself to enjoy *her* touch. It was a massive step forward. She felt confident now, that they could continue to explore ways of enjoying one another again, on a physical and emotional level.

Chapter Twenty-four

The driveway was quiet, except for the soft noises of chickens clucking as they scratched around in the dust on the other side of the hedge at Teapot Cottage. Adie had already been down to let them out, but as yet the sun had still not fully risen. There was a slight chill in the air, and Mark zipped up his fleece and put the hood up.

The front of Ravensdown House, in the small rose garden between the driveway and the house itself, had somehow become his favourite place to sit, early in a morning. It was so beautiful here, especially in that brief time between sunrise and the day warming up. He marvelled at how, in all the years he'd lived here, he'd never noticed what a lovely space this was to just sit in, and reflect, or daydream a little.

The roses were all in bloom now, along with other flowers that gave the garden fragrance and colour. Adie had put a few pretty little white wrought-iron arches around the space, for roses and other climbing flowers to take hold on, and flourish. She'd also put a lovely little birdbath in the centre. The garden wasn't formal, as such, but it was traditional and symmetrically planted. She'd done a magnificent job. Mark had always admired the garden, but he'd never fully appreciated it before, or the work that had gone into making it so lovely, before he ended up in a wheelchair and looking for sunny or shady tranquillity around his house, depending on his mood. This garden offered everything.

As he sat in the wheelchair, with a hot mug of tea on a little foldaway table beside him, he looked out across the distant fields, the ones he used to stride across without ever imagining that one day he wouldn't be capable. He always thought that the time to stop would come on his own terms – when he *declared* it would, not when fate dictated otherwise. He'd thought he was invincible, even after the previous accident when he'd been laid up for months, healing from a fractured neck and a torn liver. There had never been a question, in his mind or anyone else's, that he would get back to work when his body had healed. Adie had been concerned, of course, and so had Feen, but Mark had always been focussed on healing and getting back out there, doing the only thing he'd ever wanted to do, all his life. He was a farmer to the core, with a love of his land and his animals so deep that most people could never understand it.

The usual farm noises were starting now. They'd employed staff to run things. Mark was still the owner/manager, and he still kept a close eye on everything, thanks to Eric Tripper's conscientious reporting, with descriptive narrative about the state of every element of the farm, and photography to support it. They had drones now, too, that routinely surveyed every inch of the land, so Mark could know what was going on where, at any given time. So, the hum of the farm continued. Gates creaked, tractors thrummed, cattle made themselves heard, the rooster crowed. Certain things had stopped for *him*, but the world at large rumbled on, in much the same way as it always had and probably always would.

It's funny, 'ow how the world keeps movin,' even when yer own legs don't. The days and weeks roll on, whether yer part of 'em or not.

He flexed his hands, feeling the callouses, the strength still there.

I'm not useless. I'm not broken. I'm just… different. I feel different. I'm not the man I used to be, but I'm still a man. Last night, Adie looked at me like I was still the man she married. Not a shadow. Not a burden. Just… me.

His throat tightened unexpectedly, and he swallowed hard, as the emotions from last night took hold of him again. He'd thought that losing the use of his legs meant losing everything he'd held dear; his farm, his friends, and – worst of all – Adie herself, and what they'd meant to one another. But she'd stayed, and she'd proved many times over that she wanted him. Not Mark the workhorse, not Mark the provider. Not Mark the 'ageing stud,' as he'd always liked to think of himself, since she'd come into his life. She wanted Mark the *man*, and that was who she stayed for.

A light breeze rippled through the grass, and he closed his eyes, breathing it in, relishing the smell of flowers, earth, and silage. He grinned a little now, at how acute some of his sense had become. He was more aware of a beautiful sunrise, more absorbed by watching a ladybird scuttle across a stone wall, and more gratified by the sound of a singing bird. He'd been surrounded by nature all his adult life, and he'd always loved it, but he'd never fully appreciated all the delightful nuances that thrived within it, before his accident. He was a changed man, but it was dawning on him now that maybe he wasn't any less of one – not in the ways that mattered to the people who loved him. Maybe he was just a *different* man, now. No less worthy, just different.

So, I 'ave to see't world differently, don't I? I 'ave to look at everythin' wi' fresh eyes, in a new way.

It was becoming clearer to him that by accepting his new limitations, he'd already started appreciating the 'newness' that was slowly but inexorably filling the empty spaces within him with a different kind of joy and comfort.

He sipped his cooling tea, and turned in his chair to look again at the farmhouse. He'd restored it so painstakingly, back in the day, with Beth. They'd worked like dogs to get the house done so they could start their much longed-for family. Sadly, complications after Feen's birth had meant that she would be their only child. The big family they'd dreamed of wouldn't happen, but they'd taken that on the chin, and they'd rolled up their sleeves and got on with building a good home, a good farm, and a good life.

Beth's premature death from bowel cancer, when Feen was just fourteen, had left him to face the challenges alone, of raising their daughter and running the farm. It hadn't been an easy path to tread, but he'd battled on, and he'd made a success of it all. The farm thrived, and so did Feen. Shrewd investments had led to a solid rock of financial cushioning too, and Mark was thankful for it now, because it enabled them to stay here, on their beloved farm. Losing the use of his lower body had been a devastating enough blow. Having to lose Ravensdown too would have been unthinkable.

Adie was in the house, getting breakfast ready. This morning, they were having pancakes with batter he had whipped the night before and put in the fridge to be ready.

He gripped the wheels of his chair and slowly turned to face the front door, which was now equipped with an automatic-opening mechanism, so all he had to do was press the button on the wall. Inside, he could hear Adie humming to herself and singing a silly jingle that often came on the radio, as she was getting their breakfast and a pot of good strong coffee onto the table. She sounded happy, and he realised that this was the first time he'd heard her singing since the accident, months before. The jingle, and her hopelessly out-of-tune voice, made him smile. The memory of last night's reintroduction to intimacy warmed him, and gave him hope.

He suddenly realised that for the first time since the accident, he felt steady and solid, on ground that no longer seemed to be shifting beneath his feet.

Part III

Chapter Twenty-five

'Are you sure you've both got everythin'? Passports, money, bank cards, medicines, tickets, *underwear?*'

Adie rolled her eyes at Mark. He was fretting, and while it had been funny and quite endearing to start with, this was now the fifth (or sixth?) time he'd asked, and it was starting to wear a bit thin.

'Yes. For the last bloody time, we have everything! Trudie and I have both checked, umpteen times. We're good to go, darling. Please stop worrying. And please, for the love of God, stop reminding me of the fact that when we flew to Cancun *seven years ago now,* I forgot to pack my bag of knickers and bras, and left them here on the bed.'

He grinned at her and grunted.

'I could've run you buggers down to't airport. Yer didn't 'afta get bloody train to London at silly cost.'

'I've told you before. It's just *easier*, for everybody, and we booked well in advance so we got the tickets for less than it would cost to drive down there and back. We're staying with Mand and Max, and they'll run us to the airport in the morning, to catch our flight.'

Trudie piped up now too. 'Mark, she's with me. She's in the best hands she could be in, outside of yours. I have friends dotted about across Europe, so we'll always have somewhere to go, and we're big girls. We can take good care of ourselves and each other. The blog we've set up will tell everyone what we're up to, and when, and where, so nobody will ever have to worry about where we are.'

'Well, get in't car then, lasses. Yer don't want to miss yer bloody train. That wouldn't be much of a start t'yer big adventure, would it?'

Trudie and Adie both burst out laughing. 'God, are you always like this?' Trudie demanded.

Adie answered for Mark.

'I'm afraid his protective streak grew into a two-headed monster after the accident, Trude. It doesn't matter if I'm only going to the hairdresser, these days. He worries about it, like some great harm is going to befall me on the way there or back. Needless to say, it's been a long time since I last went anywhere without having to explain myself or promise to be back by a certain time.'

She grinned at Mark and winked at him. He responded by poking his tongue out at her, and pulling a face. The she checked her watch.

'Oh, for God's sake! The train doesn't go for another hour and a half! We have time for another pot of coffee, if you'd like to make one for us all? And maybe we could have a slice of your carrot cake?' She turned to Trudie.

'Mark makes the best carrot cake! He's even making the lavender shortbread now, for the Saturday market. He's had to make and freeze thirty double batches, to cover the three months we'll be away for, and one of Peg's part time staff is going to sell everything on her stall while we're gone. It's been a mission, but he's pulled it off. We could hardly move in this kitchen, last weekend.'

'I bet it smelled divine, though,' Trudie offered.

'It did. But wait until you taste the carrot cake. Mark has turned into quite the baker. Almost puts me to shame, but not quite.'

She turned her attention to Mark.

'And speaking of fretting, I am trying not to imagine this house burning down while I'm gone, so the concern goes two ways, but I'm not running off at the mouth about it. *Quietly* terrified, but holding it together.'

He laughed at her. 'A'reet. Point taken. But I *am* allowed to worry, aren't I? It's not every day me sexy wife goes gallivantin' around Europe wi'out me.'

'You're allowed to worry, of course. But please do it quietly, and not excessively. The last thing I need is to be worrying myself, about *you* fretting about *me!* That *is* as crazy as it sounds.'

She watched as Mark deftly started making a pot of coffee. Since his accident, he'd been forced to spend less time on the farm and had needed to find other things that interested him and enabled him to feel useful. He still found plenty of farm chores to do, thanks to his modified quad bike, and his motorized wheelchair allowed him to work on projects in the barn. He had even managed a bit of DIY in the house, installing tongue and groove panelling to a metre high, around the bottom half of the walls in the kitchen and the hallway. He'd made an excellent job of it.

But he had also allowed his 'feminine side' to shine through a little more, which delighted Adie. He enjoyed pottering around in the kitchen! He was used to cooking, after doing it for himself and Feen before she was old enough to step in and take over, but he'd never had a proper go at baking. He'd turned out to be quite good at it and regularly produced a pretty decent cake or batch of biscuits. He was never going to be a Gordon Ramsay or a Gino D'Acampo, and he always stuck to the recipes and never tried to experiment or deviate, but his baking was more than enjoyable, and whenever Feen and Gavin came to stay, he would install himself in the kitchen for an entire day, baking cakes, biscuits, fruit loaves and – always – Gavin's all-time favourite, ginger crunch.

Gavin looked across the table at Adie now, and raised his eyebrows at her.

'You don't seem particularly nervous, or excited, about this intrepid adventure? I'd be like a cat on a hot tin roof, if it were me, going on a big trip like this. It sounds amazing.'

Adie shook her head. 'I *am* excited, I think. But I'm so tired! I haven't slept properly in days, with everything to think about before I go. Once I get on the plane, I'll be fine. There's lots to look forward to. We're flying into Amsterdam, staying a few nights there, and looking around the interesting areas of the Netherlands. There are some great bus tours and things, so we can see quite a lot in a short time. I'm especially keen to see the Escher Museum in The Hague! *Longing* for that! Then, we're getting the train to Paris. I won't actually believe it's all real, until we get underway.'

'You're tired, that's true. But it won't take you long to get into the thwing of sings. Just don't forget to come home, will you?' Feen's smirk softened her plea.

'Of course I won't forget! Everything and everyone I hold dear is right here in this town! I've got my little laptop, to keep in touch with you all, and to update our blog of course, so you won't get to miss me much.'

Mark snorted. 'That's a matter of opinion, lass. This place is gonna be far too quiet wi'out yer. At least Feen and Gavin an't kids'll be 'ere to keep us company while yer gone.'

Gavin grinned at Adie. 'Don't worry. We'll take care of him.'

'I don't need takin' care of,' Mark growled. 'I'm perfectly capable on me own.'

Adie giggled at him. She knew that what he said was true. He probably *would* be absolutely fine on his own. Since the accident, he'd worked incredibly hard to push his own limits and do more and more, to get as close as he could to functioning the way he used to. He was as strong and fit as he could be, as a man with paraplegia. His ability to do most of the farm tasks was extraordinary. He still needed help, and they had well-skilled staff to do the actual 'legwork' required, and they'd been careful to employ people who were supportive of Mark doing as much as possible. They'd all been briefed to encourage him to do what he could, but also to recognise signs of fatigue or distress. Things were running as well, if not better, than they'd run before he'd been so cruelly crushed by his own combine harvester.

But the peace of mind, that Feen and Gavin and the kids would be around for the whole time she was gone, was immeasurable for Adie. The couple could work well enough from Ravensdown, and Alder and Willow were on summer school holidays now. Feen had talked to the head of the local primary school here in Torley, and they'd been accepted to start their new autumn term there until Adie returned and the family went back to London.

The twins were quite used to short stints at the local school. A lot of the kids there already knew them from times before, when Feen and Gavin had been in Torley during school terms. The school was the same one Feen had gone to herself, and they were always very flexible and helpful with meeting Alder and Willow's educational needs. It would be a different story when they started secondary school, and a greater need for stability would preclude pulling them out whenever circumstances dictated. The family would have to fit the circumstances around the academic year, instead of the other way around. But Feen and Gavin didn't seem worried or fazed by that, so Adie decided not to be, either.

'Well, you grumpy old sod, I've already told Feen not to take any crap from you. You don't get to be a prima donna while I'm gone. If you don't behave yourself, I will hear about it, and I'll be on the next plane back, to sort you out. Don't ruin my holiday by being a stubborn old goat.'

'If he wants to be a gubborn old stoat, I will pull him out of his wheelchair and bick him up the kackside. I *will*, Daddy. As Adie is my witness, I will *not* be standing for any nonsense.'

Feen's words were strident, but she had a gleam in her eye. She absolutely would put him in his place, but Adie knew it would take a lot for her to do any more than roll her eyes and shake her head at him. She adored her father, and he adored her. There wasn't going to be much to fall out about, really.

Gavin laughed. 'I'm going to be 'Switzerland,' just so you both know. Neutral shall be my middle name, in all this. You two can slug it out if you must, but I won't be taking sides. I might be a spy for Adie though, if she pays me enough.' He winked at Adie, and she winked back.

'I'm sure we can work something out. But I may have already bugged the place. You know, put a few microphones and cameras around. Every move you make, every step you take, I'll be watching you.'

Mark snorted. 'I'll not be takin' any bloody steps, will I, you daft bugger.'

'Ah, maybe not, but maybe I'll be watching for dalliances with other women. You're still a tasty specimen, and I'm not sure at *all,* about leaving you to your own devices for three months.'

He snorted again. 'Don't be daft. Even with me newly acquired prowess in't bedroom, it's only ever you, love. If it in't you, it's no bugger.'

'Urgh! *Far* too much information,' Feen spluttered, into her tea.

'That's right. 'Tee Em I,' right? Well, young lady, I'll 'ave you know that sex in't just the domain o't young an' sprightly. Us owd buggers are still capable of gettin' a leg over, when't mood takes us. One day *you'll* be in yer sixties and keen t'keep goin'. Gettin' yer Zimmer frames all tangled and what-not.'

'Oh, for God's sake!' Feen rolled her eyes and gave a mock-shudder. She was trying very hard not to laugh.

Gavin leaned forward and kissed her on the cheek. 'I'll probably still want to shag you when we're in our sixties.'

Feen tried to look haughty, and failed. 'Thank you for that. I *think* it's a compliment, so I shall take it as such. But please, for the love of God, can we please talk about something *other* than my father's sex life? Or ours?'

Trudie giggled now. 'At least you all have a sex life! I'm in the desert, a bit. Maybe I'll have a holiday fling, while we're away.'

'What, like Shirley Valentine?' Gavin grinned at her. 'Go Trude!'

'Well, why not? I can still pull. I'm sure of that. I've been ogled enough times in the Bull and Royal since word got out that I'm getting divorced. I think I can still shake my tail-feather a bit.'

Adie smirked. 'Yes, but the oglers in the Bull are all about seventy-five if they're a day, and most of them are already married.'

Trudie nodded. 'I'm sure some of them are gay actually, but they're never going to admit it at that age, are they? No. To be fair, the pickings are pretty slim around these parts, and Carlisle's not much better. I might score a nice Frenchman, like Minty Cartwright's man. What was his name? Marcel? He might have a nice friend he could introduce me to. I rather fancy living in the south of France with a bereted, stripy-t-shirted, cycling, garlic-necklaced man who calls me *'ma Cherie.'* A girl could do a lot worse.'

'No, Trudie. You need a man with a Maserati or a Bentley, not a bloody bicycle. You're too old to cride rossbar or even tandem, come to that.'

'Well, thank you for your cheek, Madam Feen! But you're probably right. Comfort has to replace romanticism, at this age. But perhaps there might be a *little* bit of romance, along the way….'

Trudie trailed off, realising that she had probably said too much about wanting to enjoy a 'dalliance' or two of her own, while they were travelling.

Feen bit her lip. 'There will be. Not with the first man you meet, who absolutely *will* turn out to be an idiot – and married to boot – but the second one you meet who feels like he might be a candidate could well be a flice one to have a ning with. Please just be careful. You're not going on holiday to have your heart broken. It will be a fling, and nothing more, so you need to know not to get too invested. That would certainly screw up the plans you'll go on to make after that.'

Trudie shook her head. 'My heart is already broken, sweetheart, remember? I'm not looking for anyone to mend it. Maybe just pour a little soothing balm on it for a bit. That'll do me nicely. But don't worry, Mark. I won't be letting Adie fall into anyone's clutches. Not that I need to try. She is still completely besotted with *you*, after a decade or so of marriage.'

Adie cleared her throat. 'You don't have to worry, on that score.'

'I know, lass.' His voice was soft, and they exchanged a long, intimate look that said all there was to say for them both, about how they felt about each other.

A horn tooted in the driveway, and Adie immediately recognised it as Bob and Sheila's Land Rover. Sheila came running in.

'Oh, I'm so glad we've caught you! I wasn't sure we'd make it in time. We planned to be here an hour ago, but Bob discovered an 'ole in one of the fences, on the way over, and we had to stop and put a temporary fix on it until he's got more to time to sort it properly. I was sure we were going to miss you. I know you've probably already got plenty of food for the train journey, but here's a few slices of Parkin, and I've got the rest for Mark to put into one of the cake tins.'

'Ooh, Parkin! D'you remember baking me a Parkin cake when I first came to Torley, and was house sitting, down at Teapot Cottage?

Sheila nodded. 'I do! That's why you've got it now. You 'ad Parkin when you came, and now you've Parkin as you're going.'

'Well... I *am* coming back, you know…'

'Oh, I know you are, love! And I'll be bloody glad to see you when you do. But it just seemed right some'ow, to bake a Parkin, to send you on your way with.'

'I'll miss you, so much!'

'Oh, don't be so bloody daft! We'll all be 'ere when you get back. Just 'ave fun won't you? Don't be worrying about us lot. Face-ache'll be fine.'

Adie always laughed when Sheila called her brother Face-ache. It was her pet name for him – a term of endearment – and, as he often said, he'd been called a lot worse.

'I know he will. He's not looking forward to being checked on every five minutes, but I appreciate you all rallying round to take care of anything he can't manage on his own, or with the farm staff. I'm trying not to feel guilty of abandoning ship.'

Bob scoffed at her. 'Don't be so silly! You deserve this trip, more than anyone else I know. We're all very much looking forward to living vicariously through your amazing adventures, so don't wait too long to start adding to your blog. We'll be hanging on every word, won't we Sheila?'

Sheila nodded, and stepped forward to give Adie a warm hug, as Gavin got up and started to take the bags out to Mark's Range Rover SV. It was a beautiful vehicle; sturdy and strong, and it had been fully adapted to suit his specific needs. He loved it, and Adie remembered the smile on his face when he got behind the wheel for the first time, after having the controls explained by one of his rehab workers. He was always keen to drive it, and that was why he'd felt a bit deprived of the chance to drive Adie and Trudie to London! But she hadn't wanted to worry about him on the return journey by himself. If he needed to stop at the services for the loo, or get something to eat, it might not go as smoothly as anticipated. As yet, he was still becoming familiar with which of the services on the M6 and M1 motorways had easier services access for people with disabilities.

As they all headed outside, Feen touched Adie's arm.

'Can I have a quick word? It's nothing to worry about. I just wanted to give you this.'

She handed Adie a piece of tissue paper, and Adie unwrapped it to find the most exquisite pendant, of a silver bird set within a pretty ring of moonstone and amethyst crystals, on a delicate silver chain. She held it up to the light. It sparked and shone in the sunshine.

'Oh, Feen! This is beautiful! These are the stones for safe travel, aren't they? Moonstone for luck and happiness, and amethyst for protection.'

Feen laughed, lightly. 'Ah! I'm pleased to see I've taught you well! And the bird is for hying fligh, and feeling uplifted as you travel. May the wind be ever beneath your wings.'

'You made this, am I right?'

'Yes, especially for you. Wear it always, and you will come to no harm. Well, you won't anyway, but this is just a little extra support for you to have a wonderful time.'

As ever, her hug was surprisingly tight. For a tiny woman, she certainly had some strength. Gavin hugged Adie next, and Alder and Willow came rushing out of the house to do the same. Sheila and Bob drew her into a group hug, and she was surprised to see tears in Sheila's eyes. The sisters-in-law shared a special bond, and Adie was well aware of how much Sheila would feel her absence, while she was away.

'I'll be back to annoy you before you even know I'm gone,' she whispered quietly in Sheila's ear.

'Well, I was saying to Bob, I might fly out and join you somewhere for a few days, in a month or so, if I can get away.'

'That would be wonderful! Peg and Carla have both said the same thing. Carla even threatened to drag her poor mum along, which would be lovely, although we'd have to meet up somewhere that wasn't too hot. Hazel's in her eighties now, and doesn't cope so well with the heat anymore. So yes! Do try! I'd *love* to see you out there somewhere.'

The were about to get into the car, when another one came up the drive, tooting its horn. It ws Kevin – Trudie's ex-husband. He got out, looking slightly worried.

'God, I thought I'd missed you! I just came to say goodbye, and I hope you and Adie have a lovely trip. I was going to come to the train station, but I forgot what time you said the train left and it all seemed a bit too… I don't know, Brief Encounter-ish, or something? I didn't want to give the wrong impression. But I have something for you. It's a debit card with a couple of grand on it. Just in case you need it to fall back on. I know you said you've got enough, but you never know, do you? It might come in handy, even if you just see a handbag you like.'

Trudie bit her lip. 'Thanks, Kev. That's really thoughtful. You didn't have to do that, but it's lovely that you have.'

'Use it for something special if you're *not* running out of money. But if you are, it might be enough to get you out of bother.'

He stepped forward and hugged her, then stepped back and looked wistful. Adie could sense there was more he wanted to say, but everyone – including him – knew it wasn't the right time. But then he smiled, as convincingly as he could, and stepped away to let Adie and Trudie get into the car.

Mark adeptly hoisted himself into the driver's seat and everyone stood waving as they set off down the drive. Adie turned back to take a last look at Ravensdown House. It would be three months before she'd see it again. She would miss home, and her family, but a longed-for adventure was about to start, so she turned her attention to that instead, and grabbed hold of Trudie's hand and squeezed it.

'Are you ready?'

Trudie squeezed back. 'Oh hell, yes! Get me onto that train, momma. Life is about to begin!'

At the station, Adie refused Mark's offer to help them get their bags out of the car.

'It's easy, and the entrance is right over there, so you don't need to get out. Just do a U-turn down there, and you'll be on the road for home. Text me when you're home safely.'

Tears sprang to her eyes. She could feel Mark's thoughts, as if they were her own. He was torn. He wanted her to go on the trip – he'd said so, many times, and she knew he meant every word. But he was apprehensive too, about being without her for three long months. He would miss her, and would feel the void more keenly for being the one left at home, while she was gallivanting around Europe, having fun.

She opened the driver's door and hugged him tight, and tried not to let her tears fall. She sniffed hard, and he patted her on the back.

'I'll be in touch. Every single day. And you just call me, whenever you want to, okay? It doesn't matter what time of day or night. Promise me, Mark?'

'Aye lass, I promise! And same goes. You ring me whenever you want. I'll 'ave me phone wi' me at all times, on vibrate and ring. I'll not miss yer calls, love. Now go. 'Ave some fun. I love you to't moon an' back, and I'll be 'ere, waitin', when you come 'ome.'

Suddenly, Adie balked.

I shouldn't be doing this! I shouldn't be leaving him. Why should I be doing this when he can't? It feels unfair.

Her sudden indecision must have shown on her face because Mark shook his head, firmly. 'Now, lass. Get yerself onto that bloody train. I'll not forgive yer if yer bottle it. Don't you worry about me. I'm in good 'ands, wi't family, and I couldn't live wi' meself if yer bottled it because o' me. This is your moment. This is your perfect moment. Take it, love, and kick fuck out o' Europe.'

She laughed now. 'Okay. We'll try. Now, Trudie is starting to do her anxious-dance about missing the train, so we better go. Love you massive, my darling. Thank you, for this, and everything else. You are my world. My *absolute* world.'

Tears threatened to fall, again, and Mark rolled his eyes at her.

'And you're mine, lass. Now get on that bastard bloody train and go and *see* the piggin' world! Or some of it, at least. I'll see yer when yer get back. Now go!'

And, with that, he moved the car forward, so she had to step back from it. He bravely blew her a kiss and swung the car out and into the traffic.

Adie tried to ignore the lump in her throat, as Trudie tapped her on the shoulder. 'We have to go. The train is already here, and leaving in six minutes.'

She took a deep breath, adjusted her handbag across her body, picked up her case, and the two women headed for the platform.

The first leg of their big adventure was about to begin.

Chapter Twenty-six

As Mark eased the Range Rover into the traffic and headed back towards Torley, his mind was unsettled. It had been harder than Adie might have imagined, for him to wave her off at the train station with a thumbs-up and a smile. He was happy that she was going off on her big European adventure, and finally getting to realise a long-cherished dream, but he was going to miss her like fire. She was his rock. He himself was almost as strong and capable a man as he'd been before his horrific accident, but he still felt more than a bit nervous at being left alone.

The reality of Adie being gone for three whole months was daunting. Thankfully, Mark didn't have many physical challenges around the house. The cleaner came in twice a week for three hours, and he was perfectly capable of cooking decent food and doing the washing up by himself. He also had a good system going for getting the laundry done and dried, and he'd become a dab hand with the ironing. Eighteen months after the accident, he'd found a way to do most things. His self-care and exercise regimen kept him as healthy, fit, and active as it was possible to be. It was nothing now, to do most of what he had done before, apart from walk. Even his tractor had been modified, for him to use with paraplegia. He loved his car, and was used to driving it now, and his adjusted quad bike had been easy to get used to again after Gavin's friend had changed the controls for him.

In the first few weeks after his accident, Mark had been in a heavy state of denial. Then came the frustration that constantly seemed to bubble over into outright fury, at the fact that he'd lost so much. Back then, the emotional overwhelm had all-but drowned him. He'd felt so much; anger and disbelief at what had happened, and the deepest confusion imaginable about *how* it had happened. It upset him a lot, in the beginning, that he couldn't remember.

He *never* got out of the combine until he'd turned the engine off and applied the brake! It was such a simple thing, to switch everything off before he got out, and then back on again when he got back in. He wasn't a 'lazy' or complacent farmer. As he'd said, many times; 'complacency on a farm'll get yer killed before owt else will.'

Bob had checked the combine over, with a fine-tooth-comb, and could find no explanation for why Mark would have got out of it. It was running well, sounding like it always did, and the mechanics, tyres, brakes, and everything else, were in good shape and working as they should. Bob had even taken a long look around the field and its perimeter, to see if there had been anything that might have distracted Mark and prompted him to get out of the cab while the machine was still running. He found nothing. He knew that his brother-in-law had long since lost the urge to go fox or badger chasing, and the field had no holes or other anomalies he might have been compelled to get out and investigate. Bob had been as bamboozled as everybody else, about what had happened and why.

The reason Mark had got out of the combine while it was still running was still a mystery and was likely to always remain so. It had taken him a while, to get past the rage and resentment, but he'd eventually come to the realisation that there was nothing good to be gained from being angry or upset at not knowing why he'd made such a foolish move.

It doesn't matter now, does it? What's done is done. There's no point in frettin' about it now. Knowing what really 'appened won't change the bloody outcome. It's not like I can say, 'oh that's right! I remember now,' an' 'ave the remembrance reverse the result. If that were even possible, I'd 'ave tried 'ypnosis, or whatever else they've got goin' that can 'elp folk remember summat they've blanked off.

The acceptance that followed, of his altered life, was also a gradual thing. To start with, he'd been worried about everything it was possible for a man to worry about. He worried about the practicalities of being paralysed from the waist down. How was he supposed to function independently? Was that even possible? He worried about his marriage. What would happen between him and Adie if he couldn't make love to her anymore? Would she leave suddenly, or drift away slowly, after realising that living with him the way he was now would simply be too hard?

He worried about his friendships. Would everyone start to see him differently now? Would they *treat* him differently? Would they all see him as just a shadow now, of the man he used to be?

He worried mightily about the farm. Farming: working manually on land he loved with every part of his heart – it was all he'd ever known. It was who he *was!* He wasn't aware, before the accident, how much of his identity was tied up with being a farmer. He defined himself by his physical work, by the achievements that farming brought. Would he start to feel differently, about his house and land? Would they stop being the comfort and familiarity he'd always been so sure of and grateful for? Would he start to resent, instead, a house he couldn't easily navigate anymore, or land he couldn't work?

So many questions – initially at least – had been impossible to answer. Mark's turmoil had left him dealing with emotions he wasn't prepared for. Grief, anger, shame, confusion, and a profound sense of worthlessness had engulfed him for many weeks. He'd also been terrified of being a burden on his family – a dead weight around the place, for them all to have to carry. For a man who'd always been stubbornly independent and self-reliant, he'd found himself in a position of having to accept help on every level. He'd been more or less relegated to 'baby' status – literally unable to do anything for himself. He'd hated the humiliation of that. It *had* felt shameful, despite everyone's assurances that it was no problem to pitch in and do whatever they could to support him and his family. He just couldn't stand the fact that it had been necessary. There was no doubt that his pride had hindered his recovery for months. He'd railed against everything, even his own wife, who was frantic in her efforts to stay close to him, and distraught at the fact that he kept pushing her away.

He'd been *testing* her, back then. He'd pushed her as far as he could, to see where her breaking point was; at what point she'd give up on him. Part of him had *wanted* her to walk away. He thought back to that now, as he drove towards home. He'd *wanted* her to leave him – as much for herself and the life she deserved, as to avoid the humiliation he'd felt at what his body had become and what it could no longer do.

It hadn't worked. Mercifully, Adie had seen his tactic, and she'd ignored his tantrums, bargaining, and every other attempt he'd made, to get her to give up. She'd weathered the worst of storms, in that. He'd put her through hell.

And she'd proved him wrong. For a long time after the accident, they hadn't touched – not even so much as a hug. He'd spurned any advances from her, terrified that a touch or a hug would lead to a desire for something more – something he knew he could no longer give. It would have been unfair to them both, to have reached a point of needing the kind of fulfilment that he could no longer give or feel himself, only to suffer the wretched disappointment of not being able to 'get there.'

But, over time their intimacy had returned, and it had been Adie herself that initiated it, the first time. That first sexual encounter had been terrifying, but ultimately satisfying and sweet, in a way that he'd never been able to even imagine before it had happened.

They'd both been left breathless, shaking, and in tears. But it had shown him – finally – after months of her trying to convince him that intimacy was still possible, that she'd been right. And, deep inside himself, the frightened part of him that always hoped she *wouldn't* give up, the part that had always willed her to stay, became more important than his dogged denial or stupid, misplaced pride.

He'd realised, much later, how brave she had been – how much of a chance she had taken, in seducing him in the way she had, that first night. She'd risked a row, a refusal, a rejection, but she'd doggedly carried on, and he knew that it had been more for him than for herself. Her love for him outstripped any need of her own, but he had been able to fulfil her need that night, and many times since. Now, they were as familiar with one another as they'd always been.

It was different now, but it was still worthwhile. Mark blinked back tears as he remembered again how close he had come to losing everything with Adie because she *did* have a breaking point, and if he'd carried on the way he was, she *would* have reached it. Everyone had their limits, of what they could endure and there were no two ways about it – he *had* been a bastard, for quite a long time.

She was a hell of a woman, and she was *his* woman. His wife. She loved him with all her heart and soul, and there had been many times, usually late into the night when they'd both found it hard to fall asleep, where he'd told her how sorry he was that he'd put her through that. She always said the same things; that there was nothing to apologise for, that if the boot had been on the other foot she'd have been more of a bitch than he could ever imagine, and he would most certainly have left. And she said that him having useless legs didn't matter to her as much as it mattered to him. She knew how *much* it mattered to him, but she tapped away at the strong part of him that had somehow fallen dormant in the process of acceptance and recovery, and she'd reawakened his drive to be successful.

He'd come to realise that life was still worth living, that he could be strong in almost as many ways as he had been before he'd lost the use of his legs. The ways in which he could no longer be strong were small, compared to what he was capable of, if he put his mind to it. Strong arms and shoulders, a strong torso, and a strong will and *mind* all made him much the same man as before. He wasn't diminished in the eyes of the people who loved him, and he let that strengthen his own resolve to not see *himself* as diminished.

The frustrations of decreased mobility in public places were ongoing though, as were the patronising or condescending attitudes of strangers in shops, restaurants, and other places he sometimes needed or wanted to go. Uneven pavements and lack of ramps on street corners were always a challenge for the wheelchair, and entryways and exits were sometimes a nightmare, especially the ones with heavy doors, when he was on his own. Having to deal with people who pretended not to see him was also tedious and frustrating. The ones who would bend down and shout in his face, presumably from some misguided idea that his disability extended to being unable to hear or have a normal conversation, were even worse. Many times, he'd said to someone; 'Bein' unable to walk doesn't make me 'ard of 'earin,' so yer can lower yer bloody tone unless yer want me to start shoutin' back.' It all turned going out in public into a challenge to be braced for, every time.

Having to 'educate' people, as he went along, was irritating but he felt it was necessary, because attitudes needed to change. People needed to be more aware of what 'disability' actually meant.

The assumption that a man in a wheelchair can only be spoken to like he's a moron is ignorant and bloody silly. If folk can't properly think about who's in front of 'em before they start wi' that caper, who's the bloody 'alfwit <u>really</u>?

That aside, going out in his local community was rarely an issue at all. He and Adie often went for dinner at one of the pubs in town, both of which were fully compliant with disability legislation, and provided good access. The Ravens were well-known throughout the community, and almost everyone they met, in the street, in the shops, or in the pubs, restaurants and other public buildings, was always happy to see them. Nobody was openly supercilious, condescending, patronising or ignorant. Even after a year and a half, Mark still always felt reassured by that, as if nothing much had really changed. Nobody treated him any differently, other than to sometimes ask how he was doing, whether he'd smashed any weightlifting records lately, or whether he or his family needed any support with something.

Some of them probably did wonder, behind closed doors, what difficulties he might have when it came to shagging his wife, or whether he could take a piss without making a mess, but nobody ever asked. To his face, at least, they were respectful, mindful, and supportive.

As he approached Torley town, his stomach growled. He'd been too nervous to eat any breakfast this morning. He decided, on a whim, to call into see Peg at Ye Olde Torley Tea Shoppe. Lunch in the café would be nice. He found a free disabled parking space close by, so he swung into it, and got himself organised to get to the pavement. Peg's café was an older building, but there was a ramp, and the door was just wide enough for him to get inside. It was a slightly tough push, to get it open, but he managed it and wheeled himself in. The café was starting to fill up with the lunchtime crowd; mostly shoppers and a couple of booted-up hikers who were peering at an ordnance survey map. Peg's assistant raised her hand in greeting then called Peg out from the back. She came out, wiping her hands on a tea towel, and beamed broadly at Mark.

'Hi, love! You've seen them off alright then? I did mean to say, you should pop in for lunch on your way home from the station. I clean forgot to mention it when I was up at yours yesterday! I swear to God, sometimes I feel like I'm headed down the slippery slope to dementia, the amount I seem to be forgetting to do or say, these days! Anyway, what d'you fancy? I've all the usual stuff but I'm also doing pizzas now. I treated the café to a little pizza oven, a month or so ago, and it's working out alright if you don't mind waiting ten minutes for me to put the toppings on and get it cooked. You can have whatever you want, for toppings. I've got most things.'

'That sounds good. Could I 'ave a meat feast, wi' some fresh tomato on it?'

'Course you can, love! And shall I bring you a pot of coffee, to be going on with?'

Mark nodded, as she moved a chair away from the table to give him room to fit his wheelchair. Within less than a minute she was back with a cafetiere, and a mug, and a jug of milk.

'I know you don't take sugar. So, the girls got their train okay, then? I bet they were a bit wobbly. They were excited, but a bit daunted too, I expect. I know Adie was in two minds about leaving you for so long, but I'm glad she's decided to go. You're fine on your own, aren't you, love? As capable as you ever were.'

'I'd have *shoved* her onto't bloody train if she 'adn't got on it 'erself,' Mark growled. 'She needs to do this, Peg. She's 'ad it as a dream for forty bloody years, and she in't getting' any younger. As wi' me – yer never know when summat can change an' chance is wiped off table. She's fit, 'ealthy an' strong, but she won't always be. I couldn't stand the idea of 'er livin' wi' regrets because she didn't do it while she were able.'

'You're absolutely right, Mark. We have to make our dreams come true while we can. Nobody knows what's around the corner for them. Interrailing doesn't just have to be for the young, either, does it? You know, I've decided to join Adie and Trudie in Rome when they eventually get there. I've always wanted to see it, ever since the days when I used to teach Latin, decades ago. I don't know why I've never gone, to be honest, but I'm going to make it happen whether Eric wants to come or not. Those two have inspired me to make one of my *own* dreams come true.'

'Good fer you, lass! I know they'll be pleased to see yer, when yer get there.' He grinned at her, as she gave him a wink and scurried back to the kitchen.

He decided, on another whim, to text Feen and see if she wanted to come down and join him for lunch. She responded straight away and, just as his pizza was being served up, she came bouncing into the café.

'Hi, Daddy! This is a nice idea. Lovely, to do something spontaneous, since I hardly ever chet the gance these days! I'm under orders to take Gavin a pizza, so I'll order that when I get my own lunch, which I think will be Peg's gorgeous deep-filled salmon quiche and salad. I think I need a cot of poffee too.'

She glanced quickly over the menu, as she spoke. 'So, Adie and Trude are on their way to London! It's good that they were able to get a direct train. It makes a difference when you don't have to fanny about with changes. I'm all for things being as easy as possible, especially when there's luggage involved.'

'Aye, Mand's pickin' 'em up from Euston. Their flight to Amsterdam doesn't go until six o'clock tomorra night, so they've got this afternoon and most o' tomorra wi' Mand an' Max. 'Appen they'll find summat to amuse theirselves.'

Feen laughed. 'Knowing Miranda, I am certain that vodka martinis will be involved.'

'As long as it's only tonight. I don't want 'em getting' on't plane pissed as farts.'

Feen giggled again. 'I'm sure they'll be right as rain, Daddy. You really must stop worrying about every little thing.'

'I know. I will. But I'll miss 'er daft face.'

'Well, you'll have *my* daft face to look at, and Gavin's, and Alder's, and Willow's. We're all going to be just fine, and so will Adie and Trude.'

She was right. He knew she was. She was nearly *always* right, especially about things like whether someone on a journey was going to come to any strife. Sometimes her 'portal' into futures that most other people couldn't see was incredibly helpful. Other times, it was profoundly upsetting – especially when it failed, like it had right before his accident. If Feen could have foreseen that – or even found a glimpse after the fact, into a realm that explained why it had happened, it would have been more than just helpful. He might not be stuck in this wheelchair now, or he could at least understand why he was.

But it wasn't fair to blame the poor woman for what she hadn't seen! For whatever reason, Feen's intuition about Mark's accident had failed. It wasn't within *anyone's* capabilities to explain why – not even Feen's herself. She'd felt terrible, initially, that something she hadn't had an inkling about had led to such a catastrophic outcome. As such, the accident wasn't something she could have prevented or even warned about. She was angry with her spirit guides for a long time, over that. She felt betrayed by them. As far as she was concerned, they had failed her over what had turned out to be one of the biggest disasters of her life.

But Mark had told her to let herself off the hook for something that wasn't a 'failure' at all! It wasn't her fault that she hadn't been give the insight. Her reminded her, on many occasions when they'd talked about it, that she did a lot of good for a lot of people, but not everyone could catch that boat. Sometimes the spiritual system simply failed, and it wasn't as if they could turn back the clock, was it? They had to adjust to and work with where they were now. Feen's intuitive guidance wasn't guaranteed to show up every time she would have welcomed it, and that annoyed her greatly. But when the insights did come, they were helpful, just like now.

'Thanks, lass. They've got each other. I'd never 'ave let 'er go alone, but when Trudie offered to go too, it seemed like the perfect solution. Both of 'em 'ave their 'eads screwed on. They *will* be fine, an' they'll have some crackin' memories for later, won't they?'

'I can just see them, on the French Riviera, swanning around in sun frocks and floppy hats, with outrageous sunglasses that cover half their faces. The matriarchs of Monaco!'

'I'd 'ate to think what a vodka tonic's gonna cost 'em, down there. Probably an arm an' a bloody leg.'

Feen nodded, grinning. 'Yes, probably more than the cost of our lunches and Gavin's pizza combined! Ah well, as the saying goes; you can't take it with you. I hope they have the time of their lives.'

'I just 'ope they don't end up on some rich bugger's yacht and decide that that's the life, and they won't want to come back to this one.'

Feen looked at him shrewdly. 'You don't really think that do you?'

'No! O' course I don't. But stranger things 'ave 'appened, an't they?'

'Daddy, you know Adie's heart as well as she knows yours. She's never going to throw you over for some rover-itch git who has to have a boversized oat to compensate for the smallness of his penis.'

Mark all but shouted, with laughter. 'At least the bastard'd 'ave one that works.'

'You don't know that for sure. Anyway, trust me when I say that it's not something you have to worry about. Kevin doesn't have to worry, either. Trudie will come back with a very different perspective on what's important. I wouldn't write those two off, quite yet.'

Mark stared at her. 'Seriously? I thought a divorce were in't bag, fer those two.'

'Nope, not according to what I'm seeing. I think this time will be a clearer case of 'absence making the heart grow fonder' than it will be about 'out of sight being out of mind.' But you mustn't say a word to Kevin, Daddy, other than to tell him not to write her off quite yet. Just tell him that bavel troadens the mind, but it also lets people value what there might be to go back to, at the end of it all.'

'Kev's one o' me best mates, Feen. 'Ow do I keep summat like that from 'im?'

'By reminding yourself that it's none of your business, and keeping his mind focussed on other stuff instead.'

Mark blinked at her, and she smiled and raised her eyebrows. He shook his head. It was decades now, since he'd even tried to fathom is strange and ethereal daughter. She was unique – a true enigma to most people and he, as her father, only ever understood so much. Curiously, Adie seemed to click with the spiritual side of Feen more than he did, and for that he was grateful. Over the past few years, the two women had spent a lot of time together, and Feen had broadened Adie's mind considerably, and guided her to develop her own intuition.

I just let it be. I don't question what I don't understand, wi' either of 'em. I let 'em be, an' that seems to work. If owt concerns me, they tell me, and if it's not summat I need to be involved with, I leave 'em to it. Best way. I've enough bloody challenges, day-to-day, wi'out wonderin' what those two are cookin' up in their 'eads.

He was simply grateful for them both. His daughter and his wife were rare and extraordinary women. He was blessed, to have them in his life. The love he felt for them both was indescribable, and he knew Feen was right when she said that he didn't have to worry about the hearts of either of them.

Chapter Twenty-seven

'Are you okay, Adie?' Trudie's voice broke through Adie's thoughts as she stared out through the window of the train, watching the countryside whizzing by.

'Yeah. I am. I know I don't have to worry about Mark. He's in good hands with Feen and Gavin, Sheila and Bob, Egg, and Peric, and all our other friends. I just feel a bit guilty, leaving him. Like, why should I have all the fun, while he's left behind at home?'

'Oh, come on; we've been through this, a thousand times! He has given you his blessing, over and *over*. He said himself, he can't be bothered with all the logistics of a trip like this, and I know you understand that! Everyone does! Flying direct to Cyprus, or even to California, for a two or three-week holiday is one thing, with the disability he has. You've done those trips together, and more besides, and there are probably more on the table, after you get back.

'But Mark doesn't want the challenge of *this* kind of trip, Adie. Doing everything by train, on-and-off, and getting between platforms; I think even you and I are going to find it exhausting, at times. He simply isn't up for it, certainly not for three whole months, but he wants you to have your dream, love. Just be thankful he's the kind of man who does.'

Adie sighed, heavily. 'You're right, and he really does. And I guess we have that Caribbean cruise to look forward to next year.'

'Yes, you do, and that is going to be *amazing*, with a state cabin and everything, room service whenever you want it, and even a dedicated pool for people with disabilities. It's important to always have something to look forward to, and Mark does have that, as *his* dream, so you're fine to come on this trip with me. Or, should I say, allow *me* to crash in on your dream and come with *you*.'

'I couldn't do it if you weren't coming with me. At this time of life, you get to a stage where you have to tell yourself that there are certain things you always wanted to do that are now beyond your reach, for various reasons. An interrail trip for three months around Europe isn't something I feel I could do on my own, in my sixties! You coming along makes this possible for me, so thank you so much for being up for it.'

Trudie pulled a face. 'Well, for what it's worth, I don't agree at all that you couldn't do it alone. I think you most certainly could, but it's all about how you *feel*. There's no point in pushing forward with something if you think it would make you feel uncomfortable or unsafe. I'm not sure I would want to do it alone, either. I'd probably feel too vulnerable. Having the *ability* to do something, and the *desire* to do it, are two completely different things aren't they?'

'When I was young, newly married with kids, I envied some of my mates their travel experiences. They'd sometimes send me postcards, which was lovely of course, but it often made me wistful for a life I could have had. I'd never want to *not* have had the kids, or the comfortable life I had before it all went tits-up. But I wish I'd been in a position to take the time to do a bit of travelling, like they did before they settled into careers or having a family. I guess I parked that dream, along with a bunch of others I put on the shelf back then and never took down and dusted off.'

Trudie smiled, gently. 'We've all got a cupboard full of dreams that need dusting off, and you're right about getting to a place in life where some of them won't be possible. I always wanted to be a gymnast.'

Adie stared at her. 'Really? Why didn't you?'

'Oh, finances, mostly. My parents didn't have the money to send me to the training classes I needed to take if I was ever going to get to competition level. Dad lost his job, and it took a while for him to get another one. Mum went out to work instead, but she didn't earn enough to keep us going and cover my fees, or my sister' piano lessons. There was a time when we didn't have a penny in the bank, so my gymnastics fell by the wayside. It's a shame really, because I was quite good, back in the day.'

'I'm so sorry, Trudie! That's tough. It's horrible to think that it was lack of money that prevented you. It's hard to have to give up on a dream, especially if you're still a child! And I guess you were?'

'Yeah, I was pretty young. I remember I spent about a week crying. Mum and Dad felt bad about it, and Dad kept apologising for years, that he'd let me down, long after *I'd* got over it! But just because you get over something, or come to terms with it, doesn't mean it really goes away. I still love to watch gymnastics on TV, on the Olympics and everything, and I still feel the longing, sometimes.'

Adie turned to gaze again at the countryside flying by, as the train rattled along. Neither her nor Trudie's story was unique. Everyone had a handful of lost or broken dreams. Trudie had been forced to come to terms with the fact that she'd have to pass her window for training for competition gymnastics. Later, she would have to come to terms with being infertile, thanks to her adenomyosis. Now, she had to face the imminent end of her marriage. Her life was littered with broken dreams, and lost opportunities to do other things.

My own life hasn't been without loss either, has it? I've been luckier than most, and I think dealing with the realisation that certain dreams won't happen depends on what other dreams you can have, to take their place. You might have to accept that you'll never do or be certain things, or go to certain places, but it's easier to bear if there are things you can *look forward to, and find a way to make them happen instead. Trudie's right about Mark not wanting to do this trip with me. As he rightly said, it would quickly turn into a challenge for us both. We'd only focus on the logistics, and how to make them work, and he wants it to be the experience I've always longed for, for myself. He wants it to be about me. The fact that I'm doing it forty years late is less important than the fact that I'm doing it at all. But 'better late than never,' as the saying goes.*

'Well, let's try to find a gymnastics festival, while we're away! There might be one in Paris, or somewhere in Germany or Italy that we could get to, if the dates line up? I don't mind making a detour to go somewhere, if that's what we might have to do. It would all be part of our adventures! Failing that, there's the London one, in October, and we'll be back in time for that. Either would be fabulous, wouldn't it?'

Trudie grinned at her. 'Seriously? That would be amazing! I didn't know you enjoyed gymnastics. I guess it's not something we've ever talked about.'

'Are you kidding? I'm glued to it, every Olympics, Commonwealth games, and any other competitions I can ever find on the sports channels. I love it! I drive Mark mad, when the games are on. If it's on at dinner time, he has to get his own food. I won't move from the telly, while it's showing.'

Trudie rocked back and forth in silent laughter. 'Oh my God! You're a closet gymnastics hound. Who knew?'

'Yeah, that and the diving. I'm off-limits to everyone while that's on, too.'

How funny, that we share a love of that! I wonder what else we'll discover we have in common, on this trip?

Adie was excited to be travelling with Trudie. They'd been down in The Feathers pub a few months ago with Peg, Sheila, and Carla. Mark had gone out to an Amalgamated Farmers' dinner with Bob, so Adie had rallied Sheila and a few of the others to come and have a meal and a drink at the pub. During a conversation about plans they'd made in their long-lost youth, the subject of interrailing had come up. Adie had confessed to always having wanted to do it, but now felt that she was too old to go backpacking and hopping on and off trains at all hours of the day and night like a teenager. She'd been intrigued by the other women's instant dismissal of that as rubbish and Trudie saying that if Adie was prepared to do it, she would tag along.

'Let's show these young things a trick or two about doing it in *style,* Adie! I'm talking about sturdy suitcases on wheels, decent hotels, and first-class train travel at sociable times. I'm talking about *taking* our time, and wandering around back-street piazzas and courtyards, finding bars and restaurants that locals go to. We could do it that way, instead of having rigid timetables and checklists for nothing other than tourist attractions and trying to survive on nothing but white rice and soy sauce for a week! We have the funds to go a bit more up-market, don't we? We could avoid the crush, and the paupers' version where we take night trains to avoid paying for youth hostels, and 'do Europe' on our own terms.'

Adie had laughed, thinking Trudie couldn't possibly be serious. But she'd looked into her eyes and realised that she was *totally* serious – and something had stirred, inside them both. Carla had quickly jumped in and supported Trudie by saying; 'there's interrailing and *interrailing,* Adie. Don't succumb to the stereotype and talk yourself out of it on that basis.'

'Yeah. Let's smash our own expectations of what it can be,' Trudie had offered. She'd sounded enthusiastic, and it was catching. Adie had felt a small, quiet pang of excitement, at the idea that Trudie and Carla thought it was possible, but she'd tried to be pragmatic about it.

'Doing it that way would take months, Trude – especially if we had a long list of places – which I do, by the way. If a trip was worth doing, it would be worth doing properly. Bite-sized chunks might work, but I'd rather do it all in one hit, because having a plan to go back to somewhere doesn't always work out, and I wouldn't want it to turn into just another dream I had to give up on. I'd rather do it in a decent block, say, two or three months.'

'No problem. Let's look at three months, then.'

'But how could you leave your shop for that long? And you're more or less footloose and fancy free, apart from that, but what about me? How would I ever get this past Mark?'

At the time, she imagined that getting Mark to agree would be her biggest challenge. If they were to plan a trip like Trudie was suggesting, Adie would need to have his blessing and, while he'd never denied her anything her heart truly desired, it was going to be a tough ask, to expect him to be happy with her leaving him for three long months! It was the chance of a lifetime for her, but how would he feel about it *really*?

'Oh, you leave bloody daft face-ache to me,' Sheila had chipped in with a grin. 'I'll soon sort *'im* out. If there's one thing I know about my brother, its 'ow much 'e wants you to be 'appy. If this is something you really want to do, 'e will want you to do it. All I need to do is give 'im a push, love, and I'm 'appy to do it.'

Her face softened, in understanding.

'Adie, 'e's fine now – a million miles from the 'opeless invalid 'e was when 'e first came 'ome from the 'ospital. If you can get Feen and Gavin to come back to Ravensdown for the time you'll be away, you can go off and 'ave the 'oliday you've always dreamed of, without any worry. Bob and I are 'ere too, remember. We'll not see the silly sod stuck for anything. Nor will anybody else, for that matter.'

Peg had also thrown her observations into the mix.

'I think it's a great idea. You've had a long slog, getting over the accident. I've seen how hard you and Mark have both worked, to get him to where he is now. But Sheila's right. You can button off a bit now, and take a reward for all the hard work you've put in, to keeping the house and farm going, seeing him through rehab, putting his needs first every time, not to mention everything else you do, like the Farmers' Market, and all that.'

She held up her hand, as Adie started to protest.

'No. Hear me out, love. I *know* it's not been a burden or an obligation. All of us know you've been happy to do all of it and more. But it *has* been a challenge, love – one that's taken all of your energy, for a long time. Maybe it's time to do something nice for yourself, while you're still young enough and fit enough to go and do it. There's nothing worse than living with regrets. I'd come with you myself if I could. It sounds like you'll have an amazing time.'

Carla had thrown her two penneth in, too. 'Don't worry, I won't offer to come with you. I wouldn't if you paid me. You'd drive me insane in a week, if *you* didn't throw *me* under the wheels of a train first.'

Adie had laughed out loud. They all had. Carla was nothing if not honest, and she was right; they were as different as chalk and cheese, and they probably *would* drive each other mad! While Adie loved and appreciated her, with her razor-sharp wit, scathing sarcasm and 'take-no-prisoners' observations about people (including herself), the idea of travelling with her was enough to make most people's hair stand on end!

'You're all talking like it's already a done deal – like it's actually going to happen! I only opened my mouth about it ten minutes ago!'

Trudie winked at her. 'Psychology, sweetie. Say something as if it's real, and real it shall be. So, Mark willing, and my ability to get cover for the shop willing too, let's *do* this!'

Carla got up from the table. 'Back in a minute. Wait for me.'

Within two minutes she was back at the table, with a bottle of what looked to be a rather expensive bottle of champagne, and five glasses. Adie raised her eyebrows and Carla raised hers back, and shook her head, as if to mock Adie, gently.

'I know! I know! We probably *should* be having bottled orange juice or flat diet coke to toast you intrepid pair, but here's my contribution to the decision. It's one worth celebrating, in my humble opinion, so get your laughing gear around a glass of The Feather's finest bubbly. Well, to be honest, it's not the finest. It's the best I can afford, which is a *long* way from being the same thing. I can't believe they've got one on the wine list for two hundred and fifty pounds! This is definitely not that, but it's good enough, I think.'

She poured bubbly into the glasses and invited everyone to take one. Then she held up her own glass.

'Here's to Adie and Trude. Queens of European rail, we look forward to living vicariously, through your eyes. Get Gavin to sort you out with a blog, and keep us abreast of developments. And please don't make the shenanigans too enviable, or we might turn up and, if we do, all hell will break loose. Believe me.'

Adie felt a sudden rush of warmth for Carla. At one time, the two women had been arch-enemies, but they'd got past all that, and Carla had turned out to be a staunch ally on her friends list – the kind of woman who never rattled your cage much and never usually seemed overly interested in what you were doing, but would be the first through the door in a crisis.

'Thanks Carla. You know, it's not a done deal yet! There are still a few hurdles to jump, but hopefully we can clear those, then maybe we can start being excited about this idea, rather than scared to death of it.'

'Hurdles, shmurdles.' Carla looked and sounded deadpan, and everyone had laughed, again.

And so, it began – the grand plan to see Europe – in style, as Trudie had suggested.

It had been easier than Adie had expected, to get Mark to say yes. Sheila had got to him first – as promised – and Adie still didn't know what she'd said to him, but he hadn't taken much convincing. He'd broached the subject himself a few days later at breakfast when he'd wheeled himself into the kitchen and found her daydreaming, and staring out though the window, across the fields at the side of the house.

'Ello, lass. Dreamin' o' the Eiffel Tower, by any chance? You've already seen that, plenty o' times. 'Appen it might be better to think about places yer *aven't* seen yet.'

She'd turned to look at him, wondering what was going to come next. Her heart had been in her mouth, because although she knew Sheila had talked to him, she didn't quite know how to *herself*, off the back of it. She'd been grateful – but also terrified – that he'd seen fit to raise it. He probably understood how awkward she felt about it, and wanted to address what was fast becoming an elephant in the room.

'So, how would you feel if I did it?'

Mark had taken a few beats to answer, but she knew she'd get the truth from him, whether she wanted to hear it or not. He would never lie to her about anything.

'I think yer should do it. I *want* yer to do it. Yer goin' wi' Trudie, an' that's good enough for me to know you'll be safe. Yer get on well together, an' she's sensible an' practical, and probably less likely to get on't wrong bloody train than you are – no offence.'

Adie had laughed with relief. 'None taken. But I'm not too much of an airhead, am I, to be let loose on Europe?'

'No, love. I never knew you'd fancied doin' a trip like this when yer were a young 'un. You've never said owt, 'ave yer?'

'No. There didn't seem to be much point. I thought I was past the age where I could do it, but the girls were right when they said that we wouldn't have to do it as a stereotype, like we didn't have a bean to our names. We *do* have the ability to do it nicely, and it never occurred to me before that it was still possible under those conditions. You know how I love trains!'

Mark's expression changed, from one of enquiry to one of reflection.

'I wish I'd known earlier, you know, back when we met. I'd 'ave done a trip like that wi' yer in a flash. Yer should o' said summat.'

She'd shaken her head. 'Like I say, it seemed like that train had left the station, if you'll pardon the pun.'

'Well, it 'asn't. But when't bugger does, you'll be on it. You an' Trudie. Yer've me blessin to go, love. Go, wi' *all* me love. In fact, I'll go so far as to say that I'll not give you any peace if yer *don't* get on't bloody train. I'll mither yer till yer go mad.'

'Yeah, you probably would. But what about you? Being left behind? I know we've done a fair bit of travelling together, and even since your accident, but this is a whole different kettle of fish, isn't it? How will you manage without me, for three whole months. You do know that's the length of time we're thinking about?'

'It needs to be that, lass. Yer need to make most of it. Even at that, yer'll still be comin' 'ome wi' a list of what yer didn't get to see! Europe's a big place.'

'Yes, but what about *you!* You haven't answered that bit of the question!'

'I'll be just fine. I've already talked to Feen. She and Gavin an't kids'll come fer't duration. But they need the dates as soon as possible so they can get organised. She said Gavin needs to arrange a few meetin's, so he'd rather get 'em out o't way before they come up. But please, please, *please* love, don't think for a minute that I don't want yer to go, or that I won't be good as bloody gold, 'ere at 'ome. It's not the kind of 'oliday I can do anymore, or would even *want* to. It doesn't interest me at all, now I'm in this state, but that's no reason to deny you yer dream. Dreams are important, love. Just make yer plans, an' do it. We're a bloody long time dead.'

She'd burst into tears then, and he'd rolled his eyes and made a big play of her being a hysterical female. The gratitude she'd felt, in that moment, was something she could never describe to anyone. Mark was a magnificent man. Through all of his own setbacks and having to come to terms with the loss of so much, he still wanted her to have her dream. She'd hugged him, with all her might, and he'd hugged her back with all of his.

They were a team, but team members often did a few solo things, didn't they? It kept things fresh, and interesting. She'd resolved, in that moment, to have the best time she could, take as many photos and videos as she could, collect and send or bring back as many mementos as she could, and make the absolute most of the opportunity so she could come home and show Mark all that she and Trudie had seen and experienced, on their travels.

So, here they were, on their first train journey, on their big European adventure. They were staying with Miranda and Max tonight, and Adie was looking forward to that. It had been a while since they'd met up, and it was a great start to the holiday, to be waved off by her oldest and dearest friend, who was also ridiculously excited for her.

I have such great people in my life. Mand and Max are going to join us for a few days when we get to Monaco, and that will be lovely. Max has a good friend there who he thinks we can all stay with. Peg thinks she can meet us in Rome for a long weekend, and two of Trudie's girlfriends are willing to fly somewhere to meet up with us, at short notice. It's going to be a wonderful experience. I can't wait to arrive in Amsterdam. It probably won't feel real until we're there.

Chapter Twenty-eight

Mark kept checking his phone. He tried to stop himself, but he couldn't help feeling ever-so-slightly lost without his wing-woman. She'd texted to say that she and Trude had arrived safely at Miranda's, but he hadn't heard anything since.

They're probably already tanked up on vodka martinis, if I know Mand. She'll 'ave 'em totterin' off to bed pie-eyed.

The house seemed a bit too big, without Adie. He chuckled to himself, a little, to try and snap himself out of dwelling on that. The reality of her being gone was a little more unsettling than he'd expected or would ever be prepared to admit.

Get over it, yer daft bugger. You know where she'll be, an' it's not like she in't comin' back! Focus, man. Yer 've plenty to be goin' on wi,' 'ere!

He'd been at great pains to get Adie to understand that he genuinely wanted her to have this amazing experience. It was a dream she'd had since she was a much younger woman, waving all her friends off on their travels, while she stayed at home with her husband and kids.

That must've been bloody 'ard. At that age, in your twenties, your dreams are everythin' aren't they?

Adie had her family (and she was very much a family woman) but she'd missed out on something important that she really wanted, that would have broadened her mind and given her something to reminisce about, while she was changing nappies and chopping vegetables. Mark would never even *consider* standing in the way of anything she wanted to do that she'd missed out on. He owed her so much.

She hadn't left him, at the most vulnerable time of his life. She'd toughed out everything he'd thrown at her; the hard denial of life being worth living, the shouting and the swearing, and the frosty silences while he wrestled with his inability to explain how he felt about being as dependent as a child, and having to somehow try and come to terms with that and everything else he had to face. He'd been scared, as much as anything else, and for a long time that had manifested as treating his loved ones terribly – like they were a nuisance he didn't want, like they had nothing to say that he wanted to hear, like they didn't matter to him anymore.

Adie had weathered all of that, and she'd stood strong in the face of it. She hadn't given up on him, and she hadn't let him give up on himself. He had faith in himself again, and his ability to still be a good strong man in whatever ways he could, and that was down to *her*, and the faith *she* had in him. He wasn't going to deny her the chance to have the joy that she deserved.

Trudie Sangster was a good sort – she'd make sure they were both as safe as they could be. She had friends dotted about across Europe, and she and Adie would be touching base with some of them on their travels. A few of their mates here in the UK would be popping out to see them too, along the way.

He could probably even get to a location himself if Feen would come with him. Maybe she would. He resolved to ask her. It would be short notice, but he reasoned that if he could manage without Adie for three full months, surely Gavin could do without Feen for a few days. They could fly to a city, and meet Adie and Trude, have a couple of nights and a catch-up, and then come home. He was sure Gavin would be happy to accommodate that, and maybe Carla and Dave, or Josie and Tony, could have the twins for some of the time so he wouldn't have too much to deal with by himself. Alder and Willow were old enough to amuse themselves a lot now, so that made the prospect easier.

Travelling was more of a challenge for Mark now than it had been before his accident. The planning took longer to sort out now, but when he and Adie flew, it did mean that they were prioritised for getting through security and onto planes. They always booked assistance now, and that helped a lot, but getting on and off their flights and getting to hotels could still be exhausting. They usually hired a car on their holidays, but it had to be a good-sized hatchback or an estate car that would accommodate his wheelchair. He was adept at getting himself in and out of the passenger seats of most cars, so that wasn't a problem and, if they'd booked a holiday at an all-inclusive resort, they didn't need one at all. They just had to ensure that airport transfers and any taxis they booked to go places could accommodate the chair. Most hotels, bars, restaurants, and tourist attractions were well set up for disabled guests, nowadays too.

Everything *worked*, it all just took a lot *longer*. He rarely encountered any big problems, usually just small frustrations that he had to make the effort to manage without going crazy in the process.

So, meeting Adie somewhere might be a plan, and he was sure she'd be thrilled at the thought of him joining her and Trudie on a 'city break.'

He fired up his laptop and looked again at their itinerary. It was a loose one, with no concrete dates. The women were 'winging-it' for accommodation, but he wasn't worried about that, because the kind of hotels they would be staying in usually had rooms available. They certainly weren't going to be on the 'budget' end of things, and scrapping for a bed. It was going to be at least 'four-star' all the way. They were doing the kind of trip that sleep-deprived teenagers would only dream about, on their low-budget fares to cities with flea-pit hostels as their destinations.

He looked over their destinations, now. The Netherlands, France, Germany, Switzerland, Austria, Italy, Croatia, Montenegro, Greece, Malta, Spain, and Morocco. It was quite a trip, that they had planned, and there was only a loose suggestion – at this stage at least – of dates for moving between countries. It really would be short notice, for him and Feen, for Peg Tripper, for Sheila, and for anyone else who wanted to fly out and catch Adie and Trudie along the way.

Mark had travelled quite a lot, with his first wife Beth, and with Adie. He and Feen had also done a couple of trips when they'd been alone together at Ravensdown, in the time between Beth dying from bowel cancer and Adie Bostock showing up as a house sitter at Teapot Cottage for Glenn and Sue Robinson, who'd owned it at the time.

He felt lucky, not just that he'd fallen in love and got together with Adie, but also that she shared his interest in travelling. It wouldn't have bothered him much if she hadn't, because he'd already been to a lot of places where he *had* been a back-packer on a budget, and becoming wealthy had sharpened his appetite for going to places he'd once though he'd never be able to afford. If that was to be his lot, he'd have accepted it, as he'd already seen more places, and in different contexts, than most people would in a lifetime. But thankfully Adie was always keen to go somewhere and their honeymoon in Bali had set the pattern for them having a nice holiday at least twice a year after that.

He chuckled now, remembering the severe 'talking-to' she'd given him, not long after the accident, when he'd made some comment about having to hang up his travel shoes for good. She'd said it was nonsense – that if he wanted to wallow in self-pity and convince himself that he couldn't do most of the things he'd once done without even thinking, he was on his own. She'd made it clear that she'd be going places on her own if he 'didn't have the guts to even try' to go with her.

She'd given him plenty of food for thought, certainly over the first six months or so, when he was involved in gruelling rehab to build his strength and trying to come to terms with his vastly altered life. But, over time, he'd found a lot of his 'mojo' again, and had started to lift his head and look at what *was* possible, rather than focussing on all the things that weren't. He'd decided that travelling again was worth a try, at least.

So, they'd gone on an experimental trip together – to Los Angeles, and a road trip beyond. Adie had organised everything to the 'nth' degree, and it had all run like clockwork. They'd seen a lot, on that trip. They'd driven as far as Las Vegas, and stayed in the beautiful Bellagio hotel. They'd seen a show, and done all the local attractions, including spending an evening in Freemont Street, which had blown his mind. They'd had a night at Caesars casino playing blackjack and roulette, visited the Titanic Museum, had dinner at the Hard Rock Café, and taken a private-charter helicopter trip over the Grand Canyon, and Monument Valley. On the way to and from Vegas they'd seen the Hoover Dam, Calico ghost town, and a long list of other places. They'd had lunch in a true-blue American airstream diner, and they'd even witnessed a mock gunfight in a 'wild west' town along the way.

Mark had sat in his chair and felt the wind in his face on the famous Santa Monica pier. He'd watched the most fiery sunset imaginable over the Pacific Ocean, and he and Adie had managed to do most of the attractions in L.A. too, including the Hollywood Walk of Fame, the Getty Museum, and Disneyland. That had been a challenge, and there were a few rides he couldn't go on, but he was delighted to see Adie's face after she'd come off one or another, buzzing with the adrenaline of it all.

'Who knew I had a passion for rollercoasters! I can't believe I never went on one before this! I'm hooked, Mark! We *have* to come again!'

Feen came bouncing into the room now, unnervingly all smiles.

'Daddy, I believe you have something to talk to me about? The answer is yes, by the way. I'd *love* to come with you on a trip to see Adie. We could make it a surprise! Not let her know, just turn up. That would be something, wouldn't it?'

Mark grimaced – at the fact that she'd picked up on his thoughts in the first place (reinforcing the fact that his private musings were rarely sacred) and the fact that she wanted to 'spring' something unexpected on her stepmother.

'I dunno, lass. Mebbe. Adie's not always fond of a surprise, but if we let Trudie know, she could pave the way for it to be a surprise rather than a shock.'

'Yes, good idea. And I see you're already looking at the itinerary. So where do you fancy? It could be anywhere that's on their list. There are only a douple of cates that I couldn't do. There's Gina's Gin Gio fashion show in London that I can't miss, because of the possibility of lucrative commissions, and the debut concert for the band Gavin's written some songs for. We have to show up for that. It's really important. But any other date would work just fine for me. I've already cleared it with him. He's fine about the two or three days we're thinking about.'

'We'll organise summat, lass. Might be short notice, dependin' on where they're goin', but I do think we can make summat work.'

'I *know* we can. And I think it will be in Montenegro. I have a very strong feeling that we'll end up in Budva, or Kotor Bay.'

Mark grinned. 'I'll take yer word fer it, lass. I've been to neither place, so they both sound interestin'.'

'Okay then. Let's see how they get on, and what their route is, and we'll organise to meet them when they arrive there.'

He was suddenly dubious about the notion of a surprise. What if Adie was having so much fun, she didn't want to see him? What if – God forbid – she'd met someone on her travels who was more interesting to her? What if she'd decided, somewhere along the journey, that she didn't want him anymore?

Feen tutted and rolled her eyes at him, intruding once again on his private thoughts. Sometimes that was so annoying! It was bad enough that she usually knew what he was thinking, but the fact that she so often commented on it was excruciating in the extreme.

Can I not have any private thoughts? D'yer 'ave to desiccate every last bloody thing' I'm thinkin'?

'Daddy, I know you're feeling insecure about Adie being gone, and you're imaging all kinds of scenarios in your head, but it's silly! Why are you expecting the worst to happen? Adie will never want someone else. I know that for a fact, and you can be sure of it too. Nor does she want to suddenly follow in Trudie's footsteps, get a divorce and be footloose and fancy-free! She has every intention of continuing to be the lock of your rife. For heaven's sake, stop fretting!'

'That's just it though, in't it? She 'as every *intention*. But intentions change, Feen, and so do people. Experiences change 'em, often in ways they weren't expectin.' What if she *does* decide she wants 'er freedom, after she's 'ad a taste of it?'

Feen's voice was quiet. 'She's not going to do that. Take that as gospel. Unless she dies, or something – God forbid – she'll be coming home just as she said she would. It will be Trude that has the big revelations about her life Daddy, not Adie. She is going to be just fine, and very happy to come home and pick up her life again as it was.'

She regarded him pensively for a few beats, and that always made him nervous. It usually came before some tirade or criticism. He braced himself, for being told how pathetic and ridiculous he was being, but what she said surprised him.

'As you know, Adie and I have grown a lot closer since your accident. Even before that, she was curious about a lot of the things I do and feel, and why. Before you came home from the hospital, she and I had a few tong lalks. She shared her deepening curiosity with me, and I've been encouraging her to open up a part of herself that she was curious about but wasn't sure she could teally rap into, and develop. But I've been kind of 'schooling' her, for want of a better term.'

Mark felt incredulous. He stared at his daughter, and tried to read her face to see if she was playing with him, but all he saw was earnestness and the intention to make him understand something.

'So, what, yer tellin' me yer've turned 'er into a bloody witch?'

Feen laughed and shook her head. 'No, Daddy. Not that. She will never be that. She has no desire for it, but she also doesn't have the gifts required, even if she did. But she *has* wanted to become more spiritually intuitive, and I've helped her to reach that part of herself that we *all* have inside us. We all *do* have intuition, and empathy and insight; it's just that most people aren't aware of their capacity to develop and use it.'

'I'm just a block o' concrete, me,' Mark muttered, half to himself.

'No, you're not. But your choice is to be more practical, and there's nothing wrong with that. Few people in the world are like me, and you know yourself how much I've suffered for it, all my life. But most people are like Adie; capable of developing intuition and insight, tapping into ibrational venergy, and so on. Adie doesn't want to be a hibrational vealer, but she does want to understand its power, and pick up on things more, in other people.'

'An' you've been teachin' 'er?'

Feen cocked her head on one side. 'Guiding her, is probably a better way to describe it.'

'She's never said owt to me about it.'

'That doesn't surprise me, Daddy. I know you don't really understand how it all works, but that's fine. The world does need down-to-earth, practical people in it too! We can't all be 'airy-fairy,' as you're so fond of describing me. But the point is – and Adie got it – that everyone is capable at least to some degree, of developing a rong stintuition about people, animals, and other things. She wanted to do that, and she asked for my help. I'm not sure she intends to do anything with it. I think she just wants to feel more enlightened so she can respond better to people on lifferent devels.'

Feen went on to remind him that many of Adie's tenants who came to Teapot Cottage were in a state in a state of crisis when they arrived. It happened more often than most people would realise. The cottage 'drew' troubled souls who were looking for a bolthole. It was built on a ley line, and had its own unique healing energy that people intuitively picked up on when they were looking for a place to run to, when they were at a difficult crossroads in their lives. Ravensdown House had good vibrations too, but the energy at the cottage was more powerful. Adie wanted to understand more about her tenants, and more about the fact that the energy within the cottage walls supported them to heal and find new direction.

Mark was surprised that she'd enlisted Feen's help to learn more. Maybe there was something in that notion of people only using around a sixth of their brain capacity because they didn't know how to develop the rest. Feen had a raft of abilities that most people didn't have, and a few that most could *never* have. Sometimes, that was more of a curse than a blessing, but she'd decided many years ago to embrace her uniqueness (many would say strangeness or outright weirdness) and do what she could with it to understand and help other people.

It seemed Adie was following suit, as far as she was able, at least. Mark figured it probably wouldn't do her any harm to be a little more in tune with the world, as long as Feen had also helped her to understand her own limitations, and when her boundaries were being tested. He didn't want to think she'd let herself be taken advantage of, by anyone.

He said as much, and Feen nodded. 'I've shown her how to put a protection ring around herself, her family, and everything else that matters to her, Daddy. She will never be able to communicate with figher horces in the same way I do, but she knows how to use vibration for self-protection as well as everything else.'

Mark didn't understand a lot of what his daughter often said about 'ethereal forces' and 'protection rings' and suchlike, but he'd long since learned to accept it. He'd lived for over twenty years with his first wife, Feen's mother Beth, before she died. For a time, Beth's mother Alice had also lived at Ravensdown, until she became too ill with dementia for him and Feen to manage at home. Alice, Beth, and Feen were all white witches, and he'd seen and heard things that passed between them that would make most people question their sanity. But they weren't insane. They were anything but, and even though most of what they talked about sailed right over the top of his head, he'd learned to greatly respect it.

If Adie wanted to tap more into that world, he wasn't going to stand in her way. As long as she didn't let it take her away to dark places in her own head, or mess with her ability to live her life the way she wanted to live it within the family framework, he had no quarrel with what she chose to dwell on or explore. Whatever made her happy made him happy. He might have to put his foot down if she started talking in tongues or something, but Feen had never done that, so he was fairly confident that Adie wouldn't have that portal either.

He was content to live in a state of ignorance, about much of it. It wasn't the same as living in denial; it was about being more grounded in the practical world, the one where he felt comfortable. Feen was right – the world *did* need practical people in it. They could take care of the real-world stuff, while the witches, the warlocks and the whimsical fluttered around – in their own heads at least – and concerned themselves with less earthly things.

Chapter Twenty-nine

Trudie decided that they should have a glass of bucks fizz, to celebrate the start of their adventure, so she went to the buffet car and came back with a chilled bottle of champagne, a pitcher of freshly squeezed orange juice, and two cut crystal glasses. Adie raised her eyebrows and Trudie chuckled.

'I went top-shelf, with the help of the son of one of Kev's friends who just so happens to be working in the buffet car today. He dug around and gave me some very impressive glasses, and then he told me off for not staying put, to wait until service came to us instead. 'Sack that,' I told him. We don't have all day to wait for them to get their hairy arses down here. That could be another hour! Besides, if we'd waited we wouldn't have crystal glasses because he wouldn't know it was me, or us. These are apparently reserved for the *really* posh people who come on board sometimes.'

'What, are we just partly posh, then?'

Trudie shrugged. 'I suppose so. Anyhoo, missus, partly posh or proper posh, let's get these drinks on the go. I ordered some sandwiches and scones with cream too. They are coming. This is a very impressive train, by the way. It's not the normal one, is it?'

Adie looked around her, at the beautiful vintage-style décor in their first-class carriage. This definitely *wasn't* a 'normal' train. It was a special service that ran infrequently, for those who could afford it, and she had engineered their departure date to take advantage of it.

'I've dreamed of taking the Statesman Service for a long time now. Mark and I were going to book a trip to London on it. We talked about it, but then his accident happened, and…'

Trudie nodded sympathetically. 'It didn't end up back on the table? Well, at least you get to go on it now, and when another date comes up maybe you could take it again wit Mark.'

'I fancy the Orient Express, actually. We've talked about that too. It's seriously expensive, but I think it would be worth it.'

'Well, you can't take the money with you, and you also can't put a price on the memories you'll have when you're old and dribbling and incapable of going anywhere, anymore.'

Adie pulled a face at her, and she laughed. 'Don't worry! I'll be sitting in the armchair next to you, in the rest home. We can do the chair aerobics together, or try to at least, and instigate a food fight in the dining room when the mood takes us.'

Adie sighed. 'I'm not ready to be old. I know we're *not* old, at least not as old as the people in those rest homes, but I'm in no rush to get there.'

'Nor am I,' Trudie admitted, and then she bit her lip. 'I certainly didn't think I'd be facing that by myself. Me and Kevin, you know? I thought we'd grow old *together*. I was looking forward to that. Not to growing old, of course, but to being in good company doing it. I didn't expect to be going into that phase of my life alone.' She kept her voice light, but Adie could keenly sense the pain in it.

'Is it really too late, Trude?'

She pulled a face, and shrugged. 'I think it is. He has talked a lot lately, about trying harder, getting counselling, and all that, but he didn't do it early enough! We've been separated for quite a while now, and the time to try and catch the horse before it bolted was *then*, when we first split up. Not now! It feels like a token gesture, or some kind of afterthought, for him to be asking for all that now.'

'Maybe it's less of a token gesture than it is a *realisation* of all he stands to lose? Men take ages to get to this stuff, you know, to work out how they really feel? They spend an aeon in denial first, and even when they've managed to figure it out, it can be *another* aeon before they feel ready to talk about it.'

Trudie nodded. 'You might be right. Maybe it is just a long process, for him to get to where I needed him to be years ago. But I was done waiting, a long time ago. Things hadn't been right for years, before I left.'

'Well, I can't remember where I heard it, or who from, but someone told me once that it's only a year or so after a split that a guy starts to feel the impact of it.'

'It's been longer than that, Adie, and for many years before, when I tried to talk to him about how I felt in the marriage. None of it made a dent.'

Trudie's voice was quiet, but she sounded resolute. It made Adie sad.

I'm going to keep trying to get her to talk about this. She's like a clam. She hardly ever says anything, and hasn't for all the time I've known her. Her marriage was in trouble for years before I even had an inkling. She always put on such a brave face. It's so true that however close we might be to somebody, we don't always know what they're going through, or trying to come to terms with.

'At least it's going to be a friendly divorce. It was nice of him to come and say goodbye to you at our place this morning. It seemed really important to him, to do that.'

'Yeah. We're on good terms. He was my best mate, you know? Not just a husband, but my best friend, for more than half my life.'

'I'd been married for twenty-six years, when everything imploded for me. I made big mistakes. I kept really important things from Bryan, for all our married life, but he'd compromised the relationship in a far worse way by having a long-standing affair. We could never even be friends, after that came to light. At least you and Kevin don't have infidelity as the cornerstone of why everything went wrong.'

'I think we've just grown apart. We've always been very different, and in the beginning it really *was* a classic case of 'opposites attract.' But he's one of those hundred-percent left-brained guys! He's fixated on numbers and balance sheets and graphs, and every other desperately boring thing to do with figures that can possibly be found on the planet. He's always been the classic nerd. I always knew he was a nerd, but he was a *loveable* nerd, back in the day. I could manage that, mostly. I just didn't know at the time that he'd stop being lovable, and just end up being a bloody *boring* nerd, with no sense of adventure and no zest for life or wife.'

She sighed heavily, and gazed out of the window.

'Somewhere along the way, he turned into a stone. Grey, immovable, and inert. It happened before my eyes, and I was powerless to stop it. He never wanted to listen to my point of view, especially if it differed from his. He wanted to be right about everything, and he did stuff without telling me; important stuff that had an impact on us, you know? He stopped taking his medication for his heart condition because he said it made him feel sick. I found out by accident that he'd stopped taking it. That was important, and yet he didn't see that. He just condemned me for being upset about it.'

'I remember you telling me at the Christmas party we had just as you and Kevin were splitting up, that you felt as if no matter what you did or didn't do or say, you ended up being the bad guy. That must have been hard to shoulder, Trudie, especially for so long. A one-off incident, maybe. But, if that was the pattern of your relationship, there certainly were some big issues there. Constantly being put down chronically erodes your self-esteem.'

'I wasn't allowed to have an opinion if he didn't agree with it. And of course, if I was emotional about something, that was intolerable for him too. He just had no idea how to deal with me, and the menopause was hell, because I was all over the place, and I tried to explain it to him, but he just didn't get it. I was on my own with that too.'

Tears sprang to Trudie's eyes. Adie was surprised, and dismayed, that she was still so angry about so much. Clearly, she was still having a tough time coming to terms with the end of her marriage.

'He never wanted to shag me either, Adie. Not for *years*, and whenever I tried to talk about the lack of intimacy and the rejection when I tried to initiate anything, and how it made me feel, he would tell me I was wrong. He said he *did* desire me, but he always tried to initiate something when he knew I would turn him down. Like, at half-past eleven at night when I was knackered, half-asleep, and literally about to start snoring! He did that deliberately, I think, because he didn't want to have sex at all, but he wanted to be able to say that he'd at least tried.'

'Kevin doesn't seem the kind of guy who'd weaponize sex, Trude.'

'No, he's not. I think he always did it to satisfy *himself* that he'd tried, even as he knew it wasn't going to happen. I'm years past the 'big bang at midnight,' and he always had a reason for not wanting to have an early night whenever I suggested it. But, you know, I don't think it had much to do with me at all. He has big issues with a lot of things, including intimacy. I did *want* to be in the mood at that time of night, but I just couldn't. I was always far too tired by then, and there's no point in letting it happen if all you can do is lie there like a sack of spuds. It has to be interactive to be meaningful, right?'

'Yeah, I guess so. Just make sure, in signing those divorce papers, that you're not tossing the bottle away with the wine still in it. I'm only playing devil's advocate here, not trying to shove you in any direction. I'll support you whatever you do. I *always* will, but you're one of my dearest friends, and I don't want you to make a mistake. I don't want you to end up any more hurt than you already are.'

Trudie gave a wry grin. 'What, are you going to suggest therapy, next?'

'Why not? As I've said before, relationship counselling isn't always about trying to get a couple to stay together. Sometimes it's about guiding them to split well.'

'I think we'll split well, anyway, Adie. We've always been friends, and I think we still are. Hopefully, we can keep that, at least.'

'Okay, just make sure it really, really is what you want.'

Trudie gave a curt nod, and Adie got the message that it was time to change the subject. She hoped, quietly to herself, that this holiday might offer Trudie a new perspective. She had the distinct feeling that her friend wasn't quite as 'done' with her marriage as she liked to think she was, or wanted everyone *else* to think she was. There may still be a way back...

*　　*　　*　　*　　*

Miranda was waiting outside Euston station when they got there, but this time Adie knew who to look for. Her friend looked casual but gorgeous, in a lightweight pale blue tracksuit and what looked to be the most expensive trainers in the world. Even as a 'jogger' she looked amazing.

Adie had always admired her friend's innate panache for looking incredible. Many moons ago, when the two of them had been at Miranda's flat one night drinking wine and eating chocolate, and crying at a soppy movie, Adie had convinced her to put on a black bin bag. It had been *hilarious!* Miranda had cut a hole in the bottom and the sides for her head and arms, then she'd cinched it in at the waist with a glittery belt, donned a pair of towering, spiky high heels, popped an outrageous black hat on, and draped herself with lots of jewellery. The effect had been incredible, and they'd rolled around laughing.

It was official. Miranda Quirk looked fabulous, even in a bin bag.

On their way to the house in Stoke D'Abernon, they stopped for lunch in a very sweet, olde-worlde country inn.

'God, look at this place! It's adorable!' Trudie seemed enchanted by the 17th century pub, with its flagstone floor, lovely original beams, and oversized stone fireplace. Max nodded.

'It's something, alright. Back in the eighties, the breweries tore the guts out of a lot of these places, and gave them what

319

they thought was a more modern feel, but it was a catastrophe for most of them. They lost so much of the atmosphere, not to mention the history, when they decided to tear everything out and replace it with a mess of different design elements that really didn't work. You had chairs and sofas in one busy fabric, carpet in another, curtains in yet another, and the lovely old bars were replaced with monstrosities made of veneer and plastic. My old local, in Hampstead, was one of the thousands of pubs they raided and ripped the character out of, and it was never the same after that.'

'Thankfully this place escaped,' Miranda observed dryly. 'Quite a few did. The ones that were independently owned tended to fare a little better in preservation and of course some of them are listed, so they couldn't be upgraded to anything beyond what was needed to make them fit for modern purpose. But most of the ones owned by the breweries were sacrificed, as Max says. Some used to have two rooms, and a central bar. That was always quite nice, I thought, and some of them had little bars off to one side that they called 'snugs.' But the rampage meant that a lot of the 'snugness' was lost. They started to feel more like barns, or someone's over-decorated living room, than the pubs they were originally designed to be.'

'I remember that;' Adie offered. 'We're lucky with the pubs in Torley. The wine bar, Whispers, is all modern with metal and glass and so on, but The Feathers, and The Bull and Royal are both still fairly old-world style. I believe the Bull has had an overhaul or two, in its time, but they haven't gone over the top. They've kept it fairly true to the old coaching inn it always was.'

Miranda nodded. 'One of our locals, The Old Plough, has been renovated but they've done it quite nicely, with wooden panelling and open brickwork, and flagstone and wooden flooring. It's light and airy, with lots of windows. Not all the pubs were bastardized, in renovations. A few of them did get it right.'

Max leaned forward now. 'Mand and I have been talking about buying another holiday home. We've got the condo in Corfu, and the funny little place I already had in Malta, but we're thinking of looking for something in the Lake District.'

Adie stared at him. 'Seriously? You do know that there are years when it rains for three hundred *days* a year, up where we are? The year before last, I think we saw the sun four times in as many months!'

Miranda laughed. 'I know you probably think we're crazy, but the truth is, I'd like to spend a lot more time with you. We're not getting any younger darling, and you're my oldest and dearest friend! Max and I are more or less retired now, and we have a lot more time on our hands. He's fond of walking and would like to explore the fells, and I'd love to spend more time hanging out with you, if you'd be amenable to that? Of course, if you don't want me …'

She trailed off, looking slightly confused, and Adie rushed to tell her not to be so silly.

'Of *course* I'd like to see more of you, you mad mare! And, as you say, you have more time on your hands than I do. I spend more time running the farm with Mark now, since he had his accident. The Farmers' Market keeps me busy as well, along with a few the other things I'm involved with. It's not so easy for me to dash off for a weekend away as often as I'd like to, and my visits here always seem a bit rushed, don't they? But I'd *love* you to be around more! I think it's a great plan if you really are serious. Don't get me all excited over an idea you're only kicking around!'

Miranda shook her head. 'No, we're serious. In fact, we've been looking online, and we've seen a couple of places we like the look of. One of them is not far from your place, Trudie. You're on the road out of town towards Carlisle, aren't you?'

'Carson Road. Just off the main Torley to Carlisle Road. Is it the place that looks like a Spanish villa, by any chance? Terracotta roof, concrete arches, set back off the road a bit, listed with Fellway Estate Agents?'

'Yes, that's the one! Do you know it?' Miranda beamed at her.

'I do! It's empty now, but it belongs to good friends of mine, Jeanette and Paul Jensen. They emigrated to Canada about six months ago, to be closer to her children, who live in Ontario. Her ex-husband was originally from there, and their kids have jobs and everything out there now. It's a gorgeous house, Trudie.'

'But it's been empty for six months?'

Trudie nodded. 'Yes, but you don't have to worry. They've got someone going in regularly to keep it clean and fresh, and maintain the garden. They wanted to sell before they left, but it didn't happen.'

'Any idea why?'

Trudie bit her lip, trying to remember. Then she shrugged.

'Nope. I don't recall that there were any issues. Jeanette never mentioned anything that sticks in my mind. It's probably just the fact that it's quite expensive, and most people don't want to spend that much, up our way. It has very little land with it, which always surprises potential buyers. I think they expect more, with a house of that size and value.'

'I suppose anyone moving for lifestyle would *want* a house like that, but I can see why they'd turn away if it doesn't have enough land to suit their vision.' Adie recall the house now. She'd seen and admired it many times, on her way to Trudie's.

Trudie nodded. 'Jeanette's frustrated. She and Paul have had several offers, but they've all been a bit insulting. It's a buyer's market out there right now, which doesn't help.'

Miranda inclined her head. 'So, they wouldn't take an offer, then?'

'Oh, I think they would. Jeanette doesn't want to drop too much, but I think she's getting a bit fed up with the hassle of trying to deal with it all from Canada. I think she'd be relieved to get rid of it, for a *sensible* offer. Personally, I think it's worth what they're asking, because it's a stunning house, but I'm not the one trying to buy it. It's always the same story, isn't it?

The seller wants the most they can get, and the buyer wants to pay as little as they can.'

'But somewhere, the twain must meet,' Max grinned. 'Maybe we should make an appointment to view the place, and a few others too, while we're up that way. But that's the one we have the best feeling about. Less land means less to deal with on holiday. Nobody really wants to spend their vacation time battling with lawns and wrestling with weeds, do they?'

'Well, there is *some* garden,' Trudie reminded him.

'There is, yes, but we could carry on with getting the place looked after in much the same way as it is now, if we bought it. It might suit us perfectly.'

'It does have a kitchen to die for, and the bedrooms all have great views of the fields and surrounding fells. I think, after all this time, the estate agency has long since lost any right to exclusivity, so you might be able to do a deal with Jeanette and Paul to buy it privately, say, if Kevin could show you around and you were still keen after you'd seen it. I'm sure they would be *very* interested in the idea of a private cash sale that avoided costly estate agent fees.'

Miranda's eyes were sparkling now. 'Ooh, yes! That might suit us *all* a lot better, mightn't it? The money's not an issue and of course there's no chain to agonise over, so she may be amenable to that. We do have to view it first, to decide, but I'm like Max – I have a good feeling about that house. Could you talk to Jeanette, Trudie? See if she's interested in that? If not, we can go through the agent, as the norm. I do hate agents though,' she added, half to herself.

Max agreed with her. 'Money-grabbing middle-men, I'd love to know what they actually *do*, to justify their exorbitant fees. In my experience, they never answer your questions properly, never return your calls when you need them to, and half the time the calls you do make get diverted to a central office where they promise to get a message to your agent in the branch you originally called, but they hardly ever do.'

'They're a nightmare,' Adie agreed. 'I bought Teapot Cottage by private sale, and happily avoided all that nonsense, but when Bryan and I sold our house in Guildford the agent was horrendous. I couldn't believe how inefficient she was, considering what we were paying for her 'services'! We lost two sales because the agency was apparently playing two buyers off against one another, trying to drive the price up, presumably to get a higher commission. Both buyers cottoned onto it, and both dumped their offers before the agent had even presented them to us! I only found out because one of them was so distraught she put a note through our letterbox, telling us what had happened. It was outrageous. I fired them on the spot, and engaged a different agency, but they weren't much better. They got the house sold, in the end, but they were terrible.'

'Teresa and Chris got their place in Keswick by private sale too, didn't they? Miranda cocker her head on one side.

Adie nodded. 'Yeah, they bought it directly from Fiona and Stuart, and their lawyers took care of everything super-fast. Actually, Fi and Stu would find you a lovely place if you decided you didn't fancy Jeanette and Pauls' villa. They buy and renovate derelict and outdated houses all across the Lake District, but they've branched into acquiring property for people who approach them. I'm sure they'd find something stunning, to suit whatever you want to spend.'

It must be nice to have the sort of money that allows you to have whatever you want.

Adie wasn't at all jealous of Miranda and Max's wealth, but sometimes it made her a little wistful, at how easily they got what they wanted. Miranda had always been warm and generous with all that she had, and she never talked about money in the same way a lot of people did, who had it. She and Max weren't ostentatious with it. They had a home worth millions, expensive holiday homes, and they drove nice cars and had a lovely lifestyle. But they never flaunted it, talked about it, or made it an issue. Adie and Mark were well-heeled too, thanks to Mark's astute investments over many years, with support from Trudie's husband. Kevin Sangster was a good friend and one of the country's top-rated financial advisors. He had apparently set Trudie up many years ago too, with her own investment portfolio, and he'd done as well for her as he'd done for Mark and Adie.

None of them had to worry about money, and it made her smile, to think back to when they were all young, and struggling. Miranda was still trying to make it as an actress, surviving on meagre wages from bit-parts in West End shows, and living in a shared dump of a flat with three other people, none of whom would ever make it big in the acting world. She'd worked her butt off for years, to get to leading-lady status and a stream of lucrative contracts and endorsements. Adie and her first husband Bryan had been living in a cramped three-up-two-down semi while Bryan was struggling too, to get his construction business off the ground. They'd all been through the struggle of wondering how to pay the next gas bill, and buying bedsheets at jumble sales because they couldn't afford new ones. She could never begrudge Miranda the success she had now.

She was grateful that Bryan had been successful enough to give his family a very comfortable standard of living. After her divorce from him, she'd fallen in love with Mark, but she'd had no idea how wealthy he was. He hadn't told her the extent of it until after they were married. So, almost unwittingly, she'd landed on her feet too. For most of her adult life, thanks to two financially clever husbands, she'd never had to worry about money. But she never forgot the lean years, when every penny had to be planned and accounted for.

She allowed herself a small fizz of excitement now, at the thought of Miranda and Max being closer for more of the time. Her dearest friend often seemed so far away, in Surrey. It was bad enough when she'd lived in London, on the edge of the West End. Now, she was even further away.

'Guys, speaking from an entirely selfish point of view, I'm glad you're at least considering it. Having you closer, at least sometimes, would be fantastic. I know you haven't moved far from your Guildford roots. You're back in Surrey, where you first started out, but after you moved out of London it seemed like you were further away than ever.'

Miranda smiled at her softly. 'It wouldn't have been a thing, would it darling, if you'd still been in Guildford yourself, when I moved to Stoke? It's just a stone's throw, but it's a hell of a long way from Torley, I'll grant you. The truth is though; I'm feeling the distance between us too. I have, ever since you moved up there. Ten years changes things, doesn't it? I didn't used to mind the distance all that much, particularly when I was always so busy myself. There were times when I had barely a week between productions, and I needed that downtime to sleep! I literally *would* sleep for almost a week, back then. But, as we get older, different things become important.'

Miranda had certainly changed her outlook a lot, from when she was younger. Until she'd met Max, she'd lived life at a hundred miles an hour, acting on stage in the West End, gallivanting around town (and exotic holiday destinations) with men less than half her age, and being as flamboyant and outrageous as she had a mind to be. Now, along with her sleek silver bob, more understated make up and infinitely classier clothes, she had also toned down her attitude to life. She was allowing her more serious side to show through, now. She was still as mischievous as ever, and just as much fun as she'd ever been, but she'd finally settled into her skin. She'd never seemed so at peace with herself. Adie marvelled, yet again, how powerful love can be, in changing so much in a person's life.

She tuned back into what Miranda was saying, now. She was laughing and saying that by the time Adie and Trudie got back from their travels, she and Max might well have found a house, bought it, and moved into it.

'I might be at Carlisle station to meet you when you get back, darling, instead of Gatwick airport! Imagine that!'

Trudie giggled. 'It is possible, I suppose, if you pushed hard. There's no chain, Jeanette and Paul are keen to sell, so if that *is* that house you end up choosing, you *could* be in before we return, or very soon after. It doesn't need much doing to it, by the way. You might want to change a few paint colours or something but trust me – *nothing* needs doing in there. I talked to Jeanette before she and Paul left for Canada, and we agreed that if the place sells, she will need to get her furniture out of there and into storage. Kevin and I will arrange for it all to be picked up, then we'll have the place deep cleaned and ready for the new owners to just step in. How funny it would be, if it turned out to be you!'

Miranda narrowed her eyes. 'How are things, with you and Kevin? You're getting divorced, aren't you? I'm really sorry about that, by the way, unless of course it's what you really want. But, even if it is, I still think it's a shame.'

Trudie nodded. 'We're getting divorced, yes, but we're on pretty good terms. We can certainly still work together on stuff like Jeanette's house. We haven't fallen out, you know, not horribly. We've just grown apart. We want different things. But we started off as friends, in the very beginning, and I think we can go back to that, when the dust settles.'

After lunch they went back to Miranda and Max's place and spent a leisurely afternoon and early evening in the swimming pool, jacuzzi and conservatory. Max cooked a wonderful paella, and they sat around chatting over a couple of bottles of wine for a few hours until they all started to feel sleepy. Miranda pointed out that they had the next morning to enjoy a leisurely stroll around the village, have a relaxed pub lunch at the aforementioned 'Old Plough,' then head out to the airport in time for Adie and Trudie to catch their flight to Amsterdam.

In the morning, before they set off, Trudie decided to challenge Max to a game of tennis. Adie was surprised, and delighted. She hadn't known that Trudie played, and she wondered if perhaps, going forward, they might join a club together, or at least meet up and play a few games when the weather might be kind enough.

She sat in the kitchen with Miranda, who remarked that she seemed a little tired this morning.

'I am. I didn't sleep that well. This trip is exciting, but it's a bit daunting too.'

'It's a huge thing, darling. You're brave and inspiring, to be doing it at this stage of your life.'

'D'you think it's silly, to be doing something like this, at this age? I do worry that I'm too old. I wonder if maybe I've bitten off more than I can chew, in believing I'll be able to keep up the pace. I can't decide if I'm being a bit reckless, or selfish even, to be wandering off and leaving everyone to cope without me, too. My head is full of conflicting stuff about this trip.'

Miranda snorted.

'Good God! Have you *heard* yourself? You're sixty-one, Adie, not ninety-one! Personally, I think this is the best *possible* time for you to be doing this trip. You might be sixty-one, but you look, and move, and think like someone ten years younger. You're as fit and healthy as anyone can be, at this age, but you never know when that might change. Things happen. I'm so excited for you, that you have the time, the courage, the ability, and the funds, to do this trip right now. To have all that in place at the same time is no small thing and that's why I think it's so important that you do this, and suck the marrow from the experience.'

'It does feel a bit like 'now-or-never,' Adie admitted.

'I prefer to describe it as striking while the iron's scalding hot. And everyone will cope just fine, darling. You know they will. You've raised good kids. They're independent, happy, focussed, and successful. You did an excellent job, and this last year and a half with Mark has taken a lot out of you. I know you're in a good place together, but that has taken a lot of effort, on your part, and I think you underestimate how much you need something just for yourself.'

Adie knew Miranda was right. The time since Mark's accident, had been intense. Getting him to a state of independence close to what he had before he'd lost the use of his legs had been a long haul. It had been the quintessential 'labour of love' for Adie; she hadn't resented a single second of the effort she'd had to put in, to getting Mark to see life positively again, pull him back from the depths of despair, and enable him to feel as if he still had a worthwhile place in the world.

After the initial shock had subsided, and they'd started getting to grips with their new reality, Mark's efforts had matched her own but there was no denying that the ordeal had taken its toll on them both – and the rest of the family too. They'd all coped well because she'd brought them up as 'copers' who could deal with what life threw at them. Yes, they'd miss her while she was away, but Miranda was right; their lives wouldn't be unduly affected by her absence. None of them needed her, at least not in any way that required her to be there beside them. It was the ideal time to go. Miranda, bless her, understood Adie's misgivings, and managed to say all the right things.

'I know older women can sometimes feel society expects them to stay home and 'be sensible,' but your family and friends aren't like that, and anyone who judges you wrongly for having the adventure of a lifetime has issues of their own, darling. It may be a jealousy thing. In fact, it probably is, for a lot of women, because they don't have the resources you have. Classic tall poppy syndrome. Most of the ones who would condemn you are probably wishing they had the guts to do more than drive to the bloody shops and back.'

'You've hit the nail on the head, Mand, as usual. I *have* been wrestling a bit over whether others will disapprove, and I don't even know where that comes from, because the ones who would look down their noses at me and accuse me of having some sort of midlife crisis are the people I no longer associate with anyway! I don't know why I'd care what they thought.'

Miranda rolled her eyes and threw up her hands. Her penchant for theatrical gestures – a habit she'd developed over half a lifetime spent on the West End stage – was always charming and amusing.

'Because they will all get wind of this, Adie. They won't hear it from me, but I know these things have a habit of coming to light, and you know they'll be gossiping about you at those infernal lunches. They live for gossip-mongering and bitching. On some level you're still affected by how those moronic women treated you after you and Bryan split up, so you do still think about them, whether you want to or not. It's probably kind of normal. And a lot of them are very envious of where you are in life now, with a big country farmhouse and a millionaire husband who adores you. Some of them would *kill* for that. They're pathetic, stuck in their dead marriages, with kids who don't acknowledge them except to ask for more money, and friends who bitch about them behind their backs. They've nothing to look forward to, and nothing positive to offer, so you absolutely *have* to stop caring what they think – or anyone else, for that matter.'

She's right, again, like she so often is. Her wisdom is second to none. There's nobody in my whole life – except maybe for Mark – who's opinion I value more. They both tell it like it is, and they both think this trip is a good idea. They're both excited for me. Maybe I am overthinking everything but, after decades of being the one who organizes, nurtures, and ensures stability for everyone else, it's surprisingly hard to step away from doing that and concentrate solely on myself.

She said as much to Miranda, who chuckled at her softly.

'You old worrywart! Get over yourself, right now. You have always put everyone else first, all your life! You've well and truly earned your stripes, darling! It's finally *your* time now, your *chance* Adie, to do something wonderful and fun and life-affirming for *yourself*.'

Adie felt a small, bubbling joy take hold now, at the prospect of discovering new places, and perhaps even new things about herself that were probably always there but hidden under the layers of years of duty, obligation, consideration, commitment, and dedication towards her loved ones. Maybe she'd get to reconnect with the youthful, dreamful Adie again, somewhere on her travels. She might even come home with more confidence, energy, and inspiration — with stories and experiences to share and inspire others too.

She and Trudie had deliberately avoided planning a tight itinerary, but she was excited at the idea of finding places to see, meeting new people, and experiencing different cultures. It lit her up inside. She was, underneath the anxiety that had gnawed at her a little, feeling almost youthful again now. She wasn't just a wife, or a mum, or a granny. She was a woman with her own dreams, and the means to achieve them. There was so much to look forward to.

'You're at a fascinating crossroads, Adie. I know you're feeling the tension between duty and desire, and fear and freedom. You're a bit guilty and anxious, and the sense of stepping into the unknown is probably giving you butterflies too, but I want you to focus on the excitement and anticipation Those are thing you *should* be feeling. As I said, you've more than earned that right.'

'I know. I just keep thinking, Mand; what if something goes wrong with the house, or the farm, or with Mark's health, while I'm gone?'

Miranda closed her eyes. 'Let me remember… well, the farthest away you'll be is Greece, right? The islands? Wherever you'll be, at any given time, you'll be less than a day from home. Three, or four hours, tops, if you have to get an emergency flight from a city, and only slightly longer if you have to *get* to a city, to catch one. Just keep it in perspective, darling, or you'll never be able to enjoy yourself and there won't be any point in going! For what it's worth, if there is some kind of emergency, I will go and handle it until you get there, if you trust me to do that.'

'Of course I do! And I know how capable you and Max are. That helps a lot; to know you'll be on hand if there's a problem that Mark, Feen, and Gavin can't deal with themselves. And I would come straight back. Of course I would.'

'I don't imagine you'll have to, Adie. Because nothing – is – going – to – happen!'

She topped up her and Adie's glasses of orange juice and held hers up as a toast.

'To your travels, brave girl. To fun, to new experiences, and to feeling free, for a while at least.'

Adie held her own glass up, and clinked it with Miranda's. She allowed her thoughts to drift back now, to a couple of days ago, when she was getting organised and putting the last bits and pieces into her suitcase.

She'd sat on the edge of the bed, looking at the suitcase, open on it like a gaping mouth. Everything she needed or wanted to take with her was in there now. She was more or less ready to go, at that point, but her heart had been pounding in her chest, with an increasingly familiar mix of excitement and dread.

Mark had been sitting in his wheelchair, looking out through the window and across the fields, with his glasses perched at an odd angle above his forehead. He'd looked up at her and given her a cheeky grin.

'Don't look so bloody nervous, lass! You'll be fine! You've been 'ankerin' fer this fer bloody years!'

She'd had to work to swallow the lump in her throat.

'Yes, I have. It's been a dream for a long time, and I ignored it for a long time. But now that it's happening … now that I'm actually, *really* going … well, I keep wondering if it's just selfish and silly. Leaving you, leaving the kids, the grandkids, the house, the farm… *everything.* I'm walking away from everything.'

He'd shaken his head, adamantly. "Don't be s'daft. It's owt but selfish! Yer walkin' towards an adventure! It's yer *time,* love! You've spent decades making sure every bugger else were a'right. It's time you bloody *did* put yerself first fer a change.'

Her eyes had prickled with tears, and she'd let them fall. 'I'll miss you,' she'd whispered.

'I'll miss you too, you soppy sod,' he'd said, reaching out his hand to brush away her tears. "But I'll be 'ere when you and Trudie get back, an' first in line to 'ear all't stories. And there's yer blog, in't there? You'll be in touch every day, an' we'll all be drinkin' it in like nectar. 'Appen you'll not 'ave *time,* to miss any of us much, love. You and Trude'll be 'avin' too much fun. That's the 'ole point o' this, in't it?'

She'd hugged him hard as the mix of guilt and excitement swirled inside her chest. She was lucky to have him. He was a treasure, and she knew that she would have a lot of fun on her travels, but there wouldn't be a single day when she wouldn't wish he was there, to share the experiences with her.

'Penny for them? Miranda's voice was soft, pulling her back to the 'now.'

'You'll think I'm crazy, but part of me thinks I should just be content with what I have. I have so much more than many. It kind of feels a bit greedy, somehow, to want more.'

Miranda burst out laughing. 'Oh, God, you really are a trick! You're fortunate, yes, but a lot of people out there who don't have much only have themselves to blame! And it doesn't help the poor to be one of them, Adie.'

Adie laughed too, now. 'I remember I said that exact same thing to Teresa, a while back, when we were talking about the first documentary she made, about the slum kids of Bangkok, and wrestling over her choice to become a videographer.'

'Well, practice what you preach then, you moron. But Trudie's a great person to be travelling with, I think? You don't have any worries on that score?'

Adie shook her head. 'Nothing much, really. We've been friends for ten years, and we know each other pretty well. Having said that, I've never lived with her, or even shared a hotel room with her before. So, if she snores, I might have to smother her in the night.'

'Or get separate rooms. That's no bad thing. We all love the idea of sharing a room, drinking wine, and telling stories deep into the night, but the reality is that sometimes you just need your own space. And you might even want to do separate things, sometimes. That's normal too.'

Addie nodded. 'Yes, I'm a hundred percent sure there'll be things we *won't* have in common, and one of us won't want to see something the other one does, that sort of thing. Being able to compromise is important, but the trip is about us *both* fulfilling a dream, and we need to do it in ways that feed both our souls, so that we both get to see as much of what's on our bucket lists as we can without getting on each other's nerves too much. I guess if that happens, we have to rethink the strategy, or make some adjustments to the schedule, or whatever. It's one of the reasons we were both keen to keep it fairly light – so we could make changes without it being too inconvenient for us, separately or together.'

'One or the other of you might need extra 'down-time' or to move along bit faster. But Trudie seems quite easy going, so I'm sure you'll work it out. The trick is to always be open and honest, so that any niggles aren't allowed to fester, and turn into more of a big deal for either of you.'

This is a big deal for both of us, and maybe learning how to travel together is part of what the adventure will become.

'We've weathered life's ups and downs side by side for a decade, and she is going through a divorce, which she seems to have accepted, but I'm sure she's going to have her wobbly moments. If we can handle that, surely we can handle the odd missed train and weird hotel room along the way. The trip might test our friendship, in fact I'm sure it *will* at times, but it might also bring us closer in ways staying at home never could. Shared experiences, and all that.'

'You seem to have a good laugh together, and it'll be lovely to share this journey with someone who you have a good time with.'

'We kind of 'get' each other, Mand. We're both sensible enough to give each other space, and respect one another's need for it. I know Trudie's going to need some of that at certain times, while she carries on working through the loss of her marriage. I think we'll be able to make it work.'

Miranda leaned forward conspiratorially. 'Max has to spend some time in Scotland over the summer. Ten days, or a couple of weeks, I think, in some obscure place up in the west with his son Tim, who is looking at acquiring an abandoned castle and some land up there, to turn into a hotel. I'm not sure of the dates yet, but maybe during that time I could come out too and see you somewhere. I know we're coming out together, to do the Monaco thing, but I'm wondering about a separate mini-break – you know, just me?'

'So, back-of-beyond Scotland in the pouring rain doesn't thrill you, then?'

'Not in the slightest, but somewhere nice in Europe does. I won't care much, where. I can get the dogs boarded, or my cleaner can take them back to hers for a night or two. She's done it before, and doesn't mind, especially if pay her extra for it. I could shoot over for a girly break.'

How funny! Almost all of my friends have said they'll come over to Europe and catch me and Trude somewhere on our travels. It's so sweet that they all want to be a part of the adventure by sharing some of it with us.

Adie understood that the opportunities her friends talked about were giving *them* something important too. Doing a trip like this for the first time, in your sixties; it *was* a big thing. None of them were spring chickens. All of them were feeling the march of time, and they were all conscious of the waning chances to *have* these kind of adventures. Peg was in her seventies now, but she still fancied a few 'European hijinks,' as she'd called them. Sheila seemed keen to meet up somewhere for a short break too, and so was Carla, with the notion of treating her mother Hazel to a trip with her.

She realised that they all wanted to feel the same thing *she* wanted to feel; the excitement of seeing somewhere new, and having the ability to do it in relative safety, by meeting up and sharing the experience with someone they cared about. It was a testament to the quality of the friendships, and if it meant that Adie and Trudie had inspired other women of their age to have a 'silver hurrah' as Hazel Walton had put it, that made her heart sing. They might inspire their other friends, to do the same thing. It could lead to a mass invasion of 'women of a certain age' taking the European capitals by storm!

The idea made her laugh. Plenty of older women were already travelling, of course, but probably not as many as wanted to or dreamed about it. If her experience was already teaching her one important thing it was that more women wanted the chance to spread their ageing wings and fly a little, before it was too late. Adie and Trudie were both fit and healthy, hopefully with many years left on the clock to enjoy life to the full. But, as Miranda had pointed out, nobody knew what was around the corner. They were all starting to go to more funerals than weddings these days, which made them well aware that any one of them could lose their health in the blink of an eye. Nobody was immune to the ravages of rogue DNA or dementia, or hereditary conditions – including those they didn't even know about until they happened. Accidents, stress-related illnesses, and all sorts of other horrible things could also turn up or be triggered without warning, and render them less able to move as freely as they did before it happened. Nobody stood before a friend's or a relative's coffin without wondering about their own mortality.

It will suit me just fine, to have a few of our mates drop in, while we're pootling about. It will keep me connected to the people I care about, in more than just a facetime chat or a blog post. Being able to share some of the adventure with them, at different times; that will all become part of the memories that Trude and I will cherish when we look back on this time. We need to make it the best it can be, and bringing loved ones into the mix is part of that, I think. I do hope they'll be as good as their word, and it won't just stay a dream for them. And, who knows? This could be the start of longer adventures for them all! Life is for living. As Mark is so fond of saying, whenever I'm dithering or procrastinating about something; 'we're a long time dead.'

*   *   *   *   *

Trudie had her feet up on her in-flight backpack, as she and Adie sat side by side in the departure lounge. She was reading a guide to Amsterdam, on her i-pad. She looked up and grinned, self-consciously.

'I know it makes sense to have this stuff more portable, like on our phones or something, but I can't be doing with peering at such a small screen, these days. I almost forgot to pack my reading glasses – can you believe that? Imagine getting abroad and finding I'd forgotten them! I only got them a few months ago, and I'm still getting used to wearing them. I always had 20-20 vision before computer screens came along and destroyed it.'

'So, what should the plan be for tonight, do you think?'

'Well, we'll get into the city late in the evening, because the clock goes forward by an hour, and we'll have to get through the airport and all that entails, and then get a taxi to our hotel. It isn't far from the Leidseplein, which is the hub of the city's nightlife. We can dump our bags then go out and get some food and unpack later, or get to the hotel, sort everything out and then go for a late meal. I don't mind whichever way you'd like to do it.'

'Let's play it by ear. I'd like to have a wander around the area near the hotel, and soak up the atmosphere, if it's bustling. That might be a nice thing to do before bed. We can decide tomorrow what we want to do. I have the canal boat tour on my list, and Anne Frank House.'

'Me too, and the Red-Light District, which is a must-see, apparently. I know you want to see the Escher Museum over in The Hague, so we'll plan for that after we've seen enough of Amsterdam. There are day tours, bus trips, where you get taken on a whistle-stop tour of different towns and cities of historic significance. That might be interesting, but we can see how we feel.'

'It's such a shame it's no longer possible to take or send tulip bulbs back to the UK. Brexit has made that impossible. I'd love to have sent some to Hazel.'

'I know, Adie. Brexit screwed everything up, didn't it? We have so much more to think about now, as we go along on this trip. I sometimes think British passports aren't worth much anymore, but at least we're able to stay three months. It's the younger ones I feel sorry for, you know, the backpackers who can't spend more than ninety days in Europe now. It's bonkers. Even if we wanted to stay away longer, we couldn't anymore, could we?'

The air around them buzzed with announcements and an endless stream of people shuffled toward the departure gates.

'Do you want to get any duty free?' Trudie asked.

'No. I've got a bottle of Baileys in my suitcase. I got it at Sainsbury's, cheaper than they've got it in here, ironically. And that's another post-Brexit nightmare, isn't it – only being able to take one litre of spirits into the EU?'

Trudie sighed, deeply. 'The nightmare is endless. Truly, it is. But I'm going to get some gin, and probably some perfume and skincare stuff. I didn't bring any because I figured I'd get it here. We have plenty of time for a mooch. If you look after the bags while I go, I'll do the same if you want to go for a wander after I get back.'

'Okay, cool.'

Trudie was back in less than twenty minutes, with a bottle of Hendricks, another of the old timeless classic perfume Beautiful, by Estee Lauder, and a very pretty coffret of Clarins skincare.

'Well, that wasn't exactly small change, but I've got what I need. Your turn.'

Adie didn't manage to find anything at the duty free, and came back empty handed. She had seen a handbag she looked but it simply wasn't practical, to be buying things like that at the start of a three-month trip. She wasn't disappointed. Her holiday was going to be more about experiences than acquisitions, although she *would* be on the lookout for something lovely to take home as a memento.

As she sat down, Trudie leaned closer, and whispered with a grin,

'Can you believe this is actually happening? Three months! Are we brave, or just plain crazy, do you think?'

Adie laughed, and tried to stop her hands from fidgeting in her lap. 'Brave or crazy, maybe a little of both.'

They shared a quick glance — the sort that spoke of ten years of friendship, of understanding how important the trip was, to them both.

She wondered if Trudie herself had had the same thoughts about it all, and decided that she probably had. But they were both here, and both up for it, and only time would tell.

Will we still be friends after three months of rubbing along together? Will we still laugh like this, and have the same rapport we've always had?

Trudie picked up on her nervousness and nudged her gently.

'Don't start worrying now. If we can survive that time when I came to your house all those years ago and rampaged through your disastrous wardrobe and threw nine-tenths of it away, we can survive anything."

The memory made Adie laugh.

'God, you did me the biggest favour! Once I'd got over being mortified at how rubbish my sense of style was, I realised that you'd rescued me from sartorial oblivion. That was worth its weight in gold. I couldn't even bring myself to be offended!'

The boarding call echoed through the hall. Trudie stood, grabbing her backpack and heaving it onto her shoulder, and lifting her bags of duty free with a flourish.

'Come on then, Missus. It's time to start our grand adventure."

Adi got up too, and tried to ignore the pounding of her heart. She willed her nerves and excitement to stay bubbling beneath the surface.

Whatever happens, we're in this together. We are going to be absolutely fine.

* * * * *

The engines roared, as the plane gathered pace for take-off. Adie's stomach fluttered as she glanced out of the small oval window. The landscape of London grew smaller and smaller beneath them. Fancifully, she imagined Miranda standing in her garden, waving at their plane. It wasn't actually happening, because Gatwick was more than twenty miles south of Stoke, and Miranda wouldn't know Adie and Trudie's plane had taken off at all, unless she was following it on the online radar system, at home.

But she might be! She was so excited for us, it wouldn't surprise me at all if she was tracking our flight.

Feen had texted her, just before she'd boarded.

Safe travels, sweetie! Go with all our love,

and have the time of your life.

As fields and rooftops shrank beneath her, taking her away from the life she knew, she had a sudden wobble.

Sixty-one years old, and I'm leaving my husband, my family, the house, my friends... everything familiar. What the hell am I doing?

She clasped her hands in her lap and ran her thumb over her wedding band. A small wave of guilt passed across her like a shadow. She thought of Mark, bravely waving her off back in Carlisle, and gave a silent prayer of thanks for his quiet strength in letting her go. But then she checked herself.

He believes I should do this. I need to believe it too. And I can, and from this point, I will. I'm not leaving my life behind. I'm carrying it, and my loved ones with me, while I go and rediscover the parts of me that somehow got buried along the way.

As the plane climbed through the clouds, something inside her lifted with it. The tight knot of fear began to loosen. For the first time in years, she felt a small but significant connection to the girl who once dreamed of adventures, who used to believe she'd one day see Europe by train. Incredibly, that girl was finally on her way.

If you have enjoyed this book, or any of my others, I would
love you to leave a review for me on Amazon
or other literary platforms.

Good reviews are the lifeblood of every author.

Thank you.

Dear Reader.

I really hope you've enjoyed this last book in the Teapot Cottage series.

It is the end of an era, at least for a while, and it hasn't been an easy thing at all, to draw it to a close. This is in fact the most poignant book I've ever written, for all sorts of reasons. But, as with people in real life, characters develop and evolve, and I was starting to feel that I had taken Adie Raven as far as I could in this series. I really didn't want her to be stuck in a rut, endlessly dealing with different tenants at the cottage, and her life *devolving* instead, into something that stopped being interesting or fresh for me to write about. She is only sixty-one, as this book comes to an end. She is still 'young' in so many ways and, like the rest of us, she still has dreams she wants to fulfil in life.

I decided that Adie is deserving of some fresh joy in her life, so I am sending her on new adventures, and a new series will start next year, again with her as our primary protagonist. I won't say any more than that about it for now, but rest assured that she'll continue to be inspiring and enjoyable to you as she dances along, and many of the characters you've come to know and love in the Teapot Cottage series will be making appearances too, along the way.

Why? Because these people are my friends now, after years of creating them and spending lots of time in their company. They are as familiar to me as some of my 'real' friends are, and there has been such a comfort for me, in getting to know this wonderful, inspiring clutch of matriarchs who offer their wisdom and insight with voices that matter and fully deserve to be heard. Oddly enough, even though I created them in the first place, it is *they* who inspire *me!* For starters, they live in a kinder and more tolerant world, where so many of us long to live, and they determinedly keep their feet on the ground to make sure it stays that way. They are beautiful to me, as ageing women, and I just couldn't bring myself to leave them all behind, as the series drew to a close. That would have felt like cutting out a piece of my heart.

This has been such a bittersweet book to write. Entitled 'The Sum of All Parts, it wraps up the current series and paves the way for the new one. Getting through that process was a real labour of love for me, especially when I was writing about Mark's accident, and how it impacted the family. I think I've always been a little bit in love with Mark Raven, since the moment I first created him as a combination of several people from my past, including a much-cherished Uncle, and my gorgeous Grandmother, both of whom came from Lancashire (as did I, in fact), and both of whom were so down to earth that their feet were more or less planted in Lancashire soil! Grandma was a white witch in her own right, and I am so proud to be descended from that, even with so few of the gifts that *she* had. But some of them have come to me, and I will be forever grateful for the rare insights they give me that *are* more of a blessing than a curse, even though it sometimes feels like the other way around!

I created this book, like many others, over a period of many months. Part One – the Christmas party – is the 'curtain-raiser,' where fans of the series get to reconnect with their favourite characters again, and find out where they are in life now. It also offers the chance for new readers to get acquainted gently with the Torley community and some of the people in it, in the happy context of a Christmas (and Adie's sixtieth birthday) party. The party setting allows everyone to touch base, catch up, chat about their lives and share the progress they have made since we first met them.

Part Two outlines a truly shocking event – the kind that most of us pray we never have to face – and details how Mark, Adie and their family manage to survive the tidal wave of physical and emotional challenges *they* suddenly all have to face. A lot of research went into this part of the book, and I did shed quite a few tears as I went along. As with all of my books, a lot of this part is written from a heart that truly feels and understands the anguish felt by those affected by such a massive, life-changing disaster. I hope I have done them justice, in guiding them through the worst of mental mazes and safely through to the other side!

Part Three is dedicated to Adie's own emotional recovery, and realising that life is short. She has emerged, in the aftermath of the catastrophe that rocked the family to the core, with a new strength and a deep appreciation for what's really important in life. She acknowledges that she still has a few long-held dreams, and comes to realise that it's not too late to make some of them real. Even as she is feeling the march of time, she comes to understand that there are still things she can do in her life, and she finds the courage to start making some of her dreams come true. This draws her towards a new chapter in her life, and a teasing glimpse of the future, for my readers. It also enables you to have a little think about where she's going next, and decide if you'd like to come along too! The final part of the book is the shortest because it tees up the new series without dragging out the concept of a new beginning. Readers feel closure, but also curiosity (and hopefully anticipation) about what comes next, and there isn't a need to 'hang around' in that part for any longer than the time it takes to do its job.

Some of you will know that I started the Teapot Cottage series as just one book, that somehow morphed into a series. I wrote No Small Change because, as a menopausal woman, I was casting around trying to find some interesting fiction to read for women of my age and I couldn't find much that inspired me. So, I decided that if I couldn't *find* a good book, I'd just go ahead and *write* one! I didn't start out intending to write eight books about Adie Bostock/Raven! But, as people sometimes do, she grabbed me, and captivated me. And then she quietly told me that there was more she wanted to be, and do, and offer, and say, if I would let her.

I am a committed advocate of older women's voices being heard in a world that consistently fails (in Western culture at least) to recognise and honour the immense value of older women and what they have to offer society with their presence, wisdom, experience, and insight. I want to be part of a revolution that changes all that. I want to be part of a movement that supports older women to stay visible and relevant in society and, if there isn't already a revolution in progress, I think I just might go ahead and start one! So, keep your eyes on the books and your ears on the podcasts, and do at least consider the help I can give you to tell your <u>own</u> powerful story – because it really is a powerful story; more than you could ever imagine, in what it can say about you, or teach other people about themselves! It is never too late to speak up, so please don't believe that it is.

So, when Adie wanted to take me on a longer ride so I could find out a bit more about her, and other women like her, I decided to go with her - and just look where we've all ended up! Eight books! Sometimes that amazes even me!

A lot of people have no idea of what it takes, to write a book. It isn't a simple process. The writing itself is simple, but the subject matter, the development of characters, the evolving plotlines, the dedication to portraying people in the most authentic way – that's all part of it. Then there is the research. I talk to a lot of professional people who guide me on how best to describe the very real issues many people face, and the impact that has on them. Along with the places and situations I visit, or revisit in my mind, all of the research I do brings true authenticity to the stories. They are all written with great heart, over many months, with a complete commitment to getting things right, especially the bits that I know will resonate with readers. There is a lot of responsibility, keenly felt, around that.

The details are important in these stories too; the colour of an Aga, the warmth and sound of an open fire, the higgledy-piggledy stacks of cups and saucers on a Welsh dresser, the prospect of a delicious homemade parkin or a mini chocolate eclair, a steaming cup of rooibos tea, the shakiness of someone's breath as they try to say something difficult, the smell of oil in the workshop, the notions of magic and serendipity…

Countless tiny details that make a story complete. A lot of people don't enjoy the finer details of what makes a story resonant, and that's fine of course. Just as I don't enjoy every genre that's written, and there are some books that I can't or don't want to get into, I know that not everyone is going to like the genres I write in. That's the way the world works. But if <u>you</u> have enjoyed this ride with me and Adie, and all her lovely, quirky, and interesting friends, please do stay with us as we enter the next phase of the lives of Adrienne Raven and the people in her world. And if you'd like to leave me a review, for this or any of the other books I've written that you've enjoyed, this humble writer (who is still pinching herself that she actually got this far) will be *eternally* grateful!

So, I'll see you next year. In the meantime, lots of love, and thank you so much for being the reason I get up every morning and write.

Annie

The Power of Notes and Spells
A Teapot Cottage Tale (#2)

**Every woman dreams of finding the love of her life.
But what do you do when yours brings baggage that
can hurt you and your family?**

Feen Raven is often described as more than just a little bit
barmy. The young 'white witch' has finally found her
soulmate, but old family wounds are opened again when she
finds out who he's involved with.

Gavin Black is on an unhappy errand that forces him to
reconnect with his estranged mother. All he wants is to claim
what's his and go home again, without any complications.

Carla Walton can't let go of a grudge. After a lifetime of
pushing everyone away, she is isolated, bitter, and blaming
everyone else for her problems. She wants to be left alone so
she can keep ignoring her demons.

But Teapot Cottage, with its mysterious ability to heal the
broken-hearted, always has a more complicated agenda for
people who don't want to rake up the past. Pretty soon, Gavin,
Feen and Carla come to question everything they think they
do and don't want in life.

Will love and a little bit of magic help them find a way
forward? Or will old family fractures be too hard to heal?

*Come to the Lake District, to a gentle place where a
beautiful blend of music and magic can heal the
hardest hearts.*

A MORAL SWERVE

Nobody comes home expecting to find intruders -
But what would you do if you did?

Alison Jones is single, lives alone, and doesn't have a lot of self-awareness. But, after coming home to find burglars in her house, she does a terrible thing without thinking, and is forced to confront some ugly truths about herself.

Darren Davies is a petty thief, stuck in the revolving door between small-time crime and prison. After he makes the biggest mistake of his life, he is compelled to re-evaluate the path his life is taking, and deal with the demons that drive him.

When Darren and Alison's lives intersect, they each find themselves on a soul-searing journey, as they struggle to come to terms with the catastrophic impact of their acts and omissions. After stumbling through the wreckage, the future for them both becomes crystal clear, but it's not what either of them expected.

As one door opens and another slams shut, choices expand and diminish.

At the crossroads of Beginnings and Endings,
who decides to go where?

When It's Meant to Happen
A Teapot Cottage Tale (#3)

Having a baby is something most women dream of and plan for. But what does it mean if you can't make it happen, no matter how hard you try?

Debby Davies longs for a family of her own. She is desperate to have a baby with the husband she adores, but fruitless years of trying to conceive have left her feeling like a failure. It's starting to make her crazy, that she can't seem to achieve the one thing she always felt destined to do.

Darren Davies is at his wits' end with his wife. Her simmering resentment is changing her in ways that really scare him, and the horrible way her parents treat him is starting to take its toll. He's beginning to question whether their marriage can survive what feels like a never-ending series of storms.

As their doubts take hold, that their love can survive, they know they're in the last chance saloon. But Teapot Cottage, with its mystical ability to pour balm on battered souls, has plans for Debby and Darren that show them what's possible in ways they could never have imagined.

Can they stay together and face a very different future from the one they had planned, or will they find the challenges too great, and go their separate ways?

Run away from home for a while! Come to the Lake District, to a place where miracles can happen, with the help of a little bit of magic!

Ruin, Reins and Redemption
A Teapot Cottage Tale (#4)

Everyone makes mistakes, and some of them are hard to come back from. When you've taken someone else's life, and destroyed your family in the process, where do you begin, to pull things back together?

Stuart Thomson is a disgraced lawyer whose catastrophic error of judgement has all but ruined his life. By the time he leaves prison, after six years, he no longer has a career, a home or a marriage, and his troubled teenage daughter is barely speaking to him.

Meghan Thomson is almost fifteen. She's a mixed-up mess of anger and confusion, and she has no idea how she feels about anything at all, especially her father. When he books a holiday to the Lake District together, to reconnect, it's the last thing she really wants to do with a man she doesn't trust.

On holiday, father and daughter both struggle to understand each other. But Teapot Cottage, with its enigmatic way of turning troubled lives around, reveals an amazing opportunity they once could never have imagined. The future on offer means a whole new level of faith and commitment from them both, to make it happen.

Stuart and Meghan desperately need a fresh start. Can they trust themselves and each other enough to make it happen? Or does the heartbreak of the past make the leap of faith too tough?

In Torley town, in a very special cottage, lives are often transformed with the help of 'a little bit of love and magic.'

THICKER THAN WATER

Earth-shattering secrets will always come out, and the truth doesn't care about the cost.

Adie Bostock has finally found the baby she was forced to give up at fifteen – the one her husband and grown-up children don't know about – and she intends to keep her secrets. But, in the wake of a shocking crime, her tightly-woven web of deceit starts unravelling and she doesn't have a clue how to stop it.

Matty Bostock boosts his graduate income with sex work. Everything ticks along nicely in his smug, self-satisfied world, until one of his clients is murdered. With another refusing to give him the alibi he needs, he can't prove his innocence, and he faces going down for a crime he didn't commit.

Ruth Stenton has a happy, settled life with her wife Gina Giordano, and she is blissfully unaware of just how big a lie she's been living. When she discovers who has been hiding a terrible truth from her, and for how long, the impact is profound and far-reaching.

Ruth is forced to face demons she didn't know she had, and Gina has to find a way to help her. Adie can't protect one of her children without destroying another, and Matty must confront the consequences of the way he has chosen to live.

As moral dilemmas start to crush a family that's been buckled by betrayal, everyone has to decide; how much does 'blood' really matter, and what can or can't be forgiven?

THE STUFF YOU FAIL TO NOTICE
A Teapot Cottage Tale (#5)

You can live your whole life without knowing what's happening around you. But how can you stop the things you haven't even seen from blowing your world apart?

Minty Cartwright is peri-menopausal, and reeling from the discovery that her husband has been having an affair with her closest friend from childhood. She takes refuge at Teapot Cottage, a quiet holiday house in the Lake District, while she considers her next move.

Fiona Winterson hates herself with a passion she once never knew she could feel. Her selfishness has shattered the heart of the 'soulmate' she's known and loved all her life. But faced with the worst of circumstances, she discovers that she needs that woman's help.

With decades of love and trust destroyed, Minty and Fiona are thrown back together in a sea of shame, fury and fear. Both women are forced to reconsider the value of a friendship that has influenced their entire lives.

Will the mysterious, healing energy of Teapot Cottage help them rediscover what's important to them both? Or is it all to painful – and too late – to even try?

Come and join new friends in the Lake District, where shattered lives can be gently pulled back together, with the help of a little bit of magic!

THE CHOICE BETWEEN SAFE AND BRAVE
A Teapot Cottage Tale (#6)

When the woman you love is ripped from your life without warning, how do you pick up the pieces if you think it's all your fault?

Chris Darcy is a mountaineer on a mission to scale the world's summits, but when his world is shattered on a climbing trip with his fiancée Daisy, he is crippled by guilt, and dealing with demons that have plagued him all his life. Bereft and broken, he goes back to Teapot Cottage, where he'd been once before, with Daisy.

Tezzie Bostock is finally home from travelling. She is reeling from a badly broken heart and reluctantly drifting towards a career she doesn't want. When epiphany strikes, she decides to do something different. She knows she has to regain her self-esteem to make it happen, but she doesn't know where to start.

As Chris and Tezzie's lives intersect, they realize they've met before. Reeling from heartbreak of different kinds, they forge a solid friendship, and form an alliance that helps to push them both forward, towards an exciting future.

But even as they find themselves edging towards romance, Tezzie has plans to be somewhere else, where her own life will be at risk. Can Chris even contemplate losing another love? Can Tezzie make a compromise that can still let her have her chosen career? Or is it all too much of a challenge for two lost souls who seem to want different things?

Come and spend some quiet time in a little house of healing in the Lake District, where lives get reinvented, with the help of a little bit of magic!

FROM RAW TO
VERY WELL DONE
A Teapot Cottage Tale (#7)

What do you do when sticking to your principles costs you the career you've spent your whole life building?

Wendy Whitelaw has just lost her job as one of the country's most brilliant chefs. Angry and defeated, with her career in tatters, she lands at Teapot Cottage, where she hopes to recover her shattered reputation and work out how to claw her way back to the only thing that gives meaning to her life.

Billy Briggs is a property developer who shows up unannounced and unwanted, with lofty ideas to clear the debt that is threatening to drown him. When the opportunity to save himself taken from him without warning, he is bitter and resentful, and looking for someone to blame.

When Wendy and Billy meet, they hate one another on sight. She wants to be left alone, to make her future plans, but he wants what she has, and he's determined to get it.

Each of them would cheerfully choke the life out of the other, but Teapot Cottage, with its uncanny way of changing people's perspectives, has a different outcome in mind.

Can Wendy and Billy set their differences aside and work together in a way that will help them both get what they want in life? Or is their animosity simply too deep to overcome?

Enjoy some gentle, quiet time in a little house of healing in the Lake District, where lives get reinvented, with the help of a little bit of magic!